1 MONTH OF
FREE
READING

at

www.ForgottenBooks.com

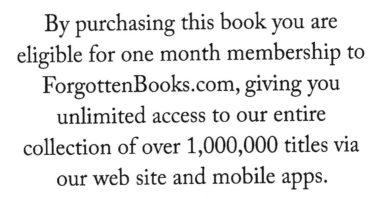

By purchasing this book you are eligible for one month membership to ForgottenBooks.com, giving you unlimited access to our entire collection of over 1,000,000 titles via our web site and mobile apps.

To claim your free month visit:

www.forgottenbooks.com/free644816

ISBN 978-0-483-70724-5
PIBN 10644816

This book is a reproduction of an important historical work. Forgotten Books uses
state-of-the-art technology to digitally reconstruct the work, preserving the original format
whilst repairing imperfections present in the aged copy. In rare cases, an imperfection in
the original, such as a blemish or missing page, may be replicated in our edition. We do,
however, repair the vast majority of imperfections successfully; any imperfections that
remain are intentionally left to preserve the state of such historical works.

A PASSAGE PERILOUS

FOURTH EDITION

A PASSAGE PERILOUS

By ROSA NOUCHETTE CAREY

Author of "The Highway of Fate," "Rue With a
Difference," "The Angel of Forgiveness,' etc.

"Be what you wish others to become; let yourself,
and not your words, preach for you."

A. L. BURT COMPANY

PUBLISHERS   NEW YORK

CONTENTS

CHAPTER		PAGE
I.	What Happened!	7
II.	An Original Wooer	16
III.	See-saw!	24
IV.	"You will have to call me Chriss"	32
V.	Adelaide plays Chopin's Funeral March	41
VI.	Number Five Grattan Gardens	50
VII.	Niobe dries her Tears	58
VIII.	The Curate of St. Cuthbert's	67
IX.	"Two's Company"	75
X.	"For Better, for Worse"	83
XI.	Jack Linacre's Wife	91
XII.	"Here endeth the Third Chapter"	99
XIII.	"The Impossible Charlotte"	108
XIV.	Near Neighbours	116
XV.	"I Have a Genius for Friendship"	124
XVI.	Under the Chestnut Tree	133
XVII.	A Woman's Mistake	140
XVIII.	A Sprig of Bell-Heather	149
XIX.	The Bowling Green	158
XX.	A Tangle of Threads	168
XXI.	Mrs. John Linacre's Début	177
XXII.	A Speck on the Horizon	186
XXIII.	The Clouds gather	195
XXIV.	Christian feels Puzzled	205

6 Contents

XXV. "I have not changed my Mind" 213

XXVI. The Breaking of the Storm 221

XXVII. "He knows it now" 230

XXVIII. Elandslaagte 239

XXIX. Waiting for News 248

XXX. Red-headed Celt, and Khaki 256

XXXI. "Can you keep a Secret?" 265

XXXII. "Who can it be?" 274

XXXIII. Sunshine and Clouds 282

XXXIV. "If it were any one else!" 291

XXXV. Letters from Durban 300

XXXVI. Christian's Diplomacy 309

XXXVII. The "Blair Castle" in Port 317

XXXVIII. Sweethearts and Wives 325

XXXIX. "I have brought you your Daughter" 333

XL. Jack has a Brilliant Idea 341

XLI. A Highland Glen 349

XLII. A Port Pleasant 358

A PASSAGE
PERILOUS

I

WHAT HAPPENED!

*It is very foolish to be gazing at the landscape when you are.
nearing the edge of a precipice.*

ALL her life long Christian Fordham had expected
something to happen.

Even when she was a mere mite of a child, with a
curly head just level with the table, her baby precocity
had astonished her mother. " Me wonders," she had
remarked in her small chirping voice,—". me wonders
what happenings baby's dot to-day." Baby's " happenings" became quite a household proverb at the Vicarage,
hoarded up with other like sayings by fond and admiring
parents.

Christian afterwards confessed to a friend that all
through her youth and undeveloped girlhood she had
never opened her eyes on a new day without a secret
hope that something wonderful and unexpected might
happen, and when evening closed in and everything had
been as usual, she would whisper confidentially to her
pillow: " It has only been a stupid common sort of day,
but to-morrow something may happen," for she was a
foolish, dreamy little soul, and being an only child, had
lived a curious inner life of her own. But as the years
went on and nothing but the grim, sad realities of life
confronted her, Christian grew less eager and hopeful,
and those bright visions which had haunted her growing
girlhood had faded into grayness.

As she sat alone of an evening—for she had many solitary hours—her work would lie untouched on her lap, as her thoughts strayed to her childish past, and then rested heavily on the monotony of her present life, and her eyes would smart with unshed tears at the bitter contrast.

"In those dear old days I was never lonely," she would say to herself; "how could I be lonely when I had mother? I daresay many girls would not have thought it much of a life," she went on; "we were so poor after father's death, and mother was such an invalid, and it was such a dull, poky little house, with no garden, and only Betty to do everything; and yet how happy we were!" And here was a lump in Christian's throat as she remembered how bright the little parlour had looked with its cheerful fireside and the dear invalid smiling a welcome as she entered: "I am so glad it is you, darling; I thought, perhaps, it might be your Aunt Caroline or Adelaide."

And then that chapter of her life had closed, and Christian, who had grown thin with fretting, had become the inmate of her aunt's house.

Mrs. Fordham was her father's sister, and was indeed her only near relative; she was the well-endowed widow of a wealthy stock-broker, who had left her sufficiently well provided with the good things of this life. She had only one daughter, and lived in a handsome house in Mandeville Street; and it was felt by Mrs. Fordham's friends that she was acting both wisely and generously in providing for the future of her orphaned niece.

"I could not turn my back on my own flesh and blood—dear Eustace's child," she remarked tearfully to her special crony, Lady Armitage. "No, my dear, of course not," replied her friend sympathetically; "your feelings do you credit, Caroline; and I cannot but applaud your sense of duty—and then the girl will be such a companion for Adelaide."

"I am not so sure of that," returned Mrs. Fordham rather quickly; "there is a difference in their ages, and Christian has never quite suited dear Addie; besides, she has so many friends; but, of course, we shall do our best for the poor child;" and according to her lights Mrs.

Fordham had acted up to her words. Nevertheless, the house in Mandeville Street was no home to the girl, to quote her own words: " for Christian was generally verbally strong. I was always a stranger and a sojourner in the Mandeville House; I was never really one of the family. No," answering an indignant protest, " they were not unkind. Adelaide was always cold—her nature is not a genial one; but Aunt Caroline tried to make me comfortable—only she had not the right knack, and somehow I always felt in the way."

Perhaps, after all, there were faults on both sides; Christian, in her secret unhappiness, may have been a little too exacting in her demands, and somewhat unyielding and aggressive with regard to the prejudice of others; Adelaide's company manners and would-be juvenility grated terribly upon her. " Why does she try to be young?" she would say to herself; " all her friends know she is eight-and-thirty; if she would leave off being sprightly and girlish, she would be so much more attractive."

Christian was in her cousin's way—Adelaide soon made this evident. There was no room in either the brougham or the victoria for three well-grown women, so Christian had generally to stay at home.

As long as she was in mourning for her mother, the Fordhams had sufficient excuse for declining all invitations on her behalf; but when the girl began to recover her spirits a little and to take interest in the people who came to the house, then the real difficulties began. Christian was no beauty; she was not really as handsome as Adelaide—who had good features, and a finely-developed figure—but people often found her attractive.

She had a beautiful complexion, and her hair was of that chestnut-brown which was so admired; her eyes were pretty too, though, as her shortsight obliged her to wear pince-nez, this was hardly so apparent, but it was when she smiled that people lost their heart to her.

Christian was rather a dangerous young woman, though she did not know it; for when she liked people she could not help making herself pleasant to them; it was not that she flirted, but that she took an interest in them.

And so it was that after some little festivity, Adelaide would follow her mother into her room. " Mother, I do wish you would speak to Christian," she would say severely; " it was really dreadful the way she went on with Mr. Masters. She was sitting in corners with him, and laughing so loudly that every one turned to look at them; she has no right to behave as though she were a school-girl at her age—Christian is seven-and-twenty,"—and so on, until Mrs. Fordham was goaded on to speak to her erring niece, and then there were ructions.

Christian, who was not submissive by nature, and had never been coerced and thwarted, had no meek answers ready, and contented herself with proudly declaring her innocence of the charge.

" Adelaide ought to be ashamed of herself, Aunt Caroline," she said once indignantly. " I never flirt; it is a wicked and cruel accusation." Christian was verbally strong again. " Those who live in glass houses should not throw stones at unoffending people; there was no harm in talking to Mr. Masters any more than to Captain Linacre; and if Adelaide is such a goose, I can't help it."

Now in Christian's position this was highly imprudent, for, as every one knew, Adelaide was the real mistress of the house, and ruled her mother, as a stronger and more dominant nature always does rule the weaker vessel.

If she had ventured to contest her mother's plan of taking Christian into the house, she could easily have carried her point, but there were limits which even she dare not cross, for what would their world have said if they had refused the shelter of their roof to the lonely girl.

Adelaide would not turn her rebellious cousin out of doors, but she could and did curtail many of her privileges. Christian more than once suspected that she had been included in some invitation and had been left purposely at home.

Mrs. Fordham, who was really a kind-hearted woman, if she had not been daughter-ridden, had tried to soften the disappointment in one case.

" You know, my dear, it is rather a big affair, and I really could not afford to give you a new dress," she said with injudicious candour; " Adelaide thinks I spend **too** much on you already; she keeps all the accounts, you know—and really, we are not so very rich;" but this was only making things worse, for Christian was quite aware that her cousin held the purse-strings, but she was pertinacious and would not at once yield the point.

" My old white silk will do quite nicely with fresh trimmings, Aunt Caroline," she said coaxingly; but Mrs. Fordham turned a deaf ear to this; it ended by Christian enacting the time-honoured rôle of Cinderella, while Adelaide went forth resplendent in gorgeous attire, to air her girlish graces, free from her cousin's severe criticism.

As time went on, Christian found herself no match for Adelaide; she was heedless and could not control her impatience; she would speak, when silence was the best policy; and to make matters worse, she always said exactly what she thought, regardless of consequence, and as her remarks generally reached her cousin's ear, Mrs. Fordham being like wax under pressure, Adelaide grew colder and more repellent in her manner, and Christian more exasperated and lonely, and then all at once, when she had left off expecting it, something happened to Christion. Captain Linacre crossed her path again, and before many days had passed he had asked her to marry him, and with her usual heedless impulsiveness Christian had said yes; and before she had realised the fact that she had signed away her freedom, the wedding-day was fixed. It was a few days before that astonishing event was to take place—that is, if Christian had not dreamed the whole thing—that the girl sat alone in the small inner drawing-room at Mandeville Street. It was a bright April afternoon, and Mrs. Fordham and Adelaide were driving in the park, and had left Christian to finish a few little odds and ends of business that had still to be done, but an hour passed and the girl sat still with her eyes fixed dreamily on the opposite windows, and her hands lying idly in her lap. She was reviewing the whole situation calmly, dispassionately, and without prejudice. What did it all mean? Had she and Jack been play-acting? How had she brought herself to such a pass, that she had actually promised to marry a man who was not in love with her, and who was up to the present moment almost a perfect stranger to her. "And it was not as though I were in love with him either," she said to herself; "if mother had been here, she would not have let me do it, and I should not have wanted to do it either; but I knew Aunt Caroline and Adelaide would be so glad to get rid of me, and so I told Jack then I would do it; but I am not sure,"—here Christian's healthy colour paled a little—"that I have done right after all, and"—for Christian was always honest with herself—"I feel less sure every day; Jack is nice, he is a dear fellow, but he is terribly erratic, and it isn't as though he were in love with me."

Perhaps this was the secret sting, and it was undeniably true; no woman who respects herself likes to be wooed in a half-hearted manner, and Captain Linacre's wooing ϑ't had been lukewarm and decidedly original.

This was how "Christian's happening" had taken place.

She had met Captain Linacre two or three times during the previous season; he had danced with her on two occasions, and had joined their party at Henley. Christian had not remembered that he had distinguished her with any special attentions, but he had been pleasant and amusing, and to use a favourite expression of Jack's, "They had hit it off." "But I am not sure that I liked him as well as Charlie Masters; and he certainly is not half as handsome." Christian said to herself Jack Linacre was not handsome; he was a dark man, with a thin, sunburnt face, and an erect, soldierly figure; he had sombre, rather melancholy eyes; only when he laughed, his white teeth gleamed pleasantly under his moustache, and there was something frank and boyish in his expression.

Christian knew something about his family; he was a younger son, and was regarded by some of his friends as a black sheep—not that his fleece was exactly sable, but it was of a decidedly greyish hue; it was supposed that he had expectations from an uncle—a wealthy and eccentric bachelor, who was generally at death's door—and that owing to Captain Linacre's recklessness and habit of contracting debts, these expectations were not likely to be fulfilled.

" When young men do not know or care on which side their bread is buttered, they deserve what they get," remarked Lady Armitage severely, for it was she who knew something of the Linacres. " They are a curious family, my dear," she went on; " the elder brother is deaf and is somewhat of a recluse, and Mr. Vigne, the uncle, is deformed and has terrible health, and never goes into society; he and Carus Linacre are both bookworms."

Christian found all this very interesting; she always liked to hear about people's lives; to be sure, she was not specially interested in Captain Linacre, and would not have given him another thought if he had not crossed her path again—that was only seven or eight weeks before, when Lady Armitage gave one of her big dances.

Christian gave Jack a friendly nod as he made his way to her between the dancers, and she was rather surprised at his evident pleasure in seeing her again; he accosted her as an old friend, told her she looked as fit as possible, and scrawled his name all over her programme.

" Well, you are greedy, Captain Linacre," was all she said, for though she preferred Charlie Masters as a man, she knew that Captain Linacre's dancing was simply perfect, and if life were only a dance and a merry-go-round, she would willingly have had Jack for her partner.

After this Christian seemed always meeting him. " The world is so small," as she said. Then he began to be attentive, and Christian wondered why he was always teasing her for dances; and then one March day she came upon him sitting rather moodily on a bench in Kensington Gardens, and he had sprung up and joined her with evident pleasure, and almost before she had finished discussing the weather—which she always did as a prelude to conversation—she found to her intense astonishment that he was asking her to marry him. In vain she strove to interrupt him.

" Captain Linacre, what nonsense! Do stop, please. I cannot really listen to you; why, we know nothing of each other."

" I have danced with you at least five-and-twenty times, Miss Fordham."

"Oh no; how can you exaggerate so And, besides, what are a few dances—we have not really talked—you know nothing about me, except what Lady Armitage may have told you, and I know even less about you?" But Jack was not to be put off in this missish way.

"We can soon alter all that," he returned quickly; "do you mind sitting down a few minutes, Miss Fordham; it is quite mild and sheltered here, and there is no wind. I have a lot I want to tell you about myself; and I know you will listen like a dear, good girl, for I am in a bit of a fix, and if I don't turn up trumps, there will be the deuce to pay—and my mother will break her heart;" the latter part of Jack's sentence was ended in a different tone. Christian glanced at him, his expression was at once pained and pleading; he looked rather like a naughty boy who had been found out.

"I will not keep you long," he said humbly; and then Christian sat down and composed herself to listen.

She was not at all flurried or discomposed, although, as it happened, this was her first offer of marriage; to her the whole thing was ridiculous and impossible; she did not really care for him; he had made no impression on her; when he had finished she would be a little severe with him and tell him that she had never given him the least encouragement; but she must listen to him as patiently as she could, and then Captain Linacre, with some difficulty and many breaks and halts, told his story.

Jack was no narrator, and nothing could be worse than his manner, but he was honest, though a little blunt; he meant to tell the truth, and he told it, though he grew rather red once or twice, as though it cost him some effort, but somehow Christian became interested. He told her that though his brother was very well off, that he himself was dependent on his uncle, who had, in a way, adopted him.

"Uncle Jasper is not a bad sort," he went on, "in spite of his cranks, but he is terribly obstinate; if he takes a thing in his head you cannot move him;" and then Jack went on to explain that he had bought him his commission and had paid his debts again and again. "Of course, I know I have been a fool, Miss Fordham; I am not trying to make out that black's white; but I give you my word, honour bright, that I don't know how the money went; there are a lot of rich fellows in our regiment, and I suppose I tried to be in the swim; anyhow, I am in no end of a mess, and there's Carus, that's my elder brother, bound over on his honour not to help me—that is one of Uncle Jasper's cranks—he will do all or nothing."

II

An Original Wooer

Of thy unspoken word thou art master; thy spoken word is master of thee.—EASTERN PROVERB.

CHRISTIAN was a good-hearted girl; one of her friends once said of her, rather prettily, that she had a genius for sympathy. She was very human, and also tolerant—real things appealed to her with irresistible force. She was beginning to feel interested in Captain Linacre. He also amused her, he was genuine, and decidedly original.

Now although this was Christian's first offer, like other healthy-minded young women she had her own code of ideas on the subject of courtship and matrimony. A judicious course of reading, notwithstanding that it included a goodly number of modern and up-to-date novels, had somewhat fostered and encouraged a certain old-fashioned taste for romance. Christian liked a lover to be a lover indeed—not a shoddy, used-up article who was an adept in pretty speeches, and whose love-making was no novelty.

No matter how old the world was, there were still roses to be gathered in Eden. Nor would the store be exhausted as long as young men and young women trod the long high road of life together. Christian, who was true to the instincts of her sex, had always nourished a secret hope that some such "happening" might overtake her, and that the old, old story might be whispered in her ear. "When He comes,"—with a capital H—"I shall know him at once," she said to herself. "Something will tell me in a moment."

And now the lover had come, and instead of being touched—embarrassed—shy—Christian had more than once to bite her lips to conceal a smile, Jack's wooing was so heavy-handed; he stated facts boldly and without embellishment, and made no attempt to round off awkward corners. He painted himself as a black sheep. " I give

16

you my word, I was an utter fool," he said once, and Christian's " Oh, indeed !" was felt by them both to be a little inadequate; but then Christian knew so little about young men, not having any brother or male cousin of her own.

Captain Linacre was so evidently in earnest that Christian gave him her full attention. To be sure, she got puzzled once or twice—he was so mixed and incoherent that she was obliged to ask for an explanation. " You are going to India, you tell me, or is it South Africa? Surely your uncle will pay your debts and help you to start comfortably." But Jack shook his head; there was a slight pallor under the sunburnt skin.

" That was the worst of it," he returned in a dull, tired voice that somehow made the girl feel uncomfortable. His uncle refused to hear reason; he would do nothing, and if things should reach his Colonel's ears, there would be the dickens to pay. " My uncle threatens to dock half my allowance," he went on; " and in that case I should have to exchange into a cheaper regiment. You see, I have been such an ass that I have tired them all out, and even my mother says she is sorry I ever went into the army."

" Are you sorry, too, Captain Linacre?" Christian asked gravely.

" No; it is the only life that suits me, and there's likely to be a lot of fighting in South Africa, for Kruger means mischief, and I am just wild to be in the thick of it; but let me finish, please, Miss Fordham, I have not much more to say," and then Jack made a bolt for it. It appeared that Mr. Vigne had come to the limits of his forbearance, and had spoken very plainly and very sternly to the prodigal, though, of course, Captain Linacre knew better than to repeat his words.

" Now, look here, Jack," he had said in a wrathful tone, " if I had not known you were more of a fool than a knave, I would never have wasted so much good money on you, and you may take my word for it that I will throw no more away, for I am about sick of it all. You are the biggest fool I know; you are so really good-natured that you can't say ' No,' and of course you are gulled and fleeced by any one who takes your measure; and this is my heir! don't flatter yourself, my fine fellow, for unless you mend your ways and manners pretty quickly, you will not touch a farthing of my money, as sure as my name is Jasper Vigne. Now listen to me, Jack. I will give you one more chance, but I shall impose a condition; you are such a fool"—Jack coloured angrily at this third repetition—"that you cannot manage your own affairs; you ought to have married long ago—the matrimonial noose is the only thing to keep you straight; get some sensible girl to marry you, and bring her to me, and if I approve of your choice, I won't be exacting, but she must have some sense in her head. I will pay your debts once more, and increase your allowance, and if you turn over a new leaf, there is no knowing what I may do in the future."

"But I don't think I am a marrying man, Uncle Jasper; and what am I to do with a wife at present?"

"What do other men do, sir?" demanded his uncle in return.

"But I don't know any one that I want to marry," continued Jack in an embarrassed voice. "I have always been civil to girls, but I never cared for one specially, unless it was——" But here Jack reddened and looked up.

"Some actress no doubt," in a withering tone, and Mr. Vigne looked stonily at his nephew.

"Well, she was not an actress exactly, though she meant to go on the stage"—Jack never could tell a lie or evade a difficulty—"but it does not matter; she is married now."

"And a good thing too," still more angrily. "When I said a sensible girl, I meant a lady, not a music-hall actress, or a ballet-dancer, or any one of that sort. Why, confound you, Jack, you can hardly have misunderstood me. Let there be no mistake on this subject."

"I have perfectly understood you, sir," returned Jack sulkily, for he was feeling sore and injured; he had been called a fool three times, and he did not like it. "But I am afraid I can't comply with this condition; it seems to me, Uncle Jasper, rather an unusual sort of thing to marry a girl when you don't care twopence about her."

"It is not more unusual than gambling and running into debt; besides, if she is a nice girl you will care for her fast enough. Why don't you ask your dear friend, Lady Armitage, to help you?" But Uncle Jasper sneered as he spoke, for he had few women friends.

"And if I prefer to remain without a wife?" But Mr. Vigne's reply is best left unquoted. It conveyed to the young man that in that case Jasper Vigne washed his hands of him—his debts would remain unpaid, his allowance reduced to half its present amount, and the sooner he exchanged into an infantry regiment the better for all parties. Truly, Captain Linacre left his uncle's house that day a sadder and wiser man.

"I suppose I shall have to do it," he muttered as he faced the situation over his cigar and a brandy-and-soda; for he wanted something to help him to pull himself together after all this rough treatment. "'Pon my soul! I felt as though he had got me down, and was trampling on me with hob-nailed boots made expressly for the purpose—I was so knocked about," he growled. "Uncle Jasper is an ugly customer sometimes. It is not fair. He has got the pull over me, and I know I shall have to do it. Confound it! how am I to find a girl?" and here Jack puffed heavily at his cigar, while his eyes followed the curling rings of smoke. And then all at once he remembered Miss Fordham. By Jove! perhaps she would do. She was rather a good sort of girl; he did not dislike her; he had danced a lot with her the previous night, and he had taken her down to supper.

He was not sure that he admired her; his taste was for dark beauties. She was not a patch on little Mabel Vaughan, his old sweetheart—a tiny brunette, with hair as black and shiny as a dowager's satin, and eyes that were brimful of mischief—"The Midget," as they called her.

How fond he had been of the little thing, and how cut up when young Donaldson had carried her off under his very nose. Well, that was all ancient history; but Mabel was the only girl he had ever wanted to marry.

He told himself a little gloomily that Christian Fordham was not his style at all—pah! what a name for a modern young lady; but of course he could call her Chriss.

And then he hated pince-nez. He wondered how she looked without them. He had a notion her eyes were rather nice. He had liked her somehow because she danced well; and it was so easy to talk to her—they always seemed to hit it off so well.

"She is better than some of them," he went on, closing his eyes and puffing luxuriously at his big cigar. "She is good-tempered, I fancy, and lively, and that sort of thing. I don't believe she is happy and comfortable either. That cousin of her's is a bit of a Tartar. Suppose I take her into confidence and ask her to give me a shove up. I shan't tell her lies—she shall know the sort of a chap I am; but, by Jove! I'll have a try, for I am in Queer Street and no mistake."

Fortune favours the brave, so Jack Linacre found his opportunity the next day; and so it was that Christian received her first offer of marriage.

Jack had finished his story, and was looking at her with undisguised anxiety. "That is all I can tell you about it, Miss Fordham," he said abruptly; and Christian started, as though she were only half awake.

"Oh, thank you, yes; I think I understand. Your uncle wants you to get married at once, or he refuses to do anything for you."

"That's about it, and I call it precious hard." Then Christian bit her lip again, or she would have laughed in his face.

"So do I," she returned after an interval. "It is barbarous, tyrannical, and very wrong of Mr. Vigne. It is infringing on your rights as a free-born Briton. One would think we were in the Dark Ages, when parents and guardians forced their sons to marry. I really do sympathise with you, Captain Linacre; but" —with a touch of embarrassment in her manner that rather appealed to Jack—"I wonder what made you think of me?"

Jack looked at her fixedly for a moment, as though he were nonplussed.

"Upon my word, Miss Fordham, I hardly know myself. When I left Uncle Jasper I felt so bowled over and knocked about that I sat down to recover a bit; and then all at once you came into my head—honour bright, I am telling you the truth—and I said to myself I will have a talk with Miss Fordham. We have always been good friends, and hit it off, and that sort of thing, and perhaps she will be good-natured and consent to marry me."

"Don't you consider that a large order, Captain Linacre? I am not at all sure that my good-nature will stretch to that extent."

"Oh yes it will," coaxingly. "Look here, my dear girl; you know all about me, and I am not really such a bad chap after all. Ask my mother and Carus."

"But I don't know them, Captain Linacre;" Christian spoke demurely, but there was still a gleam of fun in her eyes. On the whole, she was rather enjoying herself, though in her heart she was sorry for the poor fellow.

"Oh, but I shall introduce you, you see," returned Jack eagerly. "Look here, Miss Fordham; I am awfully fond of you really. Why should I have thought of you at once if I had not cared for you. I don't say," stammering and getting red, "that I am as much in love as some fellows; but then I am rather a cool sort of undemonstrative chap; but I give you my word, that if you will do this for me, that I shall be grateful to you all my life. Think what it means to me. It is like holding out your hand to some poor fellow who is drowning. Think of that, my dear girl," and Jack's voice was rather husky; his hand shook a little; his future was at stake, and he knew it, and the girl knew it too.

Then it was that Christian acted suddenly and upon impulse. Only a moment before she had been secretly amusing herself at his expense, and then the forlorn and despairing note in Jack's voice seemed to thrill through her.

Why should she not do it? she asked herself. She was very lonely; her present existence was hateful to her; no one but this man wanted her; and she could be his benefactress.

The next moment she put out her hand, and her eyes looked kindly at him.

"I am going to help the drowning man," she said in a clear sweet voice; "if you like, you can tell Mr. Vigne, that I have promised to marry you—I am my own mistress; Aunt Caroline will not object—I am sure of that."

Jack's big hands suddenly imprisoned the gray glove, no one was in sight, so he squeezed the girl's fingers, rings, and all, until Christian nearly cried for mercy. "Do you méan it? Am I a cad to take you at your word?" he gasped. She nodded her head smilingly. "By heaven! Miss Fordham, I will never forget this—this generosity," and Jack's eyes were a little misty; he got up from the seat and walked away a few steps, and when he came back, his face was beaming. "Come and let us walk," he said, taking her lightly by the arm; "you belong to me now, and I must not let you take cold." That air of proprietorship suited Jack rather well, and for the first time Christian felt a little shy, though the feeling soon passed off. "May I call you Chriss; it suits you better somehow." Then Christian laughed and gave him the desired permission.

"I am sorry you do not like my name," she said quite seriously; "mother loved it so—it was really my father's name, but he wanted his only child to have it. Adelaide, my cousin you know, says it does not express me at all; that I am not a bit of a Puritan, or like the people in that delightful 'Pilgrim's Progress'—do you know it, Captain Linacre?"

"Oh yes; I read it when I was a kid—but my name is Jack; you will be pleased to remember that."

"I have rather a bad memory, so you will have to remind me pretty often," returned Christian demurely, but after that they fell into more serious talk; to her dismay, she discovered that Captain Linacre wished her to marry him without delay.

"You see, it is just this," he explained; "I heard yesterday that we are ordered out to the Cape, and I believe we are to start in about six or seven weeks; I shall know soon—there is some talk of hurrying matters. It will not do to take you with me; but if we are married

before I go, you can leave me to arrange things with
Uncle Jasper; nothing will give him a better opinion of
your good sense, if you will only consent to be guided
by him."

"Do you mean I am to stay on in Mandeville Street?"
asked Christian.

Jack looked puzzled. "I thought perhaps you might
like to go to my mother's—at least the idea just came
into my head;" but to his dismay, Christian negatived
this quite vehemently—the young lady evidently had a
will of her own.

"Oh dear! not for worlds. I am afraid you know
very little about women, Captain Linacre; why, a mother-
in-law would be worse than Aunt Caroline; please," and
her hand touched his coat sleeve pleadingly, "when you
talk to Mr. Vigne, tell him that I should be quite comfortable living alone in lodgings—two small rooms will
satisfy me. I shall not be dull. I can go and see people,
and I shall not be in the least unhappy."

"Oh, I say!" and then Jack threw back his head with
one of his boyish laughs; they were not quite hitting it
off just now. The girl was quite honest; she did not
pretend that she was in love with him—she spoke with
a frank air of *camaraderie*.

"Suppose we leave all that, Chriss," he said pleasantly,
"until I have talked things over with Uncle Jasper and
Carus. I have got to look after you, you see, and to
make things as easy as possible for you, and I have a
notion that Carus will give me good advice."

Christian acquiesced in this, and they parted on the
best of terms. Jack said he would look in during the
evening, but Christian remembered that her aunt and
cousin were dining out, and that she would be alone.

"All right; then I will call to-morrow afternoon,"
returned Jack amiably. "I only thought I ought to turn
up on parade, you know; and that it was best to get
it over," and then Christian nodded and smiled, as she
went up the steps.

III

See-Saw!

There would be no backbiting if we looked at other people as we do at a picture—in the best light.

WHEN Christian had reached this point in her retrospection, she suddenly put her hands to her temples, pushing back her soft hair with restless, impatient fingers. " I think it must have been temporary insanity," she said aloud, and her eyes looked wide and frightened, then she felt her pulse. " Pen was quite shocked when I told her; she said it was terribly reckless—that brought me to my senses with a vengeance, for Pen is such a sensible sort of girl, and always means what she says. I did not dare tell her that I repented the moment Jack was out of sight, and that I cried half the night with sheer fright and misery. If only Jack had not been so nice the next day—so well behaved and grateful—and Aunt Caroline so pleased with him, that I could not say a word. Of course, he saw my eyes were red, for I caught him looking at me once or twice and frowning in an anxious way; and if only Aunt Caroline had left us alone, I might have had it out with him; but then the opportunity passed, and after that I was ashamed to tell him that I had changed my mind."

Christian was trying to focus the mixed sensations and inward revulsions of the past six weeks, but it was utterly chaotic and impossible.

The condition of her mind had been abnormal; it seemed to her as though some shadowy but potent influence had been whirling her through space, and that she had been too giddy to find a foot-level on which she could possibly balance herself. At night she would repent and bewail herself: she did not want to be married; she was not sure that she cared for Jack, he had so little to say—and she generally had to finish his sen-

24

tences for him. They did not seem to get on as well as they used, but when daylight came, with its duties and small feminine interests, Christian's spirits revived, and she was content to drift again.

From the first moment Mrs. Fordham had been on Jack's side; she was a stout, plethoric, rather slow-witted woman, but she was fully alive to the fact that Captain Linacre would be a desirable *parti* for her niece. "You see, Adelaide," she had said to her daughter after Jack had paid his first visit in Mandeville Street, "it will be a very good connection, and as Christian has no money of her own, and is not specially good-looking, I never expected her to do so well. Lady Armitage says the family is quite unexceptionable, though somewhat eccentric, and that if Mr. Vigne leaves his property to Captain Linacre, he will be very wealthy some day, so I really think Christian is to be congratulated."

Adelaide thought so too, but her feelings on the subject of her cousin's marriage were a little mixed; she was secretly delighted to get rid of a troublesome inmate, and she had never expected such a peaceable solution of a domestic difficulty. The daily friction had grown almost unbearable of late; Christian had become more unmanageable each day—she fairly bristled with small aggravating contradictions; it seemed absolutely a delight to her to oppose Adelaide's most cherished prejudices.

Adelaide would be devoutly thankful when her cousin took her departure; nevertheless, there was a sore spot of envy in her heart that Christian should be married first; that with all her own advantages of face, figure, and fortune, no eligible lover had ever claimed her hand; Adelaide thought too much of herself to lend a willing ear to every well-groomed nonentity who would fain have found a footing in the house at Mandeville Street—impecunious military men or needy second sons drawing a salary from the Civil Service which hardly covered their own expenses; Adelaide would have nothing to say to these gentlemanly waifs and strays.

Adelaide prided herself on her good sense and discreet knowledge of the world, and so it was that at eight-and-thirty she was still unmarried, and that, in spite of her good looks and girlish manner, people like Lady Armitage began to say " That dear Addie was a little thin and *passée.*"

Doubtless it was wormwood and bitterness to Adelaide when that provoking, heedless Christian pushed herself into the front in all the glories of a newly affianced maiden. Adelaide's congratulations were paid rather grudgingly and coldly: " You were not long making up your mind, Christian," she had said with a covert sneer, while Aunt Caroline was still wiping her eyes effusively, and the girl had winced and reddened a little.

It really had been a trying time for Christian; she had seen very little of Jack—two of the senior officers had been ill, and he had been kept hard at work. A hurried visit on his way to or from Beauchamp Gardens was all that Captain Linacre had been able to spare for his *fiancée;* nevertheless, the preparations for the marriage had been hurried on, for Mr. Vigne had been urgent with his nephew to have things settled as soon as possible. Things were certainly not going too smoothly for Jack. On his first visit, Mr. Vigne had expressed himself as much satisfied with the news Jack had brought: " You have done your part, and now I will do mine," he had said, and then he instructed him to bring a list of his debts on his next visit; and this Jack had done, but Mr. Vigne had been too ill to look over them, and had eventually to hand them to his lawyer. Week after week had passed, but Jack had found no opportunity of introducing his future wife.

" He is awfully bad, poor old chap," he said once to Christian; " I never saw him worse; he can't talk above a whisper; and they won't let me stay more than ten minutes; but I think he likes to see me. Oh, I very nearly forgot! He sent you his love, Chriss; and he hopes to see you when he is stronger."

" Is your mother soon coming back?" asked Christian rather anxiously, for as yet nothing had been definitely settled about the future.

Jack had been too harassed and overworked to attend to things, but when Christian had put this question, he had told her rather gloomily that his mother was still an invalid and unable to travel.

"I don't know how Carus is to leave them," he had continued in a vexed voice. "Heather is such a child; she is my mother's adopted daughter, you know;" and Christian nodded her head a little impatiently; of course, Jack had told her that before. "I am in a bit of a fix, Chriss," he went on; "if I could only get at Carus, we should soon hit on something, but I will write to him and see what is to be done;" but Jack looked so worried that Christian, with much tact, had changed the subject, and only relieved her feelings to her chosen confidante, a certain Penelope Mervyn.

Now this young lady had been the chief bone of contention between herself and Adelaide, as her cousin chose to disapprove of the friendship.

So only to Pen did Christian air her grievances: how Captain Linacre's people were in the south of France, and how Jack feared that they would not be present at the wedding; and he was so disgusted and disappointed, poor fellow! and how Aunt Caroline and Adelaide had decided that it must be a very quiet wedding; and that no one but Lady Armitage and a couple of Captain Linacre's brother-officers were to be invited. "I do so hate being married in my travelling dress," went on Christian rebelliously; "that is Adelaide's idea, bother her. I do believe, Pen, that it is sheer malice and envy on Addie's part, because she does not want to see me dressed as a bride." Christian's shrewdness had nearly grazed the truth.

"Walter would never hear of my being married in a travelling dress," returned Pen rather dreamily. She was a fair-haired girl, with a thin, tired face. "He says white is so beautifully symbolical of a bride."

Now the Rev. Walter Hamill was Pen's *fiancé*, and as he had only a curacy of a hundred pounds a year, and she had only her salary as an accountant in a large drapery establishment, their prospects were hardly promising; but as they were young and very much in love, and had all sorts of absurd, visionary plans in their heads —"cranks," as their friends called them—they were hardly to be pitied. Christian wished that she could have talked to Pen on this afternoon, when her head and eyes ached with all this retrospect; but though it was early closing day, Christian would have had a long walk to find her. Pen had only come once or twice to Mandeville Street, and then Adelaide had informed her cousin haughtily that for the future Miss Mervyn's visits must be discontinued; if Christian cared to make undesirable acquaintances, she could not expect them to tolerate it. Christian had fired up at once.

"Undesirable! what on earth could Addie mean?" she questioned. "Pen was as thoroughly ladylike as Adelaide or herself; she was a clergyman's daughter, and engaged to one, and a nicer girl never lived."

"Oh, I daresay," returned Adelaide, with a toss of her head; "an accountant in a drapery establishment is such a ladylike occupation. I don't say she is not a well-conducted girl, but mother and I are particular. We have our own circle of friends, and, in short—if you force me to speak plainly—we do not wish to make Miss Mervyn's acquaintance;" and in the battle royal that followed Mrs. Fordham took her daughter's side and Christian found herself defeated.

So the sacred portals of No. 25 Mandeville Street were closed on Christian's dearest friend. Christian soon ceased to do battle on Pen's behalf, but from that day she felt drearily that it would never be a home to her. "Mother was so fond of her," she thought sadly; "she never blamed Pen for being poor. She thought it just splendid of her to put her shoulder to the wheel and do the first bit of honest work that was offered her. Addie may say what she likes, but I will never desert my dear old Pen—bless her!"

Christian felt so wearied and jaded with much thinking, that she was ready to welcome any distraction that would take her out of herself, so when a knock at the door reached her ears, she sat up and straightened herself, and unfolded her embroidery, after the deceitful ways of women—for even the best of them are not above these little deceptions and subterfuges,—but the work fell from her fingers, and she uttered an exclamation of surprise when Captain Linacre walked into the room.

"Why, Jack! I never expected you this afternoon," she said, presenting her cheek for Jack's usual salutation; but Jack's moustache hardly touched her face, he was in such a hurry.

"Could you put on your hat, Chriss? Uncle Jasper wants to see you. He is better, and sitting up in his study."

"This afternoon! Oh, Jack, must I really?"

"There is no time to be lost," returned Captain Linacre, and it suddenly struck Christian that he looked nervous and unlike himself. "We must go round directly, for he will be expecting us; but there is something I must say first, Chriss. I have got my orders at last, and I don't know what you will say. They don't think the Major will pull through; at least, there is no chance of his starting on the 11th, and I have to go in his place. Don't you understand," as the girl opened her eyes very widely but said nothing, "I was expecting to leave at least a fortnight later with the 2nd battalion, and they have decided that I must go in the *Royal,* and she will sail early on the 12th." Now Tuesday, 11th April, had been fixed for the wedding, and the banns had not yet been published for the third time of asking.

"Then—then I suppose we are not to be married." Christian had grown a trifle pale, but she was conscious of no special emotion. She had not time to pull herself together, and to know whether she would be glad or sorry if the wedding were postponed, before Jack caught hold of her wrists.

"My good girl," he said irritably, "why should you suppose anything so preposterous? Of course we must be married; Uncle Jasper is determined on that. We shall only have to look sharp about it, for I must take a late afternoon train. But, Chriss,"—here Jack's voice was a little agitated—"I shall have to leave you directly after the ceremony." Then, indeed, Christian looked serious. The week's trip to Paris, which was all Jack had ventured to arrange, and to which the girl had been secretly looking forward, **was not to be carried out.**

Jack would have to leave his bride of an hour and start
with his detachment to the Cape. It was no wonder that
Christian's face lengthened, and her eyes smarted a little
behind her pince-nez. How flat and miserable it would
all be. Jack looked quite unhappy over it, but all the
same Christian's sturdy honesty would not suffer her to
make any pretence. She knew that it would not break
her heart to part with Jack; she did not want him to
go; in a way she was getting used to him; but she did
not feel as Pen would have done, if she had been in her
place, and somehow at that moment Christian envied Pen.
" It must be so nice to be really in love," she said to
herself.

Jack's big hands were still manacling the slender wrists;
he wished that Chriss would look at him and say something comforting.

" It is not my fault," he blurted out; " you don't know
how sorry and cut up I feel, Chriss."

" I am sorry, too," returned Christian slowly; " Aunt
Caroline will be so put out and shocked. You will come
back with me to the house, Jack, if it is only for a minute.
It would be so like a funeral, parting at the church door.
No; I don't exactly mean that, for, of course, there is the
churchyard service, but I don't like it somehow."

" I shall come back with you to the house right
enough," returned Jack. " What a queer girl you are,
Chriss—plucky, too; it is a pity I can't take you with
me," and for a moment a feeling of admiration, not un-
mixed with tenderness, swelled in Jack's heart as he
looked at the drooping brown head. She was a good sort
after all—he was getting fond of her—if only he could
believe that she cared twopence about him; but as this
thought passed through his mind, Christian raised her
eyes.

" Jack, you are not going to leave me with Aunt
Caroline? I could not bear to live here always; you
know I told you that before."

" Yes, and, by Jove! I quite forgot. I had a letter
from Carus yesterday; he is a decent fellow after all.
I told him when I wrote that you did not want to remain
with your people, that your cousin was a bit of a Tartar,

and that you did not quite hit it off, and that at the same time you did not much relish the idea of the Stone House, and here's his answer. I will read you what he says— the first part of the letter is only about business; just listen, Chriss. 'I quite understand your difficulties, old fellow, and it is a great pity that I cannot talk them over with you, but an idea has just come into my head. You know how litttle I use Many Bushes, and how, practically speaking, I live generally at the Stone House. My mother seems to find my presence necessary, and she never seems quite happy if I leave her. It is true, I have an affection for the place, and that I infinitely prefer a hermit's life. This is, no doubt, owing to my infirmity, but it is not well to give way to it. Why should not your wife take possession of Many Bushes during your absence? She might have some one with her if she likes. You can tell her, Jack, that the whole house is at her disposal, with the exception of my two rooms. Perhaps, when she knows us better, she will not object to my hermit ways if I come back to my old eyrie for a week or so.' There, Chriss, what do you say? Isn't Carus an old brick?"

"He is very, very kind;" and Christian flushed with pleasure. Jack suspected there were tears in her eyes. "I should dearly love to have a house to myself—and, oh Jack, if I could only get Pen to keep me company, I am sure I should be quite happy!" Then Jack winced slightly, but Christian had no idea of hurting him. "You would like me to do it," she continued wistfully, wondering why he looked so grave; then Jack roused himself.

"I think it is a capital plan. Many Bushes is not a grand house, Chriss, but I am sure you will like it. It is close to the church and opposite to the Vicarage, and the Disneys are nice people; and then, you see, Braybrooke is only three miles from the Stone House—that is in Silverton, you know; but mother and Heather drive over two or three times a week, so they would look you up:" but, to judge from Christian's looks, she hardly derived the same satisfaction that Jack did—from the close proximity of her new relatives.

IV

"You Will Have to Call Me Chriss"

And there are things that blight the soul as well as mildew blight,
And in the temple of the Lord put out the blessed light.
Mrs. C. O. Smith.

CHRISTIAN would willingly have prolonged the conversation, but Jack refused to be drawn.

"You had better put on your hat now, Chriss," he said in rather a masterful tone; "Uncle Jasper never likes to be kept waiting." And as Christian still lingered in rather a provoking manner, he took her arm and gently propelled her in the direction of the door. "He actually pushed me out of the room, Pen," she said somewhat mendaciously to her long-suffering auditor; but Pen, who had plenty of common sense, always knew how to read between the lines. Christian curtseyed and made a little *moue* at Jack when she found her arms unpinioned. "I shall be as long as ever I can," she said petulantly; but she knew better than to act on her saucy words; and they were soon walking through the squares as quickly as possible. More than one passer-by looked with interest at the tall soldierly figure and dark face of the young officer and the graceful girl beside him. Christian's colouring and hair were always effective, in spite of her lack of beauty; and then she held herself so well too, and carried herself with such a sprightly air.

Christian would willingly have questioned Jack on the subject of his brother's house. Many Bushes was such a queer out-of-the-way name. It conveyed to her mind a big barrack-like abode set like a lodge in the wilderness, with dark shrubberies coming up to the windows; but she soon found that his thoughts were engrossed with the coming interview, and that he was bent on coaching her as far as possible on her behaviour to the invalid.

"You must prepare yourself for rather an extraor-

32

dinary-looking person, Chriss," he said seriously. "Uncle Jasper is deformed, you know; and at times he suffers terribly, and he is often very irritable and abrupt in his manner. He lives alone, you see, and he has all sorts of cranks."

"I think you told me he disliked women," remarked Christian, who had already made up her mind that Uncle Jasper was an old bear and to be detested accordingly.

"Well, he is not always civil to them," returned Jack reluctantly. "I don't believe he ever sees one unless it be my mother and Lady Armitage, but of course he has Mrs. Arnitt."

"Who is Mrs. Arnitt?"

"Well, she is his housekeeper and nurse. Uncle Jasper couldn't exist without Arnitt, as he calls her. Ben is her husband and waits on him. Also there are a couple of maids, I believe, but Uncle Jasper never sees them. He hates strangers and wenches, as he calls them—girls of the lower orders are always wenches—so Arnitt and Ben do everything for him."

"But I suppose he has plenty of gentlemen friends?"

"Well, he has a few cronies—two or three learned professors, and his doctor and lawyer, and half a dozen antiquated bookworms who dine with him sometimes."

"Were you ever at the dinners, Jack?"

"Great Scot! I should think so, and of all the dreary, dryasdust banquets," and Captain Linacre made a grimace; "the old fellows enjoyed their port though; but the more they absorbed the more prosy and long-winded they became. I used to yawn until I nearly dislocated my jaws when some old duffer was riding his special hobby; and would you believe it, Chriss, there was Uncle Jasper sipping his toast-and-water and looking as fresh as paint and as wide-awake as Tossie when he has got a mouse," —and as Christian looked perplexed at this—" Tossie is the little white owl, that is Uncle Jasper's chief pet next to Sweeper, his big black cat."

"Dear me, what a very singular *ménage*," observed Christian; and then No. 25 Beauchamp Gardens loomed in view, and the girl held her peace.

A respectable gray-haired man admitted them and

glanced with some interest at the young lady. "This is Miss Fordham, Ben," observed Jack, and Christian, with a sudden impulse, held out her hand to the old servant, with one of her quick, bright smiles. Jack looked pleased, and Ben's heart was won from that moment.

"She is as fine a grown girl as one need to see," observed Ben later on to his wife. "Pity she wears glasses though; but I imagine the Captain puts up with it."

"I suppose the Missis is upstairs with Mr. Vigne?" asked Jack, but Ben shook his head.

"Not her," he returned knowingly; "she'll be in the front room taking a peep over the wire blind. Oh! here she be, sure enough," as a large-featured, plain old woman in rather a smart cap and gown came from a doorway, and Christian stepped up to her at once and shook hands.

"You are Mrs. Arnitt; Captain Linacre has told me about you," she observed in a winning manner. Mrs. Arnitt always called her that sweet young lady when she spoke of her afterwards.

"Favour is deceitful and beauty is vain," observed Mrs. Arnitt as she discussed the newcomer with her lord and master in their snug parlour; "it seems to me the Captain has shown his good sense: she is a pretty-spoken, smiling creature, and I hope the Master will take to her; it would be a blessing to have a young thing about the place, for we are both of us getting old, Ben; and we can't expect the Master to take notice of the wenches,"— the wenches at that present moment were a couple of comely country girls, who were being trained for service under Mrs. Arnitt's somewhat despotic rule.

Meanwhile, Jack had led the way upstairs; the first floor of No. 25 consisted of two drawing-rooms, at one time separated by folding-doors, but now only divided by curtains; both rooms were lined with book-shelves from floor to ceiling; escritoires and writing-tables were littered with books and papers; an invalid couch, with reading-stand and lamp, stood beside the fireplace. Christian had only time for a hasty glance before Jack, who

was preceding her, moved aside to let her pass him.
" Uncle Jasper is behind that screen by the window," he
whispered; " go on, I am following you." Then aloud:
" I have brought Christian, Uncle Jasper. I hope we
have not kept you too long waiting?"

A half-inarticulate grunt was the only answer to Jack's
polite speech, and then a short, misshapen figure in a
quilted silk dressing-gown rose with some difficulty from
the easy-chair behind the screen.

" I never expect punctuality from young people," observed a harsh, vibrating voice that rather rasped Christian's ear; it was well, she thought, that Jack had
prepared her, or Mr. Vigne's appearance would have been
a shock.

Even the loose dressing-gown that he wore could not
disguise the fact that he was terribly deformed: one
shoulder was much higher than the other, and his head,
covered with shaggy, gray hair, seemed too big for his
body. The face was distinctly handsome, and but for the
traces of suffering, and the sombre and somewhat repel-
ling expression, would have been almost beautiful; but
years of physical anguish and morbid brooding over his
troubles had left their indelible marks: he looked old and
pinched and unhappy, and the mouth was hard and
cynical—there was no welcoming smile as he held out a
thin, white hand to Christian, and then bade Jack bring
her a chair.

The girl sat down uneasily; Jack saw with alarm that
she was extremely nervous, and that the bright manner
that was Christian's chief charm had wholly deserted
her: she wished to behave well and to do her best for
Jack's sake—for the debts were still unpaid,—and yet she
sat as tongue-tied as any school-room miss.

Christian was sitting full in the sweet spring sun-
light, which turned the brown hair into gold; she was
too shy to look at Mr. Vigne, so she stared straight
before her at the pleasant, shady garden below, where
a few children were playing, while their nurses sat working and chatting under the May trees; somehow the
pleasant prospect did her good, and as Mr. Vigne watched
her grimly she suddenly exclaimed: " Oh, Jack, how de-

lightful! you never told me Beauchamp Gardens were so nice."

Mr. Vigne gave a harsh, cackling-laugh that somehow disturbed her. "Oh, Beauchamp Gardens aren't much to Jack's taste; his visits are rather like the angels— few and far between, eh, Jack? Well, it is not exactly lively for a young man, I will allow that."

"Invalids are not expected to be lively," returned Christian, feeling it incumbent to say something. "I am glad you have this beautiful garden, Mr. Vigne, although you share it with your neighbours; it must amuse you to watch the children, and the dogs," for at that moment two little fox-terriers were racing up and down the lawn in a state of perfect canine felicity.

"I think children a nuisance, and I hate dogs," was the gracious response to this, and again Christian was nonplussed.

"Oh, the dreadful old man!" she thought; "no wonder Jack came as seldom as possible."

"By the bye, sir, where is Sweeper?" demanded his nephew; "Christian wanted to see him, didn't you, Chriss?"

"Sweeper is taking a constitutional, I believe; he was here half an hour ago," and then, in a testy voice that took them both by surprise, "I wish to goodness, Jack, you would go out and smoke your cigar somewhere; Miss Fordham and I will never make each other's acquaintance at this rate," and though Jack was stricken with amazement at this unexpected order, he rose at once in spite of Christian's pleading whisper, "Oh no; do, please, stay," which Mr. Vigne overheard, and over which he smiled sardonically. "You had better let him go," he remarked; "I am quite harmless, young lady, although I look such an ogre. I never take anything on trust, and I want to ascertain for myself if Jack's future wife is endowed with that good sense of which he prates so largely, or whether it exists in his imagination."

"All right, Chriss, I'll be back presently," and Jack gave her an encouraging smile; "you have a talk with Uncle Jasper," as he closed the door: how Christian longed to run after him; in her fright and despair she

actually took the bull by the horns in an astonishing
manner; but then, as was often said, you never knew
what Christian would say next.

" I think you ought to call me Christian, Mr. Vigne,
as I am going to marry your nephew. Miss Fordham is
so very stiff." Christian spoke very coolly, though her
heart was beating rather faster than usual.

Mr. Vigne looked at her suspiciously from under his
heavy eyebrows; for the moment he thought the girl
was making fun of him, but she seemed perfectly serious.

" I have no fancy for outlandish names," he growled;
" why couldn't they have called you Betsy or Jane, or
something sensible?"

" Oh, I am so sorry you don't like my name!" she
returned regretfully; " you will have to call me Chriss
as Jack does; you won't mind that so much, will you?"

" Oh, we will see about it!" rather ungraciously. " I
have not got used to the idea of having a niece yet—
girls are not much in my line."

" No, I suppose not—what a pity!" and Christian regarded him rather compassionately. She really felt sorry
for the poor old ogre; it must be dreadful to be old and
lonely, and full of cranks. " I think," she went on in
her clear, young voice—Christian had a very pleasant
voice—"that it is well to know all sorts and conditions
of men, women, and children; it makes one more human,
and broadens your views of life."

" Oh, you think so, do you?" and Mr. Vigne leant back
on the cushions and plucked restlessly at the silken cords
of his girdle. " In your opinion, my life would be somewhat narrow, I'm afraid; I have few friends and no
acquaintances, and the world of books is all I know."

" Books are nice of course," returned Christian; " but
I like men and women better. I daresay, being an invalid, you have become somewhat groovy: that is the
worst of living alone; you ought to rub out your angles
—smooth them, you know, against your fellow creatures."

" I had no idea that Jack was marrying a philosopher,"
observed the old man cynically; but the girl's face wore
an expression of innocent goodwill that rather disarmed
him; he was inclined to be rude and snappy to **the**

young lady, because at first sight she had disappointed
him. Deep down in his sore, empty heart there was a
lurking tenderness for his scapegrace of a nephew—a
dim, troubled yearning to reclaim the prodigal. "There
are worse fellows than Jack," he once said to his friend,
Lady Armitage; "he is not a bad sort if he would only
pull himself up a bit; if he gets a good wife, she will be
the making of him."

Mr. Vigne had bargained with his nephew for good
sense, not beauty; nevertheless, as Christian came round
the screen, he had been conscious of disappointment.
Jack had not told him that the girl was short-sighted and
wore pince-nez—and he hated pince-nez; it gave women
such a strong-minded look, he thought. He had imagined Jack would have had better taste; but there, it
was no business of his; but his disillusion made him
rather short with the girl.

But as she talked, her voice pleased him; Christian was
recovering herself—she was getting more used to the
ogre; she began to have an idea that his bark was worse
than his bite—she was grasping her nettle with the usual
result.

"I suppose life teaches one philosophy," returned
Christian, and her voice was a little sad. "I have not
been too happy since dear mother died; one can't be
really happy, Mr. Vigne, unless one likes one's environment."

"And your environment does not suit you, eh?" And
the girl shook her head. "Perhaps that is why you were
disposed to listen to Jack? I suppose," and here Mr.
Vigne looked very keenly at her, "that you and Jack
are very much in love with each other?"

It was an unexpected question, and Christian grew
red to the very tips of her pretty little ears, but she was
too honest to leave him under a wrong impression.

"I don't think so, Mr. Vigne; we have seen so little
of each other, you see. Jack liked me, and asked me to
marry him, and he was rather nice that day—and somehow he talked me over; we are good friends—that is
all we are;" but with a sudden burst of frankness, "I
am so glad I am not going to the Cape with him."

Mr. Vigne looked rather taken aback by Christian's candid speech—he had not expected this. Once or twice the thought had crossed his mind that Jack was a bit cool, and had seemed to think more of getting a brush with the enemy than of leaving his young betrothed; but he had only said to himself, that Jack always was a cool customer, and that perhaps he had hurried on the thing too much. And now the girl was saying the same thing, and as though she meant it too.

" I hope you did not tell him so, young lady?" he blurted out after a moment's astonished silence.

" Oh, Jack knows all about it!" returned Christian coolly; " we don't tell lies to each other—Jack is really rather nice about that. I can always be sure of hearing the truth from him. Some men do pretend so, Mr. Vigne; they make-believe to be devoted to you, and then they go away and laugh in their sleeve. When Jack told me honestly that he wanted to get married chiefly to please you; and that though he was not a bit in love with me, that he liked me better than other girls—well, it was not exactly complimentary, but I thought it very nice and honest of him; and as I was equally frank with him, we just understood each other."

" Dear me, what a singular arrangement!" returned Mr. Vigne, but he looked rather puzzled.

" Perhaps it does not sound quite nice," went on Christian; " and of course we are not like ordinary lovers; but, really, Jack and I get on extremely well—he tells me things, and I am always interested; and if he wants me to do anything, I am generally ready to oblige him; and I don't try to make him pay me little attentions, and so he feels free and comfortable. We are just what Jack calls ' chummy"—that is what we are;" and Christian laughed in rather an amused way.

There was a quick, stern glance under the shaggy brows.

" And suppose Jack gets killed in the next battle— what then, young lady?"

" Oh, in that case I should be very, very sorry!" returned Christian without a moment's hesitation. " What put such a horrid idea into your head, Mr. Vigne; I do so hope poor Jack will come to no harm. Oh, here he is!" as the door was opened rather hesitatingly, and Jack's dark face peeped round the corner.

"You are just in time, Jack; your uncle and I have had quite a nice talk. I have been explaining things, and how I should not break my heart if you got killed, though of course I should be dreadfully sorry."

"Oh, you don't mean that, Chriss!" returned Jack good-humouredly; "you must not take her too seriously, Uncle Jasper; Chriss says lots of things she does not mean, but she is a good little girl for all that; and between you and me, sir,—for of course she is not listening,—I am getting rather fond of her;" and as Jack's hand rested on her shoulder, Christian gave an odd little laugh, but somehow she rather liked to hear Jack say that.

V

ADELAIDE PLAYS CHOPIN'S FUNERAL MARCH

A sharp tongue is the only edge-tool that grows keener with constant use.—WASHINGTON IRVING.

IT was evident to Christian that she had now paid her footing—each moment the ogre became less ogreish. A sort of dialogue ensued, and when Jack tried to put in a word, he found himself snubbed by both parties, and had to take a back seat.

It began with a growling sort of protest on Mr. Vigne's part.

" So you don't want to go with your husband to the Cape?" Here there was a mutinous curl of Christian's lip, and she edged away as far as possible from Jack. "And you do not relish the idea of the Stone House, and the society of your mother-in-law; it seems to me that you are rather difficult, young lady."

This was so obvious a truth that Christian felt decidedly cross.

" I wish you would not call me young lady, Mr. Vigne," she said pettishly; " it seems as though I were a foundling and had no name at all; if you don't choose to be friendly and call me Chriss, I should prefer Miss Fordham."

" Ah! come now, none of your airs, Chriss," remonstrated Jack good-humouredly, but Christian turned a cold shoulder to him.

" You leave her alone, Jack," returned his uncle testily; " we are getting on all right if you won't put in your clumsy oar. Well, niece-that-is-to-be, why won't the Stone House suit you; it is a big enough place in all conscience? Janet could give you a whole wing to yourself—there are eighteen or twenty bedrooms."

" Twenty-two, Uncle Jasper."

" Pshaw! who wants to know the exact number; there

is plenty of space—that is all Miss Fordham and I care
to know." But Jack was not to be repressed.

" Chriss does not care to live with strangers, you see."

" I do wish you would let me answer for myself,
Jack," returned Christian ungratefully; " I am not a bit
afraid of your mother; she could not be more trying
than Aunt Caroline and Addie,"—an audible chuckle
from the ogre here—" but I should prefer to be free,
and my own mistress."

" Rather a bad beginning to married life," remarked
Mr. Vigne grimly; " if these are your sentiments, young
—humph—Miss Fordham, I am inclined to pity Jack.
In my opinion—perhaps I am a trifle antiquated—a man
ought to be master of his own house."

" Jack's house is yet to be built, Mr. Vigne."

Then Jack gave one of his huge laughs. " Not so bad,
is it, Uncle Jasper?" But Christian was not inclined to be
patted metaphorically on the back; she did not want
Jack to laugh—she was far too much in earnest.

" It is very kind indeed of Mr. Carus Linacre to offer
me his house; and, as I told Jack, I shall accept it most
gratefully. I have a friend, a very dear girl, and I shall
ask her to come and keep me company until"—here
Christian's throat grew dry and she had to swallow something; but Jack was tired of being snubbed, and remained
obdurately in his back seat—" until"—here Christian's
eyes gleamed rather dangerously through her glasses—
" Jack has fought all his battles, and come back minus an
arm or leg, and with the Victoria Cross."

" You are to be congratulated, my boy, on having
secured an extremely strong-minded young woman for
your life-partner. No nerves or over-sensitiveness there,
I should say." But there was a twinkle in the ogre's eyes
as he spoke. It was evident that Christian amused him
—she was distinctly original. " Many Bushes is not a
grand house," he observed; " you had better wait until
you see the Stone House before you make up your mind."

" It is quite made up, thank you," returned Christian
firmly. " I should be satisfied with a cottage, if only
Pen could be with me; if Jack were not so dreadfully
busy, he would take me down to Braybrooke to have a

look at it; it is just impossible for him to get away, but I am to go and stay there as soon as ever I like."

" I expect it will be the best arrangement after all," returned Mr. Vigne, addressing his nephew. " Your mother is a bit trying at times—and she has got Heather —Carus will look after her. Well, well," raising himself jerkily, and as though the effort pained him, " I won't waste any more of your valuable time. Nicholson will be round this evening, and he will have a look at those bills; my business days are over—I think I must leave him to settle them. Now, about a wedding present for my niece-to-be," and here Mr. Vigne unlocked a drawer and took out a morocco case. " I meant Carus's wife to have had this, Jack; but as he is not a marrying man, I may as well ask this young lady to accept it," and the case was placed in Christian's hands.

Jack looked over her shoulder as she opened it; Chriss's little scream of delight and surprise was echoed by a gruff note of admiration.

It was a diamond necklace—the stones set very simply; there was no pendant, but the brilliants were unusually fine and formed a perfect collar of gems. It had been reset some years before, and had ever since then been at Mr. Vigne's bankers.

" I call this extremely handsome of you, sir," blurted out Jack, but Christian would not let him speak.

" Oh dear! I never saw anything so beautiful out of Bond Street," she gasped; " I have never had any necklace except mother's gold chain, cut in halves, with an amethyst cross, and Adelaide always sneered at it so. It is far too beautiful for me, Mr. Vigne—and you ought not to give me anything so good." Christian looked quite pretty and extremely young and girlish as she regarded the treasure with sparkling eyes.

" Tut, tut, put it away," with a wave of the hand, for Mr. Vigne was getting tired. " Women are all the same; they love bauble shops and baubles. It ought not by rights to have gone to the wife of the second son, but Carus is likely to be an old bachelor; there," as Christian held his hand with a wistful look, " never mind any more pretty speeches; I will take them on trust."

"Very well," returned the girl with a sigh; "but I had such a lot to say, and now you have put me out. I wish you would try and call me Chriss, and then we should get on as well as possible. May I come again and see you?"

"Wait a bit—wait a bit, until I send for you," he returned fussily. "You had better put the bauble in your pocket, Jack, and take her away now, and send Arnitt up to me."

"Are you sure I can do nothing more for you, sir,—wheel up the couch, or give you an arm?" But Mr. Vigne shook his head wearily, and the young people hurried away.

When Jack gave the message to Mrs. Arnitt, she looked a little reproachful. "You have stopped too long, Captain; he's got his pain again, and I must see to him. But there," as they regarded her blankly, "young folks will be young folks; and after all, it is not to be expected that you could understand the Master, for he is just a bundle of nerves; and if you set one jarring, all the rest of them go on throbbing till there is nothing but bed and silence for him."

"Poor Mr. Vigne! I am really very sorry for him," observed Christian as they left the house. "He was very dreadful at first—quite an ogre, Jack; but before he gave me the diamonds, I began to feel so full of pity for him—his life must be such a martyrdom."

"It is not much of a life certainly, poor old chap; and I am afraid," penitently, "that I have not added much to his enjoyment; it hurt me somehow, Chriss,—made me feel queer and topsy-turvy,—when he gave you the necklace. I know my mother coveted it when she was younger; but he always said it was for Mrs. Carus Linacre."

"He evidently thinks your brother will not marry."

"Well, I think he is right there; Carus always declares that he will never ask any woman to marry him, now he has grown so deaf. Carus is so painfully sensitive—he is like Uncle Jasper there; but he is such a good fellow that I am sure some nice girl would be ready to have him. Well, never mind Carus for a moment, for I

shall have to leave you directly. I want to say that Uncle
Jasper must have taken a fancy to you, dear, or he would
not have given you that necklace; you must have played
your cards splendidly."

Christian considered a moment. "I think I was rather
rude to him, Jack, but his 'young lady' was so provoking;
I did beg him so to call me Chriss, but I am convinced
that he will never do it."

"No, he will call you 'Mrs. Jack,' or if you displease
him, it will be 'Mrs. John,'—he never will use a name
unless it suits him; now, don't look so disgusted, Chriss,
for you will certainly be Mrs. Jack before another week
is over, so you may as well make up your mind to it."
And as there was no use arguing that black was white,
Christian changed the subject adroitly.

When Jack left her, Christian ran up to her own room;
the dressing gong had long ago sounded, the butler told
her, and she would have to make haste.

She dressed herself quickly, choosing a thin black grenadine, then she opened her case, and after a moment's
irresolution, clasped the necklace round her throat. Christian had a very pretty white neck, and the effect was
so striking that she would have liked to kiss the glass.
"You really do look extremely nice," she said to her
image; "and I think I admire you, my dear. 'Mrs.
Jack'"—here Christian frowned and laughed—"is quite
a graceful young woman," but she never even said in her
thoughts, "What a pity Jack cannot see me! Why should
I not wear it just to show Aunt Caroline?" she went on;
"no one is dining here this evening;" and the temptation
was so irresistible that Christian ran the risk of Adelaide's
disapproval, and a few moments later the two ladies in
the drawing-room had raised their eyes from their books
and were staring at the necklace.

"Good gracious, child, where did you get that!" exclaimed her aunt. "Why, they're diamonds, Addie!"

"Diamonds are sometimes paste, mother," returned her
daughter, but she spoke with some uneasiness; it was
evident that she knew them to be genuine.

Christian dropped a great billowy curtsey, and as she
swept the floor, the evening sunshine shone on the dia-

monds until the girlish throat seemed encircled with points
of iridescent light.

"I don't know what Mr. Vigne would say if he heard
your speech, Addie," she remarked coolly, when she had
relieved her feelings by this mocking obeisance. "What
an imagination you have! The dear, delightful old ogre
gave me this as a wedding present; he told us that it
had always been intended for Carus Linacre's wife; but
as he was unlikely to marry, he thought I had better have
it. I wanted to kiss him, Aunt Caroline, but I think he
would have had a fit on the spot, so I bottled up my
gratitude for future use."

"My dear Christian," observed Mrs. Fordham solemnly, "you really are a lucky girl; that is the Lenox
necklace that has been so long in the Vigne family. Lady
Armitage told me about it. Mrs. Linacre wanted her
brother to lend it to her for the county balls when she
was first married, but he never would do so; he told
her that her eldest son's wife should have it, and that
until then he preferred to keep it in his own possession.
I know Lady Armitage thought it rather miserly of him."

"And now it is mine—the dear, lovely thing!" returned Christian rapturously, but Adelaide interrupted
her rather sourly.

"You really are rather childish and absurd, Christian;
it is a pity that you cannot take things more quietly. Oh,
there is the gong, mother! do pray take it off, Christian,
and let me lock it up in the safe before Gray and Toppin
see it; wedding presents are never worn beforehand."

But Christian could not be induced to follow this sensible advice; she meant to sparkle for her own amusement and Adelaide's torment all the evening, and she
refused to part with it before bedtime; she even threat-
ened, if Adelaide said any more, to sleep with it under
her pillow. It was rather short-sighted and impolitic of
Christian, for her refusal offended Adelaide, and she did
not address her cousin once during dinner; and it was
a bad preparation for the evening work that was cut out
for her, but then Christian was always so heedless of
consequences.

Jack had deputed her to tell the Fordhams about the

alteration in their plans; he was full of regret at not being able to do so himself, but Christian assured him that it did not matter. There was no use beating about the bush, especially as Adelaide was in this unpleasant mood, so she stated facts as concisely as possible.

"Aunt Caroline," she said abruptly, as she put down her empty coffee cup, "Jack was so sorry that he could not stay this evening, for there is something he wanted to tell you, and which troubles him very much;" and then in few words she explained the matter—how there would be no wedding trip, not the ghost or shadow of a honeymoon, and how Jack would have to leave an hour or so after the ceremony; "and it does make him so unhappy, poor fellow!" finished Christian feelingly; but she forgot to allude to her own sorrow at the parting.

"Oh dear, oh dear!" gasped Mrs. Fordham. "I never heard of such a dreadful thing! You poor, dear child, what will you do?" And Mrs. Fordham wiped her eyes daintily with her lace-edged handkerchief; she was an emotional woman and easily moved to tears, and if only Adelaide had permitted it, she would have been really fond of her niece, but she was forced to own that Christian's presence in the house did not conduce to harmony, and above all things, Mrs. Fordham loved peace and a good digestion.

"I call it scandalous," observed Adelaide angrily. "Whatever will people say? We can explain things to Lady Armitage and the servants, but how are we to hinder gossip and talk? I always told you, mother, that Captain Linacre had no right to hurry matters on—such haste was perfectly indecent." Adelaide never would call him Jack; she said it was such a common name, and that she always intended to call him John when he was really her cousin. "Mother must do as she likes," she had said coldly; "but I shall certainly call him John, and of course your cards will be 'Mrs. John Linacre.'" Christian would have contradicted this if she dared, but public opinion was too strong for her, and the cards were printed.

Adelaide's scathing remark incensed Christian. "It is no fault of Jack's," she said, taking his part handsomely.

"A soldier must do his duty. It is mean of you to
blame him, Adelaide, as though the poor boy can help
himself; he cannot put off the wedding when the banns
have been twice read in church; and I have got my
trousseau—besides, he knows that Mr. Vigne has set his
heart on it."

But Adelaide chose to be aggravating; it made her
cross to see the glittering necklace on her cousin's white
throat; her own handsome jewellery seemed insignificant
and commonplace beside it.

"The whole affair is so ridiculous that I have no
patience to talk of it," she said in an acid tone. "Perhaps
you will have the goodness to inform us, Christian,
whether you intend to remain here on Tuesday, or if
you will go alone to the Stone House?" Then Christian
looked a little embarrassed.

"You are not very gracious, Adelaide; and under
the circumstances you might have been kinder; but I
suppose the truth is, that you want to get rid of me.
Aunt Caroline," turning to her alarmed relative, "I am
afraid I must ask you to keep me a few days longer.
Jack knows that I do not wish to go to the Stone House.
Besides, they are all abroad. Mr. Carus Linacre has
offered to lend me his house at Braybrooke; it is two
or three miles away from the Stone House. That is quite
near enough for me; and so I mean to make my home at
Many Bushes."

Mrs. Fordham opened her mouth, but she had to close
it again, for Adelaide would not let her speak.

"This is past belief, Christian!" she exclaimed angrily.
"Mother must talk to Captain Linacre. Such a preposterous idea cannot be entertained for a moment. You
must be crazy, child. Live alone at Braybrooke!"

"I do not intend to live alone," returned Christian
calmly. She was perfectly cool now; it was Adelaide
who had lost her temper. "Though, of course, if it
suited me I should have every right to do so, being a
married woman; but I shall ask Penelope Mervyn to
be my companion." Now, as Christian knew well, Penelope's name was as disturbing to Adelaide's equanimity
as the proverbial red rag to the bull; it simply made her
furious.

"I never, never heard of such a thing in my life!" she said excitedly. "Mother, why do you not speak? Christian is your niece, and you ought to have influence with her."

"Aunt Caroline has plenty of influence, and I am very grateful to her for all her goodness to me;" and here Christian squeezed the plump white hand affectionately. "But this only concerns me and—Jack—" Jack was evidently an afterthought, for the word came in rather jerkily—"and no one has any right to interfere. Dear Aunt Caroline," addressing her pointedly, and turning her back on her outraged cousin, "I have accepted Mr. Carus Linacre's kind offer, and as the house is not quite in order, Jack says I must wait a week or ten days before I go down to Braybrooke, so I shall go to Pen to-morrow and make all necessary arrangements with her. Perhaps it is unreasonable to expect her to go with me, for of course she will have to give notice to her employers, but in that case I shall not wait for her. I shall go alone;" and here Christian paused, for she was a little out of breath with her long speech, but Adelaide, with a contemptuous shrug of her shoulders as though dismissing the subject, sat down to the grand piano, and commenced playing Chopin's Funeral March as a cheerful close to the discussion.

VI

NUMBER FIVE GRATTAN GARDENS

It is far easier to see the foibles of others than to overlook them and avoid them.—MARDEN.

"In my youth," said Horace Walpole, "I thought of writing a satire on mankind, but now in my age I think I shall write an apology for them."

THERE is a certain dull, dingy-looking row of houses not far from High Street, Kensington, which is known by the name of Grattan Gardens, but the gardens are Liliputian, consisting merely of a flagged path and a strip of grass worn black by the free fights of pugilistic Toms. A wise and witty queen once explained that " The song of the nightingale and the wauling of the cat are two methods of expressing the same feeling," and doubtless this reflection must have been comforting to the inhabitants of Grattan Gardens when the night was made hideous by the ear-piercing screeches of the belligerents. In the daytime it was a quiet little back-water, into which one passed out of the stream and turmoil of traffic, from crowded pavements, with their gutter merchants and flower-girls, and wonderful glittering shops, for High Street, Kensington, was one of the time-honored Vanity Fairs of the British public. In the old days Christian had been a frequent visitor to No. 5 Grattan Gardens; on Thursday afternoons when Pen was free from her arduous work, the two girls would stroll up Kensington Palace Gardens and down the three-bordered walk, past the gray old palace, where a blue-eyed princess once dwelt, enjoying the sunshine and their own girlish fancies. Sometimes drawn by the appeal of softly-sounding bells they would turn into St. Mary Abbott for Evensong. It was Pen who would suggest this, but Christian found it soothing. As they waited for the service to begin, there was always a glorified expression on Pen's face, as though

50

she knew that at that very moment her Walter was putting on his surplice in the ugly little vestry of a Battersea church. " I like to feel we say our prayers together," she would remark simply when the service was over, for she was a devout little soul, who tried to live her religion in daily life. Pen lived with two other workers— as they expressed it, they chummed together. They were all poor and hard-working, and their modest *ménage* consisted of a small sitting-room and two bedrooms. Two of the girls shared a large top room, which was cold in winter and hot in summer, and one of them, Dorinda Chesney, commonly called Dolls, kept a small can of water handy for·use, when the cat symphony became too expressive and crescendo—at those moments Doll's language was a trifle coarse. They were both journalists, and earned their bread, like true daughters of Eve, by the sweat of their brow, working at the expense of aching heads and throbbing eyeballs.

Christian liked Gwen Stanford best. She was a good sort of girl, though somewhat plebeian, and a little free and easy in manner. She had begun life rather too early, and when other girls were under their mother's wing, " She was playing off her own bat," as she phrased it, for they talked a good deal of slang at times at 5 Grattan Gardens, and had grown rough and independent in consequence; but there was no harm in her, and she was good-natured, and would go without a meal if she knew a hungry person needed it more than she did. Christian was aware of this, so she tolerated Gwen, though she often grated on her fastidious feelings, for in her heart Christian did not love Bohemianism; but, on the other hand, she abhorred Dolls, and thought her an extremely offensive young person.

Pen used to try vainly to overcome this prejudice.

" You must not be so hard on Dolls, Chriss," she would say. " I know her manners are bad, and that she does things that Gwen and I dislike, but if you knew the home life that she had to endure. Why, her mother was hardly ever sober! She had to go to a home for inebriates at last; indeed, she died there, and the girls brought themselves up anyhow, for the father was not a nice man."

"Dolls might have brought herself up better then," returned Christian severely. " Just look at her clothes! How can any lady dress so? She looks like a factory girl out for a holiday. And her hair!" with a gesture of disgust. " And then she smokes cigarettes, and talks in such a vulgar way."

" Oh, I am afraid lots of them smoke!" returned Pen mournfully. " Walter says they do. He does not like Dolls either; but he agrees with me that there is good in her. I am not sure that even Gwen does not smoke too at the Club. I know there is a smoking-room there; but she never does it at home, because she knows I hate it."

" I cannot imagine how you and Gwen can put up with Dolls!" exclaimed Christian impatiently.

Then Pen sighed and looked troubled.

" I am sorry you feel so strongly on the subject," for Christian had actually refused to partake of any meal at No. 5 Grattan Gardens unless she were sure that Dolls would be absent. " But, really, Chriss, Dolls has her virtues. Her temper is not good certainly, and she flares up in a moment; but it is soon over, and she never sulks."

" Indeed!" returned Christian; " Addie might take a lesson from her then. When she is really put out, she simmers for hours and hours—long after every one else had forgotten what it is about."

" No, Dolls never sulks," went on Pen, pleased with the impression she had made; " and she is quite as good-natured as Gwen when she is not in a temper; and then she will put herself out to do any one a good turn."

" Oh, I daresay!" for Christian was becoming chilly again.

" I think Gwen and I took her in partly out of kindness," went on Penelope; " and just then we were so hard up, and Dolls offered to pay a month's maintenance in advance if we would only let her come and share our rooms. She talked Gwen over first, and then Gwen took her part hot and strong,—Dolls was so lonely and friendless; her sisters were all married or in situations, and her father had married again, and the stepmother was simply impossible. I spoke to Walter at last and asked his advice. Oh, it is such rest, Chriss, when you have some one belonging to you whose advice you can trust implicitly! He heard me out very patiently, and then he said: 'If this girl is really as lonely and friendless as you say, it is hardly safe to leave her to her own devices. She might get into trouble, and then you and Miss Stanford would never forgive yourselves. If she is so anxious to come you might try it for a time, but pray do not bind yourself; let it be a temporary arrangement, and you will see how it works;' and of course I acted on Walter's advice."

"And Dolls has been with you more than a year?"

Pen nodded.

"We should not find it easy to turn her out now. Besides, Gwen has grown fond of her. Their work is the same, and they have many tastes in common—so you see how it is, Chriss."

Christian was so impressed by this conversation that for some time she tried to put up with Dolls; but she never could quite conceal her aversion, and Dolls, who was perfectly aware of it, had her revenge by calling her Miss Highty-Tighty, which always hurt Pen's feelings. Pen slept in the small back room behind their sitting-room. It might have been larger and more airy, and the outlook was not particularly cheerful. The tiny slip of garden was always adorned by clothes' lines, either empty or filled; and any peg that was considered *hors de combat* became the cherished plaything of Smudge. Smudge was a forlorn waif and stray of a dog who had one day followed Pen home, and whom, with Miss Telfer's reluctant permission, she kept in a sort of kennel constructed out of an old water-butt turned on its side. The water-butt was old and leaky, and Pen and her housemates had been much put to it to keep their *protégé* dry and unfrozen on winter nights. It was Dolls who lined the big tub with pieces of old felt and worn-out mat, and who tarred the outside and nailed on bits of wood and the lids of old boxes wherever a nail could be driven in; but even plenty of clean straw, and a sack hung up as a curtain, hardly protected Smudge from cold and snow. The thought of the poor animal's sufferings prevented Pen from sleeping; and at last, with Dolls' con-

nivance and much dodging of Miss Telfer, who objected
to dogs in the house, "and wouldn't put up with one,"—
that she wouldn't for any money,—Smudge was smug-
gled into Pen's room, and spent blissful nights on an easy-
chair, covered with an old shawl. Pen did not dare keep
him there by day. Miss Telfer was not an early riser, and
when she came downstairs Smudge was always squatting
gravely on his haunches at the entrance of his kennel,
with his eyes fixed wistfully on his mistress's window,
and looking rather a sad little Diogenes in a tub.

Smudge was a long-haired, wiry dog, his coat was dark
iron-gray in colour, and his head was well formed, and
he had a handsome black nose. He had evidently good
blood in his veins, but there was the touch of the mongrel
too; but he was a gentle, friendly, and playful creature,
and his dog's heart was in the right place. From the first
moment he adored his mistress and yielded her a ready
obedience, even when he thought her commands vexatious.
Smudge found it difficult to understand why his nights
should be spent in paradise—for so he regarded that
dingy back room—and his days, except when he was
taken for walks, passed shiveringly in a felt-lined water-
butt; but a store of bones and wooden pegs buried in a
corner of the garden somewhat consoled him, and he
spent most of his time digging for them, and then gloat-
ing over them, like old Giant Pope in his den. Smudge
had one evil habit—he always growled at Miss Telfer;
but then she had met his friendly advances by threatening
him with a broom, or flapping wet garments at him,
which hurt his feelings extremely; in fact, he disliked
Miss Telfer so much that he always retired when he saw
her coming, and never ceased growling under his breath
as long as she was in sight.

As Christian walked up the flagged path that Thursday
afternoon she could hear Smudge barking blissfully—a
sure sign that his mistress was somewhere about.

"If those girls are in," she said to herself as she
knocked, "I shall make Pen come out with me, and we
will have tea somewhere, and Smudge shall come too."
And then the door was opened by the usual type of
lodging-house servant—a small, anæmic-looking girl, with

an anxious, babyish face, which lighted up with pleasure at the sight of the visitor. Susan was on the best of terms with the parlour young ladies, as she called them; but unfortunately they were not the only lodgers.

The widow of a captain in the Merchant Service lived in the drawing-room apartments. She was rather an exacting and fussy old lady, and poor Susan was often harassed to tears in her vain attempts to satisfy "the drawing-rooms." On these occasions Dolls would comfort her with small offerings of gingerbread and apples. It was even on record that one bitter winter's night, when Susan had a cold and seemed poorly, that Dolls crept past the room where Miss Telfer slept, in her stockings, with a steaming jug of hot lemonade, and a great plaid shawl that usually formed her own *couvre-pied,* which she conveyed stealthily to Susan, an act of kindness that Dolls' guardian angel probably recorded in shining gold letters, and over which the poor little drudge shed tears of gratitude. "Mother always gave me warm drinks when I got a cold," she said, with a sweet, childish smile at her unexpected visitor; and as Dolls drew up the coverings round the thin little shoulders with a whispered "Goodnight," Susan thought of the cottage in the Lincolnshire fens, and of the close little room where four of them had slept, and which somehow felt so snug and warm under the eaves on winter's night. "Just like a big bird's nest," thought Susan. "Oh, if I could only hug mother again!" sighed the little home-sick girl.

As Pen did not rush into the passage to greet her, Christian knocked at the sitting-room door. A muffled voice, as of some one awakened from sleep, bade her enter. It was rather a small room, but it had never looked to such disadvantage as it did on this afternoon.

Although it was half-past three, the remains of the midday meal were still on the table; a girl with short curly hair and pince-nez was huddled up in a rocking-chair by the open window, writing on a blotting-pad on her knee.

Another girl lay full length on the little horse-hair sofa, with her feet, shod in slovenly slippers very much down at heel, dangling over the end as though the couch was too short for her. In spite of the open window there was a faint odour as though of a cigarette, but nothing was to be seen.

"Great Scot!" exclaimed Dolls boisterously, as she scrambled up; "I thought it was the slavey. How do you do, Miss Fordham? You look first-rate; don't she, Gwen?"

Dolls was a tall girl, with rather a washed-out complexion and somewhat plain features. She had a super-abundance of coarse reddish hair, which she called auburn, and which looked as though a garden rake had been pushed smartly through it. The flaming red blouse that she wore harmonised ill with it.

"Come and sit down," observed Gwen hospitably, and she pushed Christian into the rocking-chair, and took her place on the window sill. "I am ashamed you should see the room in this untidy state, but you see, Dolls and I came in late, and we have only just had our dinner. I think you rang, Dolls, but I suppose Susan is too busy to come."

"Oh, it does not matter!" returned Christian hastily. "I hope Pen has not gone out?"

"No, she has only just come in;" and here Gwen frowned and looked unhappy. She was a short girl, with rather a thick-set dumpty figure, and her boyish head and pince-nez gave her a peculiar and strong-minded appearance, but her expression was bright and pleasant. A somewhat shapeless blue flannel blouse, with very loose wide sleeves, made her resemble an untidy pincushion.

"Is anything the matter?" asked Christian uneasily, for Gwen looked decidedly lugubrious.

"Yes, Miss Fordham," was the reply; "there is a good deal the matter. Poor Pen is in such trouble."

"Bradley and Wilson have given her the sack," explained Dolls, who never scrupled at interrupting people "Pen is crying her eyes out in the back room. Isn't it beastly of them, Miss Fordham? They are just spiteful cats. It makes Gwen and me feel sick, I can tell you," and for once Christian overlooked Dolls' vulgarity—she evidently felt so strongly.

"But why—why?" demanded Christian in a puzzled

tone. "I thought her employers were so satisfied with Pen."

"Well, she hasn't been quite the thing lately," returned Gwen. "No, let me speak, Dolls; I won't be interrupted. I think she wanted a rest, for she has had so many headaches lately. Anyhow, there have been two or three rather serious mistakes, and to-day Mr. Bradley spoke to her."

"It was sheer spite and envy on the part of one of the assistants," broke in Dolls. "It was that beast of a Miss Adkins; she has always set herself against Pen, and she wanted her place for a cousin of her own. I wish I had her here," and Dolls smiled fiendishly.

"I think myself that there was some underhand dealing," agreed Gwen; "Pen never could get on with Miss Adkins. Poor dear! she is too thin-skinned and ladylike. Anyhow, to make a short story, Mr. Bradley told Pen that she did not suit them, and offered her a month's salary if she would leave in a week, and that proves that her place is already filled up."

"Oh, my poor Pen! I will go to her at once," but to Gwen's surprise Christian's face bore no mark of sadness.

She was shocked and hurt that her dear friend should have been treated so shamefully. Nevertheless, as she tapped at Pen's door, she had some difficulty in composing her features to an expression of becoming gravity.

VII

NIOBE DRIES HER TEARS

Mists make but triumphs for the day.
                                        HENRY VAUGHAN.

If there is power in me to help,
It goeth forth beyond the present will,
Clothing itself in very common deeds
Of any humble day's necessity.
                                        MACDONALD.

"OH, Pen, my poor dear Pen!"

In spite of Christian's secret store of sunshine, the exclamation was wrung from her by the forlorn spectacle
that met her eyes as she entered the little room.

Pen was still in her walking dress, but her hat was on
the floor, and she was half-sitting, half-lying, on her low
bed, with her face so deeply buried in the pillow, that
she had not heard Christian's step, her shoulders were
heaving with sobs that she was vainly trying to repress,
for the walls of No. 5 Grattan Gardens were remarkably
thin.

"Oh, my poor dear, don't cry so!" and as Christian
placed her hand softly on the girl's head, Pen started up
as though she had been electrified; her flushed face and
swollen eyelids would have melted a harder heart than
Christian's.

"I cannot help it," she moaned. "Oh, Chriss, what
shall I do—what shall I do?" And as Christian sat down
beside her on the bed, Pen almost clung to her in her
despair—the poor child was too tired and miserable to
control herself; she was indulging in what women term
"a good cry,"—a rare luxury in her hard-working life—
and no soothing on her friend's part could check her
tears; the flood-gates were open, and her emotion must
find vent.

Christian desisted in her efforts after a time, and

58

sat by patiently until Pen could recover herself; she began to feel rather choky herself, and she had to take off her glasses and wipe them, they were so dim. Then she stroked Pen's fair hair in a comforting sort of a way, and said a cheering word to Smudge through the open window, for he had changed his joyful bark into short howls of dismay, and by and by Pen pulled herself together.

"Oh! I am so ashamed of myself; but I never expected you to come this afternoon—and—and——" More tears.

"I know all about it, dear," returned Christian soothingly; "you need not trouble to explain, the girls told me; it is a wicked shame of Bradley and Wilson. You poor little thing, to be turned away when you have always worked so well!"

"I did try so hard," sobbed Pen; "it is not my fault that I am not strong; and I think, if we could afford to live better, that I should not have so many headaches— at least Walter always says so; that is why he gives me so many new-laid eggs, but of course I share them with the girls." Pen had found her tongue now. "Mr. Bradley was not really unkind, Chriss; and I think he was sorry for me, but he said I was not the sort of girl they wanted—I was not sharp or quick enough. He said I had better try my hand at different work—be a nursery governess or something of that line; and oh, dear, when I knew the mistakes I had made on Saturday evening, I was so crushed that I could not say a word!"

"You might have told him that you felt ill that day."

"But I did, Chriss; and it only made things worse; for he said at once that I was not strong enough for the place. He promised to give me an excellent recommendation as regards honesty and good behaviour. I had always conducted myself well and like a lady—those were his words; but if I were his daughter—he has several daughters, Chriss,—he should advise me to undertake quite a different sort of work. Well, dear, I daresay he is right!" then Pen sighed heavily. "Walter always thought I should make such a splendid accountant: when I was at school I always got the prize for arithmetic and algebra!" Pen held up her head a little proudly as she spoke. "But the headaches certainly made him a little anxious, and he said more than once that he was sure I was thinner. The hours were so terribly long, Chriss; and often I was too tired to sleep. I dreamt once that I was adding up a column of figures that would not come right; and then, all at once, they seemed to be alive and change into a swarm of gnats that stung me all over. I must have called out, for Smudge woke me by licking my face."

"Did you tell Mr. Hamill this?"

"No, of course not; it would have made him so unhappy. Walter is always so anxious and worried about me. He says I am too thin-skinned for a working-woman; and that I need some one to take care of me; and he looks so sad when he says this, because he knows that it must be years before we can marry. So now I tell him as little as possible about my health."

Christian sighed sympathetically; then she looked at Pen with critical eyes. It was difficult to judge of her when she was so flushed, and her eyes were in such a condition; but she was certainly a little thinner; there were tiny hollows in her temples, where the hair had been pushed back; and she had noticed during the last few weeks that Pen had been so tired and jaded on Thursday afternoons, that she had not even proposed going to Evensong; and they had sat in the open air until they felt chilly, and had then had their tea at an aerated bread shop.

"Mr. Bradley is right," she said thoughtfully, while Pen sat in dejected silence, turning her engagement-ring round and round her finger. It was a little sapphire ring of no special value, but it was Pen's dearest treasure. "You must not look for an accountant's post—you are too weak and nervous for such hard work; besides, I know of a place that will exactly suit you." Christian tried to speak in a cool, matter-of-fact tone, but her voice was not quite under control, and Pen turned round sharply.

"You know of something—oh, Chriss!" and a gleam of hope rekindled in Pen's eyes.

" The work will be quite light and easy—ridiculously easy after Bradley and Wilson's—and the terms—well, I don't know much about that;" and here Christian stopped in rather an embarrassed manner; she could not imagine what she ought to offer Pen; they would have to talk it over together.

" I hope it will not be much less than Bradley and Wilson paid me," returned Pen anxiously. " I can only just make ends meet now; and I am afraid I am getting rather shabby," and the girl looked down at her well-worn black dress. " You know they are paying me until the end of the month, Chriss," she went on; " but I shall be free in a week's time; in fact, they do not want me after this week, so I must get something to do as soon as possible—for I would sooner starve than ask poor Walter to lend me money."

" For shame, Pen! you are not fair to Mr. Hamill."

" Oh no!" returned Pen earnestly, and the love-light came into her soft eyes; " you must not misunderstand me, dear. Walter would strip himself of everything he possessed to help me if he knew I was in need, but he has hardly enough for himself; but, Chriss, you are keeping me in suspense, do tell me more about the situation—is it teaching of any kind?"

" No, Pen, it is a lady, a friend of mine, and quite young, who needs a companion, and she has heard of you and thinks that you will suit her exactly. She is living—well, no, she is going to live in a nice place a little out of London, and——" here she paused, for Pen was gazing at her blankly.

" Shall I have to leave the girls—oh, Chriss! I would so much rather find some daily employment and stay where I am. Gwen is getting on so nicely, and Dolls has got on to a new paper; I never did much like the idea of being a companion, one is not free; and then there is Walter——" but Pen was a little mystified by Christian's reproachful look.

" Do you mean to tell me that you would rather stay with the girls than live with me? Oh, you perfidious Pen! you faithless, cold-hearted friend! And Jack is leaving me a grass widow, and I shall be so lonely at

Many Bushes all by myself!" And then, as Pen stared at her, unable to believe her ears, Christian explained the matter in more coherent fashion, narrating how Captain Linacre would be obliged to leave on their wedding-day, and how she had absolutely refused to live under her mother-in-law's wing at the Stone House.

And then she proceeded to tell her amazed auditor that Mr. Carus Linacre, Jack's elder brother, who was very deaf and extremely learned, had kindly offered her his own house at Braybrooke, as he so seldom stayed there of late years.

"It is to be got ready for me as soon as possible," went on Christian; "but, of course, no one thinks that I ought to live alone, so you must come, Pen—you really must, for I need you more than Gwen; besides, she has got Dolls; and we two will live at Many Bushes and be as happy as the day is long; and you shall ask what terms you like, for Jack says his uncle, Mr. Vigne, is sure to make us a handsome allowance, so I shall have plenty of money, and you will be able to dress nicely and look as you ought to look;" but Pen could not take it in.

"Live with you, Chriss,—by our two selves?" Pen could hardly gasp out the words, then her face grew suddenly anxious. "But Captain Linacre will come back," she continued, "and then you will have no need of me; I shall only be in the way." Then Christian gave a short laugh—that side of the question had not presented itself to her mind.

"He will not come back for a long time," she returned after a minute's puzzled silence, during which she reviewed the situation; "we need not trouble our heads about that, Pen. Even if Jack comes back, we shall not behave like Bradley and Wilson, and turn you out of the house; you shall have plenty of time to find a new berth, and we will both do all we can to help you; but perhaps by then you will be married."

But Pen shook her head; no such blissful prospect could be theirs for years and years, she assured Christian. "Walter must get a living before he could marry—and I daresay we shall be middle-aged before that happens," finished Pen quite seriously.

Niobe Dries Her Tears

There was no doubt that Pen was strongly attracted by her friend's proposal; she and Christian were devoted to each other, and for years they had been like sisters. Pen's nature was shy and reserved and she was extremely sensitive. With the exception of her lover, Christian was her only confidante; to her she could speak freely of her Walter's perfections, and of the half-dreamy, wholly ideal connection which they called an engagement, and which was as hopeless of results as it could possibly be. Walter Hamill always spoke quite frankly to his *fiancée* of the utter dearth of all prospect that lay before them.

"We are a couple of genteel beggars, Pen," he would say. "I have no one at court to back me or to give me a friendly shove in the right direction; instead of loaves and fishes, it is bread and salt. I shall be a stout, bald-headed parson, and you a prim, little maiden lady before the Vicarage is ready, sweetheart."

But once, when Pen was looking very pretty—at least in her lover's eyes—for in reality she had not the least claim to beauty, though she had a sweet, gentle expression, Walter Hamill gazed at her a little sadly.

"What a pity!" he said, and there was a touch of passion in his voice that thrilled the girl; "is it not grievous to think that I shall never have a young wife? I want you now, Pen, to be close to me, in my home—to be always near me. I should write my sermons better if I had you on the other side of the table—if I could look up and see you smile at me;" and that night Walter proved himself a very human lover, for he felt sick and sad and sorry for himself as he sat in his dull little room; but he was no coward. "This will never do," he said, after an hour's unhappy brooding, and then he took down his old felt hat and went to the Boys' Club and played single-stick with the lads, and put on the gloves and had a round with the champion player—a burly butcher lad with a fist that could have felled an ox; and the exercise did him good, and that night the foul fiend was exorcised. It was the thought of her lover that brought a distressed look into Pen's eyes.

"It would be lovely to live with you, Chriss!" she

said rather soberly; "and I know how happy we should be—but there is Walter; how am I to leave my poor boy?"

"How often do you see him, Pen?" But Christian knew quite well what the answer would be.

"Not more than once a month," returned Pen dejectedly; "we used to meet once a fortnight; but I had such long hours at Bradley and Wilson's, and Walter is so hard-worked. I think, being the youngest curate, they rather put on him;" but, brightening, "we write every other day."

"There is sure to be a post-office at Braybrooke," replied Christian drily; then a wee smile crossed Pen's tired face.

"Of course things have not been very comfortable here," she returned honestly; "we have either to turn the girls out of the sitting-room, or Walter and I have to take a walk; and if it is cold and dark and we are both tired, we go into the tea shop, just for warmth and comfort, and to have our talk out; in the summer it is much better; we take Smudge and sit in Kensington Gardens."

Christian knew all this before, but she wanted to prove her point.

"You just go out walking with your young man like any other shop-girl because you have not a decent place to receive him and make him comfortable." Christian never diluted an unpalatable truth. "Well, I call that horrid. Now, just listen to me a moment.

"Braybrooke is not quite an hour from London, if you choose a quick train. Now I have heard you say more than once that Monday is Mr. Hamill's free day, and that he could always get a few hours' leisure; but that, unhappily, you were fully engaged. Is not this the case, Pen?" And the girl nodded. "Well, what is to prevent Mr. Hamill from coming down to Braybrooke once a fortnight say, oftener if you like; but don't you think that a few hours of country air would do him good after Battersea and slums and night-schools? I shall be a married woman then," continued Christian pompously,—the words came out with a sort of relish—"and shall be quite a proper chaperon. You could meet him at the station, Pen; and we would give him such a grand luncheon,— you shall order it yourself if you like—and then you could take him for a walk or sit in the garden. There is a garden I know, though it is not large; and the church is next door and the Vicarage opposite. And we might have tea under a tree. There must be a tree—anyhow, there are bushes, or why 'Many Bushes'? And in the evening he will go back so refreshed with a basket of flowers or fruit or fresh vegetables in his hand. Well, what do you think of that?"

What Pen thought of it was translated into action promptly, for her only answer was to throw her arms round Christian's neck and kiss her and call her a darling, and then of course a few more tears were shed; and after that relief Pen dabbed her poor eyes with her common little handkerchief—bought as a bargain at four-and-six a dozen—and cheered up immensely.

"And what about Smudge, Chriss?" Then Smudge, who was sitting squarely at the entrance to his barrel, got up to wag his absurd tail and cocked his ears knowingly. Had not the beloved voice pronounced his name? The vision of a scamper with a meat pie at the end of it loomed up in Smudge's canine imagination; then he sat down squarely again and waited, for he was well used to waiting, poor fellow!

"Of course Smudge will come with us," returned Christian without hesitation. "Do you suppose we could leave him behind to Miss Telfer's tender mercies?" And then they discussed their plans seriously.

There was obviously no time to be lost, for there were only four whole days before the wedding, and one of them was a Sunday, as Christian observed; and as Pen flatly refused to move in the matter until she knew Walter's opinion, Christian suggested that Pen should play truant the next day, and that they should turn their maiden steps to Battersea and "beard the lion in his den," *alias* the Rev. Walter Hamill, B.A., in his rooms over the grocer's at the corner of Roskill Street.

"But Mr. Bradley will expect me to-morrow and Saturday," objected Pen in her conscientious way.

"Then write a little note, dear," returned Christian, "and say that you are too poorly and upset to do your work properly. It will be quite the truth, Pen, for I know you have a headache impending, and you can't deny it. You are going to lie down presently, and I will cover you up and ask Gwen to give you a cup of strong tea, for I cannot stay much longer. To-morrow I shall have the afternoon to myself," she continued. "Aunt Caroline and Addie are going to a big At Home at Chiselhurst and can't be back much before dinner. I can meet you at three o'clock at the corner of Mandeville Street, by the cab-stand. We will be extravagant for once and take a hansom all the way, and then we can come back by train or omnibus. Do you think we are likely to find Mr. Hamill in, or will it be safer to make an appointment?"

"I think I will send him a note," returned Pen, "and tell him we have something particular to say to him, and then he will be sure to be in. I will write it after tea, and lie down for a bit; and Chriss, dear, I quite forgot, Susan told me that Miss Telfer had gone out and would not be back until after tea, so will you please bring in poor Smudge, for he may as well be happy?" And then, to Smudge's delight, the door of his elysium was opened, and he spent a blissful evening curled up on his old shawl close to his mistress's pillow, with a caressing hand touching his rough coat.

VIII

THE CURATE OF ST. CUTHBERT'S

Be what you wish others to become; let yourself, and not your words, preach for you.

Let our teachers and preachers tell men plainly and distinctly that no amount of believing will do them any good as long as their lives give the lie to their belief.

MARDEN.

CHRISTIAN was punctual to her appointment the following afternoon and found Penelope waiting for her. A hansom was hailed, and then the two girls jumped in and drove rapidly off.

Christian's first act was to inspect Pen critically. The girl was still looking somewhat wan and heavy-eyed—the result of excitement and a nearly sleepless night—but she had made her toilet with some care. She wore her best hat and new gloves, and a dainty little lace tie that Christian had given her on her birthday lent the finishing touch.

Christian's mother had once said that Penelope Mervyn was a perfect little gentlewoman from the crown of her head to the sole of her foot, and as Mrs. Fordham was a gentlewoman herself, she was no mean judge. Christian always declared that Pen was lovely, and though she was neither pretty nor beautiful, the word somehow suited her, for it was an extremely sweet face, and there was a charm in her clear soft eyes and gentle expression that had won the Rev. Walter Hamill at first sight.

"I can see you have slept badly, Pen," observed her friend reproachfully. "Mr. Hamill will find that out at once."

"My head ached so," returned Pen quietly; "and I think I was too excited to close my eyes. As I lay still in the darkness I kept saying to myself that it could not be true. Oh, Chriss, how lovely for us two to live together! And though I am sorry to leave the girls, I must

67

own that I have found it rather trying sometimes. I do
so hate slang, and up-to-date talk, and literary jargon,
and cigarettes, and——"

"I only wonder how you put up with it as you did,"
interrupted Christian with her customary bluntness.

"You see, I was out all day, dear," returned Pen;
"and when I came home, I was so tired that I could
think of nothing but bed and Smudge. It was only on
Sundays that I found it so extremely trying. Dolls is so
noisy, and she never likes Sunday, and we could not
induce her to go to church. But Gwen is different; she
is really a nice girl, Chriss, and I am very fond of her."

"Then she shall come and stay at Many Bushes," observed Christian, giving herself the airs of a chatelaine;
"but not Dolls. Dolls shall never cross my threshold."

"I was afraid you would say that," was Pen's reply.
"Poor Dolls!" sighing. "Well, it is your house, Chriss,
not mine; but I should have liked her to come once, just
to show her you bore her no ill-will." But Christian was
inexorable. "She drew the line at Dolls," she returned
in a dignified tone. It was Mr. Carus Linacre's house,
and she had her position to maintain—Jack's relatives
were not far away, and all small country towns were
gossipy and narrow. A slangy, loud-voiced young Bo-
hemian like Dolls, with her bad style and free-and-easy
manner, would certainly compromise them.

"I cannot do it even for you, Pen dear," she said
decidedly; and then of course Pen yielded the point, all
the more readily that she knew Christian was right. But
she was far too happy to be damped for more than a
minute, and she presently began chirping blissfully.

"How delightful to be driving with you, Chriss, instead of adding up columns of figures in that stuffy little
office! I think the want of proper ventilation made my
head so bad. I hope Walter will see us driving up. I
daresay he will be looking out for us. Oh dear! I wonder what he will say to it all—and if he will be very
pleased?"

"I have not a single doubt, Pen. Mr. Hamill is a
sensible man."

"Yes, and he always gives such good advice. I think

few men are so clear-sighted as Walter. I know people
sometimes think him absent," went on Pen; " his manner
gives them that impression, but I never found him so
myself. When I tell him things, he always seems to
grasp them at once."

" Ah! but you are his sweetheart, you see," returned
Christian mischievously, for she always enjoyed making
Pen blush. " Of course that makes a difference. If Jack
did not listen to me when I talked to him, I should very
soon bring him to book; but you are so humble, Pen.
I believe if Mr. Hamill patted you on the head as he does
the school children and called you a good little girl, you
would not be at all offended."

" Nothing that Walter could do would offend me,"
returned Pen smiling; " but he is far too full of respect
for me to patronise me in that manner; you know yourself, Chriss, how very gentlemanly he is."

" My dear Pen," returned Christian, with a sudden
irritation that surprised herself, " I am too well aware that
all the cardinal virtues are wrapt up in Mr. Hamill, and
that there never was, and never will be, such an immacu-
late young man, and that my poor Jack cannot hold a
candle to him." Now what induced Christian to fly off at
this tangent—no wonder Pen was a little mystified.
" Jack is of the common or garden sort," went on Christian; " that is why we suit each other. We have no
yearnings after ideals. ' Life's trivial round' satisfies us
—' the desire of the moth for the star' isn't in it at all.
I am sorry if I shock you, Pen; but Jack and I are of
the earth earthy!"

" My dear Chriss, what can you mean?"

But Christian had not an idea what she meant, and
why a sort of restless dissatisfaction and impatience had
seized her at Pen's guileless speech. Pen's simple faith
in her lover, her boundless reverence, roused an envious
spirit in Christian. If she could feel for Jack in that
way—if she could believe in him, give him her girlish
fealty and adoration—then she broke into a laugh—

" Oh, how absurd we are! You are three-and-twenty,
Pen, and I am four years older, and yet we can talk all
this nonsense. Look, there is his reverence!"

As the hansom slackened speed, the grocer's shop was
in sight; and as Christian spoke, a tall, clerical figure
came out of the side door and stood on the curb, waving
his felt hat in token of recognition.

The Rev. Walter Hamill was like Captain Linacre—a
tall, thin man—and he was well built and sound of mus-
cle as Jack himself, but here all resemblance ceased.

Mr. Hamill had a smooth, boyish face and the eyes
of a dreamer or idealist. He was a little slow in manner
and speech, and sometimes hesitated as though he were
weighing his words, and this often gave people the impression that he was absent-minded; but nothing could
be further from the truth. " He was all there!" as Jack
would have phrased it.

In church his enunciation was remarkably clear; and
as he had a good tenor voice and a correct ear, his vicar
found him invaluable in training the choir and organising
Saturday concerts at the Boys' Club. In the night school,
the recreation hall, or on the cricket-field, the junior curate of St. Cuthbert's reigned supreme. His powers as
an athlete and boating man were well known to the authorities, and the rough lads looked up to him as their
champion player and leader of sports.

" He's a wunner, he is!" observed Job Pringle, a
hoarse-voiced, brawny young ruffian, who was a coster-
monger, and drove one of the smallest of donkeys. " If
parsons was all after his cut——" and in his admiration
Job indulged in a little playful blasphemy as he prodded
Jess.

Walter Hamill had made his acquaintance one wet,
blustering March day. He was standing on the curb,
waiting for a coal-waggon and a heavy dray to pass,
when he caught sight of the young coster; the contrast
between the big strapping youth and the small, weak
donkey was at once absurd and pitiable. Job was as
usual volleying oaths freely and flourishing a stick. He
wanted Jess to pass between the dray and the waggon,
but Jess had no mind to terminate a miserable existence
by so painful a death.

Walter stepped into the road, and his eyes twinkled
a little: " Don't you think you could carry the donkey,

my man; it is hardly fair to expect it to carry you?" and the expression on the curate's face was so good-natured and comical that Job, who had a sense of humour, broke into a hoarse laugh.

"Well, she is a bit young, master; but I got her cheap, and"—here Job said something about his eyes that was not exactly a benediction—"wot are you after, parson?" —another string of explosives, for Mr. Hamill had taken a bunch of carrots from the cart and was offering them to Jess.

"They are for sale, aren't they?" returned Walter absently, as Jess nibbled hungrily at the carrots. "Look here, old man, I want you to come to our club—St. Cuthbert's Club in Kempsell Street—and have a boxing match with me. I have got a lot of fellows as big as you, and there is plenty of fun going on." Job growled something, and pushed back his fur cap and scratched his head, while Mr. Hamill took out a handful of pence to pay for Jess's meal. "I shall expect you on Saturday," he said quietly; and Job drove off in astonished silence.

"Well, if that ain't the rummiest cove I ever came across," he said to himself; but when Saturday came, Job presented himself at the Club in his best velveteen waistcoat, and his hair smooth and shining with grease.

All this had taken place before Mr. Hamill had been many months at St. Cuthbert's, and since then Job had been a regular attender at the Club and night school, and Jess had become a sleek, handsome little donkey, and the pride of Job's heart.

Had not parson given her a set of new harness, when the worn-out gear had given way altogether and could not be mended? And did not the wits of Battersea and Wandsworth call Job "the dandy coster" and jeer at his smart turnout?

Job still indulged in strong language, but Jess had got used to it. Her master always walked up the hills now; her nose-bag was always well filled; and her rough coat nicely groomed—so Jess thought herself in clover. Job was always very careful not to air his remarkable vocabulary when the curate was near. Mr. Hamill never preached except in the pulpit, and his hints were brief

and few, but somehow men were always at their best
with him; and even in his Oxford days his friends felt
intuitively that a coarse story, however draped it might
be, or a little " cuss word," was extremely distasteful to
him.

And so even the night school lads dropped their rough
oaths at the door when they entered the cheery recreation
hall, or muttered them inaudibly when the " darned" ink
blotted their copy. " He be a gentleman, he be, and a
rare plucked one!" as Mat Smithers would say; and
as soon as the tall, athletic figure appeared there would
be a ring of grinning faces round the parson.

As Mr. Hamill helped the girls out of the hansom he
looked at them rather scrutinisingly, but his hands lingered on Pen's.

Christian was asking the driver his fare from Mandeville Street, so Mr. Hamill drew Pen into the little entry
and detained her a moment.

" What is the matter, dearest; you look quite ill and
worn out?" he asked rather hurriedly; but Pen smiled
at him happily.

" No, I am not ill, only very tired; but we have had
such a nice drive, and it has quite refreshed me after my
bad night. Walter dear, we cannot talk here,"—for Christian was coming towards them—" so much has happened,
and there will be such a lot to tell you," and then Pen
gently released herself and went upstairs.

Mr. Hamill waited to ask Christian if the man had
cheated her; but Christian stoutly denied this, for she
always took the part of cabmen.

" It is not his fault if I choose to give him a little over
the fare," she said defiantly; " it is my private and particular form of extravagance—my pet charity. Think what
they have to endure," she went on,—" long hours, cold,
heat, and every form of open-air wretchedness—and to
think of grudging them an extra sixpence, even if they
do spend it in hot whiskey-and-water!" Then Mr. Hamill
laughed and declared she was incorrigible, for this was
an old argument.

Mr. Hamill's sitting-room had two windows: one looking out on High Street, with its trams, omnibuses, and

ceaseless noise; the other, on the comparatively quiet Roskill Street, where passers-by were few and traffic *nil;* here he had placed his writing-table, nearly submerged under its piles of parish magazine papers, Greek Testament, lexicons, and books of reference. Here did the curate of St. Cuthbert's write his weekly sermon and bi-weekly love letters—"Dearest Pen" and "My dear friends" inscribed alternately on the blotter,—and here stood a framed photograph of Pen herself. In the other window there was a reminiscence of University days in the shape of a softly padded easy-chair, and a reading-desk and lamp-stand combined, the gift of a wealthy god-father—his sole legacy when he departed this life.

On either side of the fireplace there were book-shelves filled with miscellaneous literature—Homer, Virgil, and Herodotus, cheek by jowl with Newman's *Sermons* and the *Fathers.* Secular reading in the form of Sir Walter Scott's novels, Hall Caine, Robert Stevenson, and Crockett reposed on the lower shelves, while the top one fairly groaned under an array of silver mugs and cups, chiefly won in his public school-days.

A beautiful photograph of St. Augustine and Monica over the fireplace had been Pen's first gift. She had sacrificed a new hat to buy it, and the frame had been so costly that she had also to forego a pair of chevrette gloves warmly lined for winter.

Mr. Hamill had chidden her gently as he thanked her. "You must never do this again, darling," he had said to her. "It is my favourite picture, and I shall love to have it; but I know too well that you cannot afford to give me presents;" and Pen hung her head and blushed.

"I did so want you to have it," she sighed; but she wondered a little why her Christmas present was the very pair of chevrette gloves for which she had longed and a little dark brown muff. Walter never gave her useless presents, and somehow they were generally what she wanted most.

There was no other picture besides St. Augustine and the Monica; but the walls were adorned with foils, walking-sticks, revolvers, curiously carved pipes, butterfly nets, and racquets; while a small and somewhat rickety what-not was the receptacle for a mass of odds and ends—box-ing-gloves, tobacco-pouches, sweaters, and old caps of every description.

When Mr. Hamill had placed Pen in his especial chair, and found a comfortable seat for Christian, he paused for a moment.

" Shall I ask Mrs. Binney to bring up tea now, or shall we have our talk first?" He addressed Christian, but his eyes wandered to Pen's tired face.

" I think we had better talk first; it is really too early for tea," returned Christian, who was never long in making up her mind. " Are you going to begin, Pen, or shall I?"

" Oh, I think you, dear!" faltered Pen. She was taking off her gloves and smoothing them rather nervously. It was not easy to talk before a third person. Walter had placed himself beside her, and she felt he was watching her rather anxiously. She was afraid of breaking down or being silly, and yet she did so long to tell him. " I think you had better begin, Chriss," she said meekly; and Christian, nothing loath, plunged into her story.

IX

"Two's Company"

Without love there is no interior pleasantness of life.
                                        SWEDENBORG.

Judicious silence is far preferable to the truth roughly told.
                                        ST. FRANCIS DE SALES.

CHRISTIAN did not beat about the bush; she stated the matter very clearly and concisely. Mr. Hamill started slightly when he heard of Bradley and Wilson's dismissal, then he moved a little closer to Pen and took her hand.

"Never mind, dear," he said quietly. "I have long known that the work was far too hard for you. We must find you something lighter. I will speak to the Vicar and Mrs. Earle; they are kind people, and have a large connection. Don't lose heart, Pen; something will turn up."

Pen smiled gratefully, but she had no opportunity of speaking, for Christian was determined to finish her story in her own way.

"There is no need for you to look out, Mr. Hamill," she said in a quick, decided voice. "I have found something that will suit Pen perfectly. She is going to live with me at Braybrooke; and I shall take such care of her, and feed her up, that she will be a different girl in six months. Don't you think country air and rest and freedom, and no horrid accounts and bookkeeping, will bring back Pen's old colour?" But Mr. Hamill was too bewildered to respond suitably to Christian's triumphant speech.

"I don't understand," he returned slowly. "Has Captain Linacre proposed this? I thought you would go out to him by and by?"

"Let me tell him, Chriss; you are too abrupt, and you don't explain things properly." Pen was asserting herself now. "Walter, dear, Christian is not going out at all. Captain Linacre will be at the Cape, so his brother has

75

offered her his house, and she is going to live at Braybrooke, near her husband's family; and as she will be
dull alone, she wishes me to live with her." But again
Christian struck in in her crisp, direct way.

" Pen is coming as my friend; we shall be like sisters.
I was only joking when I called it a situation. I shall
make her a proper allowance for dress and pocket-money.
Of course that will be necessary; and when Captain Linacre returns, we can take plenty of time to find her some
other employment; but there is no need to think of that
now. I hope your reverence approves of my suggestion,"
with an attempt at playfulness, but there was just a touch
of anxiety in Christian's tone. Walter Hamill was silent
for a moment, and both the girls saw that he was greatly
stirred. Then he got up from his chair, and stood opposite Christian.

" I must shake hands with you, Miss Fordham," he said,
with genuine feeling, " and thank you in Pen's name and
my own. You are a loyal friend to both of us, and I can
fully trust Pen to your care." And he wrung Christian's
hand so hard that she winced with pain, but her eyes
sparkled with pleasure.

" I told Pen that you were a sensible man, Mr. Hamill,"
she said approvingly. " Very well, then, we may consider
the matter settled." But Pen had a good deal more to say
on the subject.

" Braybrooke is hardly an hour from town, Walter,"
she said eagerly; " we shall see each other just as often.
Christian is so kind, she wants you to spend your free
Mondays at Many Bushes—that is the name of the house.
She says country air will be so good for you; and that
we will have lovely walks and good times together."
Then the young curate's face waxed radiant.

" I am in luck's way as well as you, Pen," he remarked
with a laugh; " it won't be a bad exchange for Grattan
Gardens and tea shops; and, upon my word, I think we
may congratulate ourselves; I am not a bit sorry that
the Stanford-Chesney alliance is to be given up; those
girls were not up to your level."

" The poor things are dreadfully unhappy," returned
Pen sadly. " Gwen was so upset that she cried all break-

fast time; and Dolls was as cross as possible—that is
always her way of showing she is sorry; but of course
they know it is for my good."

" Will it make much difference to them in a pecuniary
sense?" asked Christian.

" In a way it must do so," replied Pen; " because we
clubbed together; but I think they can manage fairly well.
My room will be given up. I believe Miss Telfer really
wants it for her own use, so she will charge less for the
apartments; and now Gwen has got a rise—so altogether
they ought to get on."

" Oh, they will be all right!" returned Christian, and
then she remembered suddenly that she had a note to
write, and asked Mr. Hamill's permission to use his
writing materials. When the note was finished, she observed casually that she should post it herself; and on her
way downstairs ask Mrs. Binney to bring up the tea; and
as the young people made no objection to this, Christian
carried off her note—and if it were a little ruse to leave
the lovers to enjoy a few moments' unrestrained talk,
only Pen guessed it, and was secretly grateful.

Christian took quite a long walk; but time had passed
so quickly to the young couple that they thought she had
only been absent ten minutes. Mrs. Binney did not bring
the tea until Christian had returned; and then they gathered happily round the table.

Pen presided over the tea-tray with such modest grace
and such evident enjoyment in her face that the curate
looked at her with rapt admiration. How homelike the
shabby lodgings appeared to him with Pen's sweet face
smiling at the head of the table. No wonder the young
man sighed once or twice as he thought of the long years
that must pass before he could bring his wife home.

They stayed so long that Christian decided that they
must take another hansom back; but she was very quiet
and rather uncommunicative during the long drive to
Mandeville Street. Pen glanced at her once or twice,
then she wisely left her to her own reflections, and aban-
doned herself to a blissful reverie. Those few minutes of
unrestrained talk had brought Pen endless comfort; never
had Walter been dearer or more sympathetic. How he

had petted and praised her and called her his brave little
Pen for struggling so patiently with her difficulties!

"It will be such a relief to know you are with your
friend," he had said; "I have been very uneasy about
you, though I would not let you know it, dearest. I disliked your environment, and I knew your work was wear-
ing you out. Miss Fordham is a good creature—a trifle
original perhaps, but there is no harm in her; but somehow, Pen, I don't believe she cares much about Captain
Linacre;" but Pen had returned an evasive reply. Walter
was dreadfully clear-sighted she knew, and she did not
intend to let him find out that she shared his opinion;
from the first she had guessed that Christian was not in
love with Jack Linacre. The next moment Walter had
made her supremely happy by suggesting that they should
go to St. Mark's together on Tuesday. Christian had
begged her friend to be present. "I shall like to feel you
are there, Pen," she had said to her; "and if I can I shall
try and speak to you." And of course Pen had promised
to be there; but neither she nor Christian had expected
Mr. Hamill.

Pen had reserved this tid-bit of news as a sort of *bonne
bouché,* but Christian received it rather coldly.

"That will be nice for you, Pen," was all she said, but
her face had clouded a little at the mention of Tuesday.
The next moment she yawned and said she was tired, and
she was a little severe with the driver when he took a
wrong turning.

She parted with Pen affectionately however when they
reached Mandeville Street; but she looked out of spirits
during the evening, and that night she cried herself to
sleep, thinking of her mother. "Oh, if only mother were
here to talk to me!" she said to herself.

The next day she was a little more cheerful. Jack's
wedding present arrived—a handsomely fitted dressing-
bag, evidently Jack was flush of money just then. Lady
Armitage, who took a good deal of interest in the young
couple, had sent a case of silver salt-cellars. Christian was
so lacking in enthusiasm over this useful present that Adelaide scolded her.

"I hope you intend to take an interest in your house,

Christian," she said, rather crossly; " it is very kind of dear Lady Armitage to send you such a beautiful present, for she knows so little of you."

" The salt-cellars are for Jack," returned Christian, closing the case with an air of indifference. " I shall lock them up until he comes back; I like your present better, Addie," for her cousin had given her a very pretty bracelet. Pen's beautifully worked sachet was not on view.

Christian had not expected many presents, so few people knew she was going to be married, but the whole affair seemed to her very tame and commonplace. No bridal dress and finery, no bouquet; true, there was a white silk evening dress in her trousseau, but Christian doubted whether she would ever wear it. The two or three invited guests would be strangers to her; and when the awful ceremony was over—for in Christian's eyes it became more awful each day—she and Jack would bid each other good-bye, and then she would go upstairs and take off the pretty little white toque that was to be worn with the gray coat and skirt that had been selected as her travelling dress. Could anything be more flat and, dead-and-alive than such a programme? Christian thought. No driving off with Jack, with a satin slipper on the roof of the carriage; the nice new trunk would remain in her room to be packed more leisurely. No Parisian hotels, no sight-seeing and pleasant trips to Fontainebleu and Versailles; probably she would stay in her room the remainder of the day on the plea of a real or a pretended headache; and then Aunt Caroline would be very kind and sympathetic, and even Adelaide would show her some attention. These pessimistic reflections made Christian so low-spirited all Sunday, that she took Adelaide's dictatorial speeches quite meekly and made no effort to assert herself. More than once her cousin gave her a sharp glance, and then her manner softened.

" You look tired, Christian," she said quite kindly; " why do you not go to bed and have a good rest?" And Christian actually took her advice, as far as going to her room; but as she sat on her bed for two hours, staring out at the soft, spring darkness, it may be doubted whether she got much additional rest.

Captain Linacre was to dine and sleep at his uncle's house on Monday; and he had arranged to spend an hour or two with Christian on his way to Beauchamp Gardens. It was their only chance of a quiet undisturbed talk, and now Christian found herself dreading the interview.

On the eve of their wedding Jack would say nice things to her, and expect her to respond; he might even be sentimental for once, though sentiment was not Jack's rôle, and ask her embarrassing questions which she might find difficult to answer.

Christian's love of truth was at times somewhat aggressive—she disliked compromise. This often gave her an air of bluntness. On the previous day, when she had mentioned Jack's intended visit, Adelaide had looked somewhat surprised.

"I should have thought Captain Linacre would have preferred to spend his last evening in England with you, Christian," she said pointedly, "instead of dining with his uncle. It is rather strange behaviour on his part;" but Christian had defended him with some eagerness.

"It is not Jack's fault," she returned. "He would much rather be here, but Mr. Vigne has made such a point of it; they have to talk over a lot of business, and I believe the lawyer is to be there. Jack did suggest that he should look in later, when his uncle had retired, but I told him that I thought Aunt Caroline would not like it, so he gave it up."

"That was very sensible of you, Christian," returned Mrs. Fordham in an approving tone. "It will be rather a trying day to-morrow, and I shall be glad to go to bed early. Christian had better have the morning room, Addie, and the poor things can be undisturbed, for we are sure to have callers." And then Mrs. Fordham kissed Christian affectionately, and told her in a comfortable, motherly way that she was a good girl, and that she felt very sorry for her and Jack.

So after tea the next afternoon, Christian went upstairs to make herself smart and tidy for the impending interview.

Her new dresses were hanging in the spare-room wardrobe. Mrs. Fordham had been very generous to her niece, and had provided her with a suitable and well-stocked trousseau.

Christian had made up her mind to wear one of these gowns; and after a moment's hesitation she selected one that she thought extremely pretty.

It was a white dress, suitable for garden parties, but it also made an admirable *demi-toilette;* it was trimmed with fine embroidery and lace, and was so fresh and dainty and girlish, that Christian had declared that it would be her favourite dress. "It is a pity Jack should not see me in it," she said to herself, as she carried it off in triumph. But when the dress had been put on, and a spray of lilies of the valley slipped into her breast, Christian half regretted that she had chosen it. "I look like a bride," she thought; "Jack will see that I have dressed up for him. Well, it is too late now—I have no time to change; I only trust that I shall not meet Addie; she is always poking and prying round at wrong moments."

Christian's presentiment was realised, for as she passed the drawing-room Adelaide came out in her walking dress; her eyebrows were raised superciliously when she saw Christian's toilet.

"You had better take off that gown when Captain Linacre has gone," she said in her usual judicial manner. "It is rather ridiculous of you to put it on; and it will be such a pity to spoil the freshness." But Christian only shrugged her shoulders at this unasked advice, and hurried downstairs; her cheeks flamed angrily as she shut herself into the morning room.

"If I choose to be ridiculous, that is my affair, not Addie's," she said to herself indignantly. "I meant to take it off before dinner, but nothing will induce me to change it now; Adelaide can worry about it all the evening if she likes," for Chriss felt as cross as possible.

The morning room was a pleasant apartment on the ground floor, and was considered Adelaide's special sanctum. It was well furnished and full of pretty things, and the evening sunshine shone full on Christian as she stood in all her whiteness, her breast heaving stormily under the lilies.

"If I lived with Addie much longer I should grow

dreadfully bad tempered," she thought. " Why does she always say the wrong thing? This evening too, when she must know that I am not exactly cheerful. Why can't she be kind for once? Pshaw! what a baby! as though it matters what Addie says." And Christian walked up and down the room trying to calm her perturbed feelings. Presently her thoughts took a different direction. " I wonder what Pen would be feeling if she could change places with me," she said half aloud, " if it were the eve of her wedding day? Poor Pen! how happy she would be. Ah! there he is." And Christian started and grew a little pale as the door-bell pealed, and the next moment Jack marched into the room.

X

"FOR BETTER, FOR WORSE"

What would I give for words, if only words would come;
But now in its misery my spirit has fallen dumb,
Oh, merry friends, go your way, I have never a word to say.
CHRISTINA ROSSETTI.

JACK's thin, brown face looked a trifle worn, and his eyes were tired, as though from lack of sleep; as he put his arm round the girl and kissed her, Christian was conscious of a change in him. His greeting was warmer and more affectionate, but his first words jarred on her.

"Is this a full-dress rehearsal, Chriss?" he said, holding her at arm's length for inspection; "my word, you do look fetching!" But Christian drew herself away rather pettishly.

"Don't be absurd, Jack; why should I not put on a white frock this lovely spring day? You know I am to wear an ordinary walking-dress to-morrow." Now this was a little ungracious on Christian's part; why could she not have told him the truth: "I chose my prettiest frock to do you honour, Jack, and because I thought you would like to see me nice?" The little compliment would have pleased and gratified him; her answer did not seem to satisfy him.

"But it is all lace and furbelows," he objected, for he was sharp enough to know this was no ordinary afternoon gown; "it is tipping, Chriss, and suits you down to the ground."

"If you think it so pretty I shall wear it at the first garden party at the Stone House," returned Christian, mollified by his evident admiration; but to her surprise Jack's face clouded.

"To think my little wife will have to go everywhere alone, and that I shall not be able take care of her;" and there was a new note of tenderness in Jack's voice that made the girl flush a little. "Chriss, I could not

83

sleep last night for worrying over it. I felt as though I had been a selfish beast to hurry on the wedding as I did. I was thinking more of myself than of you; it was taking a mean advantage of your kindness, little woman." Jack was so evidently in earnest, so full of contrition and remorse for his own selfishness and want of consideration, that Christian was quite touched.

"You need not call yourself names, Jack," she said kindly; "you were in such difficulties just then; and, remember, you told me everything quite openly."

"Well, I am not a cad, you know; but somehow, Chriss, I never realised until last night that I was doing a wrong thing. I suppose it is no good saying so now when it is too late to alter things; but it is a relief to me to tell you this; you don't half know how I feel about it, and how grateful I am to you."

"I think I understand, Jack," Christian spoke very gently. Then Jack looked at her rather wistfully.

"Do you, dear? I am not so sure about that. I am not much of a hand at explaining myself, but there are one or two things I want you to know, and that's one of them."

"We will take the gratitude for granted, Jack;" Christian wanted to change the subject. Jack's grave manner alarmed her, but it was not easy to check him.

"All right," he returned easily; "we will go on to number two. Chriss, do you know I am ever so much fonder of you than I was that day you promised to marry me. We were neither of us in love; we were good friends—chummy—hit it off fairly well—but we could not say more than that."

"Well," rather faintly, Christian's head drooped a little as though she were not anxious to meet Jack's eyes.

"Well, things are a bit changed on my part," and Jack gave a short laugh as though he were embarrassed. "I believe I have fallen in love with you after all, for I hate the thought of leaving you to-morrow; it does not seem right somehow, and yet, how are we to help ourselves?"

"Of course it cannot be helped," returned Christian, but she did not look at him as she spoke, and so she missed the sad, longing look in Jack's eyes; it was far more eloquent than his words. "You must not worry about me; I shall get on all right."

"But you would rather I had stayed, would you not, Chriss?" Christian nodded, for she was thinking of the Paris trip; then she remembered Pen and Many Bushes, and was not quite so sure that she wanted him to remain. Jack did not find her curt nod very satisfying. "Can't you find something nice to say to a fellow?" he returned in an injured tone. "I am trying to make love to you, and meaning every word I say, but you don't seem to respond. Haven't you got to care for me a little, Chriss?" Then Christian turned very pale, and there was a look of fear in her eyes.

"Don't, Jack! Oh, please, don't ask me questions that I cannot answer! How do I know what I feel? Of course I care for you; have we not always been the best of friends?" But here Christian became a little agitated. "I will not deceive you, for we have always spoken the truth to each other; I know I do not care for you as Pen does for Walter Hamill; it is not that sort of feeling, Jack. Oh, dear! why do you look at me like that—ought I not to tell you the truth?"

Jack drew a long breath, as though to recover himself—Christian never knew until long afterwards that she had dealt him an unexpected blow—then he took her hand and tried to smile.

"You must always tell me the truth, dear, however much it may pain me to hear it. Poor little girl! but it is my own fault; I ought to have known better, so I am rightly punished. Chriss, listen to me a moment. Are you quite sure that you do not wish our wedding to be put off? Don't think of me; tell me exactly what you think." Jack's voice was peremptory, and he held her hands in a vice. Christian never forgot that strong, sinewy grasp, and the determined look on his face.

"I would much rather have it go on," she returned in a frightened tone. "It would be dreadful to put it off at the last minute; I could not endure the idea. Why do you look so unhappy, Jack? Indeed, I am quite content. You have arranged everything so nicely for my comfort; you have been so kind and thoughtful, that I should be an ungrateful girl if I were not satisfied."

"I wish I knew what is best to do," he returned gloomily.

"It is best to leave things as they are," returned Christian eagerly. "Jack, dear, indeed you need not worry so! I care quite enough for you—to marry you —and if you will only be patient;" but here Christian got confused and lost the thread of her speech, for her troublesome conscience was whispering that she had no right to hold out promises that she might be unable to fulfil, but Jack caught up her words thankfully.

"If I am patient, what then, Chriss? Shall I have my reward some day? Look here, darling," in his old energetic voice, "I won't tease you any more. I have got a grain of comfort anyhow, and that must last me for a bit. If you don't really wish things to be upset, I shall be too thankful to have them settled, so we will say no more on that subject. Perhaps now you know that I am so fond of you, it will draw us a bit nearer together. There is only one thing I want you to promise me, dear; that in your letters you will always be true to yourself and me. Don't say kind things if you don't mean them, because I shall read between the lines."

"I did not know you were so dreadfully sharp, Jack," and Christian laughed a little shyly. "But, indeed, you may trust me, for I shall never write a word that is not absolutely true. And, Jack," coaxingly, "I really shall take such an interest in everything; and if you do anything brave I shall be so proud of you, so won't you look a little happier?"

"And if I am killed, Chriss?" But Christian put her hand over his mouth and would not let him finish. She had passed a *mauvais quart d'heure,* but the danger was over now; she had told Jack the truth and made him miserable, and all the time she had never liked him so well.

Christian had a feeling that this little scene would haunt her all the time Jack was away; that the lean, brown face, and wistful, melancholy eyes, and the strong,

sinewy hands would be limned in her memory. " Can't
you say something nice to a fellow?" She hoped those
reproachful words would not ring in her ears; she
wondered at her own hard-heartedness and lack of expression as she recalled them.

Jack took his rebuff like a man; he kissed the soft
little hand that closed his lips so effectually, and after
this they talked more quietly.

Jack had many things to tell her—various business
arrangements. A sum would be deposited at Mr. Vigne's
banker for her use, and Jack assured her that she would
have a sufficient income for her comfort, though it would
allow of no extravagance. " Uncle Jasper is behaving
very generously," he went on. " Carus will act as your
business man and general adviser, and if you are in any
difficulty, I advise you to go to him."

" But it will be so embarrassing to confide in a
stranger, Jack."

" Oh, that's all right!" returned Jack; " you will soon
get used to him, and he will be awfully kind to you,
Chriss."

" But he is so deaf, dear."

" So he is, poor old chap! and that makes him shy
and unsociable; but I never knew any one so unselfish.
He would much rather live at Many Bushes, but he
knows our mother cannot get on without him, so he has
gone back to the Stone House; but I know it is a sacrifice to him."

" And yet it is such a fine place, Jack."

" Oh, Carus does not care for that sort of thing!"
returned Captain Linacre. " The property is his, of
course; but my father's will stipulated that my mother
should have the Stone House during her life. You see,
Carus's infirmity debars him from any enjoyment in
society; and as my mother likes to fill her house with
guests, the life is not congenial to him; and sometimes,
when he can bear it no longer, he takes refuge at Many
Bushes for a week or two. That is why his old rooms
are to be left for his use. Well, it is getting late, and I
must go, Chriss. Perhaps I ought to pay my respects to
Mrs. Fordham;" and as Christian knew that this was

expected, they went upstairs together, and ten minutes later Jack had left the house.

When Christian awoke the next morning she lay for some time trying to realise the amazing fact that it was her wedding day. " In seven hours from this moment I shall be Mrs. Jack Linacre," she said solemnly. And then the maid brought her her morning tea, and on the tray was a note from Pen—such a dear loving little sunbeam of a note—saying all sorts of nice comforting things, and this did her good.

She wondered as she sat at breakfast what she was to do with herself all those hours. Jack would be rushing about town with his best man, but she had not a notion how to employ herself. Happily, two more wedding presents arrived, and she could write notes of thanks. Then Adelaide took pity on her and asked her to help her with the flowers. Then she dressed an hour too soon, and wandered aimlessly from room to room until the carriage came. As they had no male relative to give Christian away, Mrs. Fordham had decided to do so herself; so when the right time arrived the three ladies drove to the church together. Christian looked very nice, but no one would have thought she was a bride. Her face was rather pale as she sat by her aunt's side, gazing blankly at the passers-by.

The church looked vast and empty as they entered it, and Christian thought they would never have walked up the long aisle. Jack was in his place, attended by his best man, Captain Vibart, and another young officer, and a stranger occupied the first pew. On the other side Christian caught sight of Lady Armitage, and Pen, and Mr. Hamill. Then, as she took her place, Jack stooped his tall head and whispered, " Carus is here."

Christian started visibly, but the Vicar was coming towards them, and the service was about to begin. She tried to compose herself, but she was extremely nervous, and more than once her voice shook as she made the responses. " In sickness and in health till death us do part,"—what awful words to speak lightly. Jack's voice was as clear as usual; he went through the service manfully.

It was over at last, and they were following the Vicar into the vestry. Christian was conscious that Jack was kissing her, and that her aunt and Adelaide were following his example. Then Captain Vibart and Lieutenant Harker came up with their congratulations, and she tried to smile and thank them.

The next moment Jack's hand was on her shoulder. " This is Carus, Chriss; he has come all this way to be present at our wedding," and then Christian found herself shaking hands with her new brother-in-law.

" I thought it hard that Jack should not have one of us to back him," observed Mr. Linacre. He spoke in a subdued and rather toneless voice, so that Christian could scarcely distinguish his words. He was evidently much older than Jack, and looked about eight-and-thirty, and his hair was already tinged with gray. He was somewhat short, and stooped a little, and his thin face and sallow complexion spoke of uncertain health. But his eyes were kind, and his smile exceedingly pleasant.

Christian had to sign her name, so she was spared any further effort. Then Lady Armitage took possession of her, and then Jack came up to her and offered his arm.

" There is no time to lose; we must be going, Chriss. Carus will come back with the others;" and Jack hurried her down the aisle, but in the porch they found Pen and Mr. Hamill, and Christian lingered for a moment. Pen's eyes were full of tears. " Oh, Chriss, you do look so white!" she whispered, but Christian shook her head without speaking, and let Jack settle her in the carriage. As he took his seat beside her he looked at her a little anxiously.

" I thought you were going to break down, Chriss, you were so nervous, poor little girl; but it is over now, and we are man and wife."

" Yes, Jack," but Christian shivered a little.

" Isn't Carus a trump to come all this distance? He has been travelling half the night too; he does not mean to leave me until I go on board. It is such a relief to me," went on Jack, " for I can talk to him about all sorts of things; you will not be long alone, dear; they mean to come back in another three weeks."

Christian tried to look pleased at this piece of information; then the carriage stopped, and a little road-sweeper touched his brimless hat as Jack threw him a sixpence.

The next half-hour seemed interminable to Christian. Jack made her drink a glass of champagne, but she could eat nothing. Once Mr. Linacre came and stood by her, and again she thought he had a kind face.

"I will take great care of Jack," he said quietly.

"Thank you; I am so glad you are going with him."

"I beg your pardon;" Carus looked pained and shy. Christian repeated her speech louder, but she was doubtful whether he understood her.

Christian felt as though she could not stand it much longer; every one seemed talking at once. Adelaide was laughing in her affected way; the sun was in Christian's eyes and seemed to blind her; she wondered why she felt so giddy, then Jack's voice startled her. "I want you a moment, Chriss; come into the morning room;" and the next moment they were in the cool lobby. Jack took her hand, but he did not speak, and his face looked a little drawn; but when the morning room was reached he shut the door quickly, then he took the girl in his arms. "I am going now, Chriss—say good-bye to me, darling."

Christian put her hand to her throat as though something suddenly choked her; she tried to speak, but no words seemed to come. Jack pressed her closely to him and kissed her two or three times almost passionately, then he bade God bless her, and the next moment he was gone.

XI

JACK LINACRE'S WIFE

Stand not upon the order of your going,
But go at once.

I'll make assurance doubly sure,
And take a hand of Fate.—MACBETH.

"JACK, come back, come back to me a moment!" but Christian was too late; as she opened the door she could hear quick footsteps in the hall, then Captain Vibart's voice speaking hurriedly: "There is not a moment to lose, Linacre, if you don't want to miss your train. Never mind good-byes—jump in, old fellow. I will make your peace with the ladies. Here's your brother; now you are all right—good luck to you—drive on, coachman," and then the carriage door banged. "That's a near shave, Harker," and now the voices were outside the door; "the drawing-room clock was slow—it was Mr. Linacre who found it out; he seems a 'cute sort of chap in spite of his deafness. Jack was a bit dazed and rather pale about the gills; don't wonder at it—it is rather rough on him, poor beggar!"—here the voices receded, and Christian heard no more. He had gone perhaps for months or years, and she had said nothing nice to him; she was his wife; only an hour before she had promised to love, honour, and obey this man, and yet at that hour of parting she could find no word to say to him. Jack would think her cold; he would never guess the curious sort of dizziness or faintness that had kept her silent.

"I cannot bear to send him away like this," she thought miserably; then an idea came to her. Jack had told her the name of the hotel at Southampton where he would dine that evening; he had mentioned it casually, with no particular purpose. "I shall probably have an hour or two to spare before I go on board, so I may as

well have a good dinner." Christian remembered this
speech. She would send him a telegram, there were
plenty of forms on the writing-table, and the next minute
the message was written.

Please forgive me. Indeed, I was sorry—only I could not tell
you so. God bless you.—CHRISS.

"I must go out and despatch it myself" was her next
thought. "I should not like any of the servants to see
it;" then she remembered that her purse was upstairs,
and that she must fetch it. The drawing-room door was
closed, and she could hear the sounds of voices as she
slipped past; it was very unlikely that any one would
see her from the window, but she must take that risk, for
Jack was her first consideration. She had forgotten her
gloves, but she could not go upstairs again; the post-
office was just at the end of Mandeville Street, and she
meant to leave the door ajar; it was wrong of course,
but she dare not encounter Gray; what would that extremely dignified person think of a bride running out,
without her gloves, to send a telegram on her wedding
day? Christian winced at the mere idea.
    Fortune often favours the brave, and Christian actually
accomplished her errand and had let herself in without
encountering curious eyes, but it was almost as near a
thing as Jack's train, for half a minute she would have
come face to face with Captain Vibart and Mr. Harker;
indeed, she had not reached her room before she heard
them go downstairs.
    Christian's imaginary headache had become reality by
this time, and she was only fit to lie down and close
her aching eyes; her nights had been restless and disturbed of late, and she had to make up arrears of sleep.
When Adelaide came up a few minutes later to see what
she was doing, she found her looking ill and miserable.
    For once Adelaide showed kindness and considera-
tion; she told Christian to lie still and not trouble about
anything. "I will give your love to Lady Armitage,
Chriss, and tell her that you are not fit to move; we
are going to drive with her presently when we have had

tea. I shall tell Emma to bring you a nice hot cup of coffee and a sandwich—you have eaten nothing to-day, and the headache is just worry and exhaustion;" and Adelaide shaded the light and arranged her cousin's pillows more comfortably, and even gave her a kindly kiss in token of sympathy.

By and by Mrs. Fordham crept into the room and was very tearful and affectionate. "I wish Addie would let me stay with you, my dear," she said kindly. "It seems too bad to leave you alone on your wedding day, and poor Jack gone—and both of you looking like ghosts too, poor dears!" But though Christian's lips quivered at this well-meant sympathy, she assured her aunt that it was better for her not to talk; then Mrs. Fordham gave her a hearty kiss and withdrew.

The coffee did Christian good, and after a time the pain lulled; the perfect stillness of the house soothed her, and when Adelaide returned from her drive and peeped into the room she found Christian fast asleep. It was late in the evening when she woke refreshed, and the first thing that met her eyes was a yellow envelope on the little table beside her; some one, probably Emma, had crept into the room and put it there. Christian's heavy eyes brightened at the unexpected sight. How good of Jack to send her an answer!

It was kind of you to send message. Am awfully grateful. It did me good. Take care of my wife for me.—JACK.

"I shall keep that telegram always," thought Christian, as she replaced it in the envelope. "What a dear fellow he is! It was nice of him to say that!" But Christian blushed a little as she laid her head again on the pillow. "Take care of my wife for me." It was Jack's first marital order, and she would certainly obey him.

Christian was still a little languid the next day. She half thought that she would take a hansom to Grattan Gardens, for she longed to see Pen, but at breakfast a note was brought to her by hand. Christian coloured at the inscription—"Mrs. John Linacre,"—then she

glanced at her massive wedding ring. It must be from
Mr. Vigne, she thought, and she was right. It was a
curt and abrupt note, asking her to go round that afternoon and have tea with him.

" Of course you must go, Chriss," observed Adelaide,
who never hesitated to express her opinion on any subject. " It is your duty to cultivate Mr. Vigne's acquaintance, and Captain Linacre will expect you to pay him
proper attention," and as for once Christian was not
disposed to argue the point, she wrote a civil little note
of acceptance, and postponed her visit to Grattan Gardens. The visit was to be made in unusual state and
ceremony, for Mrs. Fordham insisted on sending her in
the carriage, so Christian made her toilet very carefully,
and drove off with much dignity. " Aunt Caroline treats
me quite differently," she thought. " She never minded
my walking alone anywhere—even Adelaide did not object, and yet I know she wanted the carriage herself.
Married people certainly have their privileges;" and then
she thought that she would begin a letter to Jack that
night and tell him all about the visit, and she would
make it as amusing as possible.

Arnitt greeted her respectfully, then he took her upstairs. Mr. Vigne was not in his usual corner; he was
lying on the couch in his gorgeous silk dressing-gown,
and a quilted *couvre-pied* over his knees. The window
was open, and there was a clear little fire in the grate,
before which sat an immense black cat, with a silver
collar round his neck. Mr. Vigne looked weak and
suffering, and Christian thought he had a more shrunken
look, but he seemed pleased to see her, and bade Arnitt
place a chair near him; then Sweeper stalked majesti-
cally across the rug and condescended to make overtures.

" Sweeper does not do that for everybody," observed
Mr. Vigne. " I suppose he considers you one of the
family, Mrs. Jack."

Christian's answer was somewhat irrelevant.

" I wish I had had Mrs. Jack Linacre put on my
cards," she returned regretfully; " it is ever so much
prettier than Mrs. John. But Aunt Caroline and Ade-

laide were so shocked at the idea; but I am sure no one else would have minded it."

" Don't be too certain of that," returned Mr. Vigne drily. " My sister Janet is rather a stickler for minor morals."

" I always forget Mrs. Linacre is your sister," returned Christian smiling. " Oh, dear! a mother-in-law seems such a formidable person. I wish I knew more about her. Jack told me so little. He said it was no good trying to describe people, and that I had better find them out for myself."

" Oh, Jack was always a lazy beggar! Besides, it is not easy to describe my sister. She is rather a complex sort of person."

Christian looked grave. " I hope I shall get on with her," she returned anxiously; " but perhaps she will not like me."

Mr. Vigne shrugged his shoulders.

" I have no opinion to express on that subject. You must take your chance. Janet has her prejudices; she takes very strong likes and dislikes. I don't call her a restful sort of person, and I often wonder at Carus's patience with her. He is a good fellow, Carus, and never thinks of himself; but I know she tries him a bit."

" Mr. Linacre has a kind face. I am sure I shall like him," returned Christian in her frank way; " but I could not make him hear anything."

" He generally uses a trumpet or small hearing tube," replied Mr. Vigne. " They say that there is no hope for him, poor chap! and that he will probably get worse. It is a sad trouble to him; and if he had his way he would just shut himself up with his books and writing and let society go; but his mother won't leave him in peace—and he has such a sense of duty that he thinks it right to make the sacrifice."

" I suppose he has been deaf for some years, Mr. Vigne."

" Oh, dear, yes! He was only fourteen when it came on. I don't know if you can keep a secret, Mrs. Jack; but it is my private opinion that Carus owes his affliction to his mother's obstinacy and self-will; but perhaps Jack has told you."

" No, indeed. Jack has told me nothing about his people. We had so little time together, and Jack was so full of his own affairs. Please do tell me all you can," coaxingly; " it will be awfully good of you, and will make me feel less strange. It is rather odd and lonely for me. I feel like a daughter of Heth, going to a strange people."

Mr. Vigne's eyes twinkled with amusement, but he looked friendly.

" I am taking you behind the scenes, but you must not betray me. I have always been sorry for Janet, but it was her own fault. The boys had scarlet fever—brought it from school, I believe. Jack had it lightly, and was soon as well as usual, but Carus took it more severely. Janet was as devoted as possible, and helped to nurse them; and nothing went wrong until Carus was pronounced convalescent. She took him out one day when the boy did not want to go. I daresay he was a bit fractious from being spoilt so much in his illness; anyhow he made her angry, and she insisted that he should go. The sun was shining, but before they got far there were threatening clouds. Janet always says she turned back at once, and urged him to walk as quickly as possible, but long before they reached home they were both drenched; and in spite of every precaution and care Carus took a chill, and the first sign of deafness appeared. I believe the doctor told my brother-in-law that he had warned her that the boy would need the greatest care for the next few weeks, and that this mischief was owing to her disregard of his orders."

" Poor Mrs. Linacre! What a dreadful thing! I wonder she could ever forgive herself!" and there was a pitying expression on Christian's face. Mr. Vigne gave her a quiet, searching glance, then his manner softened.

" Come, that is acting up to your name; for, on my word, I don't know which of them is to be most pitied. Janet is a devoted mother with all her faults, and though I believe Jack is really her favourite, she does not seem able to bear Carus out of her sight. I expect her restlessness is really owing to her remorse—that she has never forgiven herself and never will. She knows she has spoiled his life by that one act of temper and self-will."

"But the sun was shining, you say. Perhaps she really thought the walk would do him good." Christian felt as though she must take the part of the absent woman; her brother was evidently a little hard on her. Mr. Vigne shook his head.

"It was March sunshine, remember, and the forecast predicted rain; but Janet took no notice of this. Well, I am glad you are sorry for her! I like women to feel for each other; but in my opinion she might leave him in peace to live the life he likes best. That is where I think she is inconsiderate and selfish. I have often told Carus not to give in to her, but he won't listen to me. Now, here is Arnitt with the tea, and we will talk of something more agreeable."

Christian had sufficient tact to say no more, but she was so intensely interested that she would willingly have pursued the subject. She was grateful to Mr. Vigne for telling her so much; it made her think more kindly of Jack's mother. "It must be so dreadful to be the means of spoiling another person's life," she said to herself, as Arnitt placed the tea-table beside her, with the beautiful old silver service and quaint oriental china. "And to harm one's own child—could anything be more dreadful? Mr. Linacre knows how she suffers, and that makes him so good to her."

Mr. Vigne had dropped all his ogreish ways that afternoon, and had evidently laid himself out to be agreeable to the young bride. He seemed to like to see her presiding at the tea-table, and paid her little old-fashioned compliments on her methods of making tea. He talked about Jack a good deal, and related many anecdotes of his boyhood. "Jack was always a pickle," he said. "Mrs. Arnitt could tell you plenty of his tricks. When his father died it was understood that I adopted him; but he led me such a life that I often vowed that I would have nothing more to do with him; but he'll turn over a new leaf, Mrs. Jack, and you will live to be proud of him;" and then he had the Atlas out, and traced Jack's probable route and the scene of his future work, and he was so keen and graphic in his descriptions that time passed like magic, and Christian was surprised when Arnitt informed her that Mrs. Fordham had driven up for her.

Christian rose at once. " I must not keep her waiting," she said hurriedly; " but I hope you will let me come and see you again before I go to Braybrooke." Then, after a moment's consideration, Mr. Vigne fixed an afternoon in the following week, and bade her good-bye quite cordially.

That evening Christian felt quite cheerful as she wrote her account of the interview. " I think Mr. Vigne and I will be good friends in time; he called me Mrs. Jack, and was quite fatherly in his manner; he is really devoted to you, though he calls you a scapegrace; and I have set my heart on your doing something very brave, to make him proud of you." And then, when she had thanked him for his telegram, and said a few nice things about it, Christian put it away to be finished another day, for she meant to send every scrap of news she could hear, that she thought would be amusing to a tired soldier after a long day's work; and if there was more description than sentiment, Christian was only keeping her promise of being absolutely true; and when it was finished, and Jack read it over afterwards, he thought it the best letter he had ever read, and far kinder than he had dared to expect. To be sure, Christian might have signed herself, " Your affectionate wife," instead of " Ever yours, Christian Linacre;" but Jack judged her very leniently. " Poor little girl! she was a bit shy," he said to himself; " but she will get over that in time." But when Jack's hasty scrawl reached her, Christian felt a little conscience-stricken when she read the closing words: " Your devoted husband, Jack Linacre."

XII

"HERE ENDETH THE THIRD CHAPTER"

The history of to-day depends upon the alphabet and the language of yesterday—ANON.

"I find nonsense singularly refreshing," said Talleyrand.

"HERE endeth the third chapter of Christian Fordham's experiences."

"Good gracious, Chriss, I thought your name was Linacre! Have you forgotten you are a married woman?" and Pen looked slightly scandalised. The two girls were in the railway compartment facing each other, and there was no other passenger in the carriage; the train had just steamed out of the great Central Station, and a little group of three had been left on the platform, waving handkerchiefs excitedly. Dolls had indeed made herself conspicuous by racing down the whole length of the train, and screaming out "Good luck!" at the top of her voice, to which Smudge had barked a joyful response, as he flattened his black nose against the window.

The Rev. Walter Hamill and Gwen had been far more decorous in their behaviour; true, Gwen's eyes were red, and her pince-nez were so misty that she was obliged to polish them with her damp handkerchief. But Mr. Hamill was very kind to her, and said so many comforting things that she cheered up a little by the time Dolls returned, hoarse and breathless. Walter Hamill was in excellent spirits; and when he parted from his two companions, his step was as free and buoyant as though he walked on air. He was overjoyed at Pen's good fortune —he knew how worn and jaded the girl was, and how unfit by nature to take her part in the rude battle of life; now for some months, at least, there would be rest and quiet and peace for her—and the young curate's good heart was much comforted at this thought.

99

When **Pen** uttered her horrified little protest, Chriss frowned impatiently.

"I wish you would allow a person to finish her sentences properly," she said rather pettishly; "you have not many faults, Pen,—I will say that for you,—but you are so staccato, and never wait for a full stop."

"I am so sorry, dear," returned Pen humbly; "but Christian Fordham sounded so oddly, you know;" and Pen with difficulty suppressed a smile, but Christian looked quite affronted.

"Perhaps you will kindly let me finish, Pen? I made no mistake in what I said. Mrs. Jack Linacre's experiences have not yet commenced; they lie in the dim future."

"Oh yes, of course, I understand your meaning!" observed Pen hurriedly. "Smudge is wanting to lick your face, Chriss, because he thinks from your tone that you are unhappy."

Then Christian patted the dog's shaggy coat very kindly.

"Smudge is a wise dog. Well, I will explain myself, Pen. The first chapter of Christian Fordham's experiences ended when dear mother died; the second closed with her marriage," and here Christian's voice grew tragical again; "and the third, when the door of 25 Mandeville Street closed upon her."

Pen nodded; she wanted to laugh, but she was not sure how Chriss would take it, so she controlled her rebellious muscles and remained silent.

"We are now beginning the second volume—'Jack Linacre's wife,'" continued Chriss impressively; "it sounds interesting; but I daresay there will be plenty of gray days in it;" then her manner changed and grew natural. "Pen, don't you think most novels are absurd? They always end with a wedding, as though the hero's and heroine's life stopped there, and there is nothing more interesting to relate. Now I call that utter rubbish."

"I remember saying something of the same sort to Walter," returned Pen; "but he only laughed and said novels were not biographies—to begin with the hero's birth and end with his death; and that as marriage **was** the central point of the drama, it was the fitting moment for the curtain to fall."

" That was cleverly said," observed Christian; " and really, Pen, when one looks round on one's married friends—they are often terribly prosy; they get children, and double chins; and they are so dreadfully narrow-minded—they can only talk about their nursery and servants. And the men too—so utterly commonplace and prosaic—one could not imagine them making love, or doing nice things; they are always at their club, or reading their paper, or eating big dinners, and grumbling afterwards."

" My dear Chriss, you are in a very pessimistic mood this afternoon."

" Yes, I know; but I can't help it, Pen; when I think of these things, it seems to me that marriage must be as serious as death, and yet how lightly we take its responsibilities on ourselves;" and here Christian's face was a little pale with suppressed feeling. " Think if Jack had not been obliged to leave me; if I had not these months to prepare myself for the inevitable change in my life! Pen, I know I am shocking you; you are so sure of your Walter, that you would marry him to-morrow without a moment's hesitation; but I know so little of Jack—he is a sealed book to me; if we were together, there would be friction; he is masterful, and I am not meek, and love my own way—there would be ructions. You shake your head, Pen, but I am speaking the truth."

" You are taking a dark view, Chriss dear, because you are feeling a little strange and forlorn at loosing from your old moorings; and though you may not choose to own it, being such a perverse young woman, because you are missing Captain Linacre. Do you know," as Christian reddened a little, " Walter has taken such a fancy to him; he says he is a fine, manly fellow, and every inch a soldier, and that he is certain that you will live to be proud of him?"

" I am sure I am very much obliged to Mr. Hamill;" but Christian spoke coldly, and she was staring out of the window. " Can't you say something nice to a fellow?" she could hear Jack's voice distinctly—a thin, brown face, and deep-set melancholy eyes, seemed to loom before her. Christian winced as though something hurt her, then she pulled herself together. "We shall be at Braybrooke directly; don't let us argue any more on abstract questions; there is plenty to interest one in life—married or unmarried. We are going to have a good time, Pen,—you and I and Smudge. Look, how pretty it is about here—meadows and trees—quite a lovely glimpse of country! I wish this were Braybrooke; but we must take everything as it comes, and then we shall not be disappointed; you know Jack told me that Many Bushes is not a grand house."

"I am glad of that, Chriss; I think a small house is much cosier."

"My ideas are not so humble as yours, Pen; I could put up with a palace with tolerable equanimity. I believe I am a Sybarite at heart. I should like a carriage and pair to meet us instead of taking a shabby station fly—not that it really matters—I only wanted to point out the difference in our taste. I amused Uncle Jasper immensely when I owned my love of the good things of this life."

"Did you really call him Uncle Jasper, Chriss?"

"Yes, I did," snapped Christian; "and I really think the ogre liked it; but he never calls me anything but Mrs. Jack. Oh, we get on capitally! I contradict him to his face, but it never seems to make him angry. I really believe he was sorry when I bade him good-bye yesterday."

"Oh, I am not surprised!" returned Pen a little absently. "Dear me, Chriss, I do believe this is Braybrooke!" And as Pen was correct in her surmise, the two girls gathered up their belongings and hailed a porter.

As Christian was hurriedly giving the man a description of their luggage, a young footman accosted her. "If you please, ma'am, are either of you two ladies Mrs. John Linacre?"

"I am," returned Christian, drawing herself up with dignity and suppressing her surprise; "but I did not expect to be met."

" Mr. Linacre telegraphed that the carriage was to be sent to the station," returned the man civilly. " If you will get in, ma'am, I will see to the luggage. There's a cart and one of our men waiting;" and the next minute the girls were piloted through a gaping little crowd of rustics to the station door, before which was a handsome carriage with a pair of dark bay horses.

" Well, you have your wish," observed Pen in an amused tone.

" I never was so surprised in my life," returned Christian, throwing herself back on the cushions with a beaming face. " It must have been Mr. Linacre's thoughtfulness for our comfort. How pleased Jack will be when I tell him! Really, it gives one a nice, homelike feeling, as though one were welcomed by a kind friend. Oh, do look, Pen!" interrupting herself, " what a dear, quaint old place!" as the carriage turned into a wide, roomy market-place, with a fine old clock-tower in the middle. As it was not market-day, the broad space was empty and deserted; but it had a pleasant old-world look, with its old-fashioned inns, and shops, and side streets, some of them bordered with trees.

" What a dear place!" echoed Pen dreamily: and the next moment they came in sight of a fine old church— a wide, flagged path, with trees on either side, led to the main entrance—the gray, venerable building stood out so grandly under the deep blue sky. It was so strangely peaceful—so still, and tranquil, and pleasant that Christian caught her breath, and her eyes grew misty: but before she could speak the carriage rolled under an imposing gray gateway, down a pleasant drive thickly bordered with all kinds of blossoming shrubs and trees, and stopped at the door of a quiet, old-fashioned-looking house, where a respectable woman and two maids were already waiting in the porch.

Christian tried to smile as she stepped into the hall: but she found it a little difficult to appear at her ease.

" I think you must be Mrs. Mills," she said rather kindly, as the little gray-haired woman curtseyed, and looked at the new mistress with bright, scrutinising eyes. " This is my friend, Miss Mervyn. We both feel a little strange, coming like this to a new place," and here Christian laughed rather nervously. "It was very kind of Mr. Linacre to send the carriage—we are so much obliged to him; and it all looks very nice, and I am sure we shall be comfortable;" and here Christian stopped to get her breath.

Now, what could there have been in this disconnected speech that appealed to Mrs. Mills's womanly sympathies? But before Christian had finished, Mrs. Mills's quick, bird-like glance softened, and she said in the pleasantest possible voice—

"I am sure my master would have been glad if he could have been here to welcome you, ma'am, for a kinder and a better gentleman never lived. He came down himself to give his orders, and to tell me about the rooms; but there, I am keeping you standing, ma'am; and you will be glad of a rest and a cup of tea before you go upstairs," and Mrs. Mills ushered them into a small, cosy-looking sitting-room, with a bay window overlooking the garden.

Many Bushes was not a large house; the old gateway was the only imposing feature. The entrance was at the side, and the principal living rooms were at the back. The drawing-room had been turned into a library, and was Carus Linacre's special sanctum, and the room over it was his bedroom. The rest of the house had been placed at his sister-in-law's disposal.

As soon as the girls had finished their tea, they made a little tour of inspection under Mrs. Mills's guidance. A moderately-sized dining-room, furnished very handsomely in light oak and red morocco, and the sitting-room, where they had had their tea, were the only rooms on the ground floor, with the exception of the library. There was a square inner hall, with a fireplace and a table, and upstairs a dressing-room, leading out of one of the bedrooms, had been converted into a pretty sitting-room. The blue cretonne covers and curtains and the writing-table and couch had an air of newness. Mrs. Mills looked at Christian rather anxiously.

"I hope the room has been done to your satisfaction, ma'am?" she observed fussily. "Mr. Linacre gave the orders himself; but we were so pressed for time that we

never thought it would be ready. You see, the master
made sure that you would choose this room, as it is the
best furnished and has such a pleasant view. The other
young lady's is in the front of the house, and we call it
the 'gate room.' Mr. Linacre's is the west room, and
this has always gone by the name of the Dormer room,
from the queer shape of the window."

" I think it is a sweet room," returned Christian; " and
it is too kind of Mr. Linacre to put himself to this expense and trouble for me."

" Well, you see, ma'am, he is so sorry for you," returned Mrs. Mills in a confidential tone. " He knows
how lonesome it must be for you without the Captain.
' We must make her as comfortable as we can, Mrs.
Mills,'—those were his very words to me—' and then,
perhaps, she will settle down and be happy amongst us.' "

" I should be very ungrateful if I were not," returned
Christian hurriedly, " when every one is so good to me.
I love my room already," and Christian leaned out of
the dormer window and inhaled the sweet fragrance of
the soft spring air, laden with the breath of hyacinths and
jonquils. The garden was not large. A terrace walk
and a few quaintly-shaped flower beds lay before the
house; some winding shrubbery walks and a small lawn
were all that could be seen, but below the terrace lay a
steep, green meadow, with clumps of trees, where an old
pony was grazing.

" I shall go and begin my unpacking," observed Pen,
when Mrs. Mills had left them, " and then I can help
you. There are two hours before dinner, and it will be
so nice to be settled."

Christian assented to this. " One of the maids is
coming up presently; I think I shall wait for her," she
rejoined, as she sat down again by the window.

April was drawing to its close, and the balmy air held
the promise of May; the borders were full of spring
flowers. Somewhere in the distance a blackbird was uttering a warning cry to his mate; down below a big
brown thrush flew across the lawn. Everywhere the tender buds of the fresh foliage and blossoming shrubs spoke
eloquently of a recreated world full of new life. The

pony had ceased to graze, and was whinnying a welcome to a boy who came to lead him to his stable. The chiming of the church clock almost startled her. The fat country sparrows, sleek and well fed, were twittering in the ivy.

Into what a peaceful, old-world corner her feet had strayed; and this quiet harbourage she owed to Jack's brother. As she glanced round her dainty little boudoir, her heart throbbed with a feeling of gratitude towards her new relation. How good he must be! She was a stranger to him, and yet, for Jack's sake, he was treating her with this generous and kindly hospitality. " Oh, I hope he will like me!" Christian said to herself. " I should wish to be a comfort, and to bring a little brightness into his life. Jack is so fond of him—and I want to do something to please Jack." And Christian remained in this softened and salutary mood until a tap at her bedroom door roused her, and a few minutes later she and Jenny were busily engaged in transferring the contents of the big trunks to the wardrobe and chest of drawers; and they worked with such a will that everything was finished by the time Pen made her appearance.

" I had not much to do," she said, as Christian showed her the well-filled wardrobe, " so I wrote to Walter and gave him a description of Many Bushes. He will read it over his breakfast," and Pen glowed with rapture at the thought. " Now, let me help you dress, Chriss, or you will be late;" and Christian graciously accepted the offer.

Mrs. Jack Linacre took her place at the head of the table with great dignity, and Brenda, the dark-eyed parlour-maid, waited on them.

Both the girls were secretly astonished at the varied delicacies provided for them in honour of the home-coming; but they had healthy young appetites, and did full justice to all the good things.

They had coffee in the bay parlour, as their sitting-room was called, and then Christian, who was too restless to work or read, proposed that they should put on their hats and take a turn in the garden; the moon was rising and the air would do them good. Smudge, too, needed exercise. This opinion Smudge endorsed by vigorously wagging his stumpy tail; so his mistresss, nothing loath, fetched a couple of light wraps which they wore after the fashion of factory girls.

They paced up and down the terrace walk under the windows; then, as the shrubbery walks looked too damp to be explored, they made their way into the front, and then Christian proposed that they should have a look at the church.

Just opposite the picturesque old gateway of Many Bushes was St. Jude's Vicarage, a curious, rather blank-looking house; near it were some almshouses and one or two other buildings—the whole place was as quiet and secluded as a cathedral close.

To Christian's disappointment, the churchyard gate was locked; but they stood for some time looking at the gray old church and its garden of graves in the dim twilight; then they slowly retraced their steps. As they did so, a door opened beside them, and a small, thin man, almost boyish in stature, came out so suddenly that they involuntarily drew back to let him pass. He was dressed as a clergyman, and wore a soft felt hat which he raised with a muttered " Good evening;" the next moment, as the girls crossed the road, he let himself into the Vicarage with his latch-key.

" That must be Mr. Disney," whispered Christian in rather a discomfited voice; " whatever will he think of us wandering about with shawls over our heads like a couple of factory girls."

" He will think we wanted to look at the church," returned Pen sensibly; " we were doing nothing to be ashamed of. Did you notice what a beautiful face he had, Chriss?"

Christian had noticed nothing but his short stature. " I thought he was a boy," she returned, " until I saw his clerical waistcoat; come, the church clock has just chimed half-past nine, so we may as well go to bed;" and, as Pen was tired, she readily agreed to this, but at the door of the dormer room Christian retained her a moment. " To-morrow, Pen," she said solemnly, " we shall begin the second volume of ' Jack Linacre's Wife';" and then she kissed her lightly on the forehead and entered her room.

XIII

"The Impossible Charlotte"

Expression is of more consequence than shape; it will light up features otherwise heavy.

> He is of stature somewhat low;
>   Your hero should be always tall, you know.
>   CHURCHILL.

ALTHOUGH Christian was very tired when she laid her head on the pillow, it was long before she could sleep. The strangeness of her new environment kept her restless; the intense silence, undisturbed by even a passing vehicle, and only broken at solemn intervals by the melodious chiming of the church clock or the drowsy twitter of a bird, added to her wakefulness, and for hours she lay open-eyed in the darkness, now following one train of thought and then breaking off suddenly as some fantastic recollection started up before her—puerile trivialities that she had long forgotten.

She had felt an odd sort of oppression all day. Pen's shrewd little speech had certainly grazed the truth; with all her courage and sense of daring, Christian had felt an inward shiver as she took her plunge into the unknown future; and Pen had actually detected the reason of her pessimism in the cleverest way.

"It is because you are feeling a little strange and forlorn at loosing from your old moorings," Pen had told her, and then she had quietly added, "and because you are missing Captain Linacre."

"Why, what nonsense!" Christian said out loud in the darkness; "how can I miss Jack when I've only seen him once a week or so—how could Pen be so ridiculous?" And then Christian banged her pillow rather irritably and shut her eyes and determined to go to sleep in the old approved fashion by counting sheep jumping through a gap in the hedge. She began systematically by collect-

108

ing her flock and driving them towards the hedge where
the jumping was to take place, and really, by the time
the thirty-fifth had jumped, she began to feel drowsy,
when lo and behold! she was wide awake again.   Such
a droll recollection had come back to her: she remembered when she was a long-legged, dreamy child of twelve
or thirteen telling her mother one day that she would like
to be a widow; she could see her mother's horrified face
at that moment distinctly.

" Chrissy, how can you say such dreadful things?" she
had remarked in a shocked voice.

" I don't think it would be at all dreadful, mammie,"
had been her answer; " of course, I should not love my
husband much—not as you love father—so I should only
feel a teeny-weeny bit unhappy when the poor man died;
and then I should be so rich and free and comfortable,
and I should do just as I liked with my children.   Oh,
dear, why does all this rubbish haunt me!" and Chriss
thumped her pillow again, this time with real indignation.
" What a very foolish, selfish little girl I must have been,"
she thought; " and even now I do not control my imagination, or it would not lead me such a dance.   Now I am
going to think properly, or else I will light a candle and
read a chapter of *Thomas à Kempis;*" and this resolution so braced and soothed her that in five more minutes
she was sound asleep, nor did she wake until Jenny
brought the tea-tray to her bed-side, and the warm, spring
sunshine lighted up her room.

It was only just seven, and as Christian sipped her
tea, it suddenly occurred to her that Mrs. Mills had told
them that the Vicar of St. Jude's always read matins at
eight; it would be a nice way of beginning her new life.
What a pity she had not proposed it to Pen last night!
But perhaps it was better to let her rest, and then Christian finished her little meal hastily and dressed herself as
quickly as possible.   She was so anxious not to disturb
Pen that she crept by her door on tiptoe, and as she gained
the inner hall she had the satisfaction of seeing Pen kneeling on the door-mat as she tied up a shoe lace that was
unfastened—she quite started when she saw Christian.

" You don't mean to say you are coming to church

too, Chriss! I thought you would be too tired to go this morning, so I said nothing about it last night."

" Of course I am going," returned Christian virtuously; " but we have not any time to spare, for there goes Mr. Disney;" and then they hurried down the drive and through the churchyard gate and up the pleasant avenue, and then through a little side door that they found open.

They passed through a side chapel into the nave and stood for a moment looking at the vast interior with awestruck eyes; it was so old and venerable with its antique carving and old monuments, but it was evidently in an excellent state of preservation; then a man, evidently the verger, came up and told them that morning service was always held in the chapel.

There was a very scanty congregation, not more than seven or eight besides themselves; as the girls took their places a lady in a gray golf cloak and a shabby black hat passed them, followed by a little girl and two boys. She had what Pen called a nice, ugly face; but Christian, who was rather critical of strangers, thought her painfully plain. She had rather prominent teeth and high cheek-bones, and was freckled; she had also reddish hair, somewhat unbecomingly arranged, and as she sat in the front row of chairs, it was impossible to overlook her; but in spite of her slightly battered hat, she looked unmistakably a lady.

The next minute the Vicar took his place at the reading-desk, and the service commenced.

Mr. Disney's voice was peculiarly sweet and clear, and his manner was so devout, and he read the Lessons so impressively and with such evident feeling that Christian was quite thrilled—never had any delivery been more to her taste. As he stood at the reading-desk and the sunshine filtered through the stained-glass window, his features looked illuminated. It was certainly a beautiful face: the features were finely cut, he had a short, curly beard, but the upper lip was shaved, and the bright, dark eyes were both keen and kindly; as she looked at him she remembered a picture she had once seen of the Beloved Apostle.

"He is like St. John," she said afterwards to Pen, and Pen had nodded.

"I was just thinking so myself," she was beginning, when, to her embarrassment, the object of their talk paused beside them and held out his hand to her.

"Am I right in thinking that I am addressing Mrs. John Linacre?" he asked in his pleasant voice; but he was evidently surprised when the girl shook her head.

"This is Mrs. Linacre," she said, pointing at her friend. "My name is Mervyn."

If Mr. Disney were disappointed, his manner did not hint at it, for he shook hands very cordially with both of them, and then walked with them to their own gate. Most strangers were attracted at first sight to Pen, and it was quite natural that he should think that the girl with the fair hair and sweet face should be Jack Linacre's young wife. Christian's pince-nez was certainly a drawback; but when she smiled, as she gave him her hand, Mr. Disney did not wonder so much at Jack's choice.

"We are close neighbours," he observed, "so you may count on us for all neighbourly help and service. I believe, Charlotte—that is my wife—means to pay her respects to you ladies this morning; she was at church with the chicks, but she always hurries off to get the breakfast ready for us. My wife is a notable woman, Mrs. John," and here the Vicar's eyes twinkled; "she is a sign-post and an example for all the thriftless young wives of Braybrooke;" and then he laughed in quite a boyish way and ran across the road.

"A sign-post and example to all the thriftless young wives of Braybrooke," repeated Christian in rather a disgusted tone. "What a preposterous and impossible Charlotte! Oh, my poor little St. John, to be saddled with such a wife; it is a new version of Beauty and the Beast, Pen, only the man has the beauty and the woman the ugliness."

"Now I call that too bad, Chrissy dear," replied Pen; "I do not deny that the Vicar's head and face are quite apostolic; but, do you know, I rather liked the look of Mrs. Charlotte—it was such a nice, ugly face."

"Oh no, Pen—not with those prominent teeth!"

" You wait until you hear her voice," returned **Pen**; " there must be something lovable about her, or Mr. Disney would not have married her. He has certainly a wonderful face, Chriss; I don't mean so much because he has classical features, but his expression is so good. What a pity he is so short! Fancy a little vicar in this great church!" And then Pen's eyes grew dreamy, for she was picturing her Walter in Mr. Disney's place.

Christian's pleasure in the appearance of her new vicar and in his kindly welcome was much diluted by the sight of his unattractive wife, and all through breakfast she indulged in little sarcasms and sly hits at " The impossible Charlotte."

" I wonder if the boys take after her or their father?" she observed presently. " I could not see their faces;" but it appeared that Pen had done so.

" The elder boy is like his mother," she returned. " I noticed it when he looked round, but the younger one is far better looking, and the little girl is quite lovely." And Christian drew a breath of relief when she heard this. Never was there a young woman more critical on other people's appearance.

When breakfast was over, Christian had a long interview with Mrs. Mills, which was highly satisfactory to both. Christian spoke with her usual frankness and candour to the little housekeeper.

" I do not quite know yet the extent of our income," she explained; " Captain Linacre will have talked over business affairs with his brother; and when Mr. Linacre returns I shall know how things are settled—until then I shall wish to live quietly."

" If you will allow me to say so, ma'am, I call that downright sensible," replied Mrs. Mills eagerly; " there's young married women I have known who thought nothing of squandering their husbands' money so that they could cut a dash and have a good time; and thankful I am that the Captain, Master Jack, as I used to call him, has not married one of these smart madams to waste his substance."

Christian laughed, for she was very much amused. " I think it would be as well to be careful until I know how much I have to spend," she went on. "Miss Mervyn and I are very simple in our tastes. You gave us such a beautiful dinner last night; but, indeed, we shall not require six courses every day,"—then a look of extreme satisfaction came on Mrs. Mills's face.

. "You just leave things to me, ma'am," she said, smoothing down the spotless white apron that she always wore in the morning. "I know exactly what two ladies need for their comfort; I never was a wasteful body, as my master will tell you, and I have always given the family satisfaction; there is no need for you to worry about things, for I have always had the keys and managed for the Master; and if you are willing, ma'am, I will just go on as we have always done."

"Indeed, I shall only be too thankful," returned Christian, who had no special love of housekeeping and very little experience; "but, Mrs. Mills, do you mean to say you do all the cooking yourself?"

"Well, ma'am, I've got a girl under me for the rough work, and she is getting quite a pretty notion of cooking, but I do most things myself. Until last week there was only Jenny for the housework and waiting; but the Master told me to look out for a good parlour-maid, and so I got Brenda; it was the Vicar's wife who recommended her."

"Oh, by the bye," observed Christian hurriedly, "what sort of a person is Mrs. Disney?"

"She is a rare manager, ma'am, and one of the best wives and mothers that I have ever known," and Mrs. Mills spoke with enthusiasm; "and she is cut out for a parson's wife, too, for the good she does, and the blessing she is to Braybrooke, isn't to be told—and there she is, ma'am, coming up the drive this moment with her little girl," and Mrs. Mills gave her apron a final smooth and hurried out to open the door.

Pen was upstairs writing as usual to her Walter, so Christian was left alone to receive her visitor. Mrs. Disney was still in her gray golf cloak and old black hat, but as she held out her hand to Christian with a pleasant smile, her homely face seemed quite transfigured, and at the first sound of a very sweet, cultured voice Christian

thought of Pen's charitable speech: " Wait until you hear
her voice; there must be something lovable about her,
or Mr. Disney would not have married her." Oh, what
a wise Pen! She was holding by the hand a pretty little
girl of about eight or nine. Christian thought she had
never seen such a lovely little face as she stooped to kiss
her. Mrs. Disney seemed well pleased.

" This is Sheila," she said, putting her arm fondly
round the child, " our one daughter, since our precious
little May died. We have lost three children, Mrs. John,
—two baby boys and May; but we always speak of our
six children."

" I think the two little boys were at church with you?"
asked Christian.

" Yes, Lionel; he is eleven, and his father says he
must go to school next year. That will be a sad wrench
to both of us, for he is the dearest little lad in the world.
Tony—his name is Antony—is our baby; he is only six.
He does not always come with me to the early service;
he is so young that I do not like to force him; he goes
on what he calls his ' goody days.' ' I am a good boy,
and mean to go to church this morning,' is the way in
which he generally announces his intention of accompany-
ing us."

" I think you are very wise not to compel him to go,"
observed Christian.

" Oh no; my husband and I think church-going should
be a privilege and a joy and not an unwelcome task; but
we believe in the force of example; we were both so glad
to see you there the first morning."

" We thought it would be a nice way of beginning
our new life at Braybrooke," returned Christian a little
shyly.

" Oh, I am so glad to hear you say that!" returned
Mrs. Disney with a sunshiny smile. " I only wish our
Braybrooke ladies would realise the blessing of these early
services. I call it winding up my clock for the day; for
somehow if I oversleep myself, or give way to indolence,
nothing seems to go right with me. By the bye, where
is your friend? I was quite looking forward to making
her acquaintance; she has such a sweet face. I believe
she is no relation of yours."

" No—only a dear friend;" and, impelled by Mrs. Disney's interested look, Christian gave her a brief sketch of Pen's virtues, her loneliness, and her hard-working life, and her engagement to the young curate of St. Cuthbert's.

" My husband is acquainted with the Vicar of St. Cuthbert's, Battersea," returned Mrs. Disney; "if you will let us know when Mr. Hamill comes to Many Bushes, he will certainly call on him. Now, I must go, for I have an appointment at the other end of the town; but I want you and Miss Mervyn to come over for afternoon tea; my husband will be free at that hour, and would enjoy a talk with you."

" You are very kind, and we shall be pleased to come," returned Christian, for she knew there was no need to consult Pen. And then Mrs. Disney took her leave, and a few minutes later Pen made her appearance.

" Has your visitor gone?" she asked in a disappointed tone, looking round the room; " I only just heard that Mrs. Disney was here."

" Yes; but she would not let me send for you, as she could not stay long. Never mind, Pen, we are going to have tea at the Vicarage this afternoon. Oh, she is very nice and friendly, and Sheila is a darling!"

" Sheila—what a pretty name! Well, Chriss, now you have really made Mrs. Disney's acquaintance, do you still think her so unredeemably ugly?"

" Well, she has not grown handsome in these two hours, and I am afraid I must still maintain my opinion that the vicaress is a very plain woman; but," as Pen's face fell at this, " you were right about her voice; it is exceedingly pleasant, and she has a charming smile, so I should not be surprised if in time we are the best of friends."

" Bravo, Chrissy! Then ' the impossible Charlotte' has found favour in your eyes?"

" She is certainly not so impossible as I thought her," returned Christian, who rather repented of her satirical speeches; " but she is still a notable woman, Pen, and a sign-post to all the silly young wives of Braybrooke. Now come out, like a good girl, and let us explore the town and its environs."

XIV

Near Neighbours

Because thou hast the power, and own'st the grace
To look through, and behind, this mask of me,
   And behold my soul's true face;
   Dearest, teach me so
To pour out gratitude, as thou dost good!
                  E. B. Browning.

THE desultory ramble that Christian had proposed only ended at the luncheon hour, when she and Pen returned almost tired out, but with fine, healthy appetites, and with spirits exhilarated by air and exercise. They had explored to their hearts' content, but nothing pleased them so well as the old market-place, with its clock tower and old-fashioned shops and inns. In the course of their wanderings they had encountered Mrs. Disney three or four times, and on each occasion she had greeted them with a friendly nod or wave of her hand.

The first time they passed her she had stopped to pacify a screaming infant, while the little nurse-girl, a mere child, stood helplessly by. " The poor mite is hungry and cold, Lizzie," they heard her say; " you must take her home as quickly as possible to her mother—nothing but her bottle will quiet her." As Lizzie dropped a curtsey and pushed at the perambulator, they saw Mrs. Disney walking beside her, and helping to propel it across the wide market-place.

The next time they encountered her she was going into the workhouse, and was evidently full of business, and later on she waved to them from the infirmary steps; half an hour later as they were passing the Dragon Inn they saw her in the centre of a group of rough lads; she was evidently scolding them for tormenting a miserable little mongrel puppy that had fallen into their hands. They were too far off to hear what she was saying, but they saw her pick up the puppy and march off with it under her gray cloak.

" What an ubiquitous Charlotte!" murmured Christian, but she uttered a mental amen when Pen observed in a feeling voice, " I am sure she is a good woman, and I mean to like her."

The bay parlour looked very inviting that afternoon, with its pleasant outlook on the terrace and meadow. The room was sweet with the scent of hyacinths and the fragrance of the hothouse flowers that had been sent from the Stone House. There were plenty of books, for the inner hall and upper passage were lined with low bookcases, so the girls provided themselves with novels, and then ensconced themselves in easy-chairs by the open window; and time passed so quickly and pleasantly that they were startled when the grandfather's clock outside chimed four.

" Good gracious, Pen," exclaimed Christian in a remorseful voice, " I had no idea it was so late! There is no time now to change our frocks, for Mrs. Disney told us to come at four;" but before Pen could reply there was a timid knock at the door, and the next minute a charming little Red Riding-Hood entered.

Sheila's lovely little face looked more bewitching than ever in the scarlet hood. " If you please, mother has sent me to fetch you," she said shyly; " and we live so close that you need not put on your hats unless you like, for it is quite warm."

" How very kind of your mother to send you!" returned Christian, delighted with this neighbourly behaviour. " I think we will put on our hats, Pen, but we must not keep Sheila waiting." Christian's hair needed smoothing, but she was soon ready, and then they ran across the road, and Sheila led them through a small hall, and then ushered them into a pleasant drawing-room, where Mrs. Disney received them with the warmest welcome.

" That's right," she said cordially; " you have taken my message in good part; you will find us very unconventional people, Mrs. John,—we like our friends to come in in their old clothes, without fuss and ceremony. Now confess, did not Sheila find you and Miss Mervyn dozing

over your novels?" And, as they both laughed at this,
"Ah, I knew it! and then you were aghast because there
was no time to put on your best-bibs and tuckers."

"I think you must be a witch, Mrs. Disney, and see
through brick walls;" but Christian was very much
amused.

"Oh, I have tolerably good sight; but, my dear Mrs.
John——"

"Oh, do call me Mrs. Jack, please; I like it ever so
much better!"

"Well, so do I. Mrs. Jack then—I want to begin as
we are to go on—we are near neighbours, and both my
husband and I wish you to feel that you are welcome at
the Vicarage at any hour of the day. I am a busy person,
and you will not always find me in, except at tea-time, or
after dinner, or before I go on my morning rounds.
Well, I hope you will both find out for yourselves our
habits and manner of life at the Vicarage."

"You are very, very kind," returned Christian gratefully; "I see we shall not long feel strangers here;
we hardly expected such a cordial welcome, did we,
Pen?"

"Is your friend's name Penelope?" asked Mrs. Disney.
"What a dear old-fashioned name! But it somehow suits
you, Miss Mervyn. Now, tea is ready, I must call my
husband in; he is playing cricket with the boys on the
lawn."

"You have a nice garden," observed Christian, as she
followed Mrs. Disney to the window. There was a good-
sized lawn, where the wickets were set, and a gravel path
ran round it. Against the walls there were broad flower-
beds full of spring flowers.

"It is more a playground than a garden," returned
Mrs. Disney. "I am passionately fond of flowers, but
I have to content myself with my borders. I wanted
dreadfully to plant standard rose-trees down the lawn,
but my husband thought they would be in the children's
way. This is the first game of the season." Christian
thought the little Vicar looked like a boy in his blue flannel
coat. He glanced up and nodded as his wife tapped at the
window.

"Why, there is the puppy!" exclaimed Pen, as a small yellow mongrel rushed after Tony with ecstatic barks.

"Oh dear—yes! we have adopted him," returned Mrs. Disney in a resigned voice. "He is the ugliest little creature I ever saw, but Tony adores him. I carried him off from those young savages, and this is the result." And then she placed herself at the tea-table, and a few minutes later Mr. Disney entered with the two boys. The youngest, a handsome little fellow, had the puppy in his arms.

"Now, Tony," observed his mother reprovingly, "I thought I said at lunch that Waif was not to be brought into the drawing-room."

"It is my fault, Charlotte," interrupted the Vicar; "Tony was taking him up to the schoolroom, but I brought him in to see the ladies. There, you may both be off, laddies;" and the boys scampered off with their new treasure.

Never had Christian felt herself more at home than in the society of these kindly people; and it was evident that Pen felt the same. She was generally rather shy with strangers, but this evening she talked more than usual.

When tea was over, they all went across to the church for Evensong; and when the short service was over, they parted at the gate of Many Bushes, with the understanding that the following evening was to be spent at the Vicarage.

"It is not our custom to have dinner company," Mrs. Disney had said frankly. "We must cut our coat by our cloth; and country vicars are not proverbial for their wealth—not that we have not sufficient and to spare, thank God! But there are exceptions to every rule, so I hope you and Miss Mervyn will take potluck with us to-morrow. Is not that the usual Braybrooke form of invitation, Graham?" But Christian shook her head.

"Thank you very much, Mrs. Disney; but to quote your own words, I would like to begin as we are to go on. So if you will allow us, Pen and I will come in at eight o'clock for a nice chat." And after a little more argument on Mrs. Disney's part, Christian carried her point.

" She is a dear woman," observed Pen, as they walked up the drive. " But I am glad you were firm, Chriss; there is not the least need to ask us to dinner; and it will be far pleasanter and less formal to take our work and spend an hour or so in the evening. They will be ideal neighbours, I can see that."

" Yes, indeed," returned Christian. " I wonder if you agree with me, Pen, but I never found it easier to talk to any one. Mrs. Disney is such a sympathetic sort of person. She seems so genuinely interested in everything one tells her. There is no humbug or make-believe about it; it is the real article and no mistake."

" Yes, of course, Chrissy; that is why she is so charming. I don't know how you feel, but I am quite in love already with Mrs. Charlotte. You did not think her quite so plain without her hat, did you?"

But Christian would not own this. " Mrs. Disney is certainly an exceedingly plain woman," she maintained; " but she has a nice figure, and her voice and manner are delightful. I shall ask her to tell me all about my new relations," she continued. " You know the Vicar has to attend a meeting, so we shall be alone with her for an hour at least." But as they sat in their cosy room that evening, more than once they laid aside their books to discuss some fresh feature in their new acquaintance. They would have been interested indeed if they could have overheard the fragment of a conversation that passed between the Vicar and his wife as the heavy gate of Many Bushes clanged behind them.

" Well, what do you think of Jack Linacre's wife, Charlotte?" asked the Vicar. " She is no beauty, certainly. Her little friend is far more prepossessing; but, in my opinion, she is rather a pleasing young woman."

" Oh, she is more than that! I think her very attractive. She is not of the common or garden sort, Graham; she has plenty of originality and character."

" Oh, you have found that out already! What a woman you are, Char!"

" Oh, but I have not grasped her yet! She is *terra incognito* to me at present; but I fancy she will repay a little study. I will come into your room a moment, dear," throwing down her hat and cloak on the settle. " The children are still upstairs, so I can spare a few moments for gossip." And then she followed him into his sanctum.

" I think they will be pleasant neighbours for us," observed Mr. Disney, as he sorted his papers.

" Oh, yes! But do you know, when I first saw the bride I was immensely surprised. Jack Linacre always seemed to me quite an ordinary young man, and I fancied his wife would be a pretty, dollish sort of woman, with no special individuality; so when I saw this well-set-up, stylish, young person, with her pince-nez, and crisp, frank manner, I was, as I remarked, somewhat surprised.'

" You are keeping something back, Charlotte," returned her husband with a quick glance at her. " Oh, I know your manner so well ! You are interested in our new neighbour, but you are not fully satisfied with her."

" Now, Graham, that is too bad;" and Mrs. Disney laughed in a somewhat embarrassed manner. " How am I to make up my mind about a person whom I have only seen for a couple of hours? I liked her very much; but it struck me that her manner was just a little peculiar when we talked of her husband."

" Indeed; I thought she seemed rather pleased than otherwise when I called him a good fellow."

" Oh yes, she was quite ready to talk about him; but all the same, I doubt if she is in love with him. There, I ought not to have said it, but my tongue is always running away with me. It is all your fault, you bad man, asking me inquisitive questions; but I really know nothing about Mrs. Jack Linacre's feelings, so I daresay I was wrong. Now, Graham, why are you smiling in that provoking manner?" But the Vicar refused to be drawn into any admission.

But as he lighted his pipe he was saying to himself, " I never knew Charlotte wrong in her intuition; she can diagnose a person more quickly and skilfully than any one I know," for this Vicar, with his wide stores of learning, and his large-hearted tolerance and charity, was absolutely loyal and devoted to his Charlotte, " his true yoke-fellow," as he sometimes playfully called her, for he had numberless names for her. When Charlotte Disney had been a young wife, and before her children were born, she once asked her husband rather wistfully how he could have fallen in love with her.

" I was just the ugliest girl in our village," she said quite seriously, for she was very frank and outspoken on the subject of her looks. " I remember telling dear mother that I should never be married, because no man would look at me. Graham," gazing very tenderly at the face that was so perfect in her eyes, " that was why you found it so hard to convince me that you really loved me."

" I remember you gave me a good deal of trouble," returned the Vicar quietly. " Why, Char, you silly child, there are actually tears in your eyes! Have I not told you a dozen times that I fell in love with you at first sight, that day old Granny Dickenson died? They told me below that a young lady, Miss Charlotte Elliott, had been sitting up with the poor old body all night. And then I went upstairs, and I saw you, my dear, with your tired, pale face, and heavy eyes, kneeling beside the poor creature. And you looked up at me with a smile, and— and"—in a voice that thrilled his listener's ear—" I had a glimpse of a beautiful soul and a loving heart, and I wanted nothing else;" and as Charlotte hid her face on his breast, he stroked her hair fondly. And so that brief moment of unrest in Charlotte's mind was hushed and quieted forever, and she knew, whatever the outer world might say, that in her husband's eyes she was fair.

The following morning, when Christian entered the dining-room, she found a letter with a foreign postmark awaiting her. Although the handwriting was strange to her, she guessed at once that it was from Carus.

Her look of pleasure and surprise arrested Pen's attention. " Is it from Captain Linacre?" she asked eagerly, but Christian shook her head.

" No, it is from my brother-in-law. I do not expect to hear again from Jack just yet, as he promised me a letter from the Cape." Christian spoke rather coolly; her manner somewhat baffled Pen. On the subject of her husband she was singularly reserved and uncommunicative; she had no confidences to impart to Pen; none of the hopes, and fears, and tremors that might well be felt by a bride of two weeks' standing.

She read her letter with evident zest, and then handed it to Pen. "He is very kind; it seems natural to him to do kind things for other people," she said quietly, but there was a pleased look on her face as she poured out the coffee.

The letter was certainly kind and brotherly.

My dear Christian—By this time you are settled in your new home, and I hope that you find your environment pleasant and to your taste. There was little time at our disposal, but I trust your rooms are fairly comfortable. When I return home you have only to suggest any alterations or additions that you may desire, and they shall be carried out. You will find Mrs. Mills absolutely trustworthy and reliable; she is an old and valued servant in our house, and you are safe in her hands. Do not scruple to ask for anything you want. Remember, I am responsible to Jack for your comfort and well-being.

Now, I must give you a message from my mother. You will, I am sure, be glad to know that she has made good progress during the last week, and is fast regaining her normal condition of health. Indeed, we hope to set our faces homeward in about ten days or a fortnight.

Now for the message. My mother thinks it a great pity (and I fully agree with her) that you should not use the carriage in her absence. The horses will be all the better for exercise, so I have suggested to her that Locock should call at Many Bushes every morning for orders, and then you and your friend can have a daily drive; in this way you will make acquaintance with the surrounding country. Locock is an excellent coachman, and he will show you everything worth seeing. My mother sends her kind love.—I remain, my dear Christian, your affectionate brother-in-law,

CARUS LINACRE.

Heather sends her love too.

But this postscript was written in a girlish hand.

"Heather! that must be Heather Bell, Mrs. Linacre's adopted daughter," observed Pen; "how sweet of her to write that!"

"Yes," returned Christian in an absent tone; "they are all very kind to me." And then for a little while she remained silent.

XV

"I Have a Genius for Friendship"

There are two elements that go to the composition of friendship, each so sovereign that I can detect no superiority in either, no reason why either should be first named. One is Truth. A friend is a person with whom I can be sincere. Before him I can think aloud. . . . The other element of friendship is Tenderness.
—EMERSON.

"SOME people have a genius for religion, others for art or literature. I have a genius for friendship."

The speaker was Mrs. Disney, the new neighbours from Many Bushes were her auditors. The three ladies were grouped comfortably in the window recess of the Vicarage drawing-room; they had gathered there to enjoy the golden lights of the evening hour.

The girls were in their pretty evening dresses. Christian had selected the plainest frock in her trousseau, but in the eyes of her companions it was a marvel of good taste and fresh daintiness. Pen, too, looked quite charming in the pale blue silk blouse that Christian had given her. Both of them had scraps of fancy work in their hands, but Christian rarely put in a stitch, the conversation was too absorbing. Mrs. Disney, on the contrary, was not idle a moment; her fingers moved as busily as her tongue. If she had added that she had a genius for needlework she would not have been far wrong, for in the manufacture of frocks and boys' suits no one could rival her in Braybrooke.

"The making of friends is a veritable art," she went on; "it must be carefully practised, or one is liable to make mistakes. In this matter, impulse is fatal; the trained intuition is far safer."

"Do you mean that you do not take to people at first sight?" asked Christian curiously.

"Oh dear no; that was not my meaning at all. On the contrary, after ten minutes' talk with a stranger, I can always tell if that person will be antagonistic to me, or *vice versa;* and though I say it as shouldn't," with a delightful little laugh, "my prognostications are seldom wrong. When my husband wishes to tease me, he tells me 'That I am a good hater as well as a good lover.'"

"And yet you say friendship is an art to be carefully practised?" asked Christian, preparing herself for an argument.

"Most surely, my dear Mrs. Jack; the heart can be trained as well as the head; if I feel conscious of a sudden drawing to a person, I do not rely on my intuitions; I make civil overtures that will not compromise me, and then I wait until I am fully convinced in my own mind that the person who attracts me is worthy of my friendship."

"I am afraid you expect too much, Mrs. Disney;" it was Pen who said this.

"My dear Miss Mervyn, what a misconception; that shows how little you know me. I am too well aware of my own failings to expect perfection from other people. 'He weighed the faults of others in the scales of charity.' Do you remember Wordsworth said that of his friend, Tom Poole? I always felt that implied such a beautiful nature."

Christian sighed. "I wish I were more like Tom Poole," she observed. "I am so terribly critical and hard in my judgment; Pen often tells me so. Once, when a party had been unusually slow and flat, and I had been terribly dull, I remember saying to her that, in my opinion, human nature was divided into two classes—bores and their victims."

Mrs. Disney laughed, but she looked at the speaker very kindly. Mrs. Jack Linacre was certainly an amusing young woman. "I am afraid that bores are to be found everywhere; Braybrooke is certainly not free from them; I have a choice collection frequently on show at the Vicarage, but I have learnt to tolerate them. Now you two dear creatures will be a perfect Godsend to me, for I have already settled in my mind that there is no danger of our boring each other. Do you suppose I should talk to some of the ladies of Braybrooke as I have been talking this evening?"

" You are paying us a very pretty compliment, Mrs. Disney!" exclaimed Christian, colouring with genuine pleasure; " but, all the same, I am not quite comfortable in my mind; when you know us better you may be disappointed in us—no, not in Pen"—interrupting herself with eager loyalty to her friend; " Pen never disappoints anyone, but I am rather a contradictory sort of person; indeed, I am not sure that I understand myself."

" That is quite possible," returned Mrs. Disney composedly; " but problems are sometimes interesting. It is rather early in the day to judge, but I think we shall be good friends, at least I hope so. Now, it is getting too dark to work, and yet I am loath to ring for the lamp."

" Please wait a little longer," pleaded Christian; " that light in the sky is so beautiful, and it will not hurt you to be idle for a few minutes, Mrs. Disney—I do so want to ask you something. Is Mrs. Linacre a great friend of yours?"

Mrs. Disney hesitated for a moment. " She is certainly a friend of mine," she returned; " and we have always been on excellent terms ever since we came to Braybrooke; indeed, we meet constantly."

" Forgive me; then why did you hesitate when I asked you the question?"

" Because you used the word 'great,' and it would hardly apply to our friendship. I have reason to believe that Mrs. Linacre is warmly attached to me; all these years she has shown me great personal kindness; possibly the affection is greater on her side, for she has very few intimate friends, but I am really very fond of her."

" Mr. Vigne told me a good deal about her," observed Christian.

" I am sorry to hear that," returned Mrs. Disney gravely. " Mr. Vigne has never done his sister full justice; their temperaments do not suit, and he certainly does not comprehend her. Mrs. Linacre has a strangely complex nature; it is not easy to understand her."

" So I imagined. I must confess that I am rather afraid of my unknown mother-in-law, and yet I am sorry for her too. Mr. Vigne told me all about Mr. Linacre's deafness, and how it was the result of imprudence on his mother's part."

Mrs. Disney sighed. " That is true, alas, poor Mrs. Linacre! She has that lifelong cross to bear, and it is by no means a light one. Still I wish Mr. Vigne had not told you this sad story; I fear it will prejudice you against her."

" No, indeed; it only makes me sorry for her; I can understand the daily trial it must be."

" You are right, my dear Mrs. Jack; it is a bitter grief for any mother to know that she is the cause of a child's misfortune. Much as I pity Mr. Linacre for his infirmity, I pity her far more; if she could only bring herself to accept more patiently the consequences of her own mistake."

" Did you know old Mr. Linacre?" asked Christian, after a moment's interval.

" Old Mr. Linacre," with a smile. " My dear, he was only forty-eight when he met with that accident in the hunting-field that caused his death a few days afterwards; there is a picture of him in the hall at the Stone House taken a few months before; such a splendid-looking man, in his scarlet coat, mounted on his favourite hunter, Brown Bess. But I have not answered your question—no, I never saw him in life. Mrs. Linacre had been a widow for two or three years when we first came to Braybrooke."

" Jack told me once that neither he nor his brother took much after their father; that seems a pity, does it not?"

" Perhaps it does, for Mr. Linacre was an extremely handsome man. Captain Linacre is very like his mother."

Christian seemed pleased to hear this; it gave her a pleasanter impression of her mother-in-law. " I wonder if Mr. Vigne was right," she observed, " when he said Jack was his mother's favourite?"

" I believe so," was the reply. " She certainly doated on him. Poor thing! she will have fretted sorely at not being able to bid him good-bye; but Carus is very dear to her too; he is her adviser and right hand; indeed, she is never happy if he is away from her. We rather hoped when she adopted Heather that she would be more willing to spare him; but I am sorry to say this is not the case."

"And is Heather nice?"

"Yes, indeed; she is a dear child, and as sweet and blooming as a rosebud. Oh, there is my husband's latchkey, and if I can grope my way to the bell I will ring for that lamp!"

The entrance of the Vicar and lights created a diversion, and there was no more talk about the inmates of the Stone House. Just before the girls took their leave, Christian bethought herself of Carus's letter, and mentioned the kind offer of the carriage.

"That must have been Linacre's thought," observed Mr. Disney, with a glance at his wife; "it would never have entered Madam's head; it is just like the dear old fellow."

"But Mrs. Linacre would be very pleased to act on the proposition," returned Mrs. Disney quickly; "she is never slow to follow his lead." And then it was arranged that she and Sheila should drive with their new friends the following day.

Carus's kind thought was the source of much pleasure to Christian and Pen; if they could have had their way, Mrs. Disney would have been their constant companion; but she was far too busy a woman.

"You must not tempt me too often," she said firmly. "I am very fond of driving; and now and then Mrs. Linacre calls for me; but if you will be content with two afternoons next week, I will try to find leisure;" and, of course, Christian professed herself satisfied.

She and Pen were settling down quite happily in their new life; in the morning they wrote letters, or walked, and they also did a good deal of needlework. Pen was trying to put her dilapidated wardrobe in order, and Christian was delighted to advise and help her. Mrs. Fordham had been so liberal to her niece that Christian had no further use for many of her old things; there were frocks and blouses in excellent condition that she could easily spare. Pen, who was very skilful with her needle, and who had plenty of good taste, was exceedingly clever in adapting them to her own use. Christian was quite astonished at some of the results. " Why, you don't mean to say that is my black grenadine, Pen?" she said once. " Why, it looks as good as new! And how well it becomes you; you are quite ' chic.' " And Pen accepted this compliment with modest dignity.

The afternoons were spent in driving, and in this way they became acquainted with the beauties of the surrounding neighbourhood. More than once they drove past the lodge gates of the Stone House, and Christian looked curiously up the long avenue, but not even the glimpse of a chimney pot was to be seen.

Now and then on their return they found a card of some caller, and then Christian would regret that they had not stayed at home. " It will be so awkward to return these calls," she said to Mrs. Disney, " when I have not even seen the people ;" but her friend assured her that the Braybrooke folk were very harmless. " You will not find either Mrs. Gregory or Mrs. Manifold at all formidable," she continued. " They are both of them dear women. I always call Mrs. Gregory Tabitha or Dorcas; she is so given to good works."

Now and then they would take their work and go across to the Vicarage for an hour or so, but they never did so uninvited; their evenings were generally spent in reading, and often closed by a short ramble with Smudge.

They had only been settled in their new home for a fortnight when Mr. Hamill paid his first visit, and thanks to Christian's tact and kind hospitality it was a complete success. As he had arranged to come early and return by an evening train, he and Pen spent a long delightful day together. In accordance with their programme Pen met him at the station, and until luncheon time they wandered about, and Pen showed him the town, and then they went into the church, and time passed rapidly as Mr. Hamill examined the beautiful carving and the few old monuments; in fact, he was so struck with everything, and so engrossed and interested, that Pen had some difficulty in inducing him to leave the building. The quaint old gateway of Many Bushes delighted him, but the sight of his young hostess coming down the drive to meet him made him quicken his steps.

"Well," she asked, holding out her hand to him with her customary friendliness, "are you satisfied that I have taken good care of Pen?"

"Pen is rejuvenated," he replied solemnly. "All the morning I have been trying to realise that this round-faced little girl is really Penelope Mervyn." And then they all laughed, and Christian led the way to the dining-room, where an excellent luncheon awaited them.

That afternoon they had their favourite drive, and the Vicar and his wife joined them at afternoon tea. They were evidently very favourably impressed with the young curate, and the two men were soon engaged in conversation. Mr. Disney questioned him on his work at Battersea.

"I have never worked among the slums," he said thoughtfully. "Since my ordination I have always been in the country, and Hodge in his smock has been a familiar figure. When the bishop gave me this living, Braybrooke seemed a city to me, for at Hatchfield there was only one shop and the village ale-house, and the life there was exceedingly primitive—but we all loved it."

"Slums are not quite to my taste," returned Mr. Hamill; "but I have always thought that one must not pick or choose one's work. I have a presentiment that I shall not be long at St. Cuthbert's. There is a rumour that the number of curates is to be diminished, and as I am the junior and the last comer, I shall probably get my *congé*. I shall be sorry," he continued frankly, "for the Vicar and I hit it off splendidly, and I am so interested in our men's club."

"Bates, my senior curate, has been trying to start one here," returned Mr. Disney; "but I am afraid it is not quite a success;" and then he looked at the young man rather fixedly for a moment and changed the subject.

Christian left the lovers alone together for an hour, and only joined them when the gong sounded. They dined earlier than usual, and immediately afterwards Walter Hamill took his leave. At parting, a small but somewhat heavy basket was put in his hand.

"Will it trouble you to carry this to the station?" asked Christian. "Mrs. Mills has put up a few things for you."

She and Pen knew how the young curate would appreciate the delicious country butter and new-laid eggs, and the home-made marmalade and potted meat, for which Mrs. Mills was famous. " Walter does so hate grocer's eggs," she had confided to Christian.

Christian had done her part nobly that day; but the sight of the lovers always made her feel dull. " It is so mean to envy any one," she said to herself; but nevertheless her conscience told her that she was not free from the hateful feeling.

" If I could only be like Pen," she thought. " Pen is so beautifully simple; she takes life almost like a child. That is why Mr. Hamill adores her; it is just her goodness and single-mindedness, and the way she struggles to do her duty. If only goodness were contagious, and I could catch the lovely disease!" and Christian's lips relaxed into a smile at her own conceit; then with a sudden impulse she sat down and read Jack's brief letter from Madeira, the only note she had received, but in ten days or a fortnight she hoped to receive another letter from the Cape. Jack had never been much of a letter-writer—the brief scrawls that had been so treasured by his mother would have failed to interest any one else, but there is no teacher like Love.

Jack's first letter to the girl he had married, and from whom he had parted an hour later, had a straightforward, manly simplicity that had appealed to Christian strongly. There were no special terms of endearment, but every word told her how she occupied his thoughts. One sentence towards the end of the letter had somewhat troubled her.

" You may take my word for it, Chriss, that there will be a flare-up soon. The Home Office is keeping it dark; but there will be a rare scrimmage presently, and I am lucky to be in the job from the very beginning."

Christian had pondered over this sentence with increasing uneasiness. What did Jack mean? He evidently anticipated some serious outbreak. Christian remembered with some compunction how lightly she had jested on the subject. She had pictured him coming back maimed or crippled with the Victoria Cross. She winced at the recollection of her girlish brutality, and she had fancied that even Mr. Vigne had been shocked. She had told them gaily that she would not break her heart if Jack were killed, though, of course, she would be dreadfully sorry, but she was glad now to remember that Jack had not taken her words seriously. " Chriss says lots of things that she does not mean," he had returned good-humouredly. Of course Jack was so sensible, dear old fellow. He did not misunderstand her girlish bravado and manner; but, all the same, " a rare scrimmage" and Jack in the thick of it was not exactly a pleasant idea.

XVI

UNDER THE CHESTNUT TREE

Nothing can bring you peace but yourself; nothing can bring you peace but the triumph of principle.—EMERSON.

CAPTAIN LINACRE was not the only person who prognosticated trouble in South Africa that spring. Everywhere there was a hush and oppression in the atmosphere which told many a prophetic soul that a storm was brewing.

While Jack, who was a born fighter, was blessing his good luck that he would be in the thick of the scrimmage, the authorities were watching the development of events with growing anxiety and alarm.

To quote from a cotemporary account: "For the last five years before the hour of conflict the British nation had felt instinctively that it was drawing steadily nearer—had watched with apprehension the enormous armament of the Transvaal, and heard with rage and shame the story of the persistent oppression by the Boers of thousands of loyal British citizens. All men had dreaded it; many had striven to avert it; many more had prayed that it might not come in their day." And yet, in spite of the general uneasiness, there was little done, and much precious time was lost, while shortsighted optimists waited in masterly inactivity in the hope of a peaceful settlement of the difficulty. A few troops were being sent to the Cape and Natal, but not until nearly six months later, not until October, when the Boer ultimatum was handed in, was mobilisation ordered in England, and the transport of troops commenced in earnest.

Jack was to register many a grumble as the months passed and the scrimmage had not begun, but he found plenty of occupation in his military duties, and Christian's delightfully descriptive letters were very comfort-

ing to him, especially when she finished them by sub-
scribing herself, "Your affectionate wife." It was only
when the war rumours were thick in the air that Christian's heart failed her, and with womanly intuition she
did the very thing that would give Jack pleasure.

"Poor little girl!" he said to himself, as he sat
smoking his pipe; "she is a bit shy and skittish, but she
will come round. I wonder if my letters bore her, and if
I say the right thing?"

But Jack had no need to torment himself, for Christian prized those letters.

One beautiful evening in May, as she and Pen were
returning from a long drive, Locock informed them that
the carriage would be required for his mistress the following day, and that he had orders to be at the station
by one.

When Christian went over to the Vicarage that evening, she found that Mrs. Disney had received a letter
from Mrs. Linacre.

"They will sleep in town to-night," she remarked;
"and come on by the midday train. Mrs. Linacre says
she has fully recovered from the effects of her long
illness, and is as active as ever. Graham and I mean
to run down to the station to give them a welcome;"
but Christian did not offer to accompany her, and
Mrs. Disney hardly liked to suggest it. "Perhaps it
might have been somewhat awkward for Mrs. Jack," she
observed afterwards to her husband; "she is a little
shy and stand-offish when she is not at her ease; and
then Mrs. Linacre would not see her to advantage."

"But all the same, the attention would have pleased
her," returned the Vicar rather regretfully, for he
thought the action would have been very gracious on
the girl's part. "It would have pleased Linacre too, if
we had brought her with us," he continued; and then
Mrs. Disney secretly regretted that she had not given
Christian a hint.

Christian herself felt somewhat restless that afternoon; for once she was alone. Pen, who was always
ready to help her friends, had undertaken to convey a
message for Mrs. Disney to a woman who lived a mile

or two out of Braybrooke, and as it was a pleasant walk, she had invited the Vicarage children to bear her company. Pen would share their schoolroom tea on their return, and Christian, who loved to lend herself to these little surprises, had enjoined her to make sundry purchases at the confectioner's on her way back.

It was the perfection of a May afternoon: Many Bushes was in its glory just then, for the drive was a mass of blossoming shrubs. Pink and white May trees scented the air with their fragrance, while the white flowers of the guelder-rose and the syringa mingled with the golden trails of laburnum and the dusky red of the ribis. The air was so sunny and warm that Christian took her book to a seat underneath an old chestnut tree overlooking the meadow; but her story soon ceased to interest her as her thoughts wandered, and she was soon in a reverie so deep and profound that even a footstep on the gravel path failed to attract her attention until it paused beside her, when she looked up with a start and met Carus Linacre's smile.

Never had she been more taken by surprise. The sight of the quiet face and kind eyes recalled too vividly the circumstances under which she had seen them last, and as she held out her hand the colour forsook her cheek, and for the moment she could not speak.

Mr. Linacre did not misunderstand her sudden emotion; he kept her hand in his, pressing it kindly, then he sat down beside her.

"I was afraid that I should startle you, you seemed so deep in thought," he said in the monotonous, toneless voice she so well remembered. But before she could answer, he put a small tube to his ear.

"If you speak quietly and distinctly I shall hear you very well," he went on; "and there is no need to raise your voice. I am still able to enjoy a *tête-à-tête* with a close neighbour; it is only in general conversation I am out of the running." He said this in a calm, matter-of-fact way, as though he and his deafness were old comrades and were quite accustomed to each other.

This had the effect of putting Christian at her ease, and she looked forward to her conversation with less trepidation.

" I drove over here directly after luncheon," he continued ; " I wanted my mother to come too, but she
thought that it would be wiser to rest. She sends her
love, and hopes that you and your friend will come over
to luncheon to-morrow and spend a long afternoon with
her. The carriage shall be sent for you, if you will
kindly tell me the time that will suit you ?"

" We can be ready by half-past twelve if that will
do ;" but Christian felt so nervous at the idea of her
visit that her voice was not quite steady, and Carus
had to ask her to repeat her words.

" I would come for you myself," he returned ; " only
I have a business interview at that hour. Well, Christian,"—dismissing the subject rather suddenly,—" what
do you think of my hermitage ?—is not Many Bushes a
peaceful little place ?"

" It is charming," and Christian's face brightened at
once ; " my friend and I have grown to love it. Oh,
we have been so happy !" and then she looked at him
with shy gratitude. " I have so often wanted to thank
you for all your kindness and consideration." His reply
touched her not a little.

" One ought to be kind and considerate to one's sister,
so you need not thank me, Christian. I told you in my
letter that Jack had placed you under my charge, and
that I felt responsible for your comfort."

" Jack knew you would be kind ; he told me so, but
he did not mean me to be a burden, Mr.——" Christian
checked herself somewhat awkwardly as she remembered
their relationship and coloured.

" My name is Carus, and any prefix is unnecessary,"
he observed quietly ; " and as for kindness, you must
remember that Jack is my only brother, and that I am
bound to do all I can for him. I have done little enough
in the past ;" and here there was a touch of pain in his
voice which Christian felt that she understood. " In
past years my hands were tied, and I could do nothing."

" I know what you mean," she returned gently ;
" Jack told me that his uncle would do all or nothing,
and that you were not allowed to assist him."

" No ; but it was rather rough on both of us, for I

had more than I needed and would willingly have shared
it with Jack. You see, he was only a lad when my
father died, and I was ten years older, and I had to
look after him, you know. He was such a plucky little
chap: he would ride my father's hunters bare-backed
in the paddock, and if he got a fall he would pick himself
up with a laugh. He broke his arm once in the hunting-
field, trying to jump his pony over a quick-set hedge.
There was a bit of a ditch on the other side, and though
the pony scrambled up, Jack rolled over and fell on his
arm. After that my mother never let him go out with
the hounds again until Uncle Jasper's reign began, and
then Jack took the bit between his teeth."

Christian listened to this with great interest. Jack
had been reckless and daring even in his boyhood. She
was quite sure that he would distinguish himself by
some conspicuous act of bravery if he ever got the
chance; she was beginning to feel proud of him already,
and quite willing to condone his faults. Her black
sheep was not so black that he could not be washed white
some day. He was not worse than other young men, she
thought; and if he had had his fling he was pulling
himself together, and then he had such a good heart.

They talked a little more and then they went indoors,
and Christian made tea in the bay window of the little
sitting-room, and Carus drew up his chair beside her
and talked to her about his books and the Disneys and
other interesting topics, to which Christian responded
with her old animation and brightness. She would soon
get used, she thought, to his level, monotonous voice.
Now and then in her eagerness she spoke too quickly
and unevenly, and then it pained her to see his patient
and puzzled look.

" I did not catch that; I am very stupid, I fear," and
then Christian would repeat her words more clearly.

Christian was at her best that afternoon. The presence of this man seemed to stimulate and elevate her;
she had never seen any one in the least like him. There
was something subdued and melancholy about him, as
though his life's pleasure was diluted and flavourless;
and yet, in spite of his limitations, a sort of peaceful

atmosphere pervaded him. " Oh, if you knew what peace there is in an accepted sorrow!" Madame Guyon had exclaimed. And Carus Linacre would have endorsed this; not that he ever put such thoughts into words, for in his case the still waters ran deep.

Years before he had looked life in the face and knew what it had to offer, and he did not flinch from the answer.

He was a reserved, sensitive man, and deafness was a greater cross to him than to many other men. It was a painful ordeal for him to feel that he was in any way a burden to his fellows; to sit at his own table, surrounded by his friends, was a martyrdom to him—the dull, distant medley of voices seemed to recede from him —and he would sit silent, watching the faces round him.

Now and then he wondered why his mother considered it necessary to give these big dinner-parties, and why she never seemed content unless she had filled the house with guests; but he never hinted at the discomfort she caused him, and very rarely beat a retreat. If she had only guessed the pain she inflicted—but Mrs. Linacre, in spite of her maternal devotion, was too self-centred and preoccupied by her own feelings not to be a little dense about the feelings of others.

Once, when Mrs. Disney ventured to hint that these large gatherings were not to Carus's taste, Mrs. Linacre had seemed surprised.

" He has not told me so" was her answer; " and it is good for him to see people, he is such a bookworm; he is quite young—only thirty-eight—and yet he leads the life of an old professor. If Heather and I did not rout him out at times he would be quite a recluse. Heather delights in dragging him out for a walk or ride; and I am sure that he enjoys them as much as she does."

" But we were not talking about his walks with Heather," returned Mrs. Disney, slightly puzzled by this; but Mrs. Linacre was a trifle obstinate and could not be induced to see that a country ramble with a congenial companion was more enjoyable to a deaf man than any smart dinner-party; for on this subject Mrs. Linacre chose to be dense.

"Of course, if Carus were to tell me that he disliked it, I should not dream of having them," was all she would say; but her knowledge of her son's unselfishness and consideration for her feelings ought to have told her that Carus would never have dropped such a hint.

Carus loved his mother dearly, and he understood her temperament. "A deep insight into your own mind gives you a knowledge of other men's," as it has been well said; and Carus, in his life of quiet abstraction and self-communing, had learnt to read human nature with some degree of clearness. Even when he had been a mere lad, and before his infirmity had developed, he had found out that his mother was not a happy woman; and as he loved both his parents, and to all appearance they lived in outward harmony, the boy was often perplexed at the signs of trouble on his mother's face. He had reached manhood before his father died, but he had not solved the problem. He had never heard his father say a cross word to her, and though at times it struck him that his mother's manner was a little cold and repellent, she certainly never failed in her wifely duty.

He remembered her dumb anguish when the accident happened, and they carried the Squire home to die. It was dreadful to him to see her despair, and for many a long day she refused to be comforted.

"If she loved him so dearly, why did my father fail to make her happy?" he asked himself, but there was only one person that could have answered that question, and that was his mother herself, though Charlotte Disney had long ago guessed the truth. But even to her, her closest friend and confidante, Mrs. Linacre had rarely mentioned her husband.

XVII

A Woman's Mistake

To err is human, to forgive divine.—Shakespeare.

Lie still, lie still, my breaking heart;
My silent heart, lie still and break;
Life, and the world, and my own self are changed
For a dream's sake.

Christina Rossetti.

Janet Linacre had been the only daughter of parents who had married late in life, and their injudicious fondness had fostered instead of repressing her natural faults of character. She had grown up with an overweening sense of her own importance, and with a strong will and arbitrary temper. With these defects she had a warm heart and much real kindliness of disposition.

Her parents died when she was only seventeen, and for a time her home was with an uncle. Janet had no beauty, but she was an heiress, and so there was no lack of suitors for her hand. But her heart remained untouched until Frank Linacre crossed her path; and his good looks, pleasant manner, and apparent devotion soon won her affection. Her guardian made no objection. The match was a sufficiently good one, and Frank Linacre was his own master. The family had lived at the Stone House for two or three generations, and never had a young wife entered it with greater prospects of happiness than Janet did that summer day. But in a few months there was a bolt from the blue. Janet, who had believed herself her husband's first love—who considered herself sure of his past—discovered one unhappy day that he had been engaged to a beautiful young widow, who had jilted him for a title and a house in town; and that the gay, frank young lover who had wooed her was in reality a reckless, embittered man, who was trying to cheat himself into forgetfulness.

140

The source through which Janet gained her knowledge was too reliable to be disbelieved—dates and circumstances were all corroborated, even the name, Madeleine Middleton, now Lady Dysart, was mentioned. Now Janet had more than once heard of the dark beauty, Lady Dysart, who was creating a furore in town that season.

"Madeleine," Janet turned cold as she remembered how, in his sleep, she had once heard her husband pronounce that name in a tone of such pain that she had woke him. She had questioned him playfully the next morning, "Who is this Madeleine, Frank?" she had asked lightly. "Oh, it was not my fancy! You said it outright in quite a loud voice, ' Madeleine, Madeleine!' "

It was his opportunity, if he had but known it; if he had told her the sad story even then, she would have more easily condoned his silence; but Frank Linacre, with all his good qualities, had one serious fault: he was a moral coward, and hated unpleasant subjects and scenes; the whole story was hateful to him; he never wished it to come to Janet's knowledge; he had found out already that her nature was exacting and jealous; she would never brook a rival; and he knew too well that Madeleine was not forgotten. He was reading his paper at the moment, and he did not put it down as he answered her. "It must have been a nightmare," he observed; and his voice sounded quite natural—probably the sense of danger helped him to steady it. "I think I told you, Janet, that my young sister's name was Madeleine, and that she died in her childhood; the curtains of her cot took fire; the nurse had been drinking; they say the child was suffocated; but my mother never got over it."

Now all this was perfectly true, and Janet had already read the inscription in Silverton churchyard to Madeleine Agnes Linacre, aged three years and a half. She never doubted her husband's veracity. She only wondered vaguely that a thing so long past—a tragedy of his early boyhood—should haunt his dreams. There had been such a thrill of horror in his tone. "How could any woman be so cruel?" these words had also reached her ear; but Frank had explained, and the episode had passed from her mind until the story of that engagement

was told. Now, indeed, the serpent had entered her paradise; jealousy, that most baleful of vices, was eating, like
the Spartan boy's fox, into her very vitals. When she
confronted her husband with this story—when she first
mentioned Lady Dysart's name—Frank quite shrank from
her hard, cold glance. "Why have you deceived me,
Frank?" she asked in a voice he hardly recognised;
"why did you pretend to love me? Was it my money you
wanted, for I had no beauty like your Madeleine?" for
in her torment of mind she was cruel to him.

Frank Linacre had little to say in excuse; he had been
a coward, and he knew it; he had taken advantage of her
trusting affection and hidden his past from her. "Let it
be; why need I ever tell her?" he had argued; "the
engagement only lasted six weeks, and we were in the
Engadine; no one in Silverton knew it;" and his facile,
weak nature plotted to keep silence.

"Who has told you this thing?" he asked fiercely; but
Janet refused to give the name of her informant; she
merely stated facts in the cold, tired voice in which there
was a note of dull anguish.

"Why did you pretend to love me?" she demanded
again; and then a man's chivalry and tenderness woke in
Frank's nature.

"I never pretended," he returned indignantly; "why
do you make things worse for us? I ought to have told
you about Madeleine. I made a mistake, I see that now;
but I wanted to marry you, Janet; you attracted me
somehow, and you were kind—kind"—and here Frank's
voice was rather husky—"and I was lonely, and afraid
of going to the devil. Why don't you believe me, my
dear? I cared for you, or I should never have asked you
to be my wife."

Poor Janet; if she could only have believed him; but
she was too dense, and too deeply wounded to respond to
this appeal for her forbearance. In her heart she told
herself that she would never be able to believe in him
again.

There was a long and painful scene, and one that
neither of them forgot; but after a time there was a
sort of reconciliation. The Squire resumed his old habits,

and soon regained his usual light-hearted insouciance, and his manner to his wife left nothing to be desired; he was always mindful of her least wish.

"The Squire makes far too much of Madam," the tenants would say; "it is not to be wondered at that she is a bit uppish with him."

Janet was a good woman; and she really strove all those years to do her wifely duty to the man whom she never truly forgave in life; but she was never the same from the day she heard of Madeleine Dysart's existence.

Her rival was living, and Frank had loved her; and the poison of this thought sapped the spring and happiness of Janet's life. There were no more scenes between the husband and wife; but her manner conveyed to the Squire that she still regarded herself as an injured woman; and no patience and tenderness on his part seemed to break down the unnatural calm and reserve in which she had impregnated herself. Then had come the accident, when they carried him home, shattered and broken, and she learnt from the doctor's lips that no human aid was of avail—that he must die. And he was her husband; and all these years she had not forgiven him. Ah! but she forgave him now.

Janet, in her dumb anguish, would willingly have remained in her husband's room day and night; but they forced her, at times, to leave him. Perhaps the doctor guessed that that white, stricken face troubled the dying man; but once, when they were alone together, and he had got a moment's ease, he made a sign to her to approach.

"Closer. There is something I want to say, and my voice is weak;" and then she knelt down beside him. "Janet, I have never made you happy," he whispered; "all these years you have not forgiven me for deceiving you about Madeleine; and yet"—his voice sank wearily—"I have forgotten her existence."

"Forgotten!" Jane started.

"Why should I remember any one so worthless? Indeed, you were wrong, my dear; and you could have been everything to me if you had only been patient, but

your pride has kept us apart; you would never believe
that I really cared for you."

" Frank, do you really mean this?"

" Yes; but I could not make you see it.   But here
comes the doctor;" and Janet rose reluctantly from her
knees.

" Forgive me," was on her lips; " forgive me the miserable jealousy and hardness that have spoiled both our
lives, for I loved you—I loved you so dearly through it
all."   But when those words were spoken, it was to deaf
ears; no other opportunity was given to Janet, for an
hour later unconsciousness set in; and the widow's
broken-hearted prayers for forgiveness were uttered beside her husband's coffin.   Janet's misery in those days
was wellnigh intolerable; when it was too late she realised the bitter truth.   She could have won him if she had
been only patient.   All these years she had been subject
to a foolish hallucination; she had lived in an atmosphere
of secret suspicion; she had lost faith in her husband and
in herself; and all the time Madeleine had been forgotten.
" Why should I remember any one so worthless?" he
had said to her, " if you had only been patient——" Ah!
no wonder she was bowed to the earth in her remorse
and misery.   It was he who had been patient; she remembered how gentle he had been with. her, when he
learnt the extent of the mischief that had resulted to
their eldest boy, through her obstinacy and denseness.
Surely any other man would have upbraided her for her
folly.

" It was a mistake," was all he said.   " My poor boy,
if only I could have had it instead of him;" and then he
told her not to fret.   " We must just do our best for him
—the rest is not in our hands;" for in his simple way
the Squire tried to practise the precepts of the great
Teacher he had learnt to serve; but even his great tenderness could not induce her to bear their misfortune with
fortitude or submission.   She only brooded over the trouble, and told herself that she had not deserved so great a
punishment.

Janet believed that her heart was really broken that
day she knelt by her husband's coffin; but though her

sorrow was intense and prolonged, it could not last for
ever. She had her sons, and by and by she adopted the
orphan child of an old schoolfellow who would otherwise
have been left destitute, and this act of benevolence
brought its own reward. Janet's sore heart found new
interest in watching over the motherless girl whom she
had taken under her roof. Janet's nature indeed would
never be a restful one—her nerves had suffered too much.
She still needed excitement; and as Heather grew up,
she made her an excuse. "We must give her all the advantages we can," she said to Carus; but Heather, who
was very simple and childish in her tastes, owned more
than once to Mrs. Disney that these gay parties simply
bored her.

"Carus hates them so," she would say plaintively; "he
always looks so dull and tired. Of course, it is very dear
of Aunt Janet to wish to give me pleasure; but," with
a laugh, "I would rather toss hay in the big meadow,
or go nutting with Lionel and Tony than put on my
smart frock and 'behave pretty,' as Mrs. Mills used to
say."

But Mrs. Disney always shook her head at this, "For
shame, Heather; you are eighteen, a grown-up young
lady now; and you ought not to be such a tomboy. Was
it true that you climbed the big pear tree yesterday? I
hope Lionel was romancing a little; indeed, my dear," as
the girl nodded, "think how shocked Mrs. Linacre would
have been if she had seen you."

"Oh, I told her all about it afterwards!" returned
Heather gaily, "and she did not mind. Aunt Janet has
so little imagination, you see; and then so much depends
on the way one puts a thing. I rather pride myself on my
finesse, Mrs. Disney."

"Indeed!" and Charlotte looked very much amused.

"I remarked on the beautiful view one can get from
the upper branches of the big pear tree," continued the
girl; "it is like a new world when one is peeping out
from them. I sat there for quite a long time enjoying
myself. Those were my very words."

Then Mrs. Disney looked up from her work with pretended severity. "Heather, how can you be so naughty?

Of course, your Aunt Janet thought you had used the orchard ladder."

"That is where the want of imagination comes in," replied Heather composedly. "It never entered Aunt Janet's head to wonder how I got there; and it was not my duty to give gratuitous and undesired information;" and then Heather ran off, and a minute later she was playing puss-in-the-corner in the Vicarage schoolroom.

"She is so nice and gamey," Toney once said to his mother; "I do love her to come and play with us."

Never had an afternoon passed more pleasantly to Christian. She was even glad that Pen was absent. This tête-à-tête with her brother-in-law was breaking the ice. He asked her presently if she had ever been into his study; and when she pleaded guilty to following Mrs. Mills in one day, he had told her smilingly that she need not have feared to look round her, for there was no Bluebeard's closet with concealed skeletons; and then he invited her to accompany him.

"There are one or two books I want," he remarked as they entered, and he placed a chair for her while he went to the bookshelves, but every now and then he interrupted himself by bringing something of interest to show her—a book of fine old engravings, or the rare edition of a classic, or an antique print he had found in a portfolio. It was evident that Carus was a booklover—he handled his treasures so tenderly.

The study was certainly a pleasant room. It was well furnished, and the few pictures and bronzes in excellent taste. A picture of Jack in his uniform was on the writing-table. Christian saw at once that it was a fac-simile of the one Jack had given her soon after their engagement.

"I thought you would like to have one of me in my war paint," he had remarked. "There is my tomahawk," pointing to his sword hilt; "but I have not got my first scalp yet, so I am not really a brave." But though Christian did not tell him so, she secretly admired the photo.

"I suppose you have a study at the Stone House?" she observed, as Carus stood beside her a moment.

"Yes, the library is appropriated to my use," he returned; "it is a big room and holds about five thousand books; but," with a wistful glance round him, "I have a fancy for my den at Many Bushes."

"But you come sometimes; Mrs. Mills told me so."

"Yes, that is true; and the room is always kept ready for me, as you see—for I never give any notice; but my visits grow rarer. My mother misses me too much, and then——" he interrupted himself, sighed, and took up the case of coins he was showing to Christian and locked them in his bureau. "Now, I must be going," he continued. "I am walking back, and Heather said she should meet me half-way with the dogs, so I must keep my tryst;" and then Christian accompanied him down the drive. "Good-bye until to-morrow," he said, as they shook hands; and then she went slowly back to the house.

"I have got a new friend," she said that evening to Pen, as they paced the terrace together. "I know now why Jack thought so much of his brother. He is unlike other men, and somehow to me he seems above them. When one talks to him one feels somehow on a higher level. Oh, I cannot explain myself, and yet it is perfectly simple!"

"I think I know what you mean," returned Pen, who was never slow to grasp an idea presented to her. "I remember Walter once saying that we create our own atmosphere, though people seldom realise it."

"I daresay he is right," replied Christian. "Anyway, there is something peaceful about Carus Linacre that I found very restful. He is kind, and his manner is very gentle, and yet one feels he can understand. In spite of his quiet life, he has plenty of knowledge of human nature, and he is lenient in his judgment."

"I am so glad you like him, Chrissy dear," observed her friend affectionately.

"Yes, and I want him to like me in return—to approve of me for my own as well as for Jack's sake. He is evidently fond of Jack; he seems to have quite a fatherly fondness for him."

"He is ten years older, you see."

"Yes; and he is twenty years wiser, and better, and

stronger than my stupid old Jack," returned Christian; but her tone was kinder than her words. " Pen, I have always so longed for a brother.   I used so to envy the girls at school when they talked of Charlie, or Harry, or Dick; it made one feel so lonely.   But now I've a brother of my own," continued Christian joyfully; and the next moment she added a little thoughtfully, " How pleased Jack will be to know I like Carus !"

XVIII

A Sprig of Bell-Heather

Her bloom was like the springing flower
That sips the silver dew;
The rose was budded in her cheek,
Just opening to the view.
MALLET.

It was natural that Christian should look forward to her interview with her mother-in-law with some degree of nervousness. She had received several messages from her, and more than one kind letter. There was no fault to find with them. Nevertheless, Christian, who was a little tenacious of her position, thought the kindness somewhat forced and wanting in spontaneity.

"She must be a very reserved person," she said to Pen that morning. "I am not sure that we shall get on together; but of course I shall do my best, or Jack will scold me;" and then, a little plaintively, "it is rather hard to have to go alone to my new relations; and I do think that, under the circumstances, Mrs. Linacre might have come to me." Christian spoke in rather an injured tone; but if Pen secretly agreed with her, she was careful not to say so.

Christian tried to settle to her usual occupations, but she was too restless; so she dressed herself early, making her toilet with unusual care, and went out into the garden. When one is excited and uneasy, there is nothing so soothing as the air and sunshine; flowers and birds seem to whisper their messages of peace and patience; and as Christian wandered down the sunny garden paths her secret irritation seemed quieted.

She was too far from the house to hear the sound of carriage wheels coming up the drive, and so she was not a little surprised to see a young lady tripping along the terrace and then quickening her steps at the sight of her. As she came closer, Christian caught sight of a pretty, blooming face under the broad hat, and such a bright, irresistible smile greeted her, that Christian at once put out her hand.

"You are Miss Bell?" she said at once.

"Yes, I am Heather," returned the girl simply, and it struck Christian that she had expected a warmer greeting. "Carus sent me to fetch you, because he thought you would like it better."

"And he was right," returned Christian gratefully. "It was a kind thought on his part, and it was good of you to come."

"Not at all," returned Heather eagerly. "I wanted to see you so badly. I was dreadfully curious, you know, for Jack was quite like my own brother, so I am anxious to make friends; and then Aunt Janet said I might come."

It was Carus's thought for her comfort then—always Carus!

"I may call you Christian, may I not?" continued the girl pleadingly, "for Carus says we must be sisters. I have never had a sister, and I have often thought how nice it would be to have one; that was why I was so glad when Jack married. I told Carus so, and he quite understood."

"I was an only child too, Heather," returned Christian a little sadly, and then, with a sudden impulse, the two girls kissed each other. "What a dear, sweet child she is!" thought Christian. "Her disposition seems as lovely as her face. She is a perfect rosebud in her pink frock and with those pink cheeks;" and she was right. Carus that very morning had called her his wild "sprig of bell-heather," for this was his pet name for her.

And indeed the girl was very winsome in her fresh, young bloom, and in spite of her eighteen years there was something extremely youthful about her, as though she still looked at life with innocent child's eyes; and yet with those she loved Heather could be womanly too.

Mrs. Linacre's tenderness for her adopted child had doubtless kept Heather from any disturbing influence. She had lived her simple child's life in unrestrained freedom, and it was only during the last three months, since she had attained her eighteenth birthday, that she had been considered grown-up and of an age to make her *début* in society; but to Carus, Bell-Heather was still a child, and the first sight of her in her ball dress gave him quite a shock. His silent look of astonishment had troubled Heather. " Why don't you tell me that I look nice?" she pouted. " Isn't this a lovely dress that Aunt Janet has given me?" and Heather laughed and shook out her silk train.

" The dress is perfect—yes—and you look very nice," —still there was a regretful tone in Carus's voice—" but my Bell-Heather is changed into a hothouse flower to-night, and somehow I cannot recognise her;" but to himself he muttered: " After all, my mother is right, and the child has become a woman;" and in some strange, inexplicable way this thought seemed to give him pain, for the childish Heather had been very dear to him, and in his darkest moments, when his infirmity weighed heaviest on him, the sight of that bright, young face had been like heaven's sunshine to him.

Pen came out of the house a few minutes later. She seemed pleased at the sight of Christian's young companion, and after a little more talk, they all three drove off in the direction of the Stone House.

The avenue was a long one, and the cawing of rooks over their heads accompanied them all the way. On either side lay the green, undulating park. Once Christian caught the gleam of water and leaned forward to catch another glimpse between the trees.

" Oh, you are looking at the lake!" observed Heather. " We call it the lake, though it is really only a big pond; but we have splendid skating there in the winter, and on hot days it is rather pleasant to sit in the boat under the willow with one's book. The dogs love it. Oh, I can hear the dear things barking! We shall be at the house in another minute."

They had emerged from the avenue, and for the moment both the girls felt a sensation of surprise. Before them stood a white, imposing-looking house, with broad wings and a heavy stone porch, but with the exception of the broad, gravelled drive, the green turf stretched to

the very walls—no shrubs, or flower-beds, or semblance
of a garden was to be seen on three sides of the house.
From the front windows one saw only the green sweep
and bosky dells and the rooks circling over the elm
avenue.

"Is it not a barrack of a place?" continued Heather, as
her companions remained silent. "Its name just suits
it. People are always surprised at first to see no gardens, but they are at the back;" and then the carriage
stopped, and the butler came out into the porch to receive
them, and told Heather that Mrs. Linacre was in her
dressing-room. "Then I will take you to her at once,"
observed Heather, leading the way with rapid steps
through an immense hall with a life-sized group of sculpture in the centre. As they went up the broad staircase
Christian paused and turned to look at the picture of the
Squire in his red coat mounted on his favourite hunter.
The good-humoured, handsome face seemed to greet her
with friendly eyes.

"That was Mr. Linacre," whispered Heather. "Isn't
he just splendid?" and Christian assented. She was in
no mood to speak just then. Heather glanced at her and
talked on gaily. "It is so absurd of Aunt Janet to call
her room a dressing-room, for there is not a ghost of a
glass or toilet table about it—nothing but a writing-table
and books and that sort of thing, but she cannot tolerate
the word boudoir; and the morning room is downstairs,"
and here she checked herself and tapped lightly at a door.
A voice said, "Come in," and as she opened it a very
small Yorkshire terrier rushed out with a welcoming bark.
Heather took him up in her arms. "Be quiet, Cheri,"
she remonstrated; and then, in her clear, young voice,
"Christian is here, Aunt Janet." A tall, grave-looking
woman in black rose from her chair and came forward
rather slowly.

"I am very glad to see you, my dear," she said, kissing Christian's cheek as she spoke. "This is your friend,
Miss Mervyn, I suppose?" as she shook hands with Pen;
but she hardly looked at her as she spoke, for her eyes
were scrutinising Jack's wife.

Christian had grown very pale. She felt a curious revulsion at the sight of her mother-in-law, for from the plain-featured and somewhat impassive face Jack's dark, melancholy eyes were looking at her.

"Oh!" she said a little breathlessly, "you are like Jack! If I had met you anywhere in a crowd I should have known you were his mother;" and then, as she said this in her quick, impulsive way, she had another moment of emotion, for lo and behold! Jack's bright, vivid smile lighted up the sad face.

"I am indeed glad that I remind you of him," returned Mrs. Linacre in a touched voice; "my boy was always considered like me. And now, will you take off your hat, my dear? Heather will show you to her room, and then you must come back to me, and we will have a little talk."

"I was so charmed when you said that, Christian," whispered Heather when the door of the dressing-room had closed behind them. "Aunt Janet was so pleased; I could see that. People say that she is a little difficult to understand at first; but then they do not go in the right way; they think she is stiff and cold, because she does not show her feelings, but she is never demonstrative."

Christian found to her dismay that Mrs. Linacre wished to be left alone with her daughter-in-law until luncheon; and Heather had orders to show Miss Mervyn the garden and hothouses, and otherwise amuse her. But Christian made the best of the situation. As she sat down in the comfortable easy-chair that had been placed for her, she felt for a moment that it resembled an imposing velvet throne, where certain unpleasant and delicate manipulations by an ogre in black had harassed her childish nerves. But then Christian's imagination often ran away with her; and surely there could be little affinity between a dentist's forceps and those grave, penetrating eyes that were studying her face.

It was a disappointing fact that Mrs. Linacre did not admire her new daughter-in-law. Christian had her good points. She had a nice complexion, and her hair and eyes were pretty. But Pen's fairness and gentleness would have appealed with greater force to Janet.

When people knew Christian thoroughly, they liked her frankness and vivacity, and did full justice to her warm heart. But at first strangers, especially older women, thought her somewhat independent and self-assertive. " I believe people think me strong-minded because I wear pince-nez," she had said once in a disgusted tone to Pen; " but what is a short-sighted young person to do?"

Mrs. Linacre was striving her best to be both conciliatory and gracious to her son's wife. " I want you to feel quite at home with us, Christian," she said with painstaking kindness. " We hoped you would have come to us during my dear boy's absence, as I knew you did not wish to remain with your aunt, but as Jack told his brother, you preferred to live alone."

" I have my friend Penelope Mervyn," returned Christian quickly. Her crisp voice and manner seemed to take Janet by surprise. The elder woman's nature was slower and denser.

" You are your own mistress, my dear;" and it struck Christian that Mrs. Linacre did not approve of her independent action. " And of course no one has a right to control you. When Carus told me that you were to live at Many Bushes, I own I was a little surprised."

" You mean that you were disappointed?" And again the girl's quickness seemed to trouble Mrs. Linacre.

" Well, yes; but perhaps I had no right to feel so. But there is so much room in this great house, and you could have led your own life even here. I think we should all have been glad if you had made up your mind to come to us."

Christian coloured painfully. Her quick perception told her that her refusal to take refuge with Jack's people had created a grievance in her mother-in-law's mind. The difficulty was how to remove it. But Christian was not deficient in courage.

" You must not be hard on me, Mrs. Linacre," she said rather pleadingly. " You were all strangers to me. Don't you see the difference that makes. Jack wanted me to come to you; he thought I made a mistake. And even Mr. Vigne seemed surprised. And then your son offered me his house, and that seemed to solve the difficulty. Oh, I hope that you do not really disapprove!" she went on earnestly. " Indeed, I should be sorry to pain or disappoint you in any way. But we are so happy—Pen and I—in our dear little Many Bushes; and we are quite near, and can come whenever you wish." Christian had spoken from her heart, and her voice was very winning; and insensibly Mrs. Linacre's manner grew softer and less judicial.

" You need say no more, Christian. After all, it is your own concern, and you had of course a right to make your own choice of a home, and no doubt your plan will answer. If I had been on the spot, if the marriage had been less hurried, I might have been able to convince you that the Stone House would have been better than Many Bushes;" and then she sighed and changed the subject. " There is so much I want to ask you, my dear. My unfortunate illness lasted so long, and left me so weak that I was not allowed to travel. And now my boy has gone, and people say there is a chance of a war in South Africa, and I have not even wished him good-bye."

" It was very hard for you," murmured Christian; but she winced at the mention of war. " But those stupid Boers will soon be brought to reason, and we shall have him back;" and then, with a sudden inspiration, " we can both come and stay at the Stone House."

Mrs. Linacre smiled, but she shook her head. " Carus would not endorse your sanguine opinion; he thinks the Boers will give us serious trouble. Still, let us pray that the difficulties may be settled in a more peaceful manner, and that these terrible rumours may die away;" and Christian said amen to this. " Yes, there is so much I want to know," continued Mrs. Linacre, in a slow, musing way. " Jack told me so little in his letter; he is such a bad hand at description too, and I could not realise in the least the sort of girl he was marrying. ' She is an awfully good sort, mother, and we hit it off like anything.' Now, do you call that a lucid description of a young lady, Christian?" but the girl broke into a merry laugh.

" Oh, that was so like Jack!" she exclaimed. " And was that all that he told you about me?"

" There was very little more, except that ' Chriss had no end of fun in her, and that my brother had given you a diamond necklace.' " Here a cloud passed over Mrs. Linacre's face. But for Carus's deafness he would have married, and the necklace would have glittered on his wife's neck; it ought not to have been worn by Jack's wife.

" It is far too grand and beautiful for me," returned Christian, answering the unspoken thought; " but Jack was so pleased."

" Jasper is so impulsive," went on Mrs. Linacre. " He is always doing such unexpected things." She spoke a little severely. " You must wear it when we give the dinner-party in your honour." She said this, fearing that her manner had been a little ungracious. She had felt that her brother would have been wiser to wait for a few years, until it was certain that Carus would not marry. " I have wondered so often how you and Jack made each other's acquaintance," she went on after a pause; " and if you knew each other long before he proposed." Then Christian's manner stiffened a little.

" We met at parties, and he danced with me a good deal, but he did not visit at my aunt's house, though both Aunt Caroline and Adelaide knew him slightly; he was a great friend of the Armitages."

Mrs. Linacre nodded. " Lady Armitage and I were schoolfellows, Christian; well, so you and Jack had a ballroom acquaintance, and then, I suppose, you fell in love with each other."

" I remember dancing with him one night a good many times," returned Christian, evading this question, " and the next day he asked me to marry him. I met him by accident in Kensington Gardens, and he made use of his opportunity."

" Dear boy !" and Mrs. Linacre mused tenderly over the imaginary scene. Jack would be an ardent wooer, she thought. Was it likely that any girl could resist him? But, poor lady, how utterly disillusioned she would have been if she had heard Jack's halting confession.

" I don't say that I am as much in love as some fellows, but then I am rather a cool, undemonstrative chap; but

I give you my word that if you will do this for me, that I shall be grateful to you all my life;" and then, with rough eloquence, he had added: "Think what it means to me; it is like holding out your hand to a drowning man;" but Jack was thinking of himself and not of the girl as he spoke, and Christian had been well aware of it.

Had any girl ever accepted an offer of marriage in the words Christian had used? " I am going to help the drowning man," and Christian kept her word; but it is hardly surprising that Mrs. Linacre, in her maternal pride and tenderness, failed to grasp the situation.

XIX

The Bowling Green

I remark that the persons most curious about my affairs are the most reticent about their own.—Anon.

No man loves the man whom he fears.—Aristotle.

What is so tedious as a twice-told tale.—Pope's *Odyssey*.

It was Mrs. Linacre's usual habit, and one that her friends found somewhat trying, to return again and again to any subject that she considered had not been sufficiently threshed out; and she would actually have done so on this occasion, only something in Christian's manner restrained her.

Fortunately she attributed the girl's evident reluctance to dwell on Jack's courtship to a very natural shyness and reserve, and as she was a shy woman herself, she showed her consideration by ceasing her embarrassing questions.

" When she knows me better she will be more ready to open her heart to me," Mrs. Linacre said to herself; but all the same she felt disappointed, while Christian, on her side, resented secretly this attempt to force her confidence.

" She may be my mother-in-law, but she has no right to ask me these sort of questions," she thought; " surely there must be some things that one may hold sacred. If dear mother had been alive I would have told her all about Jack's trouble and how I made up my mind to help him; but I would rather die—" and here her face burnt angrily —" I would rather do anything than let one of his people know how little we cared for each other then."

To change the subject effectually and to cool her hot face, Christian arose to inspect the numberless photographs and miniatures which covered the walls. To her amazement she found a perfect Jack Linacre gallery, depicting him at every possible age. There was Jack as a baby in extremely scanty attire, with his favourite fetish, in the shape of a dilapidated monkey, reposing on the pillow beside him; Jack as a miniature sailor, with his hat at the back of his curly head and his stout legs very wide apart, the very model of a British tar on a small scale; Jack as a schoolboy in his cricket flannels and carrying his bat; Jack on his pony: then a procession of manly Jacks, in uniform or out of it, alone, or with Carus; Jack with his dogs, or standing with his hand on his horse's mane; and each one was so true a presentment of him that Christian quite marvelled,—the tall, soldierly figure, so thin and muscular; the lean, brown face; the deeply-set, melancholy eyes. Christian went from one to another, while Mrs. Linacre explained and narrated the circumstances under which each photo had been taken. Here at least was a subject in which they were both interested; and now it was Christian who asked questions, who was amused and inquisitive and critical.

" But there are so many of Jack," she objected presently—" dozens and dozens; but there is only one good one of Carus, and that must have been taken long ago."

" I never could induce Carus to be taken after he grew up, except just that once," and Mrs. Linacre's face became grave; " he never could understand Jack's fancy for being photographed. There, I think you have seen all my treasures now, Christian, and we may as well go downstairs."

As they passed out of the room Christian noticed more closely a large picture on a stand with an embroidered covering thrown lightly over it; a beautiful palm seemed to overshadow it, and just above it hung a small but striking likeness of Mrs. Linacre. Christian guessed that the veiled picture was a portrait of the late squire, and she found afterwards that her surmise was correct.

As they came slowly down the wide, shallow steps of the staircase they looked down upon a picturesque little group in the hall below.

The immense piece of sculpture in the centre represented the parting of Hector and Andromache, and was the work of a well-known sculptor. Andromache had her boy in her arms, and her upturned face in its pathetic loveliness seemed to be saying those most touching words: " Father to me thou art, and mother dear, and brother too, kind husband of my heart;" surely one of the most affecting scenes for an artist's skill to portray.

Round the base of the marble ran a low, broad, circular seat, covered with dark red velvet, and known in the household with the significant name of Troy. If any one wished to assign a meeting-place where one person could wait comfortably for another, he or she invariably would say, " I will be in Troy at such and such a time."

Troy was also the favourite gathering-place before or after meals; and when the house was full of guests for the shooting or hunting season, and there was a splendid fire in the big grate, Troy was a pleasant place in which to linger, for the circular seat was broad and soft, and the rugs that strewed the hall were thick and warm, and it was a pretty sight to sit there and watch the ladies in their evening dresses coming slowly down the staircase, looking, as Jack once profanely said, " like the angels on Jacob's ladder."

The group that attracted Christian's attention was Carus and Heather surrounded by dogs of all sizes, Pen was in the background; Cheri, who was on Heather's lap, was barking furiously at a shaggy Skye terrier, whose gray coat almost swept the floor; a pure white collie, a black Pomeranian, and two little fox-terriers were seated round their master, waiting for instructions how to proceed: there was evidently some dog grievance that had to be adjusted; the Skye was on his hind legs and looked abject.

" Jock is a thief, Carus!" exclaimed Heather, reproach-fully; " he stole Cheri's biscuit and ate it before her eyes;" and then she interrupted herself and sprang to meet the newcomers, clasping Christian affectionately by the arm.

" Well, have you finished your talk, you dear people, for you both look as tired as possible?" but happily at that moment the gong sounded, and Carus, who had come forward to shake hands, offered Christian his arm, and so no one took any notice of Heather's awkward little speech.

Though food was welcome to Christian, it could not be said that she really enjoyed her luncheon. For the greater part of the time the servants were in the room and the conversation was somewhat perfunctory and formal.

Carus was very silent and rarely spoke, but Christian guessed that this was his usual habit during meals. The few remarks she made were evidently unheard or misunderstood. Heather, who seemed always watching him, invariably looked troubled at this, and tried to divert Christian's attention by asking her questions.

"It is no use trying to talk to Carus at meals," she said afterwards to Christian; "it is much better to leave him alone. I daresay you noticed that Aunt Janet never even addressed him—you see we know his ways."

They had turned their steps to Troy. As they had risen from the table Carus had suggested showing Christian the library, but his mother had claimed his attention for a moment.

"We will wait here until Carus is ready," observed Heather, placing herself between her new acquaintances, and squeezing an arm of each. "You dear things, how rich I feel to-day with two new friends!"

"Have you a genius for friendship too, Heather?" Christian asked the question with assumed gravity, but Heather laughed as she answered—

"That is borrowed from Mrs. Disney's book of philosophy. I recognise the expression," she returned. "Isn't she delightful, Christian? Aunt Janet loves her, and so do I. She is the dearest friend I have in Braybrooke. I tell her things just as though I were Sheila; and sometimes when she thinks I have done wrong she lectures me, although, as I tell her, I am a grown-up young lady."

"You do look so young, Heather!"

"No, not always. Look at me now," and Heather jumped up and disappeared behind Hector a moment. An instant later she returned with a slow and mincing step, the corners of her mouth were drawn down, and her face was preternaturally grave; her forehead was wrinkled, and her pretty hair drawn back. It was an absurd caricature, but she looked at least a dozen years older. "Here comes Miss Propriety," she said, seating herself with much dignity. "Yes, my dear Mrs. Jack, I have most certainly a genius for friendship. The cult of the good, the true, the beautiful, has been the dearest object of my life."

"My dear Miss Propriety, I had no idea you were such a mimic!" exclaimed Christian. "Was it not wonderful, Pen, the way her very features seemed to alter? I am quite sure you have done it before, Heather."

The girl nodded. "I do it sometimes to tease Carus when he treats me too much like a little girl;" and here Heather rearranged her hair, but there was still a little wrinkle on her forehead. "I do not know how it is, but Carus never will remember that I am quite grown up, and like grown-up things. I am afraid it is partly my own fault. I was such a tomboy, you see."

Perhaps Christian had played Miss Propriety too, and was a little tired of the rôle, for the spirit of mischief prompted her to say—

"Have you quite given up climbing trees, dear?" a certain anecdote having reached her ears. Then Heather gave a furious little stamp with her pretty foot.

"Now, I call that too bad of Mrs. Charlotte," she said indignantly. "The idea of prejudicing my new sister against me, and making her think I was just a hoyden! What is the good of my turning over a new leaf and making all those virtuous resolutions if my past sins are to be recalled in this way?"

"How funny to hear you say 'Mrs. Charlotte'!" observed Christian, exchanging an amused look at Pen.

"Oh, I always call her Mrs. Charlotte when she affronts me, and I do it to her face too. When she is very good I call her darling Disney, or Goody; but it was just mean of her to tell you that, Christian."

"I don't think we were particularly shocked, were we, Pen?"

"Ah! here comes Mr. Linacre to fetch me," and Heather's manner instantly changed. Carus had a tired look on his face, but he smiled affectionately as Heather met him and took his arm. Christian was touched at the sweet womanliness of her expression as she turned her bright face to him.

"You are going to show Christian the library while I talk to Miss Mervyn. I daresay Aunt Janet will join us presently." And then he nodded, and he and Christian went off together; but as they were leaving the inner hall they came face to face with a young man in a rough suit and knickerbockers, who pulled off his cap somewhat hastily at the sight of Carus's companion.

"Hulloa, Sydney! So you are back, are you?" and Carus shook hands with the newcomer in a friendly manner. "This is my sister-in-law, Mrs. Jack Linacre. Christian, let me present our close neighbour and friend, Mr. Masters."

Christian looked at him with decided approval. He was a handsome young fellow, with an exceedingly frank and open expression. He looked about two-and-twenty, and Carus's next speech told her that Sydney Masters was on intimate terms with the family.

"You will find the ladies in Troy, Syd. We will join you by and by." And then they turned into a sort of ante-room lined with books, but only furnished with a writing-table and a couple of carved oak chairs, and which looked what it was, a mere passage room.

The library was the finest room in the house. It had a grand domed roof, and with the exception of the fireplace and immense bay window, every inch of wall room was covered with book-cases. Carus's grandfather had been a book collector, and as he was an epicure in all matters relating to literature and art, he was fastidious about his bindings. The warm, rich tones of vellum and calf and Russian leather were exceedingly harmonious, and Christian praised the beautiful room in no measured terms.

"I wonder you can ever bear to leave it for Many Bushes!" she exclaimed; but Carus passed by the remark as though it were unheard, but there was an odd little smile on his lips as he took down a volume of rare prints. Dear as the room was to him, he was not safe from intrusion there. At all hours his mother would seek him, or break in ruthlessly on his occupation by some entreaty that he would join them in some expedition; and if he hesitated or seemed disposed to refuse, she would add hastily that Heather, dear child, would be so disappointed, and then he would yield. Heather never guessed how often her name was used. She had little suspicion that it was for her sake that Carus closed his books, and heroically consented to be bored; and as Heather's eyes always brightened when she saw him and a beaming smile welcomed him, he thought his mother had been right.

It was always a relief to him when his mother and Heather left home on some visit, and he could spend a week or two at his beloved Hermitage in undisturbed seclusion, only interrupted pleasantly by an evening visit from the Vicar, who came to smoke his pipe in congenial company or to play a game of chess. Now and then Mrs. Disney would bring her work, and listen with much pleasure as the two men talked of books or politics. On such occasions Carus was always at his best. When Christian had been shown the library she was taken into the gardens and hothouses; but nothing pleased her so well as the Bowling Green, shut in with a high clipped hedge, the hedge cut in the quaint old English fashion into representations of peacocks and other curious devices. At the end of the green was a summer-house, with a door and windows, which she discovered was furnished most daintily as a tea-room. The place was so green and still and secluded that Christian was charmed with it.

"Yes, it is a quiet spot," observed Carus. "Heather and I generally walk here morning and evening in fine weather. How time flies, Christian! It is nearly four o'clock, and my mother will have been wondering what has become of us."

"I suppose we shall find Mr. Masters still there?" asked Christian, as they walked down the Bowling Green.

"Oh, yes; Sydney is a tame cat about the house; we have known him from childhood. Chesterton is only a mile away. He is a nice boy, and there is plenty of good in him; but it has been his misfortune to become his own master too soon, and as his mother is a foolish woman, she has indulged and given way to him, so it will be a wonder if he is not spoiled."

"He is strikingly handsome," observed Christian.

"So all the ladies tell me; and as Sydney is good-looking, rich, and the owner of a decent property with a good house belonging to it, he is considered a desirable *parti* by the match-making mothers ten miles round. For example, my mother is devoted to him."

"And he is with you a great deal?"

"Oh yes; when Sydney is at home we see him most days; he and Heather were old playfellows;" but Carus said no more, and Christian forbore to question him. But her suspicions were aroused; and very soon after she joined the drawing-room circle, she was convinced from the young man's manner that he was certainly in love with Heather. His eyes followed her every movement, and if she spoke to any one else, he would pause in what he was saying to listen to her. But Christian was doubtful how far Heather was aware of his devotion. Her manner was as simple and unconscious as ever, and she seemed to take a delight in teasing Sydney and contradicting him. Once or twice she saw Mrs. Linacre look at her reprovingly, and then Heather coloured and became silent.

"It looks as though she could hardly do better," thought Christian, "he is very nice, and just the right age for her. Perhaps a year or two older would have been better; but what a pair they would make. Sweet thing, I hope he will be good to her."

Christian was on the couch beside her mother-in-law, Mrs. Linacre, who had been somewhat resentful of her son's monopoly of her guest; had at first been rather dignified, but Christian, who was now more at her ease, soon propitiated her with her praises of everything she had seen. "But I like the Bowling Green best," she said. "I thought at once of John Evelyn, and Milton, and Pope, and Goldsmith—all those old writers, and beaux, and wits; for, as I told your son, I am sure they walked in just such a green alley, with all sorts of beasts and birds clipped out of the box-hedge, and staring down upon them."

"I suppose Carus told you it is called 'The Lovers' Walk,'" returned Mrs. Linacre, as she put down her knitting. "In the summer we often have tea there. There is a little fireplace behind the summer-house where we boil our kettle, and we keep our tea-things there; it is too far from the house for the servants to bring them, besides, Heather loves playing at picnics."

"I never knew what gave it its name," observed Sydney in a low voice to Heather as he took his cup to be replenished at the tea-table; but Heather answered in her ordinary tone—

"Oh, it is rather a stupid sad story! Some young lady—but she was not a Linacre; what was her name, Aunt Janet?" interrupting herself.

"Ephra Fergusson. Old Roger Fergusson, her grandfather, built the Stone House and laid out the Bowling Green."

"Oh yes, I remember now! But I hate the story; do tell them about it yourself, Auntie dear." Heather spoke in a pretty childish way.

"Well, it is not a particularly cheerful story," returned Mrs. Linacre. "Ephra was an orphan cousin, who lived with the Fergussons, and unhappily both the sons loved her. She was very beautiful, but very excitable; what we should call a nervous young person in these days. Well, it never could be found out until too late which of these brothers she loved best, but she certainly encouraged both. But if the story is true, she was afraid of Roger, the elder brother, because he was so masterful and exacting. She used to walk in the Bowling Green every evening with one or other. But one night there was a quarrel between the brothers; cruel words as well as blows were exchanged between them; and Giles, the younger one, in his wrathful despair, shook off the dust of his father's house, and went out into the world. But before he went he met Ephra secretly in the Bowling Green. 'Do not marry Roger, sweetheart,' were his last words to her. 'Wait faithfully for me, for I know you love me and fear him, and my thoughts have never wronged you, Ephra. If I live I will come back to claim my bride.'"

"You can guess the rest," continued Mrs. Linacre; "all these stories are so much alike. Of course, Roger told her that Giles was dead; he had trumped up a fine garbled story, and before three years were out he had so dominated and coerced her that she had consented to marry him. But she never loved him—never. A few months after their marriage she was walking alone in the Bowling Green, when Giles suddenly confronted her. He had been to the wars, and one sleeve was pinned to his coat, and he had a fine medal hanging on his breast, and his handsome face was bronzed and pale. 'I have come for my wife Ephra,' but as he stretched out his one arm she fell at his feet like a dead thing."

"I told you it was a hateful old story," pouted Heather; "all the worse that people say it is true."

"And was she dead really?" asked Sydney blandly.

"No, she lived until she was quite an old woman," returned Mrs. Linacre; "but she was never the same after that, and she and Roger lived very unhappily together. Both the brothers died in their early prime, but Ephra lived a long solitary life. She was much respected by her neighbours, but as she grew older she became more eccentric. Whatever the weather might be—hail. snow, or frost—she would pace up and down the Bowling Green at a certain hour. An old servant would wait for her at a side door, for at times she would come in drenched, and her gray hair wet under her hood; and her servant would take her in, and dry and comfort her as though she were a child. But only once, on her deathbed, did she speak of her lifelong trouble; but just before the last, the same old servant heard her say, 'I have not been faithful, but I have sorrowed much, and I know Giles has forgiven me;" and with those words on her lips she turned over on her side and died."

"Bell Heather, why are your cheeks so hot?" and Carus came behind the girl, and put his hands on her shoulders.

Then Heather turned her glowing face to him.

"Aunt Janet is telling them about The Lovers' Walk," she whispered in his ear, for he had absented himself from the circle to read a letter that had been brought him. "I do hate that story, Carus;" and then he smiled at her, and Heather knew he hated it too.

XX

A Tangle of Threads

As the corn ripens it bends.—Anon.

Nothing is given so profusely as advice.—La Rochefoucauld.

When you are sure of the path you may quicken your pace.—Anon.

It was a lovely May evening, and Christian and Pen had arranged to walk back to Braybrooke, and as soon as tea was over they rose to take leave. To their surprise, they found themselves attended by quite a large escort—Carus, Heather, and Sydney Masters, and every dog belonging to the establishment, were all waiting in the stone porch.

"You will come again very soon, will you not, my dear?" asked Mrs. Linacre in rather a wistful tone. "Carus has monopolised you most of the afternoon, but I want to see more of you;" and Christian, who was a little touched by this, responded very amiably.

"Well, have you had a happy day, Christian?" asked Carus, as they walked down the avenue. The others were in front, but now and then Heather glanced round at them as though she longed to join them. Over their heads the rooks were circling and cawing about their nests; all round them lay the green fields, the evening shadows resting lightly on the long glades and bushy dells. The air was fragrant with woodland odours, the dogs raced each other between the trees, and Heather would willingly have joined them.

"It has been very pleasant," returned Christian, "but I think I enjoyed the afternoon best;" but Carus shook his head at this little compliment.

"I hope you got on well with my mother," he returned rather seriously. "I have set my heart on that—I want to feel that she has two daughters now."

168

"You must not be, in too great a hurry," replied Christian; "you know I have never had a mother-in-law before, and the novelty is rather embarrassing. When I was shut up in that dressing-room—'the Jack Linacre Gallery' I should call it,"—here Carus smiled,—"I felt rather like an oyster who was not in a sociable mood and wanted to close his shell."

"I know exactly what you mean, Christian." Carus was not at all shocked at this flippant answer to a serious question. Already he was beginning to understand the girl and to feel a brotherly fondness for her. If only his mother had a sense of humour, he said to himself. But what would she have thought of such a speech? It was not well always to interpret Christian's odd remarks quite literally. Jack had soon found this out.

"You see, when I have once got used to the idea that I am really and truly married," went on Christian, speaking as loudly and emphatically as she could to the edification of an aged rook, who kept his eye on her from the branch of an elm, " I shall soon play my part better. But when one's husband seems to have learnt the vanishing trick, and to go off in a blue smoke into space, it is a little difficult to realise matters and adjust one's behaviour to the circumstances." And again Carus understood the little he could catch, all the more that he was so sorry for her and Jack.

"It will all come right," he said kindly; and then he told her that he should come over to Many Bushes in a day or two for a quiet business talk with her.

"Uncle Jasper has asked me to call upon him to-morrow afternoon," he went on, "and as I have two or three engagements, I shall probably remain two nights in town. There is always a bed for me in Beauchamp Gardens. When I return I shall be able to go properly into your affairs. I suppose I shall find you in about luncheon time."

"Oh yes," replied Christian. "I have few engagements as yet, though people are beginning to call upon us. Please give my kind love to Uncle Jasper, and tell him that I do not forget him;" and Carus willingly consented to take this message. And soon after this they arrived at a rustic little corner, known as Pratt's Green, and here Heather decided that they must go back.

" Well, have you enjoyed yourself, Pen?" asked Christian, as they walked on together; and Pen's answer was enthusiastic enough.   To her the day had been simply delightful; she only hoped that she would not weary Walter with her long descriptions of the place and the people.

" They were all so kind to me for your sake, Chrissy dear," she continued.   " When you went off so long with Mr. Linacre, I had quite a nice talk with his mother; she was so full of interest, and asked me so many questions about you, that I told her all I could."

" Tell me all you said, Pen."   Christian's tone was a little sharp, but Penelope, who was full of her subject, did not seem to notice it.

" Oh, I told her all I could remember of your old life! And how happy you were with your mother, although you were poor, and she was an invalid, and how you grieved when she died."

" She would understand all that without being told, Pen," a little severely; " most girls are sorry when their mothers die."   But Pen refused to be rebuked.

" All girls do not love their mothers as you did, Chriss; and I am glad I told Mrs. Linacre what a good daughter you were, and how bright and unselfish, for she looked so pleased.   ' Good daughters make good wives,' was her answer.   ' Thank you for telling me this, Miss Mervyn.' "

." But it was no business of her's, Pen, how I treated my mother," returned Christian perversely.

" Oh yes, my dear Chriss!   She has surely a right to be interested in her own daughter-in-law.   Well, I told her how your aunt, Mrs. Fordham, adopted you, and how uncongenial the life in Mandeville Street was to you, and that seemed to surprise her, for she knew all about the Fordhams from Lady Armitage."

" All the same, I do not see why Mrs. Linacre should be surprised; I wish you would tell me exactly what she said."   But Pen, who knew her friend, was a little reluctant to do this, for Mrs. Linacre's manner had been rather judicial.

"It is a pity when young people are not content with their environments," she had remarked; "it was extremely kind of Mrs. Fordham to provide for her niece so generously. Lady Armitage assured me that her aunt treated Christian quite like a daughter. I think she ought to have accommodated herself to her situation—I do indeed, Miss Mervyn; she might have had to work for her maintenance like many other penniless girls;" but Pen judiciously watered this down, though Christian gathered that Mrs. Linacre considered her somewhat ungrateful to her relations.

"She did not ask questions about Jack and me then?" Christian put the inquiry in rather a hesitating manner.

"Oh dear, yes!" returned Pen without hesitation; "but I told her that I knew so little myself that I could not answer them. 'Christian is not the sort of girl to talk about these things'—those were my very words; 'and I was so busy, and there was such a whirl and bustle in Mandeville Street on account of the wedding party, that Christian and I hardly ever met;' and when I said this she seemed satisfied;" but Christian was not appeased.

"You seem to have had quite an exhaustive conversation?" she replied coldly. "I wonder my ears did not burn as we walked in the Bowling Green."

"Mrs. Linacre was very kind," returned Pen earnestly. "I quite liked her when she talked in a nice, motherly fashion about her son, and how she meant to be fond of his wife. I hope in time you will grow to love her, for Captain Linacre's sake; she must be nice, Chrissy dear, or Heather would not be so fond of her—the child seems as happy as possible. Oh, by the bye, do you think that delightful Mr. Masters really cares for her—I am nearly sure he does?" And this interesting topic lasted until they reached home, where Smudge gave them a rapturous and vociferous welcome.

The following afternoon, as the girls were reading on their favourite seat in the garden, Heather again surprised them. She wore the self-same pink frock, and came running down the grassy bank, with Cheri and Jack behind her. "I have come for a whole hour," she said

quite breathlessly; "Aunt Janet is at the Vicarage **and**
will call for me presently, so we can have a nice long talk.
Do you always sit here of an afternoon?" and then
Heather peeped into their books and made friends with
Smudge, and put Cheri through her tricks, and they were
all as merry as possible; and if Heather had known them
for years instead of hours, she could not have been more
friendly and unrestrained.

Presently Christian mentioned Sydney Masters' name
casually in alluding to their evening stroll, but she was
a little taken aback when Heather asked, in quite a matter-of-fact tone, what they had both thought of him.
"For though I have not known you long, I already think
a good deal of my new sister's opinion," she added affectionately.

"Oh, we both liked him so much!" replied Christian;
and Heather looked excessively pleased.

"I am so glad," she returned in the most natural way;
"he is such a dear boy, and we have always been such
friends."

"Boy! Heather!" in a tone of remonstrance. "Why,
Mr. Masters must be four or five years older than you.
Surely you ought to speak of him more respectfully!"
Then Heather blushed a little.

"Well, you see," defending herself, "we were playfellows in the old days, and I am so used to Sydney. It
was he who taught me to climb trees and do all sorts of
naughty things. Do you know, Christian, I used to cry
when he went back to school or college, because I missed
him so. It is rather nice to have a friend like that," she
continued softly, "and Sydney has always been so kind
to me."

"We thought so from his manner;" it was Pen who
spoke.

"Yes; and he seems to think so much of my opinion,"
continued Heather artlessly; "even before I was grown
up, and when I was in short frocks, he would tell me his
troubles and ask my advice; and he likes things that I
like, so of course we get on splendidly together, though
I do tease him sometimes."

"I don't think a moderate degree of teasing hurts **any**

young man," observed Christian; "I daresay Mr. Masters takes it in excellent part." But Heather looked slightly dubious at this.

"I am not quite sure—Sydney is very good-natured and patient; but Aunt Janet thinks sometimes that I try him a little. Of course, I would not hurt him for the world; but you know how it is, Christian,—one cannot always be good and well-behaved."

"No, indeed," sighed Christian, but she exchanged a meaning look with Pen. It was quite plain to them both that Heather was unconscious of Sydney Masters' devotion. Her playmate was dear to her from old associations and similarity of tastes, but the man had not yet discovered the right key to her heart—Undine had not found her soul.

While the three girls talked gaily in the sunshine, a very different conversation was being carried on in the Vicarage drawing-room. "I am so sorry Christian disappointed you," Mrs. Disney was saying; she had put down her work to listen to Mrs. Linacre's confidences.

"I would not go as far as that, Charlotte," corrected her friend; "Christian was really very nice and agreeable, and she behaved very properly; but as we sat together—shut in by our two selves—I felt as though I were entertaining a strange young lady, who was paying me a formal call. She was really very amiable and pleasant, but not at all disposed to be communicative or to meet me half-way; and when I talked to her about Jack, or asked her questions, she looked at me so oddly through her pince-nez, as though I had no right to be interested in my dear boy."

"I daresay she was merely shy," returned Mrs. Disney; "you must not forget, dear friend, that Christian's position is a little difficult; she has to make the acquaintance of her new relatives alone; it must be very trying for any girl."

"Do you think I do not understand that, Charlotte?" replied Mrs. Linacre. "I felt for her so much that I would have done anything to make her more at her ease; but how could I open my heart to her when her manner kept me at a distance?"

" Will you forgive me if I say something? Do you not
think that Christian's refusal to live at the Stone House
a little prejudiced you before you saw her?" As Mrs.
Disney said this, a slight flush suffused Mrs. Linacre's
face.

" I do not see that you have any cause to think that,
Charlotte," she replied rather stiffly. " I only recognised
that Jack's wife had a will and opinion of her own,
though I allow that her decision disappointed me; but I
am accustomed to disappointments. No, I will not own
that I was prejudiced, though I do think that my daughter-in-law is a very decided young woman."

" I think we ought to be glad of that, for Captain Linacre's sake."

" I am not sure that I agree with you, Charlotte; Jack
is undemonstrative, like me, but he is very affectionate,
and I almost think a softer and more clinging nature
would have suited him better—some one more like that
gentle little creature, Miss Mervyn." But Mrs. Disney
demurred to this.

" Christian is affectionate too, when you know her
thoroughly; she has plenty of character, and her nature
is peculiarly frank and sincere; she would never pretend
to like any one. So many people say more than they mean
just to make themselves pleasant, or because they feel
affectionate at the moment. Affection in fits and starts
is quite obnoxious to me as the ' blow hot and blow cold'
of the Traveller was to the Satyr."

" You speak warmly, dear;" and Mrs. Linacre seemed
impressed. She had a very high opinion of her friend's
good sense.

" Not more warmly than I feel," returned Mrs. Disney.
" Graham and I are very much interested in Mrs. Jack;
indeed, I may say I am very fond of her; take my word
for it, dear Mrs. Linacre, you will find that Christian
improves on acquaintance; give her plenty of scope—
she needs it—and you will soon find her a delightful companion. Now tell me about the little one? I hear Sydney
Masters is home again."

" Yes, and as much in love as ever, his mother tells
me; but I am not quite satisfied about Heather; they

only met yesterday after an absence of two months, and she was teasing him in her old way; I had to put a stop to it at last."

"Do you think that was wise? In my opinion, it would be better to let them fight it out. Heather is only playful because she is young; she will lose her kittenish ways presently."

"I was married at nineteen," returned Mrs. Linacre gravely; "and Heather was eighteen three months ago. Mrs. Masters told me yesterday that Sydney was wild to begin his courting, and that he intends to speak to Carus."

"There is no harm in that," observed Mrs. Disney; "but in my opinion it would be better to wait another six months or so before he makes his meaning plain to Heather,—you know I told you this before,—and that Sydney would do wisely if he went abroad for a time. Let the child miss him; they have been too much together, and she has no idea how necessary he is to her." But Mrs. Linacre, with her usual denseness, could not be brought to see this.

"Sydney has been away, and it has made no difference," she returned. "Heather will act childishly until her eyes are opened. You know, Charlotte, that both Mrs. Masters and I have set our hearts on this; think what it would be to me to have my dear child settled so close to me, and in such a lovely home."

"Of course I know all the advantages," returned Mrs. Disney; "and Sydney has my good wishes for his success. Now, about this invitation, Mrs. Linacre, that has reached us this morning; a dinner-party a fortnight hence seems a very big affair to my rustic mind."

"It is a big affair," was the reply. "I am asking all the best people, that Christian may make her *début* as a bride properly; I shall send the carriage for her, and then it shall call for you and the Vicar; it will be far pleasanter for Christian to come under your wing, for, of course, I have not asked Miss Mervyn."

"I suppose we shall have to go on account of Mrs. Jack," Charlotte had said that morning to her husband; but though he acquiesced in this, they both agreed that such a smart affair was in rather questionable taste. "Under the circumstances, and it is poor Mr. Linacre's birthday too," observed Mrs. Disney; "think of his mother treating him to such a martyrdom on that day." And the Vicar shook his head; in some matters Mrs. Linacre was hopeless!

XXI

Mrs. John Linacre's Début

There is a sort of instinct, a kind of freemasonry understanding with certain of our fellow-creatures that touches the mainspring of our hearts and opens it out to their confidence.—Currer Bell.

You will gain infinitely by sacrificing your own little tastes.—Lord Chesterfield.

THE return of the Linacre family to Silverton made a great change in Christian's daily life; and as weeks, and even months, passed by smoothly and happily, she felt herself drawn more irresistibly into the home circle at the Stone House. "I am no longer an outsider; I am one of ourselves," as she wrote playfully to Jack. "Poor little Pen is just a nobody who enacts the part of somebody's lady-in-waiting; even Madam, your illustrious mother, who is certainly an autocrat in her way, condescends to listen to my opinion? Think of that, my dear Jack!"

The dinner-party at the Stone House had been a complete success; and Christian had made her *début* as a bride so well and gracefully that even Mrs. Linacre's critical taste had no fault to find with her; and she had owned afterwards to Mrs. Disney, that when Christian entered the room where the guests were already assembled, that she had felt proud of her daughter-in-law.

Lady Armitage, who had come to spend a few days with her old friend, was present at the dinner, and on her return to town she called at 25 Mandeville Street and gave Mrs. Fordham and Adelaide a full description of the function, much to the secret envy and chagrin of the latter.

"You know, my dear Caroline," she observed, "that neither you nor I ever considered Christian pretty; in fact, in my opinion, she was only just passable-looking;" a murmur of assent from Adelaide endorsed this remark.

"I know many people thought she had a taking manner," she went on, warming to her theme, "and she certainly has a good carriage, though a little too self-assured
for a girl in her dependent position,"—another hum of
approval from Adelaide,—"but when she came in with
Carus—he had gone out to meet her, I believe—I was
quite taken by surprise—she looked so handsome and distinguished."

"Fine feathers make fine birds, my dear Lady Armitage," observed Adelaide with an acidulated smile.

"Well, certainly her dress was perfect," replied Lady
Armitage, "thanks to your generosity, dear Caroline;
and she wore the superb diamond necklace that Mr. Vigne
had given her. The diamond star in her hair, she told
me afterwards, had been a present from Carus; he is
very fond of his sister-in-law, and shows her a great deal
of consideration and attention."

"Dear me, what a fortunate girl Christian is!" observed Mrs. Fordham delightedly; "to think of her
making such a good match when she had not a penny of
her own—if she had only got her husband with her; but
it must have been trying for her, poor dear, to run the
gauntlet of all those eyes."

"She seemed perfectly at her ease," returned Lady
Armitage; "perhaps she was a trifle paler than usual,
but I could not have wished a daughter of my own to
carry herself better than Christian did that evening; Mrs.
Linacre introduced her to everybody, and after dinner
she had quite a little court round her. I was talking
to that deaf old Admiral Carrington, so I could not hear
what was said, but I think Christian must have been
saying amusing things, there was so much merriment;
she has a very pretty way of turning her head, and I
never noticed before that charming dimple when she
smiles; several of the Silverton ladies told Mrs. Linacre
that they admired Mrs. John excessively."

And so Christian reaped golden opinions from her
neighbours, and in so doing increased in favour with her
mother-in-law; to Pen who was sitting up for her she
gave a glowing account of the evening. "I will own to
you, my dear Pen, that I was horribly afraid when that

drawing-room door opened; but Carus, dear fellow, who knew I was nervous, whispered to me: 'You need not be alarmed, they won't bite;' and that made me smile, and the next moment I was all right, and just walked over the course as easily as possible."

"Oh, I am so glad! And you looked quite lovely, dear."

"None of your blarney, young woman;" but Christian glanced at her own reflection in the glass with some degree of satisfaction. "By the bye, Pen, mother-in-law was pleased—I could see that; she says I must have a panel photograph taken of myself in this dress, and that she will send it to Jack; it was rather decent of her, I thought."

"I suppose Sydney Masters was there?"

"Yes; and he introduced me to his mother; she is a handsome woman, but her features are heavy, and she has an indolent and self-indulgent expression. I don't think we shall take to her much: she seems to have only one idea, and that is Sydney. 'My boy Syd,' as she calls him. That dear child, Heather, ought to have a much nicer mother-in-law; she really looked almost too sweet to-night; and Sydney followed her about as though he were her shadow."

"Oh, I hope she was nice to him!"

"Oh yes, I think so! but she was not near him during dinner: and it seemed to me that she did not look quite happy. I am sure she was troubling about Carus: it was so sad to see him sitting there, looking so tired and patient, and trying to smile when any one met his eyes, and not able to hear a word of the conversation."

"But he could talk to his next-door neighbour, Chriss?"

"No, for I tried myself: I was in the place of honour, you know; but he shook his head so sadly and made me a sign to stop: and then Lady Armitage, who was on his other side, spoke to him rather loudly, but it was no use. He told me afterwards that it was impossible for him to hear anything on these occasions, as the babel of voices confused and seemed to jar on him: and that the discord and unintelligibility of the sounds at times caused him actual suffering. 'It affects the nerves in some way,' he said quite simply; 'but Heather is the only person who seems to understand.' 'But Heather will not be the only person now, Carus,' was my reply to this; and then he looked at me so kindly."

"Poor Mr. Linacre! it does seem so hard," returned Pen; "one would have thought his mother would have understood;" but Christian merely shrugged her shoulders. She too marvelled secretly at her mother-in-law's density of perception; in her opinion there was something singularly perverse in Mrs. Linacre's behaviour to her son; with all her devotion, she was both selfish and exacting, and she seemed so unconscious of this.

Christian was on her good behaviour whenever she went to the Stone House, and to all outward seeming she and Mrs. Linacre were on the best of terms; on most occasions she showed herself ready to defer to her mother-in-law's opinion, and to be willing to be guided by her on questions of social etiquette; but in other matters she was still as independent as ever, and it may be doubted whether there was any great sympathy between them.

Now and then Mrs. Linacre would drop a word to Mrs. Disney that showed that she still resented Christian's reserve, or she would complain of her want of affection. "She has a cold nature, Charlotte," she said one day; "I am convinced of it in spite of her pleasant manners. Oh yes! I know," as Mrs. Disney demurred to this, "she can be nice enough when she chooses, and with Carus and Heather she is quite charming; but there has been something in her manner to me from the very first that I might almost call aggressive."

"Oh no, dear Mrs. Linacre; you are a little hard on Christian."

"Well, not aggressive exactly—I was wrong to use that word; but, somehow, when I am talking to her seriously she seems on the defensive, as though she is afraid that I should claim more than my rights. Now she was not at all pleased when I suggested yesterday that she should invite her aunt and cousin to spend a few days at Many Bushes; she flushed up and said a little impatiently: 'That with all this gaiety going on, she was getting tired to death, and had no time to entertain visitors.' She really spoke most ungraciously."

"There has been a great deal going on," returned her friend soothingly,—" garden parties and tennis tournaments, not to mention dinner-parties and the Chesterton ball; one can hardly wonder if Christian is tired. Penelope was complaining this morning that she herself was quite fagged with pleasure."

"Oh, Miss Mervyn, I daresay!" rather contemptuously; "she has led such a different life. But I heard Christian tell Heather only the other day that she felt as fresh as possible after dancing until three in the morning at Chesterton, and she wished she could go to a ball every week; she was no more tired than you are, Charlotte; it was only just her perversity."

Mrs. Disney was silent; she thought Mrs. Linacre had some show of reason on her side; certainly Christian owed some duty and consideration to her aunt.

She tried to point this out gently when Christian next came to the Vicarage; but it was evident that Mrs. Jack was on her dignity.

"So mother-in-law has told you——" she began; but Charlotte held up her finger.

"Now, Christian, ' if you can't be good, be as good as you can,'" transposing a rude saying for her benefit; "and tell me truly if you do not think Mrs. Linacre was right in what she said."

·Now if Christian was perverse, she was also honest; and she knew that her conscience had more than once upbraided her with neglecting a duty that was uncongenial to her, so she evaded the difficulty by finding fault with her mother-in-law.

"It was not Mrs. Linacre's business to interfere between me and Aunt Caroline."

"I would not take it in that way," was Mrs. Disney's quiet answer; "so much depends on how we look at a thing. What you consider interference may be only a motherly suggestion on Mrs. Linacre's part; you may depend upon it that her intention was most kind."

"Of course you take her part," returned Christian, who was disposed to be argumentative. Then her conscience pricked her again, for she knew well that they were both right, so she heaved a rebellious sigh and yielded the point.

"Well, I suppose I shall have to do it. I have been meaning to ask them for weeks, but I have been in such a whirl; and actually, Adelaide wrote yesterday, and proposed they should come down for the day, just to see my home." Christian certainly had the grace to look rather ashamed of herself when she said this.

"Well, better late than never!" returned Mrs. Disney cheerfully.

"I will write by this evening's post," continued Christian, feeling it would be safer to strike while the iron was hot—for good resolutions soon cool—"and ask them to come to me next week. I daresay Mrs. Venables will allow me to take them to her garden-party; and as I am quite sure that Mrs. Linacre will invite them to dinner, I think we can make a few days endurable to them."

"My dear, I am quite sure that we shall do our very best to entertain your friends;" and so it was settled amicably—and Christian went off to write her letter; and the next day, when Charlotte had luncheon at the Stone House, she carried the good news with her.

"You see Christian has taken your advice after all," she said; and Mrs. Linacre seemed much relieved.

"I am very glad," she observed in her slow, serious way, for Janet Linacre was a trifle ponderous at times,— "a bit heavy on hand," as Jack used to say. "I was rather afraid, from Christian's manner, that she thought me interfering; but nothing was further from my mind. I have a fellow feeling with Mrs. Fordham; she has been so extremely good to Christian, and I was anxious that she should not be hurt; it is nearly the end of July— three months—and Christian has never even seen her aunt;" and having thus eased her mind, Mrs. Linacre benevolently turned her attention to various projects for the amusement of her daughter-in-law's guests, checking off each item gravely on her fingers.

On the appointed day the Fordhams arrived, and Christian, who was really fond of her good-natured aunt, was unfeignedly pleased to see her. Adelaide, indeed, was

less welcome, but she contrived to hide this feeling more or less successfully during the week, though it rather riled her to see that Mrs. Linacre had taken a fancy to her.

"Miss Fordham is very graceful and distinguished-looking, and I admire her extremely," she said to Christian when the visit was over; "her manners are most pleasing. She was so nice to Carus too, and seemed to enjoy his society." Here Christian bit her lip to prevent smiling; she was not the only person who had noticed that week that Adelaide showed a decided preference for Mr. Linacre's society; the only one who seemed unconscious was Carus himself. He merely tabulated her in his own mind as a pleasant, intelligent woman who had plenty of common sense, and thought that Christian hardly did justice to her cousin.

Mrs. Fordham was tearfully affectionate when she arrived, and could not make enough of her niece, and in Adelaide's frequent absences—for Pen stuck to her like a leech, and was always inveigling her into walks with herself and Heather—Christian had many nice little chats with Aunt Caroline.

In the afternoons there was generally something pleasant arranged. Mrs. Linacre would send Heather and the carriage to take them for a drive, or she would invite them to luncheon, and afterwards they would have tennis and tea in the Bowling Green. There was also Mrs. Venable's garden-party—rather a grand affair—and the small dinner-party that Mrs. Linacre had arranged was also fully enjoyed. The week had lengthened into ten days before the Fordhams could tear themselves away, and Adelaide evidently spoke the truth with all sincerity when she assured her cousin that they had enjoyed their visit extremely.

"Mrs. Linacre has been most hospitable," she continued; "she is a delightful person, and I consider you extremely fortunate in your husband's relatives."

"Dear Christian," murmured Aunt Caroline fondly as the train moved, and Christian and Heather waved to them from the platform; "I never saw her look so well—and she is wonderfully improved in appearance. Don't you think so, Adelaide?"

"Yes, she is improved," Adelaide could allow this; "and one certainly sees her to advantage in her own home; but it struck me once or twice, mother, that she and Mrs. Linacre do not quite hit it off. I thought Christian might have been a little less cool in manner."

"Dear, dear! I am sorry to hear you say that, Addie."

"Well, it was only my impression, and I may be wrong, but it does seem to me rather odd that Christian speaks so seldom about Captain Linacre. Mother,"—changing the subject rather abruptly,—" I hope you asked Mr. Linacre to call on us when he next comes to town. I hear that he often spends a night or so at Beauchamp Gardens." But Mrs. Fordham quickly satisfied her on this point. She had asked him, and indeed pressed him, to come, and he had responded very civilly he would certainly do himself the pleasure of calling when he was in the neighbourhood.

"He is very nice, but it tires me dreadfully to talk to him," she concluded; "that little tube always makes me so nervous that I never know what to say next. I am sure I do not know how you could carry on those long conversations, Adelaide; and you had to sit quite close to him, I could see that."

"Of course I had to make him hear; but we soon got on very well." Adelaide spoke complacently. Poor woman, she was not young, and the years were slipping away. Life had not brought her all she wished, and everywhere fresh young faces seemed to be—were telling her, that she would soon be old and faded. Carus Linacre was a rich man. He would be master of the Stone House when his mother died—he was virtually master now. What did deafness matter?—he was nice, a gentleman, and their ages were suitable. The elder brother's wife would take precedence under those circumstances. Mrs. John Linacre would not be quite such an important personage—but then there was the diamond necklace. Adelaide's lips were a little thin and compressed as she remembered Mr. Vigne's injudicious generosity.

"There, it is over, and now I am free!" and Christian extended her arms as if they ached from carrying too heavy a burden. "Heather, how shall we inaugurate my holiday? I want to do something—to have my fling —to work off my superabundant spirits!"

"Wait a moment and I will think," returned Heather seriously. "Oh dear! what a pity that Aunt Janet is out—but never mind, you and Penny-wise"—a sobriquet she had invented for Pen—"must bicycle over to the Stone House after luncheon, and we will have tea in the Bowling Green."

"But you won't ask any one but Carus to join us, Heather?"

"Oh dear, no! Sydney is sure to turn up whether I invite him or not. Come at four, Christian, and we will have such fun." And Christian readily promised for Pen and herself.

XXII

A Speck on the Horizon

To be loved in any fashion is to incur a great responsibility.—
ANON.

THE picnic tea in the Bowling Green was a great success, and Heather played her part of hostess very charm-
ingly. As she had predicted, Sydney Masters had made
his appearance quite early in the afternoon, and was a
very welcome addition to the little party. He helped
Heather to light her fire and boil her kettle; and as the
table was already laid and prettily set out with fruit and
flowers, Christian and Pen amused themselves by a game
of bowls with Carus, until Heather, looking as rosy and
blooming as Hebe, summoned them to the simple feast.

Never had Heather looked more radiantly happy than
she did that afternoon. Her fair young face was as un-
clouded and free from care as any child's could be, and
her mirthful laugh brought the smile continually to
Carus's lips.

There were a great many plans to discuss that afternoon. The following week Mrs. Linacre and Heather
were going to stay with some friends near Cromer for a
fortnight or three weeks, and, to Christian's delight,
Carus had announced his intention of spending the weeks
of their absence at Many Bushes. "Do you think you
could put up with me all that time, Christian?" he said
half jestingly; but her answer must have satisfied him—
her eyes had quite sparkled with pleasure as she assured
him how welcome he would be. But there was another
little scheme that Carus's benevolence had concocted with
the Vicar. The junior curate of St. Cuthbert's would
have his three weeks' holiday at the beginning of September, and, to Pen's secret rapture, these two kind
friends had arranged that it should be spent at Braybrooke and Silverton. As Carus seemed reluctant to

curtail his stay at Many Bushes, Mr. Disney had suggested that Mr. Hamill should spend the first week at the Vicarage, and that when the ladies returned to the Stone House he should go back with Carus and spend the remainder of his time at Silverton.

Nothing could have been better arranged. Silverton was only two miles from Braybrooke, and Mr. Hamill was an enthusiastic cyclist. He and Pen would be together every day. Never had the prospect of such a holiday been offered to the hard-working curate. Pen tried to express her gratitude shyly as they sat that evening in the Bowling Green, but Carus assured her that the pleasure would be on their side.

"We all like Mr. Hamill," he said in his kind way, "though we have seen very little of him." Pen had taken him to the Stone House one Monday, and he had been received very cordially by Mrs. Linacre and her son. "The Vicar tells me that he will be glad to see more of him, and that he has taken quite a fancy to him;" then Pen's face fairly glowed with happiness.

"I can hardly believe it, Chriss!" she exclaimed, as they walked home in the cool of the evening. "Never since Walter and I have been engaged have we ever been together during his holiday. He generally has a little cycling tour, and spends a few days with an old college friend in Norfolk; he has so little to spend on his own pleasures, you see; but his one idea is to get into the country and see green fields and hedge-rows."

"I can understand that after Battersea," observed Christian.

"Oh yes, and after all those terrible streets and courts. Walter always goes miles and miles the first day, and never rests until he finds some rustic little inn that looks clean and cosy, and then he spends the night there; but it is rather lonely for him, and he generally knocks himself up before he gets to Grayling, where his friend lives. But now they will make him so comfortable at the Vicarage and the Stone House, and it will be such a real rest; and for three whole weeks we shall be together," and Pen clasped her hands in silent ecstasy as though the prospect of such bliss almost overwhelmed her.

Christian fully entered into her friend's pleasure. " It
was a very kind thought on Carus's part," she said, " and
equally so on the Vicar's;" and as they had many friends
and relations of their own, she considered it was extremely good of them to give up their spare room to a
stranger. " I would have had Mr. Hamill here," she
continued, " but Mrs. Linacre thought it would not do,
and Mrs. Disney agreed with her; she said Aunt Caroline would have been shocked."

" Oh, I never thought of such a thing, Chriss!" and
Pen spoke in quite a distressed voice; " and you are so
good to Walter and make him so welcome whenever he
comes."

" Well, of course, I had to give in to the wise women
of Braybrooke and Silverton; but I half thought of
writing to Jack and asking his opinion, only the summer
would be over before I got his answer," and here Christian sighed, for she was not quite easy in her mind about
Jack. Carus had lately shown her a letter he had received
from him, and a passage in it had made her anxious.

" In my opinion," wrote Jack, " we are in for a big
job, the Boers mean mischief, and though we know
nothing definitely, for they are keeping things pretty
quiet here, a few facts leak out now and then. One
of our fellows, who has just come from Cape Town, told
me at mess the other day that cases of rifles and boxes
of cartridges in huge packing-cases, marked ' Agricul-
tural Instruments' and ' Mining Machinery,' are on their
way to Pretoria or Johannesburg. That looks uncom-
monly fishy, old fellow. It is about time the authorities
at home hurry up."

Christian turned these sentences over in her mind until
she became quite uneasy; and the next day, when she
was at the Vicarage, she repeated Jack's remarks to Mr.
Disney. She was sorry to see that he took them seriously.

" I think he is right, and that things look somewhat
menacing," he returned thoughtfully. " They have just
sent out three companies of Royal Engineers, you know.
Colonel Bramley and I were only talking over the matter
before luncheon. He has been in South Africa and
knows Natal well; he told me that in his opinion our

forces over there are absurdly inadequate for the defence of such a huge frontier, and that it was time that our eyes were opened to this fact. He declares that while all these negotiations are going on, they are playing a secret game at Pretoria, and all the time they are making their preparations for war." And that morning Christian derived little comfort, for the old Colonel was considered a great authority in Braybrooke.

This was the one speck on Christian's clear horizon, but neither she nor her friends guessed how soon the storm was to burst, and be followed by dark days of humiliation and shame, that was to overwhelm England. For it was still July and the note of alarm had not been sounded. Christian wrote long amusing letters by every mail, and Jack sent curt cheery answers. He had little to narrate, for his military duties kept him busy. He told her once " that the veldt had been burnt unusually early this year, so as to secure a good grass crop after the first rains, and that the sheep and cattle had been driven off." But he did not explain that this had been considered somewhat ominous by the authorities, neither did he mention that food and warlike stores had been accumulated by the Boers. On the contrary, he wrote more about Silverton news, and sent messages to his mother, and he took a great deal of interest in what Christian told him about Sydney Masters. " I always thought that match was to come off sooner or later," he wrote. " Well, Sydney is the right sort of chap for Heather; she is a nice little girl, and pretty as well as good; and I hope I shall be back for the wedding;" and then with an affectionate word or two he concluded his letter. Christian would sit sometimes for minutes together with her eyes fixed on the signature, " your loving husband, Jack Linacre." " I suppose it is true," she would say to herself as she laid it aside. " I think, I really think, he is getting fond of me;" but never, even to herself, did she say, " I am getting fond of Jack."

It was the day after the picnic tea in the Bowling Green that Christian first noticed a faint shadow on Heather's face; her manner, too, was a little thoughtful and constrained. It struck Christian that she was not

quite in her usual spirits, and she fancied that Mrs.
Linacre noticed it; but as they were all going to a
garden-party at a little distance from Silverton, she had
no opportunity of speaking to Heather.

Christian was to drive with Mrs. Linacre; but the
Masters' waggonette had fetched Heather, and by the
time the party from the Stone House had arrived,
Heather was already on the tennis lawn with Sydney
as her partner. Only once during the afternoon did
Christian cross her path. She had strolled down the
field with Carus to watch the archery competition, and
Heather, who had found a shady seat under an oak tree,
was looking on. Sydney and another young man, Charlie
Tressilian, the son of the house, were on either side of
her. To Christian's surprise she did not seem to be talking to either of them. Her eyes were fixed rather absently on the target, or following the flight of the arrow
somewhat listlessly. She looked tired, and the shadow
on her face was still there. She looked at them a little
wistfully, as they stood opposite to her; but the faint
smile that greeted Christian had a touch of sadness in it.
Heather drove home in the waggonette, and Christian
only saw her in the porch for a moment.

"You look tired, dear," she said as she bade the girl
good-night. "I hope you have enjoyed your afternoon."
But Heather hesitated a moment.

"I have enjoyed it pretty well," she returned in rather
a constrained manner, "and I am not at all tired, thank
you. It was rather nice watching the archery, and I had
such a shady seat."

"I thought you did not look particularly interested,
Heather; you seemed thinking of something else."

"Why, what nonsense, Christian;" but Heather coloured and looked confused. "I thought Edna May the
best competitor, though Miss Tressilian is very graceful.
Ah, there is Aunt Janet calling to me," and Heather ran
off without giving Christian time to say more.

It so happened that business and various engagements
took Christian nearly every day that week to the Stone
House, and though she seldom saw Heather alone, she
had plenty of opportunity for quiet observation; and she

was not long in making up her mind that something was troubling the girl. Her cheerfulness had lost its sweet spontaneity and seemed to Christian a little forced, and she was strangely absent at times. The evening before they left for Cromer, Christian was dining at the Stone House to meet some old friends of Mrs. Linacre's who were staying in the neighbourhood. Pen, who was not invited, was spending the evening at the Vicarage, and Christian had agreed to remain for the night. It was the first time she had slept at the Stone House, although she had more than once been pressed to do so. The carriage was to fetch her early in the afternoon; but, to her surprise, it was empty. Heather had not driven in as usual to keep her company, and somehow this omission of her usual attention troubled Christian. She was in the porch, however, to welcome her; but she made no sort of excuse for her absence. "We are having tea in Troy because it is so hot," she said, as she kissed Christian; for on sultry afternoons the great hall was the coolest place, with its open doors and wide staircase. Two or three low tables were set out, and it was very pleasant to sit on the cushioned bench and look down the green drive and the avenue, while Heather in her white frock flitted about, filling cups and handing the various dainties. Mrs. Masters was beside Mrs. Linacre, to Christian's secret disgust, for a more intimate knowledge of this lady had not softened her previous opinion. Mrs. Masters' nature was certainly self-indulgent, and she was extremely narrow-minded in her views, and at the same time decidedly opinionative. Her manner to Heather was at once caressing and monopolising; it seemed to Christian as though she had already taken possession of her, and regarded her as her son's *fiancée*. This was particularly noticeable on the present occasion, and her behaviour to the girl was so marked and pointedly affectionate that Christian thought that only an engagement between the young people could justify it. Was it possible that Sydney had spoken to Heather, and that she had accepted him?—and yet something in Heather's manner—a sort of shrinking timidity and uneasiness—made her doubt this.

When Mrs. Masters at last rose to take her leave, she drew the girl into her expansive embrace. " Good-bye until we meet at Cromer, darling," she said softly. " Of course, my tiresome Syd has given me no peace until I wrote for rooms, so I daresay you will see us by the week end if the hotel can take us in. It is dreadfully inconvenient," in a plaintive tone, " for I have had to cancel several engagements; and it is all your fault, you naughty little rosebud." But as she said this the flush on Heather was deeper than any rose-leaf.

" My fault, Mrs. Masters? It is not fair to say that. I told Sydney that he had far better stay at home," and Heather looked at once pained and injured. As she said this, perhaps Mrs. Masters felt that she had gone too far.

" Well, well," tapping the girl's cheek lightly, " I won't tease you, dear love. If Syd feels he cannot stay away, perhaps we should not be hard on him under the circumstances, and mothers have to give in." But Heather would hear no more; she sprang away, and half-an-hour afterwards, when Christian went into the library to speak to Carus, she found him in grave conversation with Heather. The girl was on a stool at his feet, and her two hands were clasped round his arm as he stooped a little towards her. Heather's face was full of wistful entreaty; her eyes were wide and anxious.

" Why do you say such things, Carus?" she asked in a worried voice, and then Christian closed the door quietly. Neither of them had seen or heard her; but what did Heather's troubled look mean? Somehow that little scene haunted Christian,—the girl's attitude, at once childlike and clinging, and the womanly pain in her face; and then Carus's expression, full of tender solicitude.

At the end of the corridor Christian came upon her mother-in-law.

" Do you know what has become of Heather, Christian?" asked Mrs. Linacre. " I want to speak to her before she goes up to dress."

" She is in the library with Carus," replied Christian. " They seemed so engrossed with their talk that I would not interrupt."

Then a relieved expression came to Mrs. Linacre's face.

"You were quite right, my dear," she said approvingly. "I am glad you had so much tact and discretion. We are not quite pleased with Heather," she continued, "and I have begged Carus to talk to her; but he has been putting it off from day to day. Heather thinks more of Carus's opinion than of any other person's. The child is quite devoted to him, and he has great influence with her."

"Oh, we all know that," returned Christian rather abruptly. "Heather's behaviour to Carus is perfect. But she has not seemed quite herself the last few days. I hope nothing is really troubling her."

"Only her own conscience," returned Mrs. Linacre rather coldly. "Christian, you are one of ourselves, and I know you are very fond of Heather, so that there is no harm in telling you that I consider that she is treating poor Sydney very badly."

"Do you mean that he has spoken to her?"

"I mean that he has tried to do so two or three times; but, as he complains, he cannot induce her to give him a fair hearing. She always turns it off, or makes an excuse to leave him. She was very trying that afternoon at the Tressilians', and gave him a good deal of trouble and annoyance. Mrs. Masters was quite put out with her, and you know how fond she is of Heather."

"I think you must all be a little patient with her," returned Christian gently. "Heather is very young for her age. She has never had a lover before, and it is quite possible that she does not know her own mind."

"That is what Carus says, but it is very strange, Christian," and Mrs. Linacre's tone was rather fretful. "I was married at nineteen, so I was only a few months older than Heather. Sydney is getting impatient. He says Charlie Tressilian is very much smitten. In fact, Heather is so pretty and engaging that she will have plenty of admirers. To my thinking, the child grows prettier every day," for Janet's heart was very soft on the subject of her adopted daughter.

"I think it is a pity that Mr. Masters is following you to Cromer. It would be wiser to leave Heather to herself for a time."

" Carus said the very same thing, Christian, but I don't agree with either of you. Girls are very often perverse, and do not know their mind until it is made up for them. At Cromer, Sydney will easily find an opportunity of having his say out. Of course, she really cares for him —there is no doubt of that. It is only just her wayward-ness, because we have all spoilt her so. Carus will soon bring her to reason, and convince her that she is treating Sydney very unkindly. He will be very gentle with her, but he will be firm too ; and I know he will tell her that it is her plain duty to listen to him ;" and then Mrs. Linacre moved away, saying that there was still a quarter of an hour before it was time for dress ; but Christian, who was unwilling to carry on the conversation, made some excuse and went up to her room.

XXIII

The Clouds Gather

A lovely flower thou seemest
So tender, sweet, and true,
And as I gaze, steals o'er me
A sadness strange and new.

Upon thy peaceful forehead
I'd lay my hands, in prayer
That God may ever keep thee
As tender, true, and fair.

From the German of HEINE.

DISCRETION is the better part of valour, and it was pru-
dence that counselled Christian to break off the conversation at this point; she knew now by experience that
when Mrs. Linacre had made up her mind on any matter
that it was impossible to move her. "She is like iron and
cotton-wool wrapped up together," she said to Pen on
one occasion when she was extremely put out with her
mother-in-law. "What is the use of firing off one's poor
little pistol shots! They never hit her. She is far too
firmly entrenched behind her prejudices. She is a good
woman," she continued, "and she means to be kind, but
she is dense—dense—dense!" but then Christian was in
one of her naughty moods.

She was not at all easy in her mind about Heather.
She was inclined to think that both Mrs. Linacre and
Carus were treating the matter injudiciously; though, no
doubt, the latter had been prompted and instigated by his
mother to reason with the girl. Carus was by nature a
peacemaker, and never mixed himself up in any domestic
factions unless he were forced to do so, and he was far
too fond of Heather to find fault with her in any way;
but probably his mother had given him no peace.

"Why can they not let her alone?" thought Christian
indignantly. "They are forcing open the bud—they are
giving her no time to expand. They have no right to

meddle with anything so sacred as a girl's affection. They are about as clumsy as a gardener would be if he tried to prune a rose tree with the shears with which he clips the grass borders. I have no patience with Mrs. Linacre. She ought to know better." Christian was working herself up now.

"What does it matter if she is childish for her age!" she went on. "She will be womanly soon enough, and it will do Sydney Masters good to wait. Why should he expect her to drop into his hand like an over-ripe plum! He has had everything his own way all his life, and I expect that foolish mother of his has done her best to spoil him, but he is too good a fellow to be ruined by over-indulgence. If they would just leave her alone, she would soon find out how much she cares for him. I have a good mind to talk to her myself. I believe I could say something to help her, but how am I to find an opportunity?" The dressing-bell interrupted Christian's reflections, and as she knew that Mrs. Linacre loved punctuality, she was obliged to commence her toilet.

On any other evening Heather would have come to her with offers of assistance, but only Mrs. Linacre's maid made her appearance and was soon dismissed. When Christian was ready she stood for a moment in the corridor hesitating whether she should go to Heather's room; then she saw Carus standing at the head of the staircase. He made a sign to her to join him.

"I think you had better come down with me," he said quietly. "Our guests have arrived, and my mother is in the drawing-room. I kept Heather too long, and she will be late, I am afraid, but Hitchens has gone to her." Then Christian went downstairs.

To her surprise, Sydney Masters was in the drawing-room. She had no idea that he had been invited to meet the Hallidays. She thought he looked a little pale and anxious, and, until Heather appeared, his look was continually turned to the door.

Just before dinner was announced Heather glided in, but before she had time to greet any one, the butler was on the threshold and Carus was offering his arm to Lady Halliday. The girl sat nearly opposite to Christian at the table. Her face was very flushed, as though she had been crying, and she was unusually quiet and subdued.

It struck Christian that Sydney, who was beside the girl, showed great tact and consideration. He talked chiefly to his right-hand neighbour, the elder Miss Halliday, and seldom addressed Heather; and there was a guarded and watchful tenderness in his manner that rather touched Christian, and she told herself again that he was a good fellow.

She was accustomed by this time to Carus's silence during meals, but this evening he seemed more than usually depressed. More than once she saw him look anxiously at Heather, but the girl seemed to avoid his eyes. She sat with her long lashes fringing her hot cheeks and puckering her napkin with restless fingers; but once, when Carus's glance was prolonged and searching, Christian saw a faint quiver pass over the girl's features. "What did it all mean?" she asked herself. "Had Carus been severe with her for once? Had he given her pain? The whole thing was provoking and mysterious." Christian grew more puzzled every minute. She had hoped to find an opportunity of speaking to Heather before the gentlemen left the dining-room, but she was soon aware that Heather rather avoided her than otherwise. She placed herself between the two Halliday girls, and presently, when Sydney joined them, the four young people went out into the garden. Christian would have liked to join them, but Heather had not even looked towards her, so she remained with Mrs. Linacre and Lady Halliday and tried to take an intelligent interest in the sayings and doings of the latter's numerous progeny—the quiverful of goodly sons and daughters that blessed the worthy baronet and his wife.

Christian soon grew weary of it all. One of the elder sons, Cecil, had gone out with the Royal Engineers, and another was with his regiment in India; Madeleine, the second girl, was engaged to one of Cecil's brother-officers, and he too had started for the Cape; and Lady Halliday was full of maternal fears for their welfare .

"By the bye, my dear Janet,"—and here Lady Halliday dropped her voice into a confidential whisper—"I

am very much struck with that handsome Mr. Masters;
he is quite charming—and—and——" here the two heads
nid-nodded more closely, but Christian heard no more.
Carus and Sir George were pacing up and down the
rose-walk; when their backs were turned to the drawing-
room window, she slipped out and enjoyed a solitary
stroll. The air was fresh and reviving after the sultry
heat of the day, and only the weird, harsh note of the
night-jar or the distant hoot of an owl broke the stillness; the moon was rising, and as Christian wandered
down the drive, the lake looked like a sheet of silver
between the dark trees. She could have lingered for
hours, the scene was so peaceful and full of beauty; but
she was afraid she would be missed, so she reluctantly
retraced her steps. She had been thinking of Jack and
wondering what he was doing. " Oh, I hope they are all
wrong, and that there will be no war!" she said to herself. " Jack is so brave and imprudent; he is afraid
of nothing, and he will expose himself to danger in the
most reckless manner;" and then she remembered a name
that one of his brother-officers had given him—" Dare-
Devil-Jack,"—and smiled and sighed as she recollected it.

She had almost forgotten Heather for the time, when
at that moment, as she was skirting the Bowling Green,
she came upon her and Sydney. They were standing
by the yew-hedge, and Sydney was holding her hands
and speaking very earnestly. Christian's footfall had
been too light to disturb them, and the next instant she
had turned into a winding walk that would lead her to
the house; no words had reached her ears, but in the
moonlight she had seen Heather's face distinctly, and the
look on it had bordered on despair; she was standing
quite still and motionless, like marble; and whether by
her own will or Sydney's strong coercion, she was making
no attempt to free herself; Sydney had found his opportunity at last, and there was no escape for Heather.

Poor little Bell-Heather! As Christian hurried through
the dark walks she wondered if the shadow of the ill-
fated Ephra lurked near the lovers; it was on that very
spot that the miserable woman had fallen at the feet of
her faithful Giles; how Heather had hated that old story;

with what childish pettishness she had uttered her protest. But it was no child's face on which Christian looked that evening; it was more like the hunted expression of some wild thing who found itself trapped and wounded.

When Christian re-entered the drawing-room she was relieved to find that no one seemed to have noticed her absence; the two Halliday girls were playing a duet, and their elders were listening to them with evident enjoyment. Once, indeed, when there was a moment's lull, Mrs. Linacre tapped Christian's arm lightly with her fan: " Have you seen Heather and Sydney?" she whispered.

" Yes," returned Christian; " I saw them in the Bowling Green."

" Naughty child, and she has thin shoes on." Mrs. Linacre spoke indulgently, but Christian did not stop to explain that Heather had not been actually standing on the grass; a few minutes later Sydney stepped in from the verandah, just as Lady Halliday was telling her husband that they must start at once, as they had a long drive before them. In the middle of the leave-taking one of the girls suddenly remembered Heather, and proposed to go in search of her, but her sister negatived this by saying that Heather was that instant coming in; and the next moment she was among them, helping them with their wraps, and giving them messages for their absent sisters; she even went out into the porch with Carus to see the last of them. When they had driven off, Carus wished his mother good-night. " Sydney is going to smoke a pipe with me," he said; " and it is such a lovely night that I shall probably have a prowl as far as Chesterton," and then he looked at Heather and held out his hand without speaking. Heather bade Christian a hasty good-night, and after that followed Mrs. Linacre to her room; but she did not remain long; ten minutes later Christian heard her pass her door. Heather's room was a little lower down the corridor, and was exactly opposite Mrs. Linacre's dressing-room; it was the prettiest room in the house, and had been beautifully fitted up and furnished for the girl's occupation as a surprise on her seventeenth birthday. Christian had often admired and marvelled at the many contrivances for the girl's comfort:

every article, every choice engraving on the walls were so many proofs of her adopted mother's thought and tenderness; if Mrs. Linacre had been her own mother, Heather could not have been more cherished and indulged.

Christian had determined not to undress until she had spoken to Heather; she only waited until Hitchens was safely shut in her mistress's room, and then she crossed the corridor and tapped at the girl's door. There was no response, and after she had repeated it she turned the handle. There were no candles lighted, evidently Heather had been unwilling to exclude the moonlight which streamed in at the large oriel window; as Christian closed the door gently, she saw that Heather was kneeling in the window recess with her face hidden in her arms. She had taken off her evening dress and wore a white dressing-gown, and she had also loosened her heavy coils, and her hair, which was very long and beautiful, swept over her shoulders and touched the ground; she might have been a St. Agnes at her devotions. For a few moments Christian stood hesitating by the door, unwilling to disturb her, and wondering if she ought to withdraw, when a low sob broke the silence—and then another. "Oh! what shall I do—what can I do?" she heard Heather say in such a tone of utter hopelessness that Christian quite thrilled with pity, and the next moment her hand was on the girl's shoulder.

"My poor, dear child, what is it?" she asked; but Heather recoiled from her touch with a suppressed scream.

"Oh, how you startled me!" she said, panting as though from fright. "Why did you not knock? I heard nothing—nothing—and then you touched me."

"Dear Heather, I did knock twice; but as there was no answer, I turned the handle, and then I thought you were saying your prayers, and I did not know whether to go or stay;" Christian spoke soothingly, for she was rather alarmed by Heather's excessive agitation.

"Oh no!" with a little shudder, "I was not praying. I tried, but I could not collect my thoughts. I was far too miserable. Why have you come, Christian? Indeed,

I cannot talk; and Aunt Janet or Hitchens will hear us."
But Christian's only response to this was to seat herself
on the cushioned bench in the window and draw the girl
gently towards her.

"Heather dear, you must not send your sister away.
I am so sorry for you, and I want to help you. I know
that something is troubling you, and that you are not
happy."

"Happy! Oh, if I could only die and go to my
mother!" and Heather broke into a passion of tears and
sobs. Strange words from the lips of that young creature whose life had been so bright and sunny. "Oh, if
I were only a child again!" she moaned, as Christian
rocked her gently in her arms. At that moment the motherly element inherent in most women's natures was
strongly developed in Christian. She felt as though she
were trying to comfort some young sister of her own, instead of one who had been a stranger to her three months
ago.

"Hush, darling! It is wrong even to think such
things," she said tenderly. "When troubles come, we
must be brave and try to bear them. You are unhappy
to-night, because they have been talking to you in a way
you do not like, and telling you that you ought to know
your own mind; and then, perhaps,"—Christian spoke in
rather a hesitating way—"Mr. Masters has been speaking too, and you are too worried and confused to know
what you wish."

"Oh, who has told you all this?" asked Heather, trying to control herself. "Christian, perhaps after all you
might be able to help me a little if I am not too bewildered to tell you things properly. How am I to make
you understand when I do not understand myself?"

"I think if you try, Heather, that we should both of
us see things more clearly. When did you begin to be
troubled?"

"It was the morning after our tea in the Bowling
Green," returned Heather in a low tone; "I had been
quite happy until then. You know what friends Sydney
and I have been. All these years, ever since we were
children, I have loved him as dearly as though he were

my own brother, and nothing has ever come between us; and when he told me, as he has done a hundred times over, how fond he is of me, I used to be as glad and proud to hear it as possible."

"And then his manner changed?" as Heather paused as though she found it difficult to proceed.

"Yes. Ever since Christmas I have noticed a change in him. He seemed nicer, but different somehow, and when we danced together, he used to make me a little uncomfortable by the way he wanted to monopolise me, and prevent other men from taking too much notice of me, but I was too stupid and childish to understand what this meant."

"And then your eyes were opened?"

"Yes. He talked to me that morning when Aunt Janet left us together. He told me that he loved me to distraction, and that he had always loved me, and that he could not live without me. Oh, I was so frightened, Christian, but I would not let him go on! I think I ran away and locked myself in my room. I daresay you cannot understand how any girl can be so silly, but from a child I never wanted to be married. I used to tell Aunt Janet when I got older that I meant to be an old maid and take care of Carus;" and here Heather dropped her face on her hand. "Aunt Janet told Carus once; but he only smiled and said that some one would gather his Bell-Heather before long. But I meant it, Christian, and I mean it now. I cannot leave Carus."

"Dear Heather,"—leaning her cheek against the girl's soft hair—"I think I understand better than any one else. Mr. Masters took you too much by surprise; it frightened you to see your old friend changed so suddenly into a lover. You were perplexed and worried, and as you had no answer ready you ran away. Well, under such circumstances, Heather, I should have done the same."

"Would you?" and Heather lifted up her hot face a moment. "But when Aunt Janet knew, she said I was a silly child, and that I had behaved very rudely to Sydney. I suppose he complained of me, for I never told her."

"Very likely she guessed it from Mr. Masters' manner."

"Well, he spoke to me again the same evening, and the very next day, but I put him off each time and would not listen. I used to get in a panic if he came near me. Oh, what a wretched week it has been! Aunt Janet got quite angry with me. She said that my behaviour to Sydney was most unladylike. Why should he not be allowed to tell me what he felt; if I did nothing else I might give him a hearing; but though I knew she was right, I got so nervous and flurried at the sight of him that I did the wrong thing again."

"You poor little thing! they ought to have left you alone."

"Oh, if they had only done so!" and Heather's voice was very sad; "but to-day Aunt Janet made Carus speak to me."

"But I am sure he would be kind to you, dearest."

"Kind! he was gentleness itself. No mother or father could have been kinder, but all the same he nearly broke my heart. He seemed to think that I was wrong too, and to be so sorry for Sydney, and he made me promise that when he spoke to me again that I would listen, and to-night, when we were out in the garden, and the Hallidays were tired and went in, Sydney made me stay out with him, and then he spoke again."

"And you kept your promise, Heather?"

"Yes, I kept my promise. Do you think I would disobey Carus? But all the time he was asking me to marry him I kept thinking of that poor Ephra. We were in the Bowling Green, just at the entrance, and there were long shadows where the moon did not shine. It was just where Ephra stood when she was Roger's wife, when she thought it was Giles's ghost that stood before her."

"Well, never mind Ephra," for Heather was becoming excited again.

"Oh, but I must mind her. She married Roger, you know, when all the time she loved his brother, and then when Giles came back—her happiness was killed—she went on loving him and sorrowing until she was quite an old woman, and people said she was not right in her head."

" Yes, dear, I know."

" It must be terrible to marry if one does not love,"
went on Heather,—" I mean love in the right way; but
I could not make Sydney understand this. He said he
would be quite content with even a little affection; that
he would not be afraid to marry me to-morrow, for he
would soon teach me to love him. He was very kind and
patient, Christian. He said he would not pain or trouble
me for worlds; and that he would wait until I got used
to the idea, and that he would not hurry me for an answer. He has promised not to speak to me again until
we return from Cromer; but he will then—but, oh!"—
burying her face on Christian's lap—" I know I shall
not give him the answer he wants, and then they will all
be angry with me, and poor Sydney will be miserable."

" Dear Heather, who knows? Perhaps you may change
your mind."

" No, never—never," and Heather spoke with strange
vehemence. " I do not love Sydney in that way,"—and
here her voice sank and became nearly inaudible—" and
nothing will induce me to leave Carus."

XXIV

CHRISTIAN FEELS PUZZLED

We often do more good by our sympathy than by our labour.—
DEAN FARRAR.

Trust God to weave your little thread into the great web,
*though the pattern shows it not yet.—*MACDONALD.

WHEN, half an hour later, Christian returned to her
room, she found herself somewhat perplexed and disappointed with the result of her conversation with Heather,
and yet she could not blame herself with any want of
kindness or tact. Her sympathy with the girl's trouble
had been very real, and she had said many helpful and
comforting things, and yet she had somehow failed in
imparting consolation. Heather had not owned herself
comforted, although she was full of gratitude for Christian's kindness, and her persistent sadness was at once
disquieting and baffling. Would it be possible that, in
Heather's undeveloped and childish nature, there might
be hidden depths of which she herself was unconscious?
Her remark about Carus had puzzled Christian.

"You know, dear," she had said very gently in reply
to this, "that when a woman marries, she has often to
give up things; not even her own people, however dear
they may be to her, ought to come between herself and
her husband." Christian said this with an air of quiet
assurance, as though she were a matron of twoscore and
ten years. It is marvellous how wise a person can be in
other folks' affairs, and it is the looker-on who sees most
of the game.

"In that case I ought not to marry," returned Heather
quickly; and as Christian looked surprised at this, she
went on in a low, earnest voice: "No one must ever come
between me and Carus."

"You do not quite understand me, dearest," returned
Christian quietly. "Of course, I do not mean that you

205

will love Carus less, because you love your husband more——" but Heather interrupted her.

" No—no—it is you who misunderstand, Christian; I shall never care for any one more than I do for Carus. Fond as I am of Sydney, he is nothing to me in comparison with Carus. Let me try and explain to you— you are so dear and kind—and I want you to understand," and then she drew Christian's arms round her in her caressing way, and settled herself more comfortably. And as the pure white moonlight lighted up the fair, girlish face, something in its soft, earnest expression reminded Christian again of St. Agnes. "You know, Christian," she went on, "that I was only a child when my mother died, and dear Aunt Janet adopted me. It was all very new and strange to me at first, and as I was a very shy child, I was rather in awe of Aunt Janet. I think, with all her kindness, most children would have found it difficult to understand her at first; and though she was so good to me, I thought her rules severe, and I used to take refuge with Carus and confide my childish troubles to him."

" And Carus was good to you."

" Good! Oh, if you only knew what he was to me!" —and Heather's eyes were full of tears—" if I were dull and lonely, he would leave his work and books to play with me. I wonder how many men would have troubled themselves about a little orphan child; but he never seemed to be weary, or to find me in his way."

" I daresay you gave him a great deal of pleasure, Heather. I know Carus loves children; he told me so."

" Oh, I hope so,"—very earnestly,—" and from the first I seemed to understand him, young and childish as I was. I always knew instinctively what would hurt him or give him pleasure; and it used to trouble me so when Aunt Janet did things which I knew he disliked. Once or twice I tried to make her understand, but I only offended her and did no good. 'If you were not a silly little child, I should be extremely vexed with you,' she said to me once; 'fancy a baby like you presuming to teach me how to manage my own son.' I am afraid she **must** have thought me impertinent, Christian." Christian smiled but made no answer. " I grew wiser after a time and held my tongue, and then my one idea was to try, in my childish way, to make up to Carus for all he had to suffer. His health is not strong, Christian, and at times he has terrible headaches; they are on his nerves, the doctors say. And there are days, too, when his deafness is worse, and then he can scarcely hear at all. That is why he shuts himself up, because the least exertion, or attempt to carry on conversation, gives him excruciating pain. And yet—can you believe it, Christian?— even at these times Aunt Janet will not leave him alone."

" I can well believe it, Heather."

" It is very trying of her—it is almost cruel—but, of course, she does not mean to be unkind. She thinks that because it is on his nerves, that he ought to be roused and interested in things, but she is quite wrong."

" But you could not convince her of that, dear?"

" No," with a sigh, " so we had to make the best of it. But however bad he was, he never minded my being in the room. I have spent hours sitting at his feet learning my lessons, or looking at pictures, and never speaking unless he addressed me. Sometimes he would forget that I was in the room, and even on his deaf days I could always make him hear," and Heather spoke in quite a triumphant tone, and again Christian smiled.

She knew Heather's methods well. At such times she would stand with her hand on Carus's shoulder, and her lips so close to his ear, that they almost touched the tube, and so her clear young voice seemed to pierce that misty silence. Heather would often take that position quite unconsciously before any one; but when there were others in the room, Carus would himself rise and place a chair for her. Christian herself had once heard Mrs. Linacre say, " That's right, Carus; Heather never will behave as though she were grown-up;" and Heather had blushed to her eyes and looked exceedingly uncomfortable.

" I think you have made me understand how you feel, Heather," observed Christian, when the girl had paused for a moment; " but there is something I must say. Carus's nature is very unselfish—it did not take me long to find that out,—and he is also extremely sensitive. I feel sure that it will give him great pain to know that **he** was in any way an obstacle to your happiness."

" But he is no obstacle, Christian," in rather a bewildered tone.

" Yes, dear; you are making him the excuse for not giving Mr. Masters the answer he wants. You cannot leave Carus—is not that what you have said? Well, Chesterton is quite near; you would be close neighbours, and could see Carus every day if you wished," but to her surprise Heather grew almost agitated.

" Oh, Christian! don't speak of it. Chesterton—Mrs. Masters. No—no; I could never do it. I know how Carus would miss me at meal-times, and then our rides, and walks, and our evening strolls in the Bowling Green, and all the dear times we have together. Why should I give these up for Sydney, when I never wish to be married?"

" But that is nonsense, dear child; you will change your mind on that point some day. You, of all people, my Heath-flower, to be an old maid. Tell me, will you, one thing? Does Carus guess the reason why you are unwilling to accept Mr. Masters?"

" Carus! oh no, Christian!" in a horrified voice. " No one must even hint at such a thing to him, or he would give me no peace until I promised to marry Sydney. And Aunt Janet would be even worse; she would pet me and scold me alternately, and call me a foolish baby, and then she would go straight to Carus, and fuss and fume until he undertook to bring me to reason. Christian, promise me that you will never betray my confidence to either of them," and Heather did not seem easy in her mind until Christian had pledged herself to silence. It was useless to say more, and Heather was looking white and exhausted, so she begged her to go to bed and leave all troublesome thoughts until daylight, and Heather was too worn out to refuse.

" I am afraid I have been very naughty," she said penitently, as Christian wished her " Good-night;" " and have said some wicked things, but I hope God will forgive me, for I did not really mean them, and I am so unhappy."

" You will be happier to-morrow, my sweet; things won't seem quite so bad to you in the daylight."

" Oh, I hope not! Good-night, you dear thing. I will try to be good;" and then Christian had stolen down the corridor on tiptoe, only just missing Carus, who was that moment coming up the stairs with his candlestick in his hand.

Christian was still trying to find a solution to the puzzle when she fell asleep, and never woke until the maid entered her room. Before she had finished dressing, a gleam of blue in the rose-walk attracted her attention, and to her surprise she found it was Heather gathering flowers for the little bouquets that it was her habit to lay on the breakfast plates. A few moments later Carus joined her, and they set off as usual to the Bowling Green. Heather always did her floral work in the arbour. She had a drawer fitted up with useful articles—gardening scissors, and apron, and string, and wire—which Carus loved to turn out and tidy while Heather sorted her flowers.

When they appeared at the breakfast table, Christian was relieved to find that Heather had recovered her composure, and was evidently making a great effort to be cheerful, and only her heavy eyes and the dark lines under them bore traces of last night's storm.

She had made a headache the excuse for her want of appetite. " I daresay it will soon pass off," Christian heard her say to Mrs. Linacre; " the air will do me good, and I need not talk in the train;" but Christian noticed that she could eat nothing.

It had been arranged that they were to start quite early to avoid the heat. Christian would remain at the Stone House until the cool of the evening, and then she and Carus would drive back to Many Bushes; and immediately after breakfast the luggage was brought downstairs, and twenty minutes later Mrs. Linacre and Heather had driven off. Carus looked after them rather wistfully; then as they went through the hall he picked up a pair of gray gloves thrown down in Troy.

"They must be Heather's," he said, and Christian noticed how gently he smoothed them out; " she has such pretty little hands. Christian, have you ever noticed them; they have dimples like a child? I gave her a ring once—sapphires and diamonds—but my mother would not let her wear it. I daresay she was right, but I know the child was disappointed."

Christian knew that too; the ring had been exhibited months before as Heather's dearest treasure. " I wonder why Aunt Janet did not want me to wear it," she had said; " it is such a beauty, Christian, and Carus and I both love sapphires. Never mind, I put it on sometimes in my own room, and when I am nineteen, Aunt Janet says I may wear it."

" I am not quite happy about Heather," went on Carus; " she looks really ill this morning."

But Christian answered in a reassuring manner: " Heather had tired herself the previous day, and the night had been hot; a headache always made people look bad;" and then she changed the subject, for she was unwilling to discuss Heather—there had been too much talk already.

As the library was the coolest place, Christian spent the morning there with her work and book. Carus was too busy to talk; he had a paper to finish for the *Spectator,* but he assured her that she would not be in the way. So she ensconced herself at the open window overlooking the lake, and the hours passed tranquilly and happily. They had tea in Troy, surrounded by all the dogs except Cheri, who had accompanied her mistress, and afterwards they drove to Many Bushes.

Never was there a happier little household during the next three weeks. Carus spent his mornings and the early part of the afternoon in his study, while Christian and Pen wrote their letters and worked and read in some shady nook of the garden; but the rest of the day Carus was always with them. The carriage was again placed at their disposal, but a charming proposal on Carus's part prevented their making much use of it: this was that Locock, the coachman at the Stone House, should give Christian riding lessons—Heather's little brown mare would be at her service—and as soon as Christian had had a few preliminary rides under Locock's tuition, Carus proposed to join them.

This was a fresh delight to Christian; she went up to town to be measured for a habit—Carus's gift—and until it was ready she wore an old skirt belonging to Heather. It had always been her ambition to ride, and she knew Jack would be glad for her to do so; he had once expressed his opinion that every girl ought to know how to ride, drive, and swim. Christian was fearless by nature, and in a very short time she could enjoy a canter in the park. Locock was quite proud of his pupil, and after some seven or eight lessons, Carus joined them for longer and more ambitious expeditions.

"Christian has a good figure and looks exceeding well on horseback," he wrote to Jack; "even now she rides nearly as well as Heather. I mean to look out for another mare—a chestnut, if possible; that is Christian's favourite colour—and give it her on her birthday. Locock thinks there is one for sale that will just do, and he is going to have a look at her; there is plenty of room in the stables, and it will always be ready for her use."

The chestnut mare was approved by both Locock and his master; she was a great beauty, and as gentle as a lamb. Carus never told any one, not even Jack, what he paid for her, and on her birthday morning Carus had the pretty creature brought round to the dining-room window while they were breakfasting—for Carus had come over to Many Bushes the previous night that he might enjoy her surprise and pleasure.

"I hope you like my birthday present, Christian," he said, smiling to see how she changed colour with pleasure; "her name is Fairy, and I trust, my dear, you will enjoy many and many a ride on her."

But Christian, in despair of expressing her gratitude, went up to him quietly and gave him her first sisterly kiss, at which Carus looked excessively pleased. Christian had her first ride on Fairy that very day—she even visited the stables to see the luxurious loose-box provided for her pet—and she wrote off pages of description to Jack, which he did not read for many a long day, being otherwise engaged, poor fellow.

Heather wrote frequently during her absence both to Carus and Christian, and her letters were always cheerful; in one of them she mentioned that Sydney had sprained his ankle badly, cycling in the dark; he had come to grief over a stone by the roadside, and had been unable to carry out his Cromer plans. She expressed a good deal of commiseration and sympathy for his misfortune, but she said nothing as to her own disappointment, though Carus took it for granted and seemed quite as sorry for her as for poor Sydney, compelled to lie up during the bright summer days.

Christian thought otherwise; she felt that though Heather was grieved for the accident, yet Sydney's absence would be a relief to her, and she was sure that she was right when she saw how contentedly she was remaining away.

Walter Hamill was now at the Vicarage, and Pen was having her good time. While Christian was riding with Carus, Pen and her lover were cycling together; and very often the two parties met at some given point and returned home in the evening. Mrs. Disney was very thoughtful on their behalf, and when Mr. Hamill did not dine at Many Bushes Pen was always invited to join the modest supper at the Vicarage; now and then the whole party adjourned to the garden at Many Bushes and sat out on the terrace in the starlight, talking of everything under the sun. One evening the Vicar asked Carus if he had read the *Times* that morning, but for a wonder Carus had been too much engrossed with a piece of library work to open the paper.

"I was keeping it for to-night," he said; "do you mean that there is any special news?"

"Nothing very satisfactory," had been Mr. Disney's answer. The answer from the Transvaal Government had been received, and it had been curt and uncompromising; the negotiations were at a deadlock. "In my opinion," went on the Vicar, "the situation is extremely serious; if the Transvaal Government withdraw their offer of the franchise and refuse to acknowledge British suzerainty, it is not difficult to predict that the storm will soon burst."

"You mean that war will be declared?"

"Yes, I mean that—and before many weeks are over," and then Carus went out to get his *Times,* and Mrs. Disney told her husband that it was getting late and that they must go home.

XXV

"I Have Not Changed My Mind"

Thank God there is always
Light whence to borrow,
When darkness is darkest,
And sorrow most sorrow.
ALICE CAREY.

God writes straight our crooked lines.—ANON.

CHRISTIAN went to Chesterton more than once during
Heather's absence. On her first visit she found Sydney
in his special sanctum; he was lying on a couch by the
window with a large table drawn up beside him covered
with fishing tackle and was busily engaged in tying flies,
for he was an enthusiastic disciple of Izaak Walton. He
seemed pleased to see his visitor, but Christian noticed at
once his air of depression; the accident had been severe,
and he told her that he was likely to be a prisoner for
another ten days; and it was evident that this forced inactivity was extremely irksome to him.

He never alluded to Heather, and Christian fancied that
he rather avoided the subject; but he sent Carus a message, begging that he would come and smoke a pipe with
him; and he took a great deal of interest in Christian's
riding lessons and gave her very valuable hints; and
when she rose to take her leave he asked her to come
again.

Christian had always been interested in Sydney from
the first, but after these visits she formed a higher opinion
of him. She thought his reticence manly and becoming,
and though she could see he was bored and unhappy, he
said little about his disappointment. Christian owned to
herself frankly that she could not wonder that Mrs. Linacre favoured his suit, or that Carus aided and abetted it.
He was a fine specimen of a young Englishman—athletic, clean-living, healthy-minded, and with a good heart.

213

Such faults as he possessed were common to a pampered only child who had had more than his share of good things, and Christian was inclined to blame Heather for her childish perversity in not lending a more willing ear to this braw young wooer.

Carus was to leave Many Bushes on the day that his mother returned home, and Walter Hamill was to accompany him. Christian was surprised to find how much she missed Carus. "I think after all it is nice to have a man in the house," she said to Pen; but Pen only smiled at this naïve admission. She had a dim suspicion that Christian was thinking a good deal about Captain Linacre just then. "Absence makes the heart grow fonder," she thought. Pen, who was devoted heart and soul to her Walter, often chafed secretly at Christian's lukewarm affection for her husband, but she was too loyal to her friend to hint this to any one.

Christian and Pen were to spend the following evening at the Stone House, so they did not see Heather until then, when she came running out into the porch to meet them.

She looked all the better for her visit, and had regained some of her old bloom, and her manner was as winsome and affectionate as ever; and yet, there was some subtle change in her, something indefinable that baffled and eluded Christian. She looked very lovely, but she seemed to have grown suddenly older, and the childish abandon and gaiety had deepened into a quiet cheerfulness. Now and then, when she was silent, Christian noticed the same faint shadow on her face, as though some secret care burdened her, but in another moment it had passed, and she was talking and laughing with her old animation. Heather never once mentioned Sydney, and Christian thought this rather a good sign. But Mrs. Linacre informed her that they were going to dine at Chesterton the next evening, and that Mr. Hamill had been included in the invitation; but though she said no more, her manner had been somewhat significant, and Christian felt convinced that an opportunity would soon be found for Sydney to renew his suit.

Christian intended to keep her thoughts to herself, but to her surprise Pen spoke of Heather at once.

" I don't fancy she is quite happy, Chriss," she observed
as they drove home; " she does not seem quite like her
bright self. I wonder if she is beginning to care for Mr.
Masters? it looks rather like it."

" How is one to find out, Pen? she never mentioned
his name to me."

" No, and it was Walter who told me that they were
going to Chesterton to-morrow. Do you know that Walter thinks Heather the most beautiful girl he has ever
seen. He says that it is so uncommon to see such beauty
with such complete unconsciousness—that he never saw
any one so free from little vanities and affectation, and so
perfectly simple. But he thinks that they ought to have
let her see the world before she accepts Mr. Masters."

" Mr. Hamill thinks her acceptance a foregone conclusion then?"

" Why, of course; don't we all think so, Chriss?" returned Pen innocently. " Mr. Masters is so nice in every
way—Walter said so at once. He really thinks Heather
could not do better, only he would like her to be free a
little longer."

" I agree with him there;" but Christian said no more
—the subject was too complex for discussion. No one
had the faintest idea where the real difficulty lay; they
must just wait patiently the development of events; it
was impossible for any one to prognosticate exactly what
would happen.

" We all want to play the part of minor providence
in our friend's affairs," she said to herself; " and a nice
muddle we should make of it. Human hearts are not
machines to be hammered out and shaped on our poor
little anvils; we may as well climb down to our own
proper level and mind our own business." And Christian
acted up to her own philosophy, for though she and
Heather rode together more than once, with only a groom
to attend them, she made no effort to find out if Heather
had changed her mind. But she was soon to be enlightened.

One morning she had bicycled over to the Stone House
on some little matter of business with Mrs. Linacre, but
on entering the dressing-room she was at once aware that

something was amiss. Mrs. Linacre's face wore its most rigid expression, and her thin lips were closed firmly. She received Christian without the semblance of a smile.

"The patterns came from Marshall and Snelgrove's this morning, and as I thought you would like to see them I came over at once," explained Christian, dismayed at this cool reception; but Mrs. Linacre waved the little parcel away almost irritably.

"You are very good to take so much trouble, Christian," she returned; "but I am far too much worried to think about silks this morning, and you will not wonder at it when I tell you the cause of my trouble. But sit down, it is far too hot for you to have bicycled over from Braybrooke; you look flushed and tired—you ought not to have done it, my dear," her manner softening as she noticed Christian's air of fatigue.

"I had no idea it was so hot, and I came early; but I shall soon be cool," and Christian resolutely fanned herself. "Please tell me what is wrong." Then Mrs. Linacre's countenance resumed its portentous gravity.

"I had quite a shock yesterday. Heather has greatly disappointed us—indeed she has behaved very badly. Sydney spoke to her again—he had my full permission to do so—and she has actually refused him."

"Refused him!" Christian's start of surprise was quite genuine.

"Yes, refused him absolutely, and desired him never to speak to her again on that subject, as she could never marry him."

"But she must have given him some reason?"

"No; that is why I say that she has behaved so badly. When the poor fellow begged her to tell him frankly the reason for her refusal, she merely said there was nothing to tell. Of course she talked the usual girlish jargon—that she only loved him in a sisterly way, and that he could never be more to her than a dear friend—why, the foolish child actually told him that she never intended to marry any one. Did you ever hear such nonsense—Carus quite laughed when I repeated that?"

"I don't think he need have laughed," returned Christian, rather nettled at this; "strange as it seems, it is perfectly true that Heather has no wish to be married."

"But that is so absurd," replied Mrs. Linacre, who never approved of anything abnormal; "why should Heather be different from other girls. I am excessively disappointed, Christian, and also mortified, that after all the pains I have taken with Heather that she should be so undeveloped and childish. It is really very hard on me," and there were actually tears in Mrs. Linacre's eyes.

"Yes, I know it is a great disappointment," and Christian was so touched by her mother-in-law's dejected look that for the first time she gave her a voluntary kiss; "but it seems to me that there is nothing to be done."

"So Carus says," with a sigh; "he is almost as troubled about it as I am. Poor Sydney has been talking to him; he will have it that there is something at the bottom of Heather's refusal to marry him—that there must be some one else for whom she cares. But, as Carus says, this is absurd. Heather has seen no·one who has paid her any special attention. To be sure young Gillespie admired her, but she would have nothing to say to him. But Carus could not reason Sydney out of the conviction that he has a rival." Christian made no answer, and Mrs. Linacre went on. "Carus is very much pained; you know how tender-hearted he is. He begged Sydney to go away for a time; but the poor boy seemed quite desperate, and declared that he did not care what became of him. He had loved Heather from a child, and if she would not marry him he could not stop at Chesterton. He was quite crushed and broken-hearted; and Carus walked back with him. And then there was such a painful scene with his mother. Mrs. Masters is so angry with Heather that she vows she will never speak to her again—that she has spoilt her boy's life."

"Oh, I hope not; Sydney Masters is not the only man who has to bear a love disappointment."

"Oh, but he has loved Heather for so many years, and it will go very deep with him. Even Carus says that that is why he is so troubled. And to think we can do nothing to help him."

"It is very sad," replied Christian; "but you must see for yourself that there is nothing to be done, and after all even a young creature like Heather must know what is best for her own happiness." But Mrs. Linacre evidently did not agree with her. She was excessively angry with Heather, and thought her both unreasonable and incomprehensible. With her usual pertinacity she declined to believe that nothing remained to be done; for she was one of those people who persist in trying to shape other folks to their own pattern idea, and who would hammer at them on their own little rusty anvil everlastingly. It was this want of perception and adaptability that had in a great measure made the misery of Janet's life. It would be well for some of us if we would add a clause to our morning petitions: " Give us grace to see ourselves and other people in the true light, and with that knowledge help us to be kind."

There was little use in prolonging the conversation, and after a few minutes Christian suggested going to Heather. To her surprise Mrs. Linacre made no objection.

"You will not do any good," she said mournfully. "As both Carus and I have failed in bringing her to reason, it is not likely that she will listen to any one;" but though Christian had her own doubts on this point, she wisely let this pass.

She found Heather in her own room. She was sitting in the window recess in an attitude of dejection, with an open book in her lap; but she jumped up with a little cry of pleasure when she saw Christian.

"Oh, I am so glad you have come," she said, throwing her arms round her. To Christian's relief she was quite calm and like herself, only there were again dark lines under her eyes, as though she had not slept; but it was at once evident to her that there was to be no return of the stormy scene of five weeks ago, and this was a great relief.

"I am indeed glad I came—if you wanted me, Heather."

"I always want you," returned Heather simply. "I do not know how it is, Christian, but you seem to understand better than other people; and you never make a fuss, or seem shocked if one differs from you in opinion."

"I am glad you think me so large-minded," returned

Christian, smiling at this. "Now, dear, we have not much time before luncheon, so we had better get our talk over. Mrs. Linacre has been telling me that poor Sydney Masters had been sent about his business. Oh, you cruel little child, how could you have had the heart to do it;" then Heather grew very pale.

"It was dreadful," she returned, in a low voice; "but it had to be done. One must do either right or wrong, Christian."

"How do you mean, dearest?"

"It would be wrong for me to marry Sydney, because I could never love him in that way; and it was right to tell him so straight out, and in such a manner that he would never ask me again. Indeed, I was very gentle; but the truth had to be told."

"But you gave him no reason, Heather." But as Christian said this, she was struck with the girl's womanly bearing. There was no trace of childishness or excitement in her manner; but she looked very sad.

"Did they tell you that? I knew how Aunt Janet would harp on that string. But was it not sufficient reason to give that I could only love him in a sisterly way."

"But if Mr. Masters were content with that."

"That is what he said. Oh, poor Sydney, how he begged and prayed me just to marry him, and let the love come later! But I knew the love would never come, Christian, and I was firm. I asked God to make me so, and I think my prayer was answered. But oh," with a pained contraction of her forehead, "it was horrible to have to hurt him like that—it just tortured me to do it; and at last my nerves gave way, and I got hysterical, and that frightened him, and he ceased to press me."

"Dear Heather, how you must have suffered."

"Yes, indeed; and for a long time there will be little comfort for me. Mrs. Masters is quite ill with worry, they tell me, and Aunt Janet is so angry with me;" and here Heather sighed heavily. "I wonder if people always have to suffer when they are grown up; but of course not, or Penelope would not be so happy. I suppose it is somehow my own fault."

" I don't know that; one cannot help one's nature."

" Oh, that is comfortable doctrine; but it does seem a poor return to make to Aunt Janet after all her goodness to me." And here Heather's voice was a little choked, in her youthful way she was evidently going through a slow martyrdom.

" And Carus, dear;" then a painful flush came to the girl's face.

" He is troubled too. He cannot bear to see any one suffer; and he is so fond of Sydney. And though he would miss me terribly, I think he would have been glad if I had accepted him."

" In that case you are sacrificing yourself and Sydney to no purpose," began Christian, but Heather stopped her.

" Hush, hush! It is no sacrifice on my part. What do you mean, Christian? It is quite true that Carus does not understand. He told me once or twice yesterday that I puzzled him; and then," here Heather became crimson, " he asked me if I had seen any or for whom I could care more."

" Well!" for Heather paused here.

" I was quite angry when Carus said that, and would not talk to him any more. I suppose he meant Robert Gillespie. But it was too ridiculous; he made it up with me afterwards, and was as dear as possible; but I can see he is puzzled."

" You think he has really no idea that you cannot bring yourself to love him;" but here Heather's hand was laid upon Christian's lip.

" Not another word, Christian. You promised, and I know I can trust you. This is our secret—your and mine. No; I have thought it all over. It has never been out of my mind day or night, for my dreams have been full of it. I have not changed my mind. I never shall, however angry they may be with me. I will not leave Carus to marry any one."

XXVI

THE BREAKING OF THE STORM

Sing of war, and deeds of heroes, and the crash of battle drum,
Praying always for the dawning of the happier days to come.
        ALEXANDER CLUNY MACPHERSON.

THE autumn days were passing rapidly away, and September had merged into October, when Christian, who had been visiting two or three old people in the Infirmary wards, stood on the steps a moment to inhale the fresh evening air. From the first days of their arrival at Braybrooke, Penelope had volunteered to help Mrs. Disney in her parish work, and in her quiet way was proving herself a most valuable coadjutor. But Christian, who had no parochial yearnings, had held aloof.

" I have no vocation for district visiting," she observed once. " I don't mind talking to people after my own fashion; but it really isn't my business if their children are not baptised, and I could not pretend it was. Pen is different. She is going to marry a clergyman, and she is just getting her hand in; but I belong to the church militant."

" Well, we all have our gifts," returned Mrs. Disney tranquilly, for this mutinous speech had been addressed to her; " neither can we all work in the same corner of the vineyard, or there might be some danger of treading on each other's heels; but it would not trouble you, I am sure, to read the paper or an interesting book to poor old Oliver in the Infirmary. He is quite blind now, and he is such an intelligent man."

" I should not mind if it were not the thin end of the wedge," returned Christian reflectively; " and if I could be sure that you would not give me a shove on. You are a dangerous woman, Mrs. Disney;" but Charlotte only laughed and promised faithfully that there should be no such shove given.

And so it came about that Christian often spent an
hour or two reading to three or four old men in the Infirmary, and in her own quaint, original way bringing
a good deal of brightness into their dim lives; but she
did even this excellent work by fits and starts, and could
not be induced to use any method on her visits. " I don't
want them to expect me," she said once. " I mean to be
a constant surprise—a parochial Mrs. Jack-in-the-box,"
and she certainly acted up to her words.

On this afternoon in question she had been in a restless, dissatisfied mood, and she thought that even reading *The Land and the Book* to old Oliver would be better
than staying at home alone; and yet, as she stood on the
Infirmary steps, the weight on her spirits had not lifted,
and in spite of the evening freshness, it seemed to her
that the atmosphere round her was charged with elec-
tricity—that a brooding stillness pervaded everything like
the hush before a storm. In her little world things were
not going well, and her visits to the Stone House were
somewhat trying. Mrs. Linacre had not yet forgiven
Heather. It was never easy for her to condone an offence,
and without being the least vindictive, she had a morbid
habit of brooding over an injury and treating the offender
with marked coldness and dignity. It was no wonder
that Heather drooped in such an atmosphere, for the girl
fretted sorely at her adopted mother's displeasure.

Chesterton was shut up. Mrs. Masters and her son
had gone abroad. Sydney had told Carus that they were
probably going to Berlin, as his mother had relatives
there, but he seemed uncertain as to their plans. He had
not called to say good-bye, but had sent a message to the
ladies, and Heather had thought this extremely unkind.

" I suppose he is angry with me too," she said to
Christian, " and yet, what have I done? They are all so
terribly hard on me, except Carus, and he does all he can
to make me happy." But though Christian was full of
sympathy there seemed nothing to be done. Heather
must wait with what patience she could muster until the
cloud passed and Mrs. Linacre forgot her grievance.

Christian thought she would call at the Vicarage before she went home, but as she turned into the market-

place she met Colonel Bromley,—he was a great ally of hers,—so she stopped to speak to him.

"Have you heard the news, Mrs. John?" he said at once as he shook hands with her; but as Christian shook her head, she knew instinctively what he would tell her.

"The evening papers are in," he went on. "The Boers have crossed the Free State borders. War has begun."

"War has begun!" Christian repeated the words slowly as though she would fix them in her mind. Oh, no wonder the atmosphere had been electric if such news were on the way! . "But I thought," she added in a bewildered voice, "that our Government was negotiating with President Steyn?" Then, as they crossed the Market Square, the Colonel expounded the matter to her, bringing it carefully to the level of her feminine intellect.

While the British Public was trying to shut its eyes and hope against hope, things had been drifting to this sad end.

The garrison at Natal had been increased by troops from Europe and five thousand troops from India. As early as July, Queensland had offered a contingent of mounted infantry with machine guns, and the other colonies had, in like manner, proffered help.

On 7th October the army reserves were called out; and two days later an audacious ultimatum had been received from the Boer Government; and on the 12th, as the old Colonel informed Christian, twelve thousand of the Burghers broke up their camps at Sandspruit and Volksrust and crossed the borders with Piet Joubert at their head.

Christian listened in silence as Colonel Bromley dilated eloquently on the craft and cunning of the Boers, their courage and bull-dog tenacity. "They will be formidable foes," he finished, "and we shall have our work cut out for us. I am no pessimist, but I know something of the country. It is a bigger thing than John Bull guesses at the present moment. We have only about twenty-two thousand men in South Africa to defend that huge frontier."

"Oh, we shall be sure to manage them!" returned Christian obstinately. "They are most of them farmers."

" My dear young lady, mark my words. You will soon
alter your opinion of the Boers. Some of these men from
the veldt are the finest natural warriors upon earth. ' The
sunburnt, tangle-haired, full-bearded farmers,' as I have
read somewhere; ' the men of the Bible and the rifle.'"
And future experience proved that Colonel Bromley was
right.

Christian hurried off to the Vicarage and found Carus
there; they were all discussing the news.

" Jack will have his wish," he said to her; " he was
longing for a brush with the enemy. And then he told
her that his mother seemed in low spirits; the outbreak
of the war in Natal made her extremely anxious. And
Christian said at once that she would go over to Silverton
the next day.

" I shall be glad if you will do so," returned Carus;
" it is rather unfortunate my being away just now;" for
Mr. Vigne had been ill, and had begged his nephew to
come to him for a few days. " I wish," looking at her
wistfully, " that you would stay for a night or two;" but
Christian would not promise to do this, though she undertook that either she or Pen would go over daily for an
hour or two.

She went over to luncheon the next day. Mrs. Linacre, who was much depressed, seemed very glad to see
her; but she could talk of nothing but the war. Colonel
Bromley had called at the Stone House the previous day,
and his prognostications had filled her with alarm.

" The Colonel says it will be a terrible business," she
began at once; but Christian, who had regained her usual
bright optimism, after the first few moments of panic,
could not be induced to take a gloomy view of the situation.

" It is a righteous cause," she said proudly; " we are
fighting on behalf of the oppressed. Oh, I am not afraid
of the results! The Boers will have to give in; there
will be a few battles first, and Jack will have an opportunity of winning his laurels." But as Christian made
her little speech, she was in happy ignorance of the long
and bloody strife that was to follow,—of the humiliating
disasters and inglorious defeats that were to make Eng-

land veil her eyes in sadness and shame, and to shroud many a happy home in sorrow.

" How you talk, my dear," returned Mrs. Linacre fretfully; " I should have thought Jack's wife would have shared my fears. Do you know, I have been awake all night, thinking of all Colonel Bromley told us? He seems to think those Boers will be formidable enemies, and of course he is an authority. I have been reproaching myself for encouraging Jack in his wish to be a soldier. If anything happens I shall never forgive myself, Christian."

" But that is nonsense," returned Christian in her most bracing manner; for she was not going to give into that sort of false sentiment; as though Jack could ever have been anything else. Why, the word soldier is written over him from head to foot! " I wonder," speaking half to herself, but yet aloud, " if I could have cared for him if he had been a curate, or a stockbroker?"

" My dear!" and Mrs. Linacre looked quite scandalised, " what will you say next? The idea of a Linacre being in trade—the very notion is preposterous."

" But stockbroking isn't a trade," returned Christian, who felt rather disposed for an argument. " I think they do buy stocks or shares or something over counters; but it is a highly respectable business if they don't gamble; and they have a lot to do with bulls and bears." Mrs. Linacre looked mystified, but made no observation on this; and Christian went on recklessly: " It is very different, you see, from weighing out pounds of tea, or cutting yards of silk; but all the same, I am rather glad that Jack is not a stockbroker—and his uniform is so becoming."

" The Linacres have never been anything in the city," returned her mother-in-law stiffly; " the second son has generally gone into the army or the Civil Service. I cannot recall at the present moment that one has ever taken orders."

" Then there is no Dean or Bishop Linacre?"

" No, I think not, but Carus will know. There has been a sailor or two; and there was a Carus Linacre who was in the Diplomatic Service; but in every generation there were Linacres in the army, so I suppose Jack has inherited the taste;" and as Christian supposed so too, the discussion ended amicably.

There was no doubt that Mrs. Linacre was becoming fond of her daughter-in-law, though it could not be said that she understood her in the least; but Christian's bright manner was a great charm; and somehow it always happened that even if people criticised and found fault with her at first, and called her a free-spoken, independent young woman, they generally succumbed to her fascinations at last.

So when day after day Christian turned up at the Stone House on all sorts of pretexts, Mrs. Linacre welcomed her quite warmly, and was always willing that Heather should accompany her for a ride after luncheon. Christian was glad to see that Mrs. Linacre was visibly relenting to the poor little culprit, and spoke to her with her old kindness—evil is seldom unmitigated; and the war had one good effect, it made Mrs. Linacre forget her small grievances—her mind was too full of Jack and South Africa to brood over minor disappointments.

Meanwhile events marched on. Talana Hill had been stormed and carried—a victory dearly bought by the death wound of the gallant General Penn Symons, and the loss of Colonel Gunning, and several other brave officers.

Hungry, breakfastless men had crossed the open grass-land and the nullah, and fought their way up the hill among the boulders; it was a soldier's battle, and the valour of the troops carried it through; but a serious disaster to the small cavalry force marred the victory.

They had wandered too far—had been surrounded by a superior force—and had been compelled after some hours to lay down their arms. When Carus brought the news to his uncle, Mr. Vigne expressed his thankfulness that Jack was with General French—but he little knew how small cause he had for thankfulness. Christian was in high spirits over the news of the victory of Talana Hill; she insisted that Pen should accompany her to the Stone House and spend the afternoon with Mrs. Linacre, while she and Heather had a glorious scamper; for Christian had grown quite an expert horsewoman, and could jump a ditch or a low fence, to Locock's great pride and satisfaction.

It was one of those sober, sunless October days, when Nature wore her brown and russet livery, and there was a sense of decay in the rotting heaps of leaves under every hedge row.

The trees in the avenue were thinning, but their tawny and yellow tints were still marvellously beautiful; a frosty finger had not yet been laid on the oaks, and they had not yet hung out their dark red pennons.

Heather, who was looking a little pale and subdued, brightened at the idea of the ride, and ran to put on her habit; Mrs. Linacre and Pen went into the porch to see them start.

"Christian rides as though she had been accustomed to it all her life," observed Mrs. Linacre, as the horses cantered out of sight; "she has a very graceful figure, and she looks extremely well on horseback. I wish Jack could have seen her just now," and Mrs. Linacre's voice was quite motherly. "Do you know, my dear Penelope," she went on, as they ensconced themselves cosily by the drawing-room fire, for she and Pen were great friends, "that when I first saw Christian I could not make out why Jack had fallen in love with her?"

Pen smiled. Mrs. Linacre had more than once hinted at her dissatisfaction with her daughter-in-law.

"Well, Chrissy is not exactly pretty," she returned; "but she is very taking."

"Oh, yes; and she wears her clothes well, and knows exactly what becomes her—that is quite an art, and a very important one; but I was not thinking of her looks, Penelope; she is certainly not responsible for her lack of beauty. But at first I thought her rather cold and decidedly flippant; she was always saying such extraordinary things, and so I got it into my head that she was rather shallow, and that she had no real depth."

"My dear Mrs. Linacre, that is quite a mistake."

"Well, I am beginning to find that out for myself— that brusque, decided manner of hers hides so much. When there was all that trouble about Heather and that poor boy Sydney, she showed a good deal of feeling. It is very nice of her coming over every day like this; and I am sure she is doing it out of pure kindness, because she thinks I am dull without Carus; and yet it is rather odd that she is not a bit anxious about Jack?"

"I am not so sure of that, Mrs. Linacre; however anxious she might be, I am pretty sure that Christian would show us a bright face."

"But it is not quite natural," objected Mrs. Linacre. "All the summer Christian has been as light-hearted and as full of frolic as a child; from the first she never seemed to miss or fret after Jack; I have so often puzzled over this."

"But she spends hours writing to him; she has never missed a mail yet," returned Pen. "I don't think you can quite judge of Christian by the ordinary standard—her case is rather exceptionable; she and Captain Linacre have seen so little of each other."

"But they had time enough to fall in love," returned Mrs. Linacre rather sharply; but, happily, Pen was spared the embarrassment of a reply, for at that moment some visitors were announced, and the rest of the afternoon was spent in discussing local topics. Tea was nearly over, and it was growing dusk when Christian and Heather returned from their ride; Pen thought they both looked a little excited. Christian stood for a moment beside Mrs. Linacre, drawing off her gloves.

"I wish we were nearer town," she said slowly; "there is a placard up at Silverton Station. Another battle has been fought under General French. What was the name, Heather? Oh, I remember, Elandslaägte; I was spelling it over the last mile."

Mrs. Linacre dropped her knitting; she had turned rather pale. "Do you think Jack was there?"

"Oh yes, he would be there!" returned Christian, but her voice was not as clear as usual; "it must have been the same day as Talana Hill—we ought to have heard about it yesterday. Come, Pen, it is getting late, and the carriage is waiting for us,"—for they were to drive home,—"I will just drink a cup of tea, while you put on your hat; we may as well go to the Vicarage and see if Mr. Disney has the evening paper."

"If he has, will you ask him to send it back by Locock?" exclaimed Mrs. Linacre eagerly; "I have half a mind to drive back with you myself." But both Christian and Heather dissuaded her from this.

But as Christian and Pen drove home through the autumn dusk, they little knew that at that moment Carus, with a white set face, was perusing the list of killed and wounded at the War Office.

" Killed in action—Captain Linacre."

XXVII

"HE KNOWS IT NOW"

Grief will come, and loss will come,
Saddening many a morrow;
But through all, though often dumb,
Blessing even sorrow,
Love, that knits the souls of friends,
Makes for all divine amends.
ANNIE MATHESON.

THREE hours later Carus was in the Vicarage study, and at the sight of his dazed, white face, the Vicar had started to his feet; and Charlotte, with womanly quickness, had gently pushed him into her husband's chair.

"You have some bad news to tell us?" she said, keeping her hand upon his arm; "do not hurry, take your own time," for Carus was breathless with haste and agitation; but he shook his head in a hopeless way, as though he failed to hear her.

"I have bad news; and my mother and Christian must be told," he said in a dull, thick voice. "I was at the War Office three hours ago, and I saw his name myself in the list; it was at Elandslaagte—killed in action. Jack—my only brother——" and then Carus's head went down on his crossed arms on the table with a stifled sob; and Charlotte looked at her husband and softly left the room. When she returned, he was calmer, and the two men were talking quietly together.

"Must they be told to-night?" the Vicar was asking; "it is nine now, and by the time we reach the Stone House, your mother will have gone to her room."

"We cannot help that," returned Carus; "anything will be better than the shock of seeing it first in the morning papers. The Fordhams might write to Christian, or some one in town might telegraph the news; it would not do to leave it."

"Then I will send a note to the King's Head at once

230

for a fly," replied Mr. Disney; "of course I shall go with you, my dear fellow; and Charlotte had better come across with us to Many Bushes," and then the three friends went out on their mournful errand.

The evening was chilly, and Christian had ordered a fire to be kindled in the sitting-room, and she and Pen had drawn up their chairs beside it, and were talking quietly. Christian had felt too restless and excited to read, so Pen had laid down her own book.

"I wish the London papers came earlier!" Christian was saying as the street door opened, and the next moment Mrs. Disney entered the room, followed by Carus. The Vicar was behind them.

"Why, Carus!" exclaimed Christian delightedly, "what a surprise! Whoever thought of seeing you to-night?" Then, as he saw his face more distinctly, her manner changed, and a frightened look came into her eyes. Mrs. Disney tried to say something, but Christian pushed past her and took hold of Carus with both her hands. "What is it?" she said in a hard voice. "Why don't you tell me quickly; it is something about Jack— he is hurt—wounded in that battle. Oh no—no!" as Carus looked at her sorrowfully,—"impossible! Jack is not dead!"

"Killed in action,"—the words came from Carus in the same dull, muffled voice. What was the use of trying to prepare her when she had guessed the news from his face?

An exclamation of horror broke from Pen, and the tears were running down Mrs. Disney's cheeks; for though she was by no means an emotional woman, the sadness of it all overwhelmed her. But for a moment Christian uttered no word; she stood there, her face paling perceptibly, clasping and unclasping her hands in a nervous manner. But the next minute she said something so strange that they all looked at her with alarm; only Carus failed to hear her. "Can't you say something nice to a fellow?" and then a dry little mirthless laugh followed the words.

Had the shock turned her brain? As that miserable little laugh rang in her ears, Mrs. Disney quietly put her arm round the girl.

"Come with me, dearest, to your own room," she said gently; "it will be better for you to be quiet;" but Christian looked at her in uncomprehending surprise.

"Why should I be quiet? There is no need for you to look so frightened. I am well—quite well—only a little bewildered—and Jack!" she pressed her hand on her forehead as though she were perplexed.

"It is for us to leave you," observed the Vicar hastily, as his ears caught the sound of carriage wheels in the drive. "Come, Linacre," taking his arm as he spoke; "Charlotte, my dear, you will stay as long as Mrs. Jack needs you. God bless you, my poor child, and give you strength for your heavy trial;" but as he took her cold hand and pressed it kindly, Christian made no sort of response—she seemed almost dazed.

When the gentlemen had gone, Mrs. Disney took hold of her with gentle force and placed her in a chair close to the fire. Then she knelt down beside her and gently chafed her hands—they were icy cold. Perhaps Christian felt the comfort, for she made no resistance.

"Have they gone to the Stone House to-night?" she asked presently.

"Yes, dear; it is late, but Mr. Linacre thought it would be better; he was so afraid that the news might reach them another way." Then Christian shivered.

"He was right; it is kinder—far kinder, but I ought to have gone too. Why did I not think of it—it was very selfish?"

"You go, my poor child!" Charlotte could hardly believe her ears.

"Yes, of course, isn't she Jack's mother?" Then with sudden nervous irritability, "Oh, Pen, do sit down; why are you hovering about me in that way?"

"I was bringing you some wine, dearest, because you looked so white."

"But I do not want it; I am well—quite fit as Jack would say. And Jack, poor fellow, is lying out on the veldt; he has fought his first and last battle. Are you sure there is no mistake?" turning almost fiercely to Charlotte. "No one has told me anything; they treat me as though I were a child or a lunatic. I don't want to be hushed up and petted—I want to know every-thing."

"But there is so little to know, Christian; I can only tell you what Carus said to us."

"Yes, yes!"

"He was at the War Office; he has a friend there, you know, and he showed him the list."

"Do you mean the list of the killed and wounded?"

Mrs. Disney nodded. "His brother's name was there, so you see there could be no mistake. Carus got into a hansom and drove at once to Beauchamp Gardens. He kept the cab; for Mr. Vigne was so upset by the news that he had to stay with him some time, and then he took the next train to Braybrooke. His uncle urged him to come, but Carus did not like leaving him; he says he will have to see him to-morrow."

"I hope it will not kill him," returned Christian in a low voice; "he is such an invalid, you know, and he was so fond of Jack, and so good to us both." There was a curiously pained expression about Christian's mouth as she said this: it reminded Charlotte of a child who felt very unhappy and could not cry.

"I trust it will not make Mrs. Linacre ill too," went on Christian. "I think Jack is her favourite; I must go to her to-morrow."

"Dear child, you must think of yourself," returned Mrs. Disney affectionately. "Mrs. Linacre will have her son and Heather; there will be no need for you to go too soon;" then Christian gave another of those dreary little laughs.

"You mean that I ought to stay at home and pull the blinds down, because I am Jack's widow; but I have never been a hypocrite—never. Do you know that Jack once told me that I was the truest person he had ever met. 'There is no humbug about you, Chriss; you are always absolutely sincere;' those were his very words."

"It was very high praise, Christian."

Mrs. Disney was trying to follow the girl's lead; but surely no newly-made widow was ever behaving in such a strange, unconventional fashion; but for that look of pain round her mouth and her exceeding paleness, Christian would have looked as usual.

"Yes, and I must always try to deserve them. I was so pleased and proud when Jack said that, and I want always to be true and like myself."

"To be sure you do, dear;" but Charlotte was clearly puzzled.

"You must not make me do things because other people do them, for that would be wrong. Listen to me, both of you, for I want you to understand, and when I see Mrs. Linacre I shall tell her too, when I married Jack I did not love him. Pen found that out, though she was kind and never told me so; but she was always so sorry for Jack."

"Oh, Chrissy dear, how can you say such things?" and Pen's cheeks were flaming.

"Why should I not say what is true? In your heart you were pitying us both, because you knew I did not care for Jack as you did for Walter."

"Oh, but—Chrissy!"

"Hush! we must not argue about it—not to-night—not to-night, when he is lying out there in the cold and mist;" and Christian's voice brought the tears again to Mrs. Disney's eyes.

"I married him because he was in trouble and needed help; and we were friends, and he was nice to me; and I was glad to help him, but,"—pausing a moment—"I am not sure it was the right thing to do."

Mrs. Disney was silent—Christian's words were no new revelation; she had grasped the truth instinctively a long time ago; but she knew it was better to let her talk. The girl was working off some torment of thought that was harassing her; but Christian had not much more to say.

"We were together so little," she went on, "and then he went away; but before he left, I knew he had begun to care for me in the right way."

"Yes, dear,"—it was Mrs. Disney who spoke—"you must have been glad to know that?"

"Glad!"—and now there was a look of anguish in Christian's eyes that filled Charlotte with dismay,—"it is that one thing that is troubling me—that he was nice to me, and that I never said a kind word to him, and now——"

"Stop, dearest! I cannot let you go on; you are torturing yourself needlessly; it may be all true what you have told us: that you did not absolutely love Captain Linacre when you married him; but, Christian, I have seen it for a long time—you have begun to care for him; and if he had come back, poor fellow!"—and here Charlotte choked a little—"he would have seen it for himself."

"Do you mean it?" and Christian grasped her dress; for the moment her face looked radiant. "Say it again—those very words."

"Not those very words, love; they shall be better ones. Dear Christian, you have grown to love your husband dearly, though perhaps you have never told him so; but you must not fret about that—he knows it now."

"He knows it now," Christian repeated the words as though she were a child conning a lesson. "Oh, Jack, Jack, if I had only been nicer to you!" and then for a little while Christian hid her face on her friend's shoulder; but though Charlotte and Pen could not restrain their tears, the young widow's eyes were quite dry.

There was very little more said. Christian would not hear of Mrs. Disney remaining the night.

"Why should you think of such a thing?" she said wearily; "I have Pen—but, indeed, I shall be better alone. You have done me good, and I am very grateful; and now you must go home," and so she sent her away.

Neither would she let Pen stay with her.

"You must not be hurt with me, dear," she said very gently; "but I want to be alone with Jack—and——" but though Christian never finished her sentence, Pen understood her.

"Then I will go and pray for you, my darling," was Pen's answer.

"Yes, we must all do that; but some of us will not pray well;" and then Christian closed the door resolutely and prepared for her long, sleepless night.

She was down at her usual time the next morning. Pen, who was making the coffee, looked at her anxiously; she thought Christian looked worn and ill, and there was a touch of nervous irritability in her manner as she drew up the blind and admitted the soft October sunshine.

" We are not in a town square, Pen," she said quickly;
" and the thrushes and blackbirds won't be shocked if we
show our faces at the window. Please give me some
coffee, for I am so parched;" but Pen noticed that the
piece of toast on Christian's plate was broken up into
fragments and left uneaten.

Pen waited for a few minutes, she had a message for
Christian; but she hardly knew whether it would be
wise to deliver it, but the next moment an opportunity
came.

" Will you send some one round to the King's Head,
Pen? I shall want a fly to take me over to the Stone
House."

" Oh, there will be no need to do that, Chrissy!" returned Pen eagerly; " I have had a note from Mrs. Disney just now—Mr. Linacre is driving in, as he means to
take the 11.11 train up to town, and Locock is to call for
any orders or message."

" That is very thoughtful of Carus," returned Christian. " I will be ready then; but there is no need for you
to go too." But Pen was not to be shaken off; she
pleaded so earnestly to accompany her friend that Christian reluctantly yielded. The drive was taken in silence;
but when the old butler, Hyde, came forward to assist
them to alight, Christian's lip quivered for a moment at
the sight of the old man's red eyes and shaking hands.

" Oh, Mrs. John, that I should have lived to see.this
day—my dear young master!" But Christian only bowed
her head in silence. At the head of the staircase Heather
met her, and gave her a long, loving kiss.

" How is she, Heather?" and the girl shook her head.

" She has been very ill all night. Carus never left
her until three. But she would get up this morning; and
Hitchens was helping her to dress, when she nearly
fainted. She is better now; but she is still on the couch
in her bedroom. She knows you are here, and would
like to see you."

The blinds had been lowered, but even in that dim
light Christian was shocked to see the alteration in her
mother-in-law's appearance. It was not only that she
looked ill, but she had suddenly become an old woman;

never all her life long did Janet Linacre recover wholly the effects of that sudden shock.

As Christian knelt down by her, she put out her arms with a feeble yearning gesture: " Oh, my poor child!" she said in a broken voice; " it is good of you to come to me; we must be much to each other—you and I—my dear boy's wife and his mother; we must try to comfort each other," and she would have drawn the girl into her embrace, but Christian shrank back.·

" No," she said a little wildly; " there can be no comfort for me until you know the truth—you are Jack's mother, and you have a right to know it;" and to Heather's dismay, Christian repeated the same dreary little confession that she had made the previous night to Mrs. Disney—saying almost the same words, as though her tired brain could find no others; but as she listened, there was a strange expression in Mrs. Linacre's sunken eyes, and she half raised herself on her pillows.

" What is this you are saying, Christian? Tell me again, you poor child. You married my boy without loving him, because you wanted to help him."

" Yes," returned Christian in the same dull, monotonous voice, as though she had set herself a task. " I knew he was nice, but I did not care much for him; but he was in trouble, and his uncle wished him to marry."

" Yes, yes; it was a whim of Jasper's. Go on—go on, my dear."

" He had made it a condition, and Jack was in a dreadful hole; and then he asked me to marry him. ' It will be like holding out your hand to a poor fellow who is drowning;' those were his very words—your son's words."

" And your answer, Christian?" Mrs. Linacre whispered the question.

" I said to him: ' I am going to help the drowning man,' and you know the rest. Mrs. Disney says I have begun to care for him, and that if he had come back——" but here Christian caught her breath with a little sob, but her eyes were bright and dry. Then she felt her mother-in-law's arm round her again, trying feebly to draw her
· closer.

" Christian, my poor child, why did you not tell me

this before? I should have understood things better. You helped my boy—you did your best to save him, and I never thanked you, my dear. Charlotte is right; if my Jack"—here the tears streamed from the mother's eyes— tears that relieved the oppressed brain and heart,—" if my poor boy had come back, you would have had a wife's love ready for him. Don't turn from me, my child; we must love and comfort each other for Jack's sake;" and Janet pressed the girl-widow to her breast with the utmost tenderness, and at that moment Christian felt something like peace steal into her sore heart; never again would those two women misunderstand each other.

XXVIII

ELANDSLAAGTE

A wicked old world, sirs, but all the same,
It's not for the soldier to bear the blame;
And duty is glory, and sweet is fame,
And we carried the ridge that day.
ALEXANDER CLUNY MACPHERSON.

THE midday meal was over at the Vicarage, and Mr. Disney had retired to his study for a quiet half-hour before it was time for him to go on his rounds, for he was a model parish priest, and the sick and feeble ones of his flock were never neglected. Night or day he was ready either to attend a dying bed or to listen to the tale of sorrow. "Our Vicar is the poor man's friend," observed one of his most faithful adherents; "he is never too busy to harken to an ould chap that is in a peck of trouble; he is like his Master, is parson; he is always going about doing good."

Mr. Disney was tired and sad at heart, and needed a rest sorely; but just as he had unfolded his *Times*—his one luxury—his wife entered the room; she looked anxious and disturbed.

"Graham," she said in her quick way, "here is a letter from Mr. Linacre; it has been brought by hand by a commissionaire. I am so afraid there is further bad news, and that Mr. Vigne is worse;" and it was evident from her husband's face that he feared it too.

Carus had remained the night in town, as his uncle's state caused great anxiety. He had sent a telegram to Heather, and Christian had at once telegraphed back that she would stay at the Stone House until his return.

"Troubles never come singly," muttered the Vicar, as he opened the envelope. Charlotte watched his face with undisguised anxiety; but she looked alarmed as a loud exclamation startled her.

"Good Heavens!" burst from his lips; "read it—read

239

it, Charlotte;" and the Vicar's face was strangely excited as he pushed the letter towards her. This was what
Charlotte read:—

I am sending this by hand, as I cannot leave my uncle; he had
a sort of seizure early this morning, and the doctors are somewhat
apprehensive of the consequences. I have wonderful news to tell
you. Herbert Frere, my friend at the War Office, has been down
to Beauchamp Gardens. Jack is alive. Oh, thank God! thank
God! It is Lieutenant Linkwater of the Lancers who is killed—
the similarity of names led to the mistake. Jack is wounded
rather severely in leg, and is probably in Ladysmith. That is all
we know, as I am kept here. I must ask you and Mrs. Disney to
break the news gently at the Stone House—Christian is there.

"Graham, Graham!" but for the moment Charlotte
could say no more; both husband and wife bowed their
heads reverently in silent thanksgiving for this great
mercy vouchsafed to their friends; but Charlotte's tender heart breathed a prayer for that other woman, to
whom, perhaps, the ill-fated officer had been nearest and
dearest. Alas, alas! she little knew how many women's
hearts were to ache and bleed before that cruel war was
over. How that pitiless veldt would be strewn with the
bravest of our men and officers—gallant young hearts
stilled in death—fighting for their Queen and their oppressed countrymen.

"Charlotte, we must go at once;" the Vicar's eyes
were bright and resolute; "if you will put on your hat,
I will get the bicycles ready;" and Charlotte needed no
second bidding. When did she ever delay when there
was an errand of mercy to be done? And these were
dear friends.

Braybrooke folk looked a little scandalised at the reckless speed of the two cyclists as they flew down the country roads; the commissionaire was still refreshing himself
in the Vicarage kitchen as they rode up the long avenue,
while the rooks cawed wildly over their heads. Not a
word had passed between them; but as the Vicar walked
up a steep little bit of hill, near Silverton, propelling his
machine, he hummed a bar or two from a well-known
oratorio: "How beautiful upon the mountains are the
feet of them that bringeth good tidings, that bringeth

good tidings, that publisheth peace!" And Charlotte, trudging on behind, smiled, well pleased, for she knew her husband's heart was glad within him—that it was given him to be the minister of consolation. Half-way up the avenue they came upon Heather; she was sitting on the stump of a tree, with the dogs round her, looking very sad and dejected; she brightened up a little at the sight of her friends.

"Oh, how kind of you to come!" she said, walking beside them, for they showed no intention of dismounting. "Christian will be so pleased; but you will not be able to see her just now, as she is with Aunt Janet. Carus is not coming home to-night," she continued in a melancholy voice; "Mr. Vigne is worse, and he cannot leave him."

"We heard from Mr. Linacre just now," returned the Vicar; and then they quickened their pace, and Heather found it impossible to keep up with them. When she reached the porch they had given up their bicycles to the footman, and Mr. Disney was talking to Hyde in a low voice; Charlotte had seated herself in Troy, and was trying to recover her breath.

"Dear Mrs. Disney, you ought not to have ridden at such a rate," remonstrated Heather, and she stopped in surprise, for the Vicar was behind her humming in quite a cheerful manner—rather a strange proceeding in a house of mourning.

"How beautiful are the feet of them that bringeth good tidings," chanted the Vicar, "that bringeth good tidings of good!" then, as Heather turned in great astonishment, she saw the gladness in his eyes.

"Oh," she said with a gasp, "you have some more news, good news!" Then Hyde joined the little group; and the Vicar, in a voice that would tremble a little in spite of all his efforts, read aloud Carus's letter; and as the news leaked out, quite a little army of servants, from the housekeeper to the scullery-maid, gathered in Troy. Hitchens was the last to hear the news; and it was to her that Heather presently turned a radiant face.

"What are we to do, Hitchens?" she asked. "If

16

Aunt Janet is asleep, we ought not to disturb her; but there is Mrs. Jack."

"My mistress is only dozing a bit, Miss Heather," returned Hitchens, sniffing with suppressed emotion, for she was a faithful soul and devoted to her mistress. "If Mrs. Disney were to go up and take her chance, there could be no harm done, to my thinking. Good news never kills, I'll be bound."

"Oh, you are wrong there, Hitchens!" returned Charlotte gravely; "there have been cases when the heart was weak,"—she stopped as one very sad instance recurred to her memory—"I could not take the responsibility without my husband;" then it was decided that Heather should creep into the room and tell Christian that the Vicar and his wife were below, and, if possible, induce her to come down to them. As soon as Heather had gone upstairs the servants dispersed, with the exception of Hyde and Mrs. Townsend, who, as old retainers, considered themselves privileged to remain; a few minutes later Heather came down to them alone.

"You may both go up," she said breathlessly; "Aunt Janet is awake and would like to see you; you will find Christian there. I shall be here if you want me," she continued; "but I had better not come in with you. Christian asked me to remain below; Aunt Janet is very weak still."

"Peace be to this house and all who dwell in it," said the Vicar with unusual solemnity, as he paused on the threshold with uplifted hand; it was his usual formula in a sickroom; the words thrilled Christian, who had never heard them before; it was at her the Vicar looked as he came forward into the room, but his strangely significant glance told her nothing.

Janet held out her hand with a pathetic smile. "It is good of you to come again, dear friends," she said in a low, hollow voice. "I was too ill to see even Charlotte yesterday; but I had Christian—I seemed to want no one but her."

"We hardly expected to see you," returned the Vicar, placing himself so that the dim light should fall on the invalid's face; he wondered how many hours Christian had sat in the darkened room, her face looked drawn and pale, and her eyes were heavy.

"God's hand is very heavy on us, Mr. Disney. My son—my dear boy;" but Janet could say no more; then the Vicar took her hand in his.

"Dear lady, I have a word for you and for Christian too—let me speak it now; heaviness may endure for a night, but joy cometh in the morning."

"Yes, I know," returned the poor mother; "but Christian is young, and the morning will be long in coming to her. I know that I shall go to him, but he will not return to me."

"Dear friend, you must not be too sure of that," returned Mr. Disney slowly; "there are strange things in life; people make mistakes sometimes in the rush and hurry of events—wrong names get into the lists——" he stopped, somewhat afraid that he had been too sudden, for Janet was sitting bolt upright with her sunken eyes fixed on him, and Christian had started to her feet, her figure swaying a little as though she were suddenly giddy.

"You have something to tell us? Jack! oh, Jack!" Christian could not articulate another word, for as the old Biblical expression has it, "Her tongue clave to the roof of her mouth;" then the Vicar took a hand of each of the excited women.

"I am the messenger of good tidings," he said clearly and distinctly; "your son, Mrs. Linacre, is still living; he is wounded, but not severely, we hope; it was a Lieutenant Linkwater who was killed at Elandslaagte."

Did Janet grasp the truth? A gray, ashen tint came over her face, but though her lips moved, no words were uttered, but the Vicar felt the pressure tighten on his hand, then she fell back on her pillows as though she had suddenly collapsed from weakness; but before anything could be said, Christian had knelt down beside her and taken her in her strong young arms.

"Do you hear that, dear?" she said in a broken voice. "God is good, so good to us. Jack—our Jack—is alive. Oh, the dear fellow!" And then, for the first time, Christian broke into a passion of tears.

An hour later Heather and Penelope were sitting to-gether in Troy, and Mr. Disney was with them. Penelope had ridden over earlier in the day to see how Christian had passed the night, but she had not remained long, and this was her second visit; she had walked over with some letters that had come by a later post, and had just heard the wonderful news. Heather had no wish to go into the drawing-room, so Hyde had kindled a fire in the big hall grate and lighted the lamps, and had just set out the little tea-table when Mrs. Disney came down to them; she looked tired but relieved.

"Christian is better now," she said cheerfully; "she is lying down in her own room; we have made her com-fortable, and Hitchens has brought her some tea. Her head is bad, but her fit of crying has relieved her; all these two days she has pent up her feelings, and the sudden joy has opened the floodgates. Poor dear! she cannot speak without the tears running down her face. Graham was afraid she would go into hysterics, but she controlled herself wonderfully."

"May I go to her?" asked Pen eagerly; but Charlotte shook her head.

"I have promised her that no one shall go near her for an hour—after that, I daresay, she will see you."

"And Mrs. Linacre, Charlotte?" asked her husband.

"Oh, I looked in as I passed! She is lying in the firelight looking so beautifully calm and happy, but so weak she can scarcely lift her hand; she thinks only of Christian, and is full of regret that she cannot take care of her. Now, Heather, will you give us some tea, and then I shall go back to her?" And then, as they sat under the shadow of the marble Hector and Andromache, they talked softly of the marvellous news that had reached them.

It was settled that Pen should remain for the night, and that the Vicar and his wife should be driven back later in the evening; but more than two hours passed before Pen was summoned to Christian's room. Mrs. Disney had very wisely persuaded her to go to bed—two nearly sleepless nights had exhausted her, and she was only fit to lie perfectly still; when Pen kissed her,

Christian opened her heavy eyes and put her arms round Pen's neck.

"Oh, I am so happy!" she whispered; "but I am so tired I cannot talk; I shall sleep like a baby to-night. God is so good—so good to spare me such a sorrow." A tear trickled down Christian's face as she spoke, and Pen did not dare say more.

"You were wise not to stay," observed Mrs. Disney; "nature is exhausted, and sleep will be the best restorative. Mrs. Linacre wanted Dr. Morton to give her a composing draught, but he knew there was no need. 'Mrs. John is young and healthy, and youth has plenty of recuperative power,' he said to me; 'it is Mrs. Linacre who will require care—her constitution has received a shock.'"

"I wish you could remain here to-night too," returned Penelope wistfully, for she had the greatest confidence in Mrs. Disney's judgment and good sense.

"I would gladly have done so," replied Charlotte; "but Mrs. Linacre will not hear of it—she is strangely thoughtful and unselfish. 'Go home with your husband, my dear,' were her words; 'I have my two daughters, and I know the Vicar is lost without you.' Isn't it delightful, Pen, to think how all this has drawn those two together?" And that night peace brooded over the inmates of the Stone House.

While Christian slept like a worn-out child, how was it faring with Jack Linacre? His first battle had been fought, but it might not be his last, as Christian feared; but though they little knew or guessed it, it would be many a long day before Jack would be able to tell them the story of Elandslaagte.

It was at eight o'clock on a bright summer morning when the first skirmish took place, but it was long after noon before the real advance began. French had sent to Ladysmith for reinforcements, and a couple of hours later the Lancers—Jack amongst them—were galloping amongst the billowy, russet-coloured hills, and a little later came Ian Hamilton, with the Devons and the Gordon Highlanders, and then the deadly fight began.

To add to the horrors of the scene, a dense black

cloud obscured the sky, and presently a torrent of rain lashed the faces of the men. To quote a contemporary account: "And now, amid the hissing of the rain, there came the fuller, more menacing whine of the Mauser bullet, and the ridge rattled from end to end with the rifle fire. Men fell fast, but their comrades pressed hotly on."

Khaki-clad figures swarmed up the ridge among the boulders. "What price, Majuba!" was the cry of some of the infantry as they climbed to the edge of the plateau.

There were gallant feats done that day which thrilled all English hearts as they read of them. Amid the litter of bodies a major of the Gordons, shot through the leg, sat philosophically smoking his pipe. Chisholm, Colonel of the Imperials, had fallen with two mortal wounds, as he dashed forward waving a coloured sash in the air.

"Retire be damned!" shrieked a little bugler, when the crafty enemy had sounded the British bugle call, "Cease fire and retire," and he blew "the advance," with all his strength.

It was while the Lancers and Dragoon Guards were prowling round the hills in the fading light that Jack got his wound. Lieutenant Linkwater of the Dragoons had had his horse shot under him, and was trying to mount another when a shot brought him to the ground, and the horse galloped away.

Jack, who was riding past, saw his plight and helped him to mount his own horse. As he did so, a company of retreating Boers dashed past them; one black-bearded fellow stooped and fired straight at the wounded officer. "I am done for, save yourself, Linacre," groaned the dying man; but Jack, wounded, but undaunted, clambered up on the saddle behind him and carried him into shelter. The white flag was up, the battle was over, camp-fires were lighted for the soldiers and prisoners, and fatigue parties were searching the hillside for the wounded. But it was morning before they found Jack, lying under a huge boulder, with stiffened limbs from the drizzling rain and cold. Beside him was the body of the young officer he had tried to save. "For God's sake, give me a drink and don't touch my leg!" were his first words when they found him at last. All his life long Jack would never forget that long, dark night on the veldt, when the tortures of thirst and the throbbing of his wounded leg made rest impossible, while the wind blew round his stony shelter, and the icy rain beat pitilessly on him. The next day Jack was in the hospital at Ladysmith, his wound aggravated by the night's exposure, and he, poor fellow, light-headed from pain. " You can give my love to Chriss," he said to his nurse; " Chriss is my wife, you know;" and then he lay and muttered to himself about a dark night and a lonely hillside, and some poor fellow lying stark and cold beside him; but the busy nurse could make nothing of his talk, and when she had given him a cool drink, she turned away to another patient.

XXIX

WAITING FOR NEWS

Forward! but not in gladness;
Sorrowful, hating the need;
Not with the brute-brave madness,
Throwing life as a worthless weed.
*   *   *   *   *
Forward! with straining sinew,
Saxon, or Norman, or Kelt,
With the grand young manhood in you,
Rocky slope or burning veldt!
ALEXANDER CLUNY MACPHERSON.

FOR some days Mr. Vigne's life hung in the balance, and for more than a week Carus found it impossible to leave the house even for a few hours; but when he was at last able to run down to Silverton to see his mother, he found Christian still at the Stone House.

"I shall mount guard here until your return," she said in her old crisp way; "your mother does not wish to part with me yet. Heather is getting jealous, but that cannot be helped;" but there was no trace of that ignoble passion on Heather's bright face.

"Oh, she is such a comfort to us!" she returned softly; "she manages Aunt Janet far better than Hitchens and I do. When Christian says a thing Aunt Janet seems to think it ought to be done, and she is quite meek and obedient, isn't she, Chriss?" but Christian only laughed in an amused way.

She knew well how necessary she had become to her mother-in-law. There were times when Janet could hardly bear her out of her sight, when her one pleasure was to talk of her boy Jack; Christian was quite content to listen. She suppressed bravely her longings for her dear little Many Bushes, and took up her day's task cheerily; here at least was something she could do for Jack— if she could do no wifely duty for his comfort, she could minister to his mother.

248

Janet had been very meek and submissive in the hour of sorrow, but with returning convalescence the old nature at times asserted itself—perhaps it was owing to her weakness; but she had hours of depression when it was almost impossible for her to battle against her despondent fancies—when she took dark views of everything. On these occasions Christian was a tower of strength to her, and her talk, at once breezy and full of cheerful energy, was an immense relief.

They had all gathered in Mrs. Linacre's dressing-room, for she was still too weak to move downstairs, and she was unwilling to lose her son's company; Carus was to return to town by an evening train. Mr. Vigne had been pronounced out of immediate danger by the physicians, but his state was still sufficiently critical to need the greatest care, and the doctors still forbade any conversation.

" And he does not know about Jack?" asked Mrs. Linacre in an astonished voice.

" My dear mother, the excitement would kill him; we must wait until he is strong enough to bear it; we none of us realised how fond he was of the dear fellow. We have all been so accustomed to Uncle Jasper's bad health and frequent illnesses that we forget how these repeated attacks must tell on him in the long run. Dr. Myrtle says ae will pull through this time, but another such seizure must carry him off."

" I wish I could see him," observed Christian wistfully; " he has always been so nice to me."

" It is very sad," sighed Janet. " Poor dear Jasper! but perhaps it is as well that he is spared our anxiety;" for Mrs. Linacre fretted sorely at the lack of news.

" Now, mater, how can you be so naughty?" Christian had adopted Jack's name for her mother-in-law; Janet always smiled when she used it. " Didn't we see in the papers that Jack was going on all right,—'Captain Linacre wounded severely in leg, doing well,'—and yet you can be so ungrateful?"

" Oh, I am not ungrateful, Christian!" Mrs. Linacre seemed quite distressed at the idea; " in my heart I am singing my *Te Deum* all day long, but I cannot always quiet my tears. My boy is wounded and in the hospital, and we cannot get news of him." Then Christian's face became grave, though she still strove bravely to maintain her bright optimism.

"We must be patient, mater; we cannot expect things to be done like magic. Jack will take no harm even if Ladysmith is surrounded. Why don't you tell her so, Carus—that there is no need to be anxious?" But Carus was cunning for once and feigned not to hear. For in his opinion things looked sufficiently black; the battle of Ladysmith had been fought, and the miserable disaster at Nicholson's Nek had occurred; about nine hundred British soldiers and their surviving officers were on their way to Pretoria. England was aghast at the woful news. Later on they were to read with aching hearts "How haggard officers cracked their sword-blades and cursed the hour they had been born;" while privates sobbed with their shamed faces buried in their hands. "Father, father, we had rather have died!" cried the Fusiliers to their priest; no wonder if men's eyes grew misty as they read the harrowing tale of Nicholson's Nek.

Carus knew well that twelve thousand British troops were shut up in Ladysmith, and that telegraphic communication with the town was interrupted; only that morning he had heard that the railway line was cut, and that the previous day the last train had escaped under a brisk fire, and as yet the relieving army had made no sign. A labyrinth of mountains closed round it—some near, others distant—and very soon the Boers had established "their circle of fire" and commenced shelling the devoted town. Carus might well be silent, his only word of comfort concerned Jack.

"It is very seldom that evil is unmitigated," he said presently; "perhaps, after all, it was better for Jack to be in the 'hospital;' he might have fared worse in the last scrimmage. Cheer up, mother; what would poor Mrs. Linkwater give to be in your place? Frere was telling me about her only yesterday. She is a widow; and that poor lad was her only son, and one of the finest young fellows you could meet anywhere;" and then Janet wept, and accused herself of ingratitude; but Christian soon coaxed her into a calmer mood.

It was only at the last moment that Carus found opportunity for a quiet word with Christian; he had gone into the library for a book he had left there, and she followed him; he turned at once to her.

"That is right, dear," he said, taking her hand; "I wanted to say something to you, but I could not get you alone. Christian, I won't thank you for your goodness to my mother, for I know you are doing it for Jack's sake, and one day he will thank you himself when he knows how unselfish you have been."

"Oh no, you must not praise me, Carus!" returned Christian, colouring up. "I have done so little; besides, I have grown so fond of your mother now. I shall stay at my post until you relieve me; indeed," as he looked at her a little keenly, "I am quite happy and comfortable here. Pen comes every day to see us, and dear Heather is so sweet and good to me, and—and I try not to let them see when I am a little down and anxious about Jack," and now there were tears in Christian's eyes.

"You are very good and brave, dear," he returned. All day he had been telling himself how greatly Christian had improved; she had lost her quick, brusque manner and had grown softer and gentler; the events of the last few weeks had stirred her nature to its depths. Christian was learning her woman's lesson of patient hopefulness under a somewhat heavy discipline, for only Pen guessed her anxiety on Jack's account.

"You have been very good—you see, I am praising you again; but, Christian, there is one thing I want to ask you: I am rather troubled about Heather—even in this short time she seems somehow changed."

"Changed! my dear Carus, what can you mean?"

"Well, not changed exactly, but all the same she is not the old Heather—the child Heather—who has been the sunbeam of the house. She has grown older and quieter, and seems to have lost some of her old frankness. You are smiling, Christian, as though you were incredulous, but indeed I am conscious of some difference; never before when I came home has Heather held aloof from me."

"Carus! indeed, this is only your fancy. Heather was

so happy and excited last night when she knew you were coming to-day. Things have been rather upsetting lately, and that affair with Sydney——"

" Oh, by the bye!" interrupting her, " that is one of the questions I wanted to ask you. Do you think the child repents her decision?"

" No, indeed, I am quite certain she does not," and Christian spoke with a decision that admitted of no doubt; " she is a little troubled about Mrs. Masters—of course you know she is ill at Berlin."

" Yes, but I have heard no particulars."

" Mrs. Linacre thinks it is her old complaint, but Sydney seemed anxious when he wrote; they are with some cousins—a Dr. Koch and his wife—extremely kind people. Heather answered the letter at once and told him about Jack. I saw her letter."

" Well!" there was a trace of anxiety in Carus's voice.

" It was extremely kind and sisterly—just such a letter as Heather would write; but when I told her so she looked a little sad. ' But it will not please him, Chriss, however kind it may be; nothing that I can do will ever please him again;' it is easy to understand what she meant by that."

" Yes, I see; still it was nice of her to write—she is a loyal little soul, Christian;" and then he got his book and bade her good-night. " Take care of yourself," he said affectionately, and Christian smiled and nodded. But her face was a little grave when Carus had left the room.

" Why are men so blind?" she said to herself; " women see much more quickly; if one could open his eyes, but I dare not—I dare not! We must do as we would others should do to us. Dear little Heather! but you shall be safe with me, darling;" and then Christian went to the book-shelves to look out another volume of the book she was reading to her mother-in-law, for she and Heather took it in turns to read aloud to the invalid during the long evenings.

It was a month before Carus was free to return home; Mr. Vigne had recovered from his severe illness, and had, in some measure, regained his normal condition; but those who were with him noticed there was more excitability and restlessness, as though he were conscious himself of added infirmity. " I am a poor old stick," he said to Christian, on her first visit to him; " I am not worth any of this fuss and care;" but when Christian spoke of Jack, Uncle Jasper's eyes grew moist at once. " Ay, I am glad the lad's alive; somehow it did not seem natural that he should be in his grave—the young scamp—while I am left like a scarecrow in life. Shut up in Ladysmith! Pooh! what of that? Haven't we Buller and an army? Jack will have a tale to tell us when he comes home;" and Mr. Vigne wrapt his gorgeous dressing-gown round him with his shaking hand; " a young scamp," Christian heard him mutter again; " but for pluck and daring he'll beat the record."

It was not until the beginning of December that Christian returned to Many Bushes, and settled into her quiet home life again with Pen. The last week of her stay at the Stone House had been saddened by the intelligence of Mrs. Masters' death, which had taken place very suddenly. Mrs. Linacre felt the loss of her old friend and neighbour acutely. She had long been aware that Mrs. Masters suffered much at times from a painful malady that must eventually become fatal; but the poor woman had kept this knowledge from her son, and it was only towards the last that Sydney realised her critical condition. The young fellow seemed quite crushed by this fresh misfortune; and in the brief note that he wrote to Heather in return for her kind letter of sympathy, he seemed to have lost all interest in life. " I can make no plans," he wrote. " I think I shall stop on here with the Kochs; they are kind people. I cannot face the idea of coming back to Chesterton without my mother."

" This is a lesson to me not to judge people so harshly," observed Christian one day to Heather. " I never could bring myself to like that poor woman. I thought her self-indulgent and rather artificial and affected—you know what I mean; and all the time, poor soul, she was making those heroic efforts for her son's sake."

" I don't think I loved her very much myself," returned Heather frankly; " but from a child she has always been so good to me. I don't like to think how I must have pained her. You know, she would not let me go and bid her good-bye."

" But, she sent you a message, Heather."

" Yes, a very kind one;" but Heather told no one but Christian of the little note scrawled by a feeble hand that had been enclosed in Sydney's letter.

Heather, darling, be good to my boy when I am gone. How is he to live alone at Chesterton? Oh, he is so unhappy, but he tries to hide it from me! Do not harden your heart against him. With my dying breath, dearest, I beg you to comfort him.—Your loving friend,

                         Lydia Masters.

" I wish she had not written it," sighed Heather. Her young face looked quite careworn as she spoke.

" It was only natural that she should try to do her utmost for her son," returned Christian. " It is very painful of course; but you must not allow it to influence you against your judgment."

" Oh, I am so glad you say that!" in a tone of relief. " Of course, even this can make no difference. It would be wrong for me to marry Sydney—every day I realise that more. I could not do it, Christian,—I could not—I could not." And Heather shuddered as though she were under the influence of some strong emotion.

Christian was thankful to be at home again, though she missed her daily rides. But Carus, who was always thoughtful for her comfort, arranged that Fairy should be sent over to Braybrooke twice or three times a week, so that she could ride with him and Heather; and as she generally remained to luncheon at the Stone House, Mrs. Linacre would not feel herself neglected.

Christian felt happier at Many Bushes. The daily services were a comfort to her, and the society of her friends at the Vicarage a never-failing pleasure. Charlotte thought that Christian showed both good feeling and good taste in refusing any form of gaiety that winter.

" I cannot understand how people can have the heart to go to balls and parties with all these dreadful things happening," she said one day at the Vicarage. " I cannot help it if people are offended. I am not going to dance and enjoy dinner-parties while poor Jack is starving perhaps in Ladysmith."

Christian adhered firmly to this resolution. " The black week," as it might well be called, had just ended, with its terrible record of defeat and disaster. The massacre of the Highlanders, and the death of the gallant Wauchope at Magersfontein; the defeat of Gatacre at Stormberg; and a few days later, of Buller at Colenso. And a bitter sense of humiliation and dismay prevailed through the Empire—men began to realise the magnitude of the task that they had undertaken with such light hearts.

But in spite of crushing defeats, the indomitable English pluck refused to own itself beaten. The old British lion rose from his lair and shook his shaggy mane with a roar of defiance. The latent resources of the vast Empire were to be employed. The grand old veteran, Lord Roberts, with the briliant Kitchener as his chief of staff, was to be entrusted with the direction of the campaign. The remaining army reserves were called, and ten thousand men were sent out; and amongst other provisions, a strong contingent of volunteers, and a yeomanry mounted force, were to be despatched to South Africa. And so the weary weeks passed on.

" I think we only lived to read the papers," Christian said long afterwards to Mr. Vigne. " When I woke in the morning that was my first thought; and when they had been read, the work of the day seemed over, and I only looked forward to the morrow."

But when Christian said this, she was minimising her daily duties. There were her constant visits to the Stone House, to cheer and enliven Mrs. Linacre; and her spare afternoons were always spent at the Infirmary. The Vicar noticed with approval that she was seldom absent from Evensong. Indeed, in those sad days of anxiety, Christian's energy never failed; and it was only in the evening, as she and Pen sat by their fireside, that she would ever own herself tired.

And so the last days of December passed away, and the New Year dawned somewhat gloomily on England. Ladysmith had not yet been relieved; and Christian and the inmates of the Stone House were still waiting for news of Jack.

XXX

Red-Headed Celt, and Khaki

Nothing makes a man strong like a call upon him for help.—
MacDonald.

The love of an innocent soul is often the guardian angel that
guides a man's steps to the best actions of his life.—Anon.

Early in January, when Heather came over to Many
Bushes one morning with a message from Mrs. Linacre,
she told Christian that they had heard that Sydney Masters was at Chesterton. "He has been there three or four
days," she went on; "and he has not let us know, or
Carus would have gone to him at once. Don't you think
it is rather strange,—and after all our letters too?"
Heather spoke in a pained voice.

"How did you hear of it?" asked Christian.

"Dugald met him in the Market Square on Tuesday.
He was coming from the station and seemed in a great
hurry; he passed Dugald without speaking, and a moment later he ran after him and asked how they all were
at the Stone House. 'If you see any of them,' he added,
'would you tell them that I shall be too busy to look in
for a day or two?'"

"Did Dugald say how he looked?" Dugald was a
young Scotchman who had been for some years a confidential servant to Carus. He was an educated man, and
had helped him in copying papers, and looking out refer-
ences for his literary work. He had lately married, and
he and his wife had a small stationer's shop in the market-
place. His wife had been the national schoolmistress;
and the Vicar and Mrs. Disney thought very highly of
her.

"Dugald said he looked pale and fagged, but not otherwise ill. 'He looked older, and a bit sober,' were Dugald's
words. Carus went over to Chesterton after dinner that
evening, because he and Aunt Janet could not bear to

256

think of Sydney sitting alone in those big rooms; but he was up in town, and was not expected back that night."

"And he has not turned up yet?"

"No! I can't think what makes him so busy. Carus saw Robarts—he is the gardener at Chesterton,—and the man told him that the Master went up to town every day and seldom came back until the last train. So Carus, of course, says it is no use trying to find him. We must just wait until he comes of his own accord."

"Yes; and then he will explain things for himself. Don't worry, Heather; he will be sure to come sooner or later." Christian would not own that she thought Sydney's behaviour to his old friends somewhat strange. She hardly wondered that Mrs. Linacre and Heather felt rather hurt.

But a few days later the mystery was cleared up. Carus, who had been to town for a few hours, came face to face with Sydney in the Great Central Station, and they travelled down to Braybrooke together. The compartment was empty, and Carus had his tube, and Sydney soon explained matters to him. He had enrolled himself in a company of the Imperial Yeomanry who were going out to the front, and his visits to town were to procure his outfit and uniform.

"I was coming over this evening to tell you about it," he observed; "we are to start next week."

"What put it into your head?" asked Carus. He was very much surprised at Sydney's news.

"Well, I was getting pretty sick of idleness, and my life at Berlin bored me, and yet I could not make up my mind to come back to Chesterton. It seemed to me as though I hated the thought of the place, and had lost interest in everything."

"Oh, but that sort of thing always passes, you know!" replied Carus.

"Yes, I daresay, but I am a coward, I suppose. Well, I had a letter from Rupert Blount; he is the son of that old Ralph Blount who used to kick up such a shindy at the vestry meetings."

"Oh, every one for ten miles round Silverton knows old Blount!" observed Carus with a smile.

" Of course they are only farmers," went on Sydney;
" but Rupert is a nice fellow, and he is a chum of mine.
He told me that he had joined the Imperial Yeomanry,
and meant to be off as soon as possible; and that night
I made up my mind to go too."

" Do you think you will like soldiering, Sydney?"

" That remains to be proved; anyhow, it will be occupation and take me out of myself. You know I can ride,
and I am a very fair shot, and I have had some training
too with the Volunteers. I am up to my eyes in business,
for there is a good deal to settle, but I will come over for
an hour after dinner."

Carus told his mother and Heather that he thought it.
was the best thing Sydney could do. " It has roused him
already," he went on; " he looks better and less depressed
than I expected to find him; but he certainly feels his
mother's death a great deal."

The meeting with his old friends tried Sydney, and at
first he was very silent and constrained; but they were
all very kind to him. And after a time he recovered himself, but it was evident that he could not trust himself
to say much to Heather. He spent Sunday evening at
the Stone House, and on this occasion he brought Heather
one or two valuable ornaments belonging to his mother
which he knew had been put aside for her. They were a
pearl and gold chain, and a cross of sapphires and diamonds. Heather's face wore rather a distressed expression as she stood with the open case in her hand.

" You need not scruple to wear them, Heather," observed the young man, reddening as he noticed her reluctance to accept the gifts. " My dear mother always
intended you to have them; they are not from me;" the
last words were said with a little bitterness.

" He is quite right," interposed Carus hastily. " You
must not refuse them—the gifts of the dead are sacred;"
and then Heather closed the case and said a few words
of thanks in a low voice.

Sydney had promised to say good-bye on the day he
was to leave Chesterton. Heather had expressed a wish
to see him in khaki, and it was understood that he would
dine at the Stone House and go up to town by the last

train; and Mrs. Linacre had asked Christian to come for the night. But in the afternoon Sydney sent a message to Carus to tell him that he was likely to be detained by some necessary business with his lawyer, and that he should only be able to look in on his way to the station. Heather seemed much disappointed, but Carus and Christian mutually agreed that Sydney wished the leave-taking to be a hurried one, and they were right.

Dinner that evening was rather a dismal affair. Heather looked pale and ate little, and Mrs. Linacre, who felt the parting excessively—for Sydney was like one of her own children—scarcely responded to Christian's attempts at conversation. They were all assembled in the drawing-room when Sydney at last made his appearance. No one had heard the carriage drive up, and as he was unannounced, they were all a little startled at the sight of the khaki-clad figure in the doorway. He came forward, his handsome young face white with suppressed emotion.

"I have not a moment to spare," he said hurriedly; "Blount is outside, and we must not lose this train. Mr. Horsley kept me until half an hour ago;" and then, as Janet gave him her motherly embrace and blessing, he said a few fords to her in a low voice, and then shook hands with Christian. The next moment he was beside Heather; for a second he hesitated, but Heather quietly put up her face and kissed him before them all.

"God bless you, dear Sydney, and bring you back safe to us!" she said very gently.

No one present—certainly not Sydney himself—misunderstood that innocent, childlike caress. The young man looked at her sweet face a moment with an expression of mute reverence and love; then he raised the little hand to his lips and left the room, followed by Carus. No one but Christian saw Heather again that night, for the girl fretted sorely over parting with her old playmate.

"If he should get killed, will it be my fault?" she kept saying over and over again. Heather was so downcast the next day that Christian suggested that a little change might do her good, and as Mrs. Linacre made no objection, she took her back with her that afternoon; and Heather spent a peaceful week at Many Bushes.

Christian's plan had been so successful that she was emboldened to make a further proposition. She had promised to spend ten days or a fortnight with Mr. Vigne, and she begged Mrs. Linacre to let Heather accompany her. Her society would do Uncle Jasper good, for the girl was a great favourite of his, and a longer change would be beneficial. And as Mrs. Linacre was rather uneasy at Heather's dejection and drooping spirits she readily consented to this, and a pleasant fortnight was spent in Beauchamp Gardens.

Christian adhered steadily to her resolution of refusing all gaieties; she mortally offended her cousin by declining to appear at a large dinner-party in Mandeville Street. "Until Ladysmith is relieved, and we know that Jack is safe, I will accept no such invitations," she said firmly. But though Adelaide pretended to sneer a little, in her heart she respected her cousin's scruples.

Christian dined once or twice quietly in Mandeville Street, while Heather remained with Uncle Jasper. And on two afternoons Mrs. Fordham took her for a drive. "It is such a treat to have you to myself, my dear Christian," she said on one occasion; "there is so much I have to tell you. I am very much worried, my dear, about Adelaide; she is very self-willed and headstrong, and I am afraid she will do the wrong thing."

Now Christian already had an inkling that something was in the wind at Mandeville Street. Her aunt had dropped mysterious hints from time to time in her letters, and Adelaide seemed anxious and preoccupied. A certain Cluny Macgregor had appeared on the scene. Christian had encountered him once when she had run in one morning, and had found him alone with Adelaide in the morning room. He had taken his leave almost at once, and Christian had only seen him for a moment. He was a big, rather hard-featured man, apparently between fifty and sixty. And Christian had certainly not been prepossessed by his appearance—red hair and high cheekbones not being her idea of manly beauty. She had a strong presentiment that it was on the Macgregor subject that Mrs. Fordham wished to talk to her.

"I hope there is nothing wrong, Aunt Caroline?"

" Well, my dear, I suppose most people would not consider it wrong; but it is a heavy trial to me, I assure you. You may remember, Christian, that in my recent letters I mentioned a Mr. Cluny Macgregor."

" I remember it very well, Aunt Caroline; you told me that Adelaide had seen a great deal of a Mr. Macgregor, and that he was a widower, and a very clever man. I rather guessed from the way you wrote that he was paying Addie a good deal of attention."'

" My dear, he is perfectly devoted to her; and I must say in my opinion that it is very ridiculous for a man of that age, with four grown-up daughters, to want to marry again. It is all very well for Adelaide to say that he is full of energy and in the prime of life, for I know he is sixty, if not more. Why, his eldest daughter is Adelaide's age, and a plainer set of young women I never saw in my life; it is not likely that any of them will be married, though they are amiable enough, poor things."

" And do you really think that Adelaide intends to accept Mr. Macgregor?" asked Christian in some surprise; for it seemed to her that Adelaide, with her money and good looks, ought to make a better match; a big raw-boned Scotchman, with four plain daughters, did not sound very attractive.

Aunt Caroline heaved a billowy sigh. " My dear, I am certain she intends to marry him, and every day I expect her to tell me that they are engaged. I have said all I can on the subject, but I can make no impression on her; when I pointed out to her that his age and family were decided obstacles, she was quite annoyed with me. ' I consider our respective ages quite suitable,' was her answer; ' you forget I am not young, mother; and as I am already much attached to the Macgregor girls, the family will be no difficulty to me.' "

" I wish you liked him better, Aunt Caroline."

" My dear, I never did like red hair, and I am quite sure he has a temper, though Adelaide has not found it out. Look at his massive jaw, and his mouth is like iron. I am certain those poor girls dare not contradict him. It is ' Father says this,' and ' Father likes that,' as though they had not a will of their own; I must say, Christian, that, with all my old-fashioned notions, I do not care to hear women over thirty talk as though they were in the schoolroom; and to listen to her, Minna Macgregor might have been a slip of a schoolgirl."

" I don't quite understand why Adelaide wishes to marry him, unless she is in love with him," returned Christian; but Mrs. Fordham negatived this at once.

" She does not pretend to be in love with him: she only professes to respect and admire him. Not that there is anything to admire," continued Mrs. Fordham dejectedly; " unless she values weight, and I pity the horse that carries him, for Cluny Macgregor is the heaviest man I know."

" Is he rich, Aunt Caroline?"

" No, my dear, he is fairly well off, and I believe Macgregor House is rather a big place; but he is not nearly such a good match as Mr. Linacre would have been. Do you know,"—dropping her voice mysteriously—" I have always had an idea that Adelaide had a fancy for Mr. Linacre, in spite of his deafness? She was very much put out that he was all those weeks in Beauchamp Gardens, and only called twice, and refused all our invitations. I cannot help thinking she would have preferred him to Cluny Macgregor, if she could have had the choice. And he is certainly the last son-in-law that I would have selected."

" It is really very hard upon you, Aunt Caroline."

" Would you believe it, Christian,"—and here Mrs. Fordham's voice dropped again—" Addie actually wanted me to promise that I would live with them? I told her that there were limits to everything; and that nothing would induce me to leave my comfortable home. If you choose to leave me, that is your affair, I said to her; but there is no reason why, if you are doing a foolish thing, that I should do another."

" That was rather strong, Aunt Caroline," returned Christian, smiling; but even a worm will turn, and much-enduring, placid-tempered Aunt Caroline was asserting herself for once.

Adelaide had been a little taken aback by her mother's plain speaking. " If you have made up your mind to marry Mr. Macgregor, you will do it, I suppose, and nothing I can say will turn you; but I am not going to live with a son-in-law of my own age, so you may as well say no more about it." And for once Adelaide had held her tongue.

"I really cannot understand it," reiterated Christian thoughtfully; but she changed her opinion five minutes later, when Mrs. Fordham informed her that Mr. Macgregor would probably have a baronetcy before long.

"His old cousin is eighty-five," she observed; "so he cannot live many years. I am afraid it is sad to say this of a daughter, but I am sadly afraid, Christian, that this has some influence with Adelaide." And Christian agreed with her; but she was very kind and sympathetic, and after a time Aunt Caroline seemed more comforted.

Christian had merely laughed at the idea that she should break up her establishment because Adelaide intended to be married. "You must be firm and not let them impose on you," she said; and Mrs. Fordham, with much solemnity, assured her niece that nothing would induce her to live in Scotland.

Aunt Caroline's prognostications were soon verified. For the day following this conversation, Adelaide came to Beauchamp Gardens to announce her engagement. Christian gave her congratulations with due decorum.

"I do hope you will be happy, Addie," she said a little wistfully.

"Oh, as to that," returned her cousin composedly, "I am old enough not to expect married life to be all roses and sunshine! Most people have their troubles, and I shall have mine, I daresay; but as every one says that Cluny made an excellent husband to his first wife, he is not likely to turn Bluebeard now. I told him that I was rather a determined sort of person, and that he must not expect me to yield to an opinion unless I saw the force of it. But he said I should have as much of my own way as would be good for me."

"Your mother thinks Mr. Macgregor has a temper, Addie."

"I daresay he has," replied Adelaide coolly; "I don't care for meek men; I would much rather have a strong man with a touch of the devil in him. I was only scolding Minna the other day for letting her father tyrannise over her. I mean to stand up for those girls when I am married and not let Cluny put on them so much," and Adelaide looked very handsome and resolute as she spoke; "they lead such dull lives, poor things! It is quite an event for Minna to come up to London; but I mean to change all that. Now, Christian, I must go; I have only called to tell you the news, and to know if you will dine with us to-night—Cluny and Minna will be with us." Then Christian promised to join the family gathering.

"Well, Chriss, what do you think of your new cousin?" asked Heather rather mischievously when Christian returned that evening; but Mrs. Jack made a little grimace.

"He is a red-headed Celt, and I am not sure that I would care to offend him," was the reply; "I think his language would be rather powerful. All the evening I was saying to myself, 'Poor Addie, poor deluded Addie!' But I am not sure, Heather, that she will not come out grandly in the character of a stepmother."

XXXI

"Can You Keep a Secret?"

If thou art blest,
Then let the sunshine of thy gladness rest
On the dark edges of each cloud that lies
Black in thy brother's skies.
    If thou art sad,
Still be thou in thy brother's gladness glad.
                              A. E. Hamilton.

"Pen, do you believe in presentiments?"

"I don't know—yes—I think so;" but Pen looked a little preoccupied as she answered the question; an open letter lay beside her plate, and she was giving her breakfast a very divided attention.

"Well, I have a presentiment that something pleasant is going to happen to-day," continued Christian; "I felt so when I woke—there was a touch of spring in the air; I could hardly believe it was February; and the blackbird was singing quite loudly too."

"Yes, I heard him;" Pen still spoke absently.

"You are not attending to me one bit," with a touch of impatience; "you had better finish your letter, and then we can talk afterwards."

"Oh, I finished it long ago!" returned Pen hastily; "I was only thinking over something Walter has written. He has given up the idea of St. Philip's, Chriss; he is afraid he would not be able to work happily with the Vicar. He thinks the ritual excessive; Walter is only a moderate High Churchman, you know, and he does not quite like the way things are done at St. Philip's."

"Then he was right to give it up; but it seems a pity, as the pay is so good."

"Yes, that is the worst of it; but from all one hears, Walter would have been dreadfully hard-worked. He says two curates are needed for the work; I cannot help being thankful that he should be spared such a strain;

265

but it is rather serious if he cannot get a curacy soon—
he is to leave St. Cuthbert's in the middle of May."

"Oh, there is plenty of time—nearly three months—
so you need not look so anxious! You are not Penny-
wise this morning, but Penny-foolish; and I wish Mr.
Hamill could see that little furrow in your forehead."
Then Pen laughed; Christian looked so unusually bright
this morning that she wished that she could feel more
cheerful. Christian could have given no adequate reason
for her good spirits.

The situation in South Africa was still causing anxiety.
Buller, beset with difficulties, had not yet made his final
advance; but Kimberley had been relieved, and why not
Ladysmith? And so the promise of spring and the blackbird's song seemed to lighten her burdens, and to give
her a renewed feeling of hope. Pen felt a little ashamed
of her depression, but she always shared her lover's
moods. On his last visit to Braybrooke, Walter Hamill
had seemed dull and out of spirits; he felt leaving St.
Cuthbert's, as the work had been congenial to him, and
he liked the Vicar and his fellow-curates, and he knew
how the men and boys at the Club would miss him.

"That is the worst of being a curate," he had said to
Pen; "one has to move on at the will of other men;
not that I have a word of blame against the Vicar. I
know he would keep me if he could; but it is a world
of change, Pen," and Walter sighed as though he found
life somewhat difficult.

Christian knew Mrs. Mills would be waiting for her,
so she left Pen to read her letter over again in peace;
but half an hour later she looked in to say that she was
going across to the Vicarage to ask for an address that
Mrs. Disney had forgotten to give her.

She found Charlotte at her writing-table, surrounded
with housekeeping books; but she pushed them aside
and greeted her visitor with a very bright face.

"I am afraid I am interrupting you!" exclaimed Christian, rather repenting of her early visit.

"Not at all; I am always busy, as you know, and I am
always pleased to see my friends. I wonder what put it
into your head to come across this morning; I was long-

ing to see you, but 'I had no opportunity of speaking to you after service."

" Why not!" in some surprise; " we walked together to your door."

" Oh, but Pen was there!" was the somewhat perplexing answer, " and I did not want to say anything before her. Christian, can you keep a secret?"

" Better than most people, ma'am."

" Well, it is only for a few hours, and Graham said I might tell you. You know he went up to town yesterday."

" Yes, to attend the meeting at St. James's Hall."

" Oh, he had other fish to fry as well! Mr. Hamill was at the meeting too, and Graham had tea with him in Roskill Street."

" Pen had no idea of that!" returned Christian, rather surprised; " she had a letter from Mr. Hamill this morning, and he never spoke of Mr. Disney's visit."

" Oh, I can explain that!" returned Charlotte. " Mr. Hamill had written his letter the previous night, and had omitted to post it; he found it under a book when Graham had gone, and sent it off at once."

" And he kept Mr. Disney's visit for his next letter?"

" Oh, of course he means to tell her! Well, Christian, rather an important piece of business was settled during Graham's visit. You know, how grieved we are to lose Mr. Bates; he is such a steady worker and takes such an interest in things. Well, Graham went down to Battersea yesterday with the fixed purpose in his mind of asking Mr. Hamill to take the curacy."

" Mrs. Disney!" and Christian's eyes quite sparkled with pleasure; this was good news indeed.

" You may be sure that Mr. Hamill was not long in making up his mind, and that he accepted it gratefully. He and Graham are capital friends already; Graham has had this in his thoughts ever since he knew Mr. Bates would have to leave us. ' Hamill is just the man for me,' he said the very first day he saw him; Graham has always been fortunate in his curates."

" It is a wonderful piece of good fortune for Mr. Hamill," returned Christian; " he was only a junior curate at St. Cuthbert's."

"Mr. Bates was an older man, and Graham gave him a hundred and eighty pounds a year. Mr. Hamill is to begin at a hundred and thirty, but he will probably be raised in a year or two's time. Graham means to have a deacon as junior curate; he rather thinks Edgar Allonby will suit him; he is a nephew of Mrs. Allonby at Broom House; there is some talk of his being ordained on Trinity Sunday."

"Oh, I am so glad; I always liked the look of him!"

"He will be like a son to Graham; you have no idea how he fathers the young curates. Well, I see you approve of my secret, Christian, but I have not quite finished my yarn; I have such a nice plan in my head for Mr. Hamill's comfort. The Dugalds are going to let their two best rooms—the one overlooking the market-place is so pleasant and cheerful, and really quite nicely furnished, and the bedroom behind it is quite large enough for a gentleman; and I want Mr. Hamill to take them."

"What an excellent idea! and the Dugalds are such a thoroughly good sort of people."

"Alice Dugald is one of the best people I know," returned Charlotte; "I am really attached to her, and her husband is a most intelligent man. Mr. Hamill will be in clover with them. Graham and I sat up quite late last night discussing things, and I could hardly get to sleep; I was so hard at work trying to choose a position for Mr. Hamill's writing table."

"It is almost too good to be true," observed Christian. "Dear Pen, how happy she will be at the thought of seeing him every day! So my presentiment was true;" and she told her friend how she had awakened with the feeling that something pleasant would happen.

"I am a devout believer in presentiments," returned Charlotte; "coming events, pleasant or otherwise, often cast their shadows before them. Now, Christian, you must promise not to let out a word of this to any one; it is a secret, and must be faithfully kept until to-morrow evening."

"Do you mean that Mr. Hamill will not write to Pen to-day?"

"Most assuredly he will not; but he is coming down

to-morrow afternoon, and will occupy our spare room for the night. Graham wants some more talk with him; but he means to call at Many Bushes on his way here to tell Pen everything."

" And what time will that be? Pen will be in the school until four."

" I should think Mr. Hamill would hardly arrive before five, or a little after."

" Then Pen will be at Evensong !"

" Well, never mind," smiling at Christian's excitement; " he will probably follow her and attend Evensong too, and you can give him his tea afterwards; he need not turn up at the Vicarage until half-past seven, so they can have time for a nice talk. Now I really must send you away, while I do my accounts; and do, pray, try to look a little less cheerful, Christian, or Pen will guess something;" but the next moment they both started like a pair of guilty conspirators, for there stood Pen on the threshold, with a pink woollen shawl drawn over her head, and framing her soft, delicate face.

" I could not think what kept you so long, Chriss," she said innocently; " I thought you had only gone across for an address; have you forgotten that you arranged to go over to the Stone House this morning and help Heather with her work?" for a young woman at Silverton, in whom she was interested, had recently given birth to twins, and Heather, who was skilful with her needle, had set herself to add largely to the babies' scanty wardrobe.

" I don't think I actually promised, Pen," returned Christian; she did not like to own that the matter had quite slipped her memory.

" I am quite sure that Heather will be expecting us," replied Pen decidedly; " and we ought to take over the flannel wrapper that you finished last night; the baby boy has nothing but an old shawl."

" Oh dear !" sighed Christian; she was not at all in the mood to sit and sew in Mrs. Linacre's dressing-room, and to talk to her and Heather about all kinds of extraneous things; but Charlotte came unexpectedly to her rescue.

" Why should not Pen go over alone," she observed sensibly; " surely Heather will be satisfied with that, and you can stay here and have luncheon with us; it is Graham's leisure afternoon, and we rather thought of going over to Broom House. I am sure you owe the Allonbys a visit;" and this proposition was so attractive to Christian that she eagerly accepted it, and Pen was allowed to have no voice in the matter.

"I shall leave you in peace for an hour to finish your accounts!" she exclaimed, as she followed Pen out of the room, but she came back for a final whisper.

"You did that very cleverly; I did not want to go to the Stone House. Heather is so quick, and so is Carus; they would both have guessed something from my face. You need not hurry back, Pen," she said carelessly as she gave her the wrapper; "the evenings are much lighter now—the Allonbys are sure to keep us a long time; tell Heather to send me another night-dress to make;" and Pen nodded and rode off.

Christian spent a delightful day with her friends; she was able to discuss Mr. Hamill's prospects freely with the Vicar, and to make all sorts of arrangements with Mrs. Disney for his comfort. "Dear little Pen, I do love to think how happy she will be to-morrow!" were her last waking thoughts that night.

Pen was rather mystified by Christian's high spirits the next morning; she seemed to have put her own anxieties in the background; and as they sat at work in their sunny little sitting-room, she was quite the Christian of old.

"I wish it were not your day at the school, Pen," she remarked when luncheon was over; "it is such a lovely afternoon, and we might have done a little gardening;" but Pen was far too conscientious a young person to be seduced into playing truant, neither could Christian induce her to stay away from Evensong.

"I am sure you are tired, Pen; you look quite flushed," said the temptress artfully; "those children take it out of you."

"They were a little troublesome certainly," observed Pen.

"Then why not stay at home and have a rest, dear?"

"Oh, church always rests me!" returned Pen, for she

was a pious little soul and lived her religion in a sweet, unobtrusive way, and then Christian ventured to say no more. Charlotte gave them a quick look as they took their seats in the chapel, and the service had hardly begun before a tall, clerical figure came in and took the vacant seat behind Christian. Pen flushed up and looked round at Walter as though she were very much startled; but a smile reassured her. " It frightened me a little to see you come in like that so unexpectedly," she said to him in the porch; "I thought something had happened, and I was obliged to look at you." But all the rest of the service Pen's fair head was bent devoutly over her book, and if now and then she paused in her responses to listen to the deep voice behind her, the venial offence might be condoned by her guardian angel. Christian had fully intended to leave the lovers alone, but Walter Hamill called her back as she was opening the door.

"Please do not go for a moment, Mrs. Linacre," he said; "I have something to say to you and Penelope— that is partly why I have come down, Pen, to tell you of my good fortune."

" Oh, Walter, do you mean you have a curacy already?"

" Yes, dear;" and Walter's eyes glowed with pride and tenderness as he looked at her; " when I leave St. Cuthbert's, I am coming here. Mr. Disney has engaged me as his curate."

" Walter, Walter!" Pen was a little spent and tired with her day's labours, and the surprise and joy were too overwhelming; she tried to speak, to express her pleasure, but the tears would flow; " it is because I am so happy," she sobbed when Christian scolded her.

" It is because you have overtired yourself," returned Mrs. Jack severely; " but I shall leave Mr. Hamill to manage you," and Christian flashed a bright look at the young curate as she passed him. " I knew all about it; oh! I am so glad—so glad," and then she called Smudge and went across to the Vicarage.

Pen soon grew calm when she was left alone with Walter, the tears had relieved her, and as she nestled against his broad shoulder, she cooed to him as happily as a little bird.

" To see you every day," she broke out presently; " to be always together in church."

" No, love, you forget that I shall often be at St. James's;" for there were two churches under the pastotal supervision of the Vicar of Braybrooke; " my junior will only be a deacon."

" But you will be often at the services at the parish church?" returned Pen with tender rapture; " that will be the most precious privilege of all, Walter. Christian will not mind my going to St. James when you preach;" then Walter smiled and pressed her closer to him.

" The Vicar is worth a dozen of me, sweetheart;" but Pen was not going to believe him; to her Walter Hamill was the finest gentleman and the truest Christian, and the most noble-hearted man in the world; Pen in her simplicity thought his sermons miracles of wisdom and cleverness. Mr. Disney was older and more experienced perhaps—she would allow that—but Walter would one day take the world by surprise. If any one had prophesied that he would be a bishop, Pen would not have been the least astonished. Walter himself was amused by the girl's transparent flattery, but it touched him too.

" I wish I could live up to it, Pen," he said once rather wistfully; " but we clerics are only human."

The hour passed only too rapidly. Pen declared that Walter's watch must be wrong.· When he showed her the time, " We have scarcely begun to talk," she said regretfully.

" But I shall see you after breakfast to-morrow; I need not go back before the afternoon; we can finish our talk then," and then Pen was obliged to let him go.

What an evening that was! Christian told her all about the plan that Mrs. Disney had proposed, and Pen was charmed at the idea.

" I have always liked the Dugalds so much," she returned. " Oh, I do hope Walter will take me to see the rooms!" But she need not have had any doubts on the subject.

There was quite a little procession to the Dugalds' shop the next morning; the Vicar and Mrs. Disney, Christian, and Pen and Mr. Hamill, and Sheila; quite a little mob filled the shop, and then mounted the steep little staircase, preceded by the comely smiling young wife. Pen and Walter were charmed with the rooms; they were so cheerful and pleasant, there was plenty of room for all Walter's possessions—his writing-table, bookcase, and pictures.

"What a change it will be after Battersea!" observed Walter. He drawled the words somewhat slowly, after his usual dreamy fashion, but there was a look of extreme satisfaction on his face as he stood at the window with Pen beside him. Just opposite was the clock-tower and the gray old market-place; except on market days it would be quiet enough. "It is better than Roskill Street, Pen;" and then the young curate drew a long breath; no one except Pen knew what the change meant to him, and how, as he had worked manfully in the slums and streets of Battersea, his strong young manhood had sickened for fresh air and the sweet sights and sounds of country life; but Pen understood and squeezed his hand secretly before they left the window to join the little group round the fireplace.

XXXII

"Who Can It Be?"

I love thee
By love's own sweet constraint, and will forever
Do thee all rights of service.

SHAKESPEARE.

ALL these weeks Carus had had his own secret anxieties, which he had concealed carefully from his mother and Christian. The total absence of all news from Jack filled him with uneasiness, but only to Colonel Bromley did he hint at such fears.

"It seems very strange," he said one day; "other people have heard from their relatives in Ladysmith from time to time, but we have not even had a message from Jack. I cannot help fearing that there must be something wrong."

"Very likely he has written and the letter has never reached you," returned the Colonel—they ascertained afterwards that this had been the case. "The Hardcastles are just as anxious as you, Linacre; they have not had a line from Philip since the end of November; poor Mrs. Hardcastle is working herself up into a fever. If I were you I should not trouble too much about Captain Linacre's silence; his wound was not a very severe one."

"I was not thinking so much of that," observed Carus. "Jack has a good constitution and is as wiry as possible; but think of the privations they are undergoing; half-starved men are not able to resist disease; there are hundreds down with enteric and dysentery;" then the Colonel shook his head a little gravely; he was forced to admit that Carus had ample reason for uneasiness; nevertheless, with his wonted unselfishness, Carus kept a bright face in his mother's presence.

But doubts of his brother's safety was not his only anxiety; he was still worried about Heather. The girl's cheerfulness was certainly forced; she no longer carolled

274

about the house like a lark, and he even fancied that her step was less springy; a few months ago she would have danced in and out of the library, or run up the staircase singing as blithely as possible, and now she walked about the place quite soberly, with a thoughtful, abstracted look on her young face.

Carus was patient by nature, but he also had some of his mother's pertinacity; as Jack once observed, " he never was satisfied until he got to the bottom of a thing." He would take any amount of time and trouble to solve a difficulty that perplexed him, but he would never rest until it was surmounted. Christian was beginning to realise this trait in Carus.

A few days after Walter Hamill had paid his momentous visit, Christian walked over to the Stone House to take Heather some more articles of clothing that she and Pen had made for the twins. As usual she was kept to luncheon, and later in the afternoon Carus walked part of the way back with her.

Christian had been offered the carriage, but she had refused, alleging as her reason that she was growing fat and needed exercise. " I don't want Jack to find a stout young woman on his return," she had observed to her mother-in-law, and Janet had smiled in reply; there would be no fear of that, she thought, as she looked at the trim, graceful figure.

It was a damp, sunless afternoon, and as Heather had a cold, Mrs. Linacre would not hear of her leaving the house, and though the girl protested that it was nothing, that she hated fuss and stuffiness, and that air never did any one harm, she was obliged to yield; but she stood at a window watching them until they were out of sight. How she would have loved the walk back with Carus in the soft gloom and twilight. Heather felt quite childishly disappointed, and disposed to be pettish for once with Aunt Janet.

Meanwhile the two went on silently. Carus was in a brown study, and seemed almost oblivious of his sisterin-law's society; he walked on mechanically with his hands behind his back, as though he were pacing his study. He quite started when Christian touched him.

" Is there anything troubling you, Carus?" she asked;
" I spoke to you just now, but you did not seem to hear
—you were thinking so hard."

" I am afraid I have been rude," he returned, trying
to rouse himself; " but I am poor company just now."

" You are never that at any time," she replied affectionately; " but I always see in a moment when you are
worried." She took his arm as she spoke, with a little
sisterly pressure of it, that told him of her sympathy and
readiness to help.

" It is the old subject," he said with a sigh; " I am still
troubling about Heather. Christian, even you have no
idea what that child is to me; if she were my own daughter she could not be more. I would give five years of my
life to have the old Bell-Heather back again."

" But she has not gone, Carus—how often have I said
the same thing to you. Heather was unusually young
for her age in spite of her years; she was hardly as grown
up as other girls; she took childish views of life, and now
she has suddenly become older—that is all."

" But it is not only that," he objected; " no doubt what
you say is correct, but it does not account for the change
in her. For a time I thought as you do; I said to myself
that the affair with Sydney had given her a shock, but
that she would regain her cheerfulness after a time."

" But she is very cheerful, Carus; she was laughing
and talking all through luncheon. It was natural that she
should take Sydney's disappointment to heart, and of
course she feels parting with him; but I must say that
in my opinion Heather is behaving very well.. She has
gone through a good deal, we must allow that."

" Of course we know all that," with a touch of impatience that he rarely showed; " but there is something
beyond this, Christian; it will always be a puzzle to me
why Heather refused Sydney Masters. Do you think—
can it be possible that he was right, and that there is
some one else for whom she cares."

If Christian had only been prepared for this, she would
have had her answer ready; but if Carus had held a re-
volver to her ear, she could hardly have been more startled
at the unexpected question. They had reached the lodge

gates by this time, and as Carus had spoken, he had stood still looking at her; the lodge door was open, and the light fell full on Christian's face. She felt herself change colour, and dropped his arm with an air of annoyance.

"You have no right to ask me such a question," she said angrily; " only God who makes women's hearts can read what is in them. If I had the knowledge you imagine I have, do you suppose I should tell you." It was not a very wise answer; it left too much to be inferred; but it was not easy for Christian to tell a fib, and there was a searching look in Carus's eyes that seemed to read her very thoughts.

" I am answered," he said, turning away; " you are a poor actor, Christian. Then there is some one—good Heavens! that child—and who can it be?" but Carus said the last words to himself.

Christian felt a hot tingling in her veins; she was enraged with her own want of readiness; in her anxiety to shield Heather she had said the wrong thing. If only she had kept cool and fenced a little; men were so dense, and she could easily have thrown dust in his eyes. There would have been no necessity to tell an untruth—a little shocked exclamation of surprise and wonder, a doubtful shake of the head, a laugh even, at such a preposterous idea, and Carus would have been put off the scent, instead of which she had spoilt all with her air of tragedy and her quick temper. " You are a poor actor," he had said almost scornfully; but though Christian scolded herself for her gaucherie, she felt that it would have been impossible to do otherwise—Carus's keen eyes seemed to probe to the very depths. She had never before realised the strength and force of his will; he had sprung this mine upon her, and there had been no escape; and poor Heather's unconscious confidence had been in some measure betrayed by her. There was no doubt that Christian was extremely angry; as they walked on she determined that no further word should be spoken by her; but the next moment Carus put his hand on her arm with his old kind smile.

" I see I have said the wrong thing, Christian; but you must not be cross with me. I will ask you no more questions; but it was necessary for me to know that."

" I do not agree with you," she said stormily; " it is no business of yours or mine either." In a cooler mood Christian would have seen that this speech was absurd, for if she were correct in her surmise, it was certainly Carus's concern; but she was too much put out to measure her words.

" Well, well, we will not quarrel about it," he returned good-humouredly. " Some other time, when we are both cooler, I will prove to you that I am within my rights. Now I must go back, dear; good-bye, and don't be hard on me." But Christian was not to be so easily appeased; she wished him a curt good-night, and marched off with her head in the air.

Carus smiled again as he walked back in the February gloaming—that soft obscurity which was neither dark nor light; he did not misunderstand Christian, he liked her all the better for her fierce loyalty to her sex. " Who can it be?" he asked himself. " How am I to help her if I cannot find out?" And each time he woke that night the question rose to confront him in the darkness—" Who can it be?"

Morning brought no solution; he could recall no one in whom Heather had taken any special or abiding interest. George Gillespie—pooh—the child had laughed at him! He had admired her, of course—how could any one help admiring Bell-Heather; every day she was growing sweeter and more lovely—but George Gillespie was not to be compared with Sydney Masters.

Carus gave it up at last in despair; he would not speak to his mother on the subject, and it was clearly impossible to ask Heather; but there was one thing he would do: he would say a word to Heather that she would be able to understand; he would tell her that any confidence she chose to repose in him should be secret, and that she might be sure of his help and sympathy under all circumstances. " You have no father or mother," he would say to her; " let me be both to you;" and perhaps she might be induced to tell him her secret.

Carus watched for an opportunity all that day, Heather's cold still hung about her, and a slight drizzling rain kept her again in the house. In the afternoon, while

Mrs. Linacre was resting, she went to the library to ask Carus to give her another book. From the first he had directed her reading; he had taken a great deal of pains in forming her girlish tastes, and encouraged her to read the best authors. Christian had been quite surprised at the extent of Heather's information.

Carus pushed aside his papers with unusual alacrity and went to the bookshelves; he made his selection carefully. "I think that will interest you, Heather," handing her *The Intellectual Life* by Hamerton. Heather thanked him and was about to withdraw, but he detained her.

"I thought you were going to keep me company this wet afternoon," he said in a disappointed tone; "you have only paid me angels' visits lately—few and far between. Why have you given me so little of your society, Bell-Heather?"

"I don't know," she stammered; "I thought you were unusually busy, Carus, and I was afraid of interrupting you;" but Heather grew as pink as her namesake at this little fib, over which Carus opened his eyes rather widely.

"Why, what nonsense is this you are talking?" he said, quite surprised; "you know I always work all the better when I have you near me;" then he pointed suggestively to the little oak stool that Heather always occupied—it stood beside his easy-chair; but for a moment the girl hesitated.

"I am afraid I cannot stay now," she faltered, looking wistfully at her dear old stool.

"Shall I bring you a chair," he returned quickly, with an odd sort of laugh; "I forgot you were grown up, Heather, and that I ought to treat you with due deference." Then Heather shook her head deprecatingly, and crept to her corner like a little mouse.

Carus sat down with a sigh of contentment. "That's right, dear; I like the old ways best. You do not know how I have missed you, little one."

"Have you, Carus?" and Heather brightened perceptibly. Of course she knew it, but she loved to hear him say it.

"I have had some dull hours lately because my little

sunbeam refused to shine on me," laying his hand fondly on the soft brown hair. "Heather, there is something I want to say to you, and which I hope you will not take amiss; for you know, dear child, that I would not hurt you for worlds."

"I am quite sure of that, Carus."

"I don't want to touch on any vexed questions—let the dead past bury its dead, eh, Heather?—so we won't even mention Sydney's name." Then a relieved look came to Heather's eyes, and she breathed more freely. "No, no! we will leave all that alone. But, Heather, now that the poor fellow has had his *congé* and gone, why do you still seem so thoughtful and unlike your bright self? If there is anything troubling you, dearest, if there is anything that I can do to help you——" Then the girl started nervously.

"No, no! there is nothing; you are very kind, Carus, but I am happy—quite happy."

"Do happy people cry themselves to sleep?—for that is certainly what you did last night," continued Carus quietly; "no, you need not trouble to invent any pretty little plausible fib," as Heather tried to stop him; "your cold is better, so it was not that. But do not look so alarmed, I am asking no questions, I am not trying to force your confidence."

"What do you mean? Why do you speak so strangely?" Heather's face was burning. "You look at me as though you thought I had a secret——" but Heather could not finish her sentence.

"If you have one, dear, I will not ask you to tell it to me," he returned gently, "unless you do so of your own accord. But, my child," and he took the hot, little hand in his, "there is one thing I do want to say, that under any and every circumstance you may be sure of my sympathy—that help and advice are ready for you when you need them. No father, no brother, would ever give them more ungrudgingly than I would, Heather."

"Yes, yes! I know it," but Heather covered her face with her hands.

"There is nothing—nothing that I would not sacrifice for your happiness," he went on, in that subdued, tender voice that was so sweet to her ears; "every year you become dearer to me; and if you were my own child——"

"Oh, if I only were," she murmured with a choking sob; but he misunderstood her emotion.

"There is little difference—these adopted ties are often as strong as the natural ones. I think I could not love you better, little one, if I were really your father; I am certainly old enough," with a forced laugh; but a slight shiver was the only answer. "Now I am not going to say anything more; if you can bring yourself to trust me, perhaps I should be able to help you. And if there be any one else, Heather, now, or at any future time, for whom you could care, and you judge me worthy of your confidence, there is nothing——" but Heather jumped up from her seat; her eyes were wet and her sweet lips quivering with pain.

"Oh, how can you! how can you!" in a broken voice. "You mean to be kind; but you are cruel; I cannot bear it," and Heather burst into tears and left the room.

Carus sprang up in dismay. For once she had forgotten his defective hearing, and her words had failed to reach him; but those tears, and that look of reproach, what could they mean?

"That you of all others could hurt me so,"—that was what her eyes had said to him, and yet how gently and considerately he had spoken. Nothing in his words could have offended the virginal instincts of any girlish mind. In his perplexity he repeated the latter part of his speech, "If there be any one else, now, or at any future time, for whom you could care, and you judge me worthy of your confidence." Well, could any words be more brotherly and faithful. And yet she had flashed that look of reproach at him and rushed away. Carus sat down in his chair with a heavy sigh, "There is some one, but she will not confide in me," he said to himself; "my well-meant attempt has only frightened her away. But who can it be? who can it be?"

XXXIII

SUNSHINE AND CLOUDS

Then rise from thy sad miserere
Unburdened, no longer distrest,
There's a light that can shine thro' **the drear**;
For thyself, for thy land,
There's a Heart and a Hand
That can lead thee to glory and rest.
ALEXANDER CLUNY MACPHERSON.

CHRISTIAN had no presentiments, either of good or evil, when she woke on a certain eventful day which was to fill the country with rejoicing. She went about her daily tasks as usual, performing all her little self-imposed duties with her customary energy and cheerfulness. The twins were sufficiently clothed by this time, and she and Pen had launched into a more ambitious undertaking—a set of new cretonne covers for the sitting-room. Pen, who had developed quite a talent for upholstery, was the chief manager, and cut out and fitted and sewed and strewed the carpet with pins, that imperilled Smudge's life, while Christian presided at the sewing-machine, only pausing now and then to look with secret amazement at Pen's absorbed face.

" It it were your own house I don't think you could take more interest," she said once, smiling, as Pen regarded her work with pride.

" It is such a pretty pattern," she observed; " I do love these little blue flowers with their golden hearts, and the room will look so nice when it is finished. Look, Chriss, the cover of this easy-chair fits quite perfectly; there is not a crease anywhere." Then Christian got up to look and admire.

" It is just beautiful; I had no idea that you were so clever, Pen; don't you wish they were for a little house of your own?" rather mischievously. Then Pen blushed guiltily. More than once the thought had crossed her

282

mind as she had fitted the blue cretonne; and dim sweet dreams had come to her of a cottage home which she would beautify and make ready with her own hands. No dwelling would have been too humble, no fear of poverty would have daunted her loving heart. If Walter Hamill had asked her to marry him at once and begin life with him on a hundred and thirty pounds a year in the room over the stationery shop in the market-place, Pen would have raised no scruples. She would have packed her trunks, and bought her modest wedding-dress without any hesitation. But Walter, much as he longed for his wife, knew better than to suggest such a thing. Christian, who was very sharp-sighted, soon detected her thoughts.

" I don't believe you would mind living in the Dugald's rooms one bit, Pen," she said presently; but Pen took the observation quite seriously.

" I don't think I should mind anything with Walter," she returned simply; " and you know Mrs. Dugald said there was another room they could spare, so he could have a study," which proved to Christian that this was no new idea to Pen. And indeed she was for ever building up her small visionary air-castles.

" I am afraid it would not be wise to take such a step until Mr. Hamill's income is larger. If he could take pupils; but that is not possible, for Mr. Disney's curates have so much to do."

" I daresay you are right, Chriss," and Pen sighed as she saw her dream ruthlessly brushed away like an empty cobweb. Then she turned the subject bravely. " I wonder if you and Captain Linacre will go on living at Many Bushes," she went on; " there is really no need for Mr. Linacre to keep the house for his own use, as his mother and Heather will not let him live here."

" I think Carus begins to realise this," returned Christian; " indeed he was saying as much to me the other day. ' I don't know where you and Jack intend to live,' were his words. ' Of course he may have to go to Egypt or India; but if you like, Many Bushes can be your head-quarters. We will have a talk with Jack when he comes back,' he went on, ' and if he cares for the idea, I will cart away my belongings, and you can have the whole house. That little room by the front door would make a capital smoking den.' Wasn't it kind of him to say that?"

"Yes, indeed, but I do hope that you will not have to go to India, Chriss."

"Oh, as to that, I must go where Jack goes; and I have an idea that Indian life would be rather fun for a year or two; but I should like to feel that we have an English home ready for us. I should not care to stay at the Stone House, or in Beauchamp Gardens; and you know, Pen, that we are not likely to be rich until Uncle Jasper dies, which I hope will not be for years and years. So Many Bushes will be quite large enough for us." And then, in womanly fashion, they reorganised Christian's future home. Carus's library was to be the drawing-room again, and the sitting-room was to be called the morning-room. Time passed rapidly over this delightful employment; and Christian was even beginning to lay out a fresh flower border when the luncheon bell rang. Carus had gone up to town that day, and there could be no ride with him in the afternoon, so Christian went to the Infirmary, and afterwards she and Pen had a stroll in the twilight. They were just re-entering their own gate, when they caught sight of the Vicar hurrying after them. He was waving his hat wildly.

"Hurrah, three cheers for Buller! Ladysmith is relieved," he shouted. Christian turned quite pale. "Oh, are you sure; is there no mistake?" she said breathlessly.

"There is no doubt of it," he returned. "The city is quite crazy with excitement. They are waving flags and shouting themselves hoarse all over the place. Dundonald and his horsemen are in Ladysmith."

"Oh, thank God," murmured Christian, and her eyes were full of tears. At last, at last that gallant town was relieved. "But what of Jack?" she continued.

"Oh, we shall have news of them all soon," returned the Vicar cheerfully. "Carus begged me to give you his love and congratulations. We came back together, but he has gone on to the Stone House; he is so anxious for Mrs. Linacre to share the grand news. You will hear the church bells ring directly, and in another hour we shall have the flags up in the market-place."

Christian was almost too moved to answer. She went up to her room, and threw open her window. After all that bloodshed and disaster the riddle of the Tugela was solved at last, and the dauntless emaciated garrison was crowding round its deliverers. "Oh, thank God! thank God!" murmured Christian as her tears flowed in the darkness, for the great burden of fear that had oppressed her for so many months had now rolled away. Later in the evening Charlotte came over to rejoice with her friends. She told them that Braybrooke was perfectly wild with excitement. Boys were letting off squibs and crackers in the market-place; flags were flying and bands playing; the lads' brigade was marching through the town with pipe and drum; the bells of Silverton Church were pealing. Christian would have liked to have stood in a quiet corner and seen the excited, huzzaing crowd go by; the children, with their penny whistles, beating toy drums, and shouting "Hurrah for Buller!" in their shrill baby voices. "I must go to the Stone House to-morrow," she whispered, when Mrs. Disney took her leave.

"Graham and I will come too," returned Charlotte. "Dear Christian, if you knew how happy we all are; it has been such a long, trying ordeal; but it has ended well."

"But we have not heard from Jack." This was the one drop in her cup of gladness. If only the long, strange silence could be broken, and a message come to them from Jack himself.

"Carus says we shall have a telegram soon" were Mrs. Linacre's first words as she greeted Christian. Janet's eyes were bright; she looked ten years younger; but Christian, who had lain awake for hours, trying to calm her excitement, was weary from the very stress of feeling.

"Oh, the relief of it all, mater!" she said softly. "If only Jack had sent us a message." This was the burden of her cry, but Carus reassured her.

"We shall hear soon," he said cheerfully. "You know

it is only Dundonald and his troop who are actually in Ladysmith. Buller and the main army have not made their entry. We must be patient a little longer, dear Christian."

But Christian, who had waited so bravely for news all these months, felt as though the hours of silence were interminable.

When the telegram came at last, he went into the library to open it; but Christian, who was on the watch, followed him at once.

" It is·as I thought," he said, as he handed it to her. But the message Christian read so eagerly was not from Jack. " Captain Linacre recovering enteric fever,"— that was all.

" Oh, Carus!" Perhaps it was the sudden revulsion from the excitement of the previous evening, but Christian felt a strange sinking of heart.

" Why do you look like that, dear?" asked Carus gently. " This is what I have feared all the time— that Jack was down with enteric. But he is recovering; can any news be better than that?" But Christian still looked troubled and anxious.

" Yes, I know; but if he has not all the care he needs —if he is not well nursed and should have a relapse. All this time they have been without comforts for the sick;" but Carus stoutly combated her fears. There would be no lack of care; officers' lives were too precious; Jack was convalescent; he was probably only suffering from weakness. Christian listened gratefully, but she could not at once recover her spirits. Mrs. Linacre was far more sanguine. Colonel Bromley did more to re- assure her than any one else when he came up to the Stone House to congratulate his old friends.

" They will send the sick and wounded down to the sea; you may be sure of that. I expect they will go to Durban," he said to Carus. " You will hear from Captain Linacre when he gets there. Buller will know better than to leave them in such a fever pest-house;" and subsequent events proved the truth of the old Colonel's words; and a little later a second telegram informed them that Jack was going to Durban.

Christian chid herself for her want of faith; but she could not regain her old happy confidence. Strange to say, she and Mrs. Linacre seemed to have exchanged natures for the time. Janet, who had been so full of fears—who had suffered so cruelly—now displayed a marvellous cheerfulness and confidence. "The sea air will do wonders for him," she would say almost daily. "As soon as he is strong enough, they will put him on board and send him home. Colonel Bromley was saying so yesterday. The dear boy will be home soon; and then we must nurse him and feed him up. You will let him come here, Christian,"—looking at her daughter-in-law rather wistfully—"you will not keep him from his mother."

Then Christian promised rather reluctantly that Jack should go to the Stone House first for a long visit. "I would so much rather have had him at Many Bushes," she said afterwards to Mrs. Disney; "but I knew I ought not to be selfish."

Charlotte quite understood her. After this long separation, the young wife would have liked to have kept him to herself. "I daresay the country air and the large rooms at the Stone House will be very good for an invalid," she returned sensibly. "Of course it will be self-denial on your part, Christian; but I think Mrs. Linacre will fully appreciate your self-sacrifice."

Christian smiled faintly, but it was evident to Charlotte that the self-sacrifice was by no means light. Christian's charming little plan was to be ruthlessly demolished. She meant to have asked Mrs. Linacre to have Pen for a week or two, and then she and Jack were to enjoy their long postponed honeymoon at Many Bushes. "When I have him all to myself, I can tell him things," she thought; "and there will be no third person to interfere with us, and we shall get to understand each other thoroughly; and if he be still an invalid, I shall so love to take care of him;" for Christian's wifely instincts had come to life now.

But at the Stone House Mrs. Linacre would never be long away from them. The beautiful suite of rooms that she had already set apart for them would be dominated by her maternal presence. Janet would not intend to interfere with Christian's prerogative; but with her customary denseness she would forget that Jack was not her sole charge. Christian would be hampered and fretted by advice given in season and out of season; her judgment would be questioned and her want of experience lamented. "Dear Christian, I am quite sure that Jack ought to do this or that;" and then she would appeal to the doctor. Christian had quite a struggle with the old rebellious feeling before she yielded the point.

"I know things will be spoilt for us both," she said quite mournfully to Charlotte.

But before many hours were over she would thankfully have accepted any conditions if she could only have him back. Christian, who was just then staying for a few days at the Stone House, had come over to Braybrooke for the day. She had driven in with Carus. He was going up to town to see his uncle, and would call for her on his return. Christian had not expected him until late in the afternoon. She was rather surprised then when she left the Vicarage to see him coming towards her on foot. She went at once to meet him.

"I thought I was not to expect you before half-past five!" she exclaimed. "It is only half-past four now."

"Yes, I know," he returned hurriedly. "I came back earlier; when I got to the station the telegraph-boy stopped me—they have cabled from Durban,—it is not nice news, Christian; Jack has had a relapse—he is in the hospital, and I am going out to him."

For one moment Christian did not seem to take it in. She had never seen Carus so moved and excited. There was an alert, resolute air about him; he was no longer dreamy or subdued; but as the meaning of his words became plain to her, she looked at him pitifully.

"Oh," she said, "what is this that you are telling me, Carus—that Jack is worse—that he has had a relapse?"

"Yes," he returned briefly; "I wish I could have spared you this fresh anxiety, Christian; but I could not hide it from you if I would; you are his wife and have a right to know everything."

"Thank you for saying that, Carus."

"But he is also my only brother, and therefore I mean to go to him."

"Will you take me with you? Indeed, I will be a help and not a hindrance," and Christian clutched his arm as she spoke. But Carus shook his head.

"Come in for a moment, dear; the carriage will be round directly, and I must make this clear to you. Christian, I cannot take you with me. How can I tell in what state we may find the town? Rather than have you with me, I would stop at home." Carus's voice was almost stern.

"But you cannot go alone. My dear brother, you forget——" Then Carus's face flushed a little.

"If you mean my infirmity, I am not likely to forget that; my old servant Dugald has promised to accompany me. He is wild to go, and his good little wife has promised to spare him. Christian, you are always brave and helpful: I shall rely on you not to raise difficulties. If I am on the spot I can do my best for Jack, and if God spares him to us, I will bring him back to you. Tell me I am right to go."

"Oh yes—oh yes!" she sobbed. "If I could only go too and be nice to him."

"Your share of work will come later, dear. Let me tell you all I have done this morning. When I read the telegram I felt that I must go to him. For days the thought had been with me, but I was afraid of missing him, so I just waited. But when I knew that horrible fever had got hold of him again, it flashed across me that I must go, and I made up my mind. I was standing in the station waiting for the train to come in, when I saw Dugald and his wife; they were going up to town to see a brother of hers who was going to the front. I made them get into my carriage, and before we reached town the whole matter was settled. Dugald went with me to take our berths,"—here Carus paused a moment—"we start to-morrow, Christian. I went in for a moment to see Uncle Jasper; he took the news better than I expected, and seemed glad that I should go. 'You are right, Carus; go yourself and bring the poor fellow back. There, I won't keep you,' and he almost pushed me from him. But, indeed, Christian, I have not let the grass grow under my feet. Dugald is doing the rest of my business; he will not come back until late. Now, if you are ready, I see the carriage turning in at the gate."

"I must just speak to Pen," she returned. "She is upstairs and has not heard us." But as Christian mounted the staircase, her limbs felt as though they were weighted with lead.

"Are you going already?" exclaimed Pen in surprise. She was folding up the blue cretonne and laying it in the press.

"Yes," returned Christian in a tired voice, and her face was very pale. "Carus cannot wait. Jack is worse; he has had a relapse, and Carus is going out to him."

XXXIV

"IF IT WERE ANY ONE ELSE!"

Mine! O heart dost thou know it? dost thou grasp the gift I
    gain?
Strength for my weakness, calm for my turmoil, solace for pain,
Love for my love.

E. M. L. G.

WHEN Christian and Carus arrived at the Stone
House, they found Mrs. Linacre alone.

"Heather is spending the evening with the Hardcastles," she explained to them. "Rose and Mildred
came over this afternoon and carried her off. They
were so anxious for her to remain to dinner that I made
Hitchens put up her things. They have promised to
send her back."

Christian exchanged a look with Carus.

"It is a good thing," he observed in an undertone,
which, however, reached his mother's ears.

"Of course, it is a good thing," she returned in a decided tone. "Heather leads far too quiet a life for a girl
of her age. I had to insist on her going back with them;
she actually wished to refuse; poor Rose looked so
disappointed; they wanted her to help them with some
tableaux."

"I daresay she will not be very late," returned Carus;
he was telling himself that he would be no loser by
the girl's absence—he had to superintend his packing,
write a few business letters, and set his affairs generally
in order—and he would have had no time to spare for
the child. Nevertheless, he felt unaccountably chilled
and disappointed; if only she had known that this was
his last evening, he thought nothing would have induced
her to go. "No, she would not be late," he repeated to
himself; he would try and get forward with his business, so that he could spare half an hour to talk to her.
Carus knew there would be little sleep for him that

night; that he would not be able to rest until he had
settled things to his own satisfaction. He was as orderly
and methodical as an old bachelor, and prided himself
on his own good management. " Mother," he said
gently, " I have something to tell you about Jack;" and
then very carefully and tenderly the news was broken
to her.

It was a great shock to Janet, and she was very much
upset; it was almost too cruel, he thought, that her cup
of happiness should be dashed so ruthlessly from her
lips. All her fears were magnified a hundredfold.
" Jack would die; she would never see her boy again!"
she exclaimed, almost in despair.

" Hush, mother, you must not say such things; you
are distressing poor Christian; once before we thought
we had lost Jack, but he was only wounded."

" Yes, but—but we may have to undergo all that agony
again!" exclaimed the poor woman. " Carus, you must
not go; I cannot bear it. Why should I be deprived
of both my sons?" and Janet's face was drawn with
pain.

Carus sighed a little wearily; as usual, his mother
was adding to his burdens. He looked at Christian
with a mute entreaty for help, and Christian was not
slow to respond; she pushed back her own fears and
troubles into the background and set herself to soothe
the poor, weak soul.

" Mater, dear, we must only consider Jack," she said
quietly. " Think what a comfort it will be to him to
see Carus's face; they love each other so dearly"—
Christian gave a little sob, but recovered herself bravely
—" and Jack thinks so much of his brother!"

" Yes, for Carus was like a father to him," murmured
Janet.

" And so he feels that he must go to him," went on
Christian. " Mater, do you know, I would have gone
with Carus if he would have taken me?"

" My dear child—impossible!"   ·

" Why should it be impossible? It cannot be wrong
for a woman to go to her husband when he is lying
on a bed of sickness. I should not have been afraid,

only Carus refused to take me; he said I should be a
burden to him."

"Christian, you must not think of such a thing; Carus
is right;" but Janet loved her all the better for the
thought; then she melted into tears, and said if he must
go—and she knew that all her prayers and entreaties
would not keep him if he was set on doing this thing—
he must promise her to keep nothing from them, even
if he spent half his substance in sending her news; and
Carus was quite ready to promise this.

"Now, you must let him go and do his business,"
observed Christian, and Carus withdrew, with a glance
of gratitude at his sister-in-law. Christian's task was
not an easy one that evening—she had simply to efface
herself and banish all reflections; she sat beside Mrs.
Linacre listening patiently as she bemoaned her own
and Christian's troubles.

"I know I deserve to be punished," she kept saying
over and over again; "but, my poor, dear child, why
should you have to suffer too?" But Christian refused
to be drawn into any such discussion.

"If trouble came," she said, "they would have
strength given them to bear it; but it was wrong, wicked,
to give way to despair. Jack had been spared once and
might be given back to them again; so many people had
had enteric and recovered, though, of course, their
progress might be slow." Christian said this quietly,
almost mechanically, and all the time a voice seemed to
say within her: "Perhaps when Carus arrives it will
be too late; perhaps when he goes to the hospital to look
for Jack he will not find him——" but Christian would
not let herself finish the sentence. What was the use
of hoping and fearing?—women had to wait and pray in
those days. "Give peace in our time, O Lord!" that
was the ceaseless petition that was to rise from thousands
of anxious foreboding hearts—"Give peace in our time,
good Lord!"

Christian's quiet fortitude gave Janet fresh courage,
and as soon as dinner was over she set herself to work
—packing for Carus. Christian left her busy with
Hitchens, and made herself extremely useful on Carus's

behalf.   Everything was finished, and the luggage was in the hall ready for the early start when Heather returned.

"Where are they all, Hyde?" she said to the old butler as she stepped into the hall; then she caught sight of the luggage heaped together in a dark corner. "Oh, has any one arrived?—no"—interrupting herself —"that must be Mr. Linacre's Gladstone! What does it mean? Is he going away?"

"The mistress has gone to her room, and Mrs. John is upstairs," replied Hyde discreetly; "but you will find the master in the library, Miss Heather; he said he should be up late."

The opening door did not disturb Carus; it was not until a shadow fell upon his paper that he raised his eyes and saw Heather standing beside him. How often he recalled that fair, girlish figure as he paced the deck, night after night, in the starlight. The white dress; the pearls that were not whiter than the soft, round throat they encircled; the pretty evening wrap, falling from her shoulders; and lastly, the sweet, anxious face—how well he remembered them.

"What does it mean, Carus?" she asked. "There is luggage in the hall, and Hyde is so mysterious, and" —looking at the table strewn with papers—"you are so dreadfully busy."

"No, I shall soon have done. It is you who are dreadfully late, little one,—half-past eleven. Why, what giddy doings, Bell-Heather?"

"I could not help it," she said wearily; "Aunt Janet made me go. They wanted me for those stupid *tableaux vivants* that Laura Bromley is getting up. Rose said that she and Mildred could do nothing without my help; they are not very clever at that sort of thing, so of course I could not refuse."

"Why should you refuse?" he said, looking at her with fond admiration; it seemed to him that Heather looked strangely beautiful to-night. "Do you know what my mother says?—that you lead too quiet a life. We must alter this, dear."

"No, we must alter nothing," she returned impa-

tiently. "Why do you listen to Aunt Janet, Carus?
Don't you know that this quiet life is just perfect? That
I want nothing else? Only for us three to be always
together,—just you, and me, and dear Aunt Janet."

"Why! this is a pretty sort of thing," he said, playing with her fancy for a moment, for he was loath to
tell her his news. "What would people say if we kept
our young princess shut up in this grim captivity?
They would call me an ogre, and my mother a witch."

"I prefer the society of ogres and witches to stupid,
humdrum people," she returned with a charming pout.
"Oh, those girls were so silly and tiresome! They
wanted me to be Andromache in that parting scene, and
Bertie Hardcastle was to be my Hector. Just fancy that
ridiculous boy!"

"Boy—Bell-Heather! Do you call that muscular
young giant a boy?"

"Oh, he is only a lad!" she returned disdainfully,—
"an awkward great lout of a lad, with more inches
than brains. Fancy Bertie Hardcastle trying to per-
sonify my favourite hero! No, I would not agree. I
told Mildred that I would take no part in such scenes.
Just fancy!"—and Heather's eyes shone like stars in her
indignation—"just imagine me hanging on Bertie's arm,
and saying dumbly to him with my eye: 'Father to me
thou art, and mother dear, and brother too, kind husband
of my heart,'" and Heather laughed. Perhaps she was
a little excited by the controversy, but she seemed more
at her ease with Carus than she had been since that last
talk. "It was all so provoking——" but interrupting
herself—"You have not explained about the luggage?"

"Oh, the luggage!" and a shade came over Carus's
face. "Sit down, dear, and I will tell you all about it.
A great deal has happened to-day. We have had news
from Durban that has greatly troubled us—Jack has had
a relapse, and I am going out to him."

"You—you!"

"Yes; there is no one else. It seems only right that
his brother should go to him. Do you know, Heather,
Christian wanted me to take her? But I told her that it
was impossible. Poor girl! she was dreadfully disappointed."

"But you of all people; you—you!" Heather could scarcely bring out the words.

"Oh, I shall have Dugald!" he returned cheerfully; "Dugald knows all my ways. I am a good traveller, Heather, and a long voyage will just suit me. We may have to rough it a little when we get there, but what of that?" Carus was talking in a cheery way, because he did not like to see the sudden fading of the girl's bright colour and the frightened look in her eyes. "My mother was very much against it at first," he went on, that she might have time to recover herself. "As you know, she never likes to trust me out of her sight; I think in her heart that she considers us boys still," and Carus forced a little laugh. "Christian has talked her into a more reasonable frame of mind, and she has promised to make no further difficulty."

"And Christian helped you, and encouraged you to go! Christian!"

"To be sure she did; Christian is a sensible little woman. She knew better than to keep me; she has been hard at work for me all the evening, and now she has gone to her room to write to Jack."

"And I was away while all this was happening. Carus, Carus! how am I to bear it? If it were any one else; but you—you!" The last words were rather breathed than spoken, but Carus heard them. The next moment the truth flashed upon him, and he knew!

The grandfather's clock in the hall was chiming twelve, and Heather drew her cloak round her with a little shiver; the poor child had no idea that she had betrayed herself. "I must go now," she said in a dreary voice; "Aunt Janet will be vexed if I stayed longer. Good-night, Carus," putting out a shaking little hand to him.

"Good-night. Sleep well, dear child; I shall see you to-morrow." He dropped her hand hastily and turned to the writing-table. Carus made no attempt to detain her, though he knew well that she would lie awake for hours in her girlish misery; she must dree her woman's weird, and he must be alone.

"Good God!" he said, as the door closed and he was left in that shadowy solitude; "how can it be possible?"

and then his head sank on his folded arms, for he was
wellnigh blinded and overwhelmed by that sudden flash
of joy. Not for worlds would he have looked her in the
face as he touched her hand, for if he had, how could he
have let her go? "I must be dreaming!" he exclaimed
aloud a few minutes later; "it is madness! I am deceiving myself!" but all the time he knew well that it was
no deception, and that this great and unexpected blessing
had come to him,—that he, Carus Linacre, the shy
recluse, no longer young and set apart by his infirmity,
was to be so crowned and honoured!

No; it was no mistake. It was he who had been
blind, who, in his clumsiness and crass ignorance, had
probed and wounded that innocent young heart. His
very unselfishness and affection had made him stern with
himself and her. She had been the dearest thing in life
to him, and yet, for her sweet sake, he would have
sacrificed all that he most valued; and yet he had been
almost angry with her because she had refused to marry
Sydney. He would have given her to him without a
murmur, although he knew well that there would be no
more sunshine for him. "What does it matter if I
have to walk in the shade, if only my child is happy?"
he would say to himself.

There was a strange, deep glow in Carus's eyes as he
mused in that midnight silence. Now and then a board
creaked, or there was a faint scurry behind the wainscot,
or a restless dog turned himself with a sleepy groan on
the rug, but Carus's ears were impervious to all outward
sounds. If the old house were haunted, as some said,
they were only the spirits of youth, and hope, and joy
that glided round him. "Who could it be?" he was
saying to himself; "I asked myself that a thousand
times. Night and day I was perplexing myself with the
question, and all the time it was I! Oh, the miracle!
the wonder of it! I—myself!" Carus was quite dazed
and giddy; he got up from his chair and paced the long
room to calm himself. There was something indescribably pathetic in the man's happiness. Hitherto the future
had seemed a colourless blank to him; sooner or later
Heather would leave him for a home of her own. How

could he hope to keep such a little bud of blossoming
loveliness beside him? She would go away with her
chosen husband, and leave him to his books and his loneliness; there would be no wife, no child, for him; and
yet few men could have loved a woman better. And now
the gray curtain had lifted, and he was standing himself
in the glowing sunshine, for he knew, with that sure
knowledge that only love can give, that he and Heather
must never more be parted—that no one must come
between them. "My sweet one, I am not worthy to kiss
the dust off your little feet; but if you will have it
so——" he murmured, and then he gathered his papers
together, and locked them up, and went to his room for
a few hours' rest. Heather, weeping heartsick tears on
her pillow at the thought of the long parting, and the
perils by land and sea, knew nothing of the long pause
and whispered blessing as Carus passed her door.
"Heaven bless and guard my darling for me!" he said
softly.

The next morning there was little said during the
hurried breakfast. Mrs. Linacre had had a wakeful
night and was unable to rise, and Carus went up to
see her. The carriage was at the door when he came
down.

Christian met him at the foot of the staircase and
slipped the note into his hand. "Give him this, with
my dear love," she said quietly. "And Carus, promise
me one thing, that you will hide nothing from me."

"Dear Christian, you may trust me—you need not
fear, you shall know everything;" and then she thanked
him and let him go.

The next moment Heather glided out from the porch.
"Good-bye" was all she said; but the sadness in her
eyes went to his very heart. Oh, if only he had not to
leave her!

"God be with you, my dearest," he said gently; and
then a sudden uncontrollable impulse made him draw
her closer to him and kiss her quivering lips: "Take
care of yourself for me, Heather;" and then he put her
away from him, and a moment later the carriage door
closed after him.

" Come in, Heather dear, the wind is so cold," and Christian shivered as she spoke; but Heather did not hear her; she stood there, with the March wind blowing round her, and her eyes fixed on the receding carriage. Was it her fancy, or did a hand wave to her? She smiled, and then her arms dropped to her side, and with a languid step Heather re-entered the house.

XXXV

LETTERS FROM DURBAN

Dost thou thus love me, O thou all-beloved,
In whose large store the very meanest coin
Would outbuy my whole wealth? Yet here thou comest,
Like a kind heiress—from her purple and down
Uprising—who for pity cannot sleep,
But goes forth to the stranger at her gate,
The beggar'd stranger at her beauteous gate,
And clothes and feeds; scarce blest till she has blest.

MULOCK.

CHRISTIAN remained at the Stone House during Carus's absence; she knew he would wish her to do so, though he had said to her no word on the subject. She went over to Many Bushes the next day to pack her things and talk to Pen. The sight of the pretty room with the new cretonne covers gave her a pang.

"Oh, how cool and fresh and sweet it all looks!" she said, burying her face in a great bowl of yellow daffodils that Pen had just arranged. "I wish I had not to go away; but I feel it is my duty to take care of Jack's belongings."

"You always do your duty, Chriss dear," returned her friend affectionately; "and I will not say a word to keep you; but of course you know how Smudge and I will miss you." Smudge endorsed this by wagging his stubby little tail vigorously.

"You must come over as often as you can. I do hope you will not be dull, Pen?" But Pen scouted the very idea; how could she be dull with Mrs. Charlotte?—they still called her Mrs. Charlotte between themselves, and the children constantly running in and out. But for her friend's anxieties, Pen would have been radiantly happy that spring, knowing that every day was bringing her nearer to the blissful time when Walter was to take possession of the rooms in Market Place.

300

Pen felt ashamed of her own light-heartedness when she saw Christian's worn face and tired eyes. " Of course I love to have you with me," she said presently, as she was helping Christian to fold her dresses. " We are always so happy together; but I know Mrs. Linacre needs you most. I really think, Chriss, that she depends far more on you than on Heather." Christian smiled.

" Heather is so much younger, you see, and then she has not married Jack; there is another reason for my staying, Pen: Heather is not well; her head was so bad this morning that I persuaded her to remain in bed. I think she is fretting about Carus."

" Yes, I daresay;" but Pen was too busy at that moment to give full heed to Christian's remark. A headache! well, what of that? Most people suffered from them at some time or other.

" Oh, how troublesome this chiffon is!" she said with a little frown of anxiety; " you must use plenty of tissue paper, or you will have your gown crushed."

" Oh, never mind, Pen—get on!" returned Christian impatiently; " Hitchens will unpack for me and put things right."

Christian was in no mood for such trifles—the mint and anise and cumin of life were nothing to her; just then she could only remember that Jack was lying on his fever-bed, and that Carus was speeding across the ocean; she dropped her end of the skirt a little petulantly and went downstairs, leaving Pen and Brenda to finish, and wandered out into the garden.

" Pen does not understand how all these little paltry, insignificant things fret one," she said to herself as she walked down her favourite path, with its wide border full of sweet-smelling spring flowers—hyacinths and daffodils, and clumps of reddish-brown wall-flowers; some pigeons were circling round the church tower; a pair of doves were building their nest in a young elm by the gate. Christian could hear the male bird cooing to his mate; a little robin came fluttering out of a bush and hopped down the path, with his red breast shining in the sunshine. The sweet air, the wholesome scents, the soft twitterings, the busy bird-life round her seemed to soothe Christian, then came the chiming of the church bell. "Be still and do your best," it seemed to say to her. "God is everywhere, and you and yours are alike in the hollow of His hand—be still—be at peace."

"No news is good news!" was her usual morning greeting to her mother-in-law; and, indeed, as the days went on, she grew more hopeful. It is so impossible for youth not to be sanguine; in the spring one believes in miracles, in all sorts of prodigies and wonders, when buds are bursting, and flowers blossoming, and trees putting forth their tender leafage. Hope is unloosening her bandage, and looks round her with timid expectant eyes.

So Christian set a good example of cheerfulness to Mrs. Linacre and Heather; she insisted on carrying off the girl for long rides. She was secretly dismayed at Heather's unusual lassitude and drooping spirits.

"We must put some colour into those pale cheeks," she would say, as she urged Fairy into a gallop; and then, in spite of herself, Heather would come back refreshed and cheered.

At last another message reached them; Christian's lips were quite white as she tore open the envelope, and for a moment the words danced before her eyes. "Better —doctors more hopeful." But when Christian tried to repeat that brief message to her mother-in-law, her breath seemed to fail her; and Janet snatched the paper from her hands and read it for herself.

Christian had Fairy saddled, and rode over to Braybrooke to tell Pen and the Disneys the good news.

"He will get well; I know he will get well, Pen!" she exclaimed, and her eyes were very bright. "I think Fairy sympathises with me, for she has been dancing on three legs most of the way; haven't you, darling?" and Christian kissed the brown glossy neck of her favourite.

Heather did her best to rejoice too, but she was not well, and could not combat her secret sadness. Mrs. Linacre, with her usual pertinacity, insisted that she was fretting after Sydney. "You may depend upon it, Christian, that she regrets her childish refusal," she said quite seriously one day; "she is not the only girl who has sent a lover away, and then wants him back. Sydney never did a wiser thing for himself than when he enrolled himself in the Imperial Yeomanry. When he comes back, we shall see results for ourselves," and Janet nodded mysteriously.

Christian tried to combat this perverse notion, but in time she gave up the attempt to convince her of her error. Janet was quite happy in her belief; she was extremely kind to the girl, and petted and made much of her. " The war will soon be over, and then we shall have him back," she said one day; but she was somewhat surprised at the faint smile that was Heather's only response.

" Of course he would come back," the child said to herself impatiently; "what could Aunt Janet mean? Poor, dear Sydney! how pleased she would be to see him again!" But, after all, it was not Sydney she wanted. There was only one face for which she was longing, and which was more to her than any other face on earth. Heather would wander into the library and stand looking round her forlornly; how big and empty it looked without the well-known figure bending over the writing-table. How the quiet, thoughtful features had brightened at her entrance. " Is that you, Bell-Heather?" in the subdued, pathetic tone that was so dear to her; " you are welcome, little one,"—a kind smile would accompany the words, and then she would sit down beside him, so content and happy, and tell him all her doings. But a strange cloud had come between them, and those childish happy days were over. Carus no longer understood her; when they talked together, she could often detect a perplexed and troubled expression on his face, as though he had lost some clue.

" He is still as fond of me," she once murmured to herself, as she arranged the flowers on the table—this was her daily occupation. " I could not doubt his love if I would; but I no longer make him happy. Is it my fault, or is it his, that there is a barrier? And yet, how kind he was that morning. He has never kissed me like that before," and Heather blushed very sweetly, as she remembered how Carus had held her to his breast;

but dearly as she loved him, she never guessed, poor innocent child, the passion of worship that was in Carus's heart. At that moment Christian was quite aware of these long lingering visits to the library, and that the flowers were always kept fresh—even in the master's absence—but she never made any remark.

One morning as they were all sitting together at work in Mrs. Linacre's dressing-room letters were brought to her and Heather. They were both from Carus. He had arrived at Durban a few days before, and two more reports had already reached them. " Decided improvement all round" was the first, and the second was even better—" Improvement steadily maintained. Sends love." Oh, no wonder Mrs. Linacre shed tears of gratitude as she read them!

" It is to both of us, Christian!" exclaimed Mrs. Linacre excitedly. " ' Dearest mother and Christian,' that is the beginning, and there is a note inside for you." Then Christian knelt down beside her, and she and Janet read it together.

Heather sat and watched them. She had opened her envelope and peeped at the closely-written pages. " He has written all that for me," she said to herself with secret rapture, but she made no attempt to read it; she must hear about Jack first.

Christian's arm was round her mother-in-law; the two heads were quite close together. First one and then the other read out little scraps aloud.

I have just been to the hospital. Of course it was rather a shock at first. The poor, dear fellow is a perfect wreck. One can see for oneself what he has been through.

" Oh, Christian, my poor boy!" and Janet's voice was choked with emotion. It was Christian who went on.

The doctors say that his recovery is a perfect miracle; that it is very rarely that any one who has been so bad and has had a relapse is restored to health, but that Jack had such splendid recuperative powers and such tenacity of life; but I cannot help thinking that he owes his recovery mainly to Nurse Gillman's devotion and care.

"Oh, mater, do you hear that? Nurse Gillman! We must send her a present—a watch and chain, or something of that sort. You see, Carus thinks she has saved Jack's life."

"Oh, do go on, Christian!" exclaimed Heather, half amused and half provoked at these interruptions. "How is one to understand if you break off at every sentence?"

But Christian's pince-nez needed manipulation and readjustment, and it was Mrs. Linacre who took up the thread of Carus's narrative.

Jack knew me at once, though he was almost too weak to speak, and, of course, I could not hear a word. I had to get Nurse Gillman to tell me what he said.

"Dear old chap, how good of you to come! How's the mater and Chriss?"

And then he told Nurse Gillman to speak louder. They would not let me stay long; he was so weak, you see. I gave him your letter, Chriss, and he made me a sign to put it under his pillow. "The captain will read it himself when he is a little stronger," nurse said in her cheery way. Jack grasped my hand when I bade him good-bye, and his eyes were full of tears. In another minute he would have been sobbing like a child, for he was as weak as a baby, but nurse hurried me away. I shall go to-morrow, and every day, and—and——

"You can go on, Christian." Janet was a little out of breath.

Heather listened patiently to some more fragments. She made out that Carus was fairly comfortable, and had a small room which he was obliged to share with Dugald, and that one of Jack's fellow-officers had introduced him to a friend of his who lived there, and who showed him a good deal of hospitality and kindness.

I think Dugald is enjoying himself. He is keen on everything.

"What does this mean, Christian? Humph, humph, I cannot make this sentence out;" but Heather waited for no more. They were too much engrossed to miss her, she thought, and she could safely slip away and read her own letter in peace.

Heather closed the door so softly that no one heard

her, then she shut herself in her own room and curled herself up on the broad window seat by the open window. " To think of his taking all that trouble for me!" she said with a soft sigh of satisfaction as she glanced at the well-covered pages.

Heather had quite a store of letters from Carus, which she kept with her dearest treasures during his rare absences from home. He had always written to her " paper talks," as he would call them,—delightful descriptions of places and people, clever criticisms on the books he had read, little fanciful sketches with picturesque touches, for Carus had the pen of a ready writer, and dearly had Heather prized these letters.

And now she had this fresh proof of his thought for her. Heather was in no hurry to begin her letter. She leaned out in the sunshine and inhaled the warm fragrance of a great bed of wall-flowers under her window, and then her eyes rested on the Bowling Green. How long would it be before he would be walking there again with her? Jack was getting better. He would bring him back, and then—— Heather's girlish heart gave a sudden leap of joy as she thought of that return, then she settled herself to read her letter, but before she had finished the first sentence she laid it down with a little gasp of astonishment. This was no ordinary letter of chit-chat and description; he had never written to her in this way before.

My dearest (wrote Carus), I must call you that again, for I know now that for years you have been just the dearest thing on earth to me, though fool that I was, I never guessed what such knowledge meant. Oh, no wonder you were out of patience with me, my sweet, for I was utterly dense and stupid, and yet the handwriting of my fate was legibly inscribed before my eyes!

" What can he mean? ' Out of patience with him.' And could it really be true that she, foolish little Heather, should be the dearest thing in the world to him." The loveliest flush came to Heather's face. She covered her eyes with her hands as though she were dazzled. No, he had never written to her before in this manner, and there was a rising sob of excitement in her throat.

It is night, and I am/writing alone in my little room. Dugald is asleep. This morning I went again to the hospital. Perhaps I am getting a little used already to Jack's changed looks, for to-day he seemed a little more like himself, but his voice is so weak that even the nurse and doctor can hardly understand him, and with my deafness too. Well, for the present we must be content to look at each other. I have just written very fully to my mother and Christian, and by this time you will have probably heard all that there is to tell; but this letter only concerns you and me—you and me.

How many years is it since my mother brought you to the library that day—ten or eleven? I quite forget. Such a blue-eyed mite of a child, with brown hair flowing over your shoulders, and such a wistful little face. "I have brought you a new little sister, Carus," she said, with such a pleased expression on her face. "I have adopted Heather, and she is going to live with us." Indeed, I never saw my mother so excited. "Will you be my sister, little one?" I said to you, and I remember quite well the confiding way in which you slipped your tiny hand into mine. "Oh yes, for you have a nice, kind face, and I am not a bit afraid of you!" and when I placed you on my knee, you nestled up to me as though you had known me all your life. You see, I have a good memory, Bell-Heather.

From that day you seemed more my child than my mother's. She was very good to you, but I think she did not understand the workings of your childish heart as I did. You brought me all your troubles and difficulties. Sometimes I had to mend a broken doll, and sometimes a broken heart; you were so sensitive, Heather, so easily wounded, and yet a happier little creature never existed.

What dear days those were! We had a little sunbeam in the house. I never wanted you to grow up, for the child Heather seemed all my own, and I feared that when you came to your woman's kingdom that I should lose you. That fear always lay heavy in my heart.

And then what I dreaded came to pass, when your young lover came to me and besought my help.

I will not hide from you now that it was a sore trial to me. I felt as though I were shutting out the sunshine with my own hand when I promised to do my best for him, but I would not think of myself.

I liked Sydney Masters, and I thought he would be a fit mate for you, Heather; he was such an honest, clean-living boy. Such a goodly sample of a young English gentleman, full of energy and manly pluck, and he loved you so dearly. Was it any wonder that I deceived myself and him?

Forgive me if you can, dear child, for I see now with the clearer knowledge that has come to me that I must often have pained you. Once or twice I remember how reproachfully you looked at me. You thought it so strange, did you not, that I, of all people, should not understand? Child, child, I understand now!

But how did the knowledge come to me? Do you ask me that question, Heather? But, indeed, it is difficult to answer. Sometimes in life we walk on blindfold, and then some unseen hand tears away the bandage, and we see plainly, or it may be, there is a sudden lightning flash and the truth is revealed to us. It was so that night when you stood beside me in your white dress. Was it something you said? Was it only intuition? But all at once the truth came to me that you were not for Sydney or any other man—that you were mine.

The paper fluttered from the girl's trembling hands, and Heather's eyes were blinded with tears. For some minutes she could read no more.

" Carus, Carus, at last !" she whispered.

Oh, my child, can it be possible? All these weeks I have been asking myself this. Can it be true that you can ever bring yourself to give me what you refused to Sydney?

Think of it a moment, dearest. I am nearly twenty years older —a staid, elderly bachelor, and then my sad infirmity. Is it right? Is it even reasonable that such a one should offer himself as your mate? What will my mother and Christian and all the rest of our little world say? Will they not tell me that I am doing a selfish and cruel thing?

And yet I love you, Heather, as I have never loved any woman yet, and something tells me that my affection is returned; that you will not be unwilling to give yourself to me. Am I right or am I deceiving myself?

Darling, this is all I have to say, but not for worlds would I have you answer me yet. When I come back I shall look on your face and shall read the answer for myself. Until then I would like you to think over my letter very quietly and calmly. It shall be as you wish, dear child. If, after due consideration, you make up your mind that you prefer to keep me as your friend and brother, you shall never be troubled by a word from me. Your will shall be mine, and no brother shall be more faithful and fond. But if—oh! my Bell-Heather, my hand trembles as I write the words—if a closer love is to unite us, and you will be content with a deaf, middle-aged husband, you will know some day what a man's worship means. One more word. I have an odd fancy; it has just come to me. Will you do this one thing, Heather? If you decide to accept my life's devotion, will you let me see on your hand the sapphire and diamond ring I once gave you and that you never wear. If I see it on your finger I shall know. God bless you!—Your faithful friend always, and if you will, your devoted lover,

CARUS LINACRE.

XXXVI

CHRISTIAN'S DIPLOMACY

Let me not to the marriage of true minds admit impediments.—
SHAKESPEARE.

> The shadow of his presence made my world
> A paradise. All familiar things he touched,
> All common words he spoke became to me
> Like forms and sounds of a divine world.
> SHELLEY.

THE morning wore away, and still Heather sat there
in the sunshine oblivious of time, her eyes full of a sweet
wonder, for a marvellous thing had befallen her—Carus
loved her. Carus wished her to be his wife, and Heather's
simple, girlish heart seemed hardly large enough to con-
tain her happiness.

Deaf, middle-aged, what did it matter? He was Carus,
and it was she who was not worthy of him. Heather
set little value on her own young beauty. It seemed to
her nothing in comparison with other gifts. "If I were
only clever like some women," she was saying to herself; "but that he should stoop to me—a foolish, ignorant child, who owes all she has learned to him—it is this
that is the wonder."

A knock at her door startled her, and the next minute
Christian entered. She gave a quick glance at the girl's
flushed face and the closely-written sheets that lay in
her lap. Heather tried to fold them, but her hands shook
over the task.

"Is it late? Does Aunt Janet want me?" she asked
a little tremulously.

"No, you need not go to her," returned Christian.
"I do not think she has missed you, but it is quite two
hours since you left us."

"Oh no; impossible, Chriss!"

"Indeed I am right, dear; it is nearly luncheon-time,

309

and we have done nothing—the mater and I—but read and re-read that letter," and Christian gave a happy little laugh.

"You had a note all to yourself, had you not, Chrissy dear?"

"To be sure I had; it was private and confidential, and only for my own eyes. Is your letter private too, Heather?"

"Oh yes," returned the girl hurriedly; "why do you ask that? I never care to show Carus's letters; he often writes to me, you know."

"Does he? I am glad of that; but there is no need to look so frightened. Suppose I were to tell you that I know what is in that letter, and the reason why your eyes are shining like sapphires. You have been crying, Heather; but they were only happy tears that you have shed."

"What do you mean, Chriss?"

"Hush, I do not mean to tease you; no one has told me anything, not even Carus—but all the same, I know your secret. Dear Heather, you need not speak. I am only so glad—so glad that Carus has found it out for himself." No answer, only Heather's head was bowed and Christian could not see her face. "Dear little sister," laying her hand on her shoulder, "if you only knew how thankful I am for that. Men are so dense; they do not always understand; and Carus thinks so little of himself, but now he has found it out."

"Oh, please stop, please—please!"

"I will not say a word more; your secret shall be safe with me. Oh, there is the luncheon bell and we must go down, or the mater will guess something!"

"You go, Christian, and I will follow directly;" and Heather jumped up and smoothed her hair and hid away her letter.

"Where have you been, dear child?" asked Mrs. Linacre innocently, as Heather took her place; "you need not have gone away. Our letter had no secrets in it; they were reserved for your note, Christian," and Janet smiled as she spoke.

"You know I had a letter too," returned Heather

bravely; "but there was nothing about Jack in it." To Christian's surprise Mrs. Linacre took the matter quite coolly.

"Heather is such an odd child," she said in an amused voice; "she will have her little mysteries and reservations; would you believe it, Christian, she never will show me Carus's letters? She says it would spoil all her pleasure to share them with any one; and he actually indulges her in this whim."

"Oh, I have my mysteries too!" returned Christian lightly. "Mater, I wonder if you would mind being alone this afternoon, for I feel I must work off my restlessness in some way. Shall we have a ride or a walk, Heather? Oh, I forgot! Locock thought your mare ought to have a day's rest, so I am afraid it must be a walk."

Heather would rather have indulged in a solitary stroll, but she did not venture to say so, for fear she should arouse Mrs. Linacre's suspicions, so she agreed to the walk with at least an outward semblance of willingness.

She was somewhat taken aback, however, when Christian remarked coolly as they went down the drive together, attended by all the dogs as usual: "Now, Heather, you shall go one way and I another; so take your choice, my dear;" then as Heather stared at her, "I may be selfish and stupid, but there are limits even to my stupidity; and I certainly never intended to inflict my society on you. I only made the walk a pretext for getting you out into the sunshine, so that you could escape a long afternoon in the drawing-room, and possibly uninteresting visitors; you ought to be very grateful for my tact and finesse—a fellow-feeling makes us wondrous kind." But Heather protested that she would do nothing so ridiculous, and it ended by their sitting down on a mossy tree-trunk in a sunny little glade, where no one coming up the avenue could see them, and having a long confidential talk. "You are sure that you do not mind my knowing all this?" asked Christian a little anxiously, when the talk had drawn to a close.

"No, indeed, Chrissy dear; you are so understanding and comforting. Oh, you are laughing at my odd phrase; but when I was a small girlie I used to say that

to Carus. ' You are so understanding ; such a big lump
of comfort,' I once said to him, and I remember he
laughed too."

" I think you would be surprised, Heather, if you
knew how absurdly pleased I am about this."

" Are you, dear ?"

" It seems to me the most beautiful thing I have ever
heard. Not that Carus loves you—for indeed how could
he help it,—but that you are going to make up to him
for all he has missed in life—so much has been denied
him."

" Do you think I do not realise that?" and Heather's
face wore a sweet, womanly expression that was good
to see.

" I think no man ever needed a wife more ; you will
give him back his youth, Heather, and shield him from
his mother's trying little exactions ; the mater will not
be able to stand up against you both, and you will lead
the life you both wish. How do you suppose that she
will take the news ?"

" I am afraid she will be a little shocked at first.
You see, Aunt Janet has always believed that Carus would
never marry ; she always talks as though he were a
confirmed old bachelor, and he has encouraged her in
this idea ; she likes to manage him and make him do
as she pleases—that is why she never will let him stay
long at Many Bushes. I think he has given in to her too
much, Christian."

" Oh, there I agree with you! No one is perfect ; and
I think Carus has yielded to her for the sake of peace—
but things will be different now."

" Do you think so ?"

" Yes, I am sure of it ; as a married man Carus will
be quite masterful ; he has plenty of spirit if he cares
to assert himself—he is not really meek."

" Oh no, he can be quite stern, Christian ; but is it
not foolish of him to speak of himself as though he were
elderly, and he will not be forty until next January? I
am nearly nineteen, you know."

" That makes him twenty years older—but what of
that? Do you know, Heather, I have rather odd ideas

on the subject of matrimony. In my opinion, when two people really love each other, I do not think that anything should be regarded as an insuperable obstacle to their marrying—neither disparity of age, nor want of health, nor small means. I only draw the line at two things: when there is hereditary insanity, or a decided tendency to intemperance."

"I think you are right there."

"Of course I am right; but I am afraid many people would be shocked at my views. I would let a woman marry a man who was eight or ten years younger than herself—if they really loved each other,—and I would not be afraid of comparative poverty if they were young and strong."

"I really like your ideas, Christian; but Aunt Janet would be shocked at them."

"Yes, I daresay; for in her way the mater is a very worldly-wise woman and thinks a lot of the loaves and fishes. Now look at Pen and Walter Hamill. Could any two people be more in love with each other—they are just an ideal couple? But if their friends do not help them, they will not be able to marry for years and years, for I am not unpractical enough to suggest their beginning life on a curacy of a hundred and thirty a year."

"No, I suppose not."

"No, indeed, I have no such absurd Utopian ideas; but all the same, I mean to get them married as soon as possible. Mrs. Charlotte and I were talking about it the other day. She said it would be impossible for him to take pupils, as his parish work would occupy all his time; but she thought that Pen might do something, if we could hear of some Indian children who wanted a home, or an orphan who needed mothering—anything of that kind to eke out their small income. Pen is so clever and managing, and up to now she has never been used to luxuries; and so we both made up our minds to keep our eyes open and to leave no stone unturned. If they took a small house in the Cheetham Road,—where the Infirmary is, you know—they might begin on three hundred a year; the houses are so cheap there—and we could all club together for the furniture."

" What a nice idea, Christian! I am sure Aunt Janet would contribute handsomely; she is so fond of Pen. And as to Carus——"

" Oh, Carus will be our *pièce de résistance*—he is generosity personified! Now you have been a good child, Heather, and I am going to reward you; I am going to carry off the dogs for a smart run to Hammersley's Mill, —three miles there and back,—and you can stay in your hidie-hole and read your letter until you have learnt it by heart and feel chilly, and then you can come and meet me."

" Oh, Chriss, what a perfect darling you are!"

" I always was, mademoiselle, and my tact and finesse are simply beyond words. Adieu—*au revoir,*" and Christian summoned the dogs and set out for a brisk walk. Heather watched her until she was out of sight, and then she took the precious letter from its hidden receptacle. Learn it by heart! why, she knew every word already! Nevertheless, those pages would be read and re-read daily until Carus came back; and so engrossing was her occupation, and so delightful her musings, that Heather never remembered that she was to meet Christian until Cheri roused her by thrusting her little black nose into her hand.

" What, back already?" but Heather looked rather ashamed of herself.

" It is past four o'clock, and I am yearning for the cup that cheers but not inebriates," replied Christian in her usual crisp manner; " have you actually not moved all this time, my dear child? I hope you have not taken cold? This is only the first week in April, and that hollow is rather damp."

" Oh, I am as warm as a toast, Chriss; I am only just a little stiff; but I hope Aunt Janet will not question us too closely."

" Oh, you can leave her to me!" and then they walked quickly up the avenue and found Mrs. Linacre and tea waiting for them.

" Where did you walk," she asked, as Christian established herself cosily in a corner of the big Chesterfield couch,—" you have both such nice colours? After all, there is nothing like exercise for young people."

"I went to Hammersley," returned Christian; "Heather was lazy and did not go so far, so I left her on a log while the dogs and I tramped a bit farther."

Artful Christian! she put it so cleverly that Mrs. Linacre never discovered that Heather had not walked many hundred yards, and that the chimneys of the Stone House had been visible to her all the time.

"Did you have any visitors, mater?"

"Only Charlotte; she came up on her bicycle with Sheila; she left a message for you about old Armstrong: he died last night in his sleep." Armstrong was one of Christian's special *protégés* in the Infirmary.

"Oh dear, I am so sorry! but it was a nice, easy death. Poor old man! I shall miss him—and so will matron. Why did you not keep Mrs. Disney to tea?"

"Because she and Sheila were to have tea with the Hardcastles; but they stayed quite a nice long time. I read her part of Carus's letter, and she was so interested; she says we shall soon have them back now; that when Jack is a little stronger that they will put him on board. Do you know, Christian, I am sure that we ought to begin getting the rooms ready for Jack; we will go up to-morrow morning and see what alterations you will like made?" For Janet, with her usual pertinacity, was determined to keep the young couple as long as possible at the Stone House, and quite a palatial suite of rooms in the left wing were to be set apart for their accommodation. Christian was quite aware of what was in her mother-in-law's mind, but she was content to bide her time; she knew that Jack shared her opinion, and hated the idea of a mixed household—they would pay a long visit, and then have a little home of their own. Christian would prefer Many Bushes, but she meant to leave the decision with Jack.

Christian spent the entire morning in the west wing admiring her mother-in-law's arrangements for their comfort and adding a few suggestions.

No better quarters could have been found for an invalid: the large, sunny bedroom and spacious dressing-room and bath-room, and a pretty little sitting-room, with a view of the lake and the Bowling Green; there

was even a small room where his servant could sleep,—
if he needed one,—and the whole was shut in with baize
doors apart from the rest of the house; it was always
called the west wing.

"I do not think that we have forgotten anything,"
observed Mrs. Linacre, looking round with pardonable
pride at the luxurious dressing-room; there was the
comfortable couch, where Jack could stretch his long
limbs, and the big easy-chair by the window. "The dear
boy can have his old smoking-room; but until he is
strong enough for the long passage, I daresay you will
not mind his smoking here?"

"Oh, of course not, mater!" there was a touch of impatience in Christian's tone. "Jack will do as he likes
in his own special domain; do you suppose I am going
to interfere with his little pleasure?" Then she repented
of her petulance and put her arm round her mother-in-
law's matronly waist. "Dear mater! you are so good to
us both, and we are not half grateful enough;" then
Janet's eyes filled with tears.

She was dense and at times almost stupid, and she
loved her own way, though it was not always the best
way; but, after all, her heart was in the right place; she
responded instantly to kindness.

"You have been a dear, good daughter to me, Christian," she said affectionately, "and I shall tell Jack so;"
and then they went downstairs arm in arm, and found
Heather waiting for them in Troy. A week or ten days
later Mrs. Linacre received another telegram:

Leave Durban to-morrow in *Blair Castle.*—LINACRE.

XXXVII

THE "BLAIR CASTLE" IN PORT

A great content's in all things
And life is not in vain.
W. E. HENLEY.

When first I saw your face, a year ago,
I knew my Life's Good.
BROWNING.

All's well that ends well.—SHAKESPEARE.

WHEN Charlotte paid her next visit to the Stone House, three bright faces welcomed her; but it was not until afterwards that she recalled how little Christian and Heather had contributed to the conversation. It was Mrs. Linacre who had talked and explained and who had carried her off to see the glories of the west wing. Christian did not volunteer to accompany them; she sat over her embroidery frame listening and putting in a stitch here and there, but she made no attempt to stem the steady flow of words; as for Heather, she scarcely opened her lips until the two ladies had left the room.

"How excited Aunt Janet is, Chriss! I never saw her like this before; she has never stopped talking for an hour."

"She is so happy, you see."

"Yes; but we are happy too," and Heather glowed like a rose in the sunshine.

Charlotte was saying that very moment to her friend above, "How wonderfully Heather is improved! Graham was noticing it the other day; he says she is quite a little beauty."

"We are happy too, Chriss; but somehow I don't feel as though I could talk about it."

"Nor I," and Christian looked up with the beaming smile that Jack loved. "I feel that nothing could induce me to enter into all those particulars. When the mater

begins I just long to run away and hide myself somewhere. I am afraid I don't hear half she says, and sometimes I answer at random. Do you know what I said
yesterday when she pulled out one of those apple-green
curtains from the press and asked me if it would not do
splendidly for a *portière* in Jack's room to keep out the
draught? I said yes, certainly, that it was just the thing;
and then I remembered that Jack had a perfect horror
of apple-green, and so I had to get out of the muddle
somehow."

"Whatever could you say, Chriss?"

"Oh, I said it was extremely handsome, but hardly
suitable for a gentleman's dressing-room, and that I was
afraid the green would make him look sallow. I was
obliged to say that, for she was so set on the hideous
thing; but she gave in at that. Oh, Heather, I hope you
won't think me horrid; but all this talk and fuss seem
so to spoil things!"

"I feel just the same, Chriss."

"Sometimes I wonder if the three weeks will ever
come to an end," went on Christian; "if it were not
unkind I would go to Many Bushes for a week or so;
it would be so nice and refreshing to be there with Pen;
and I should not feel so nervous and jumpy."

"Then why not go, dear? Aunt Janet and I will be
quite happy together."

"No, I won't be so selfish; the mater wants me.
Hush, Heather, they are coming down now—right about
face—attention," and Christian threaded her needle afresh
with silk. "Well, madam," as Mrs. Disney re-entered
the room, "do you think the British soldier will be well
housed?"

"I think Captain Linacre will be delighted with his
quarters, Christian," returned her friend.

But Mrs. Linacre went on eagerly: "Charlotte admires
everything; she says it is all just perfect; and she is
quite of your opinion about the *portière*, Chriss, and that
the brown *plushette* will be better."

"Yes, indeed; but I must go now, for I am to meet
Graham at Moss-side at half-past four."

Then Christian threw down her work and said **she**

would walk to the gate with her. "You can come too, if you like, Heather," as the girl looked up wistfully; but she shook her head.

"It seems almost too good to be true, does it not, Christian?" observed Charlotte, as they walked down the avenue. "Who would have expected such a happy ending last October? Do you remember that quaint old saying: 'A passage perilous maketh a port pleasant'?"

"Jack is not in port yet;" Christian's voice had a break in it, and Charlotte looked at her quickly.

"I know what you mean—and the days seem long, do they not? But remember every day of those sea-breezes will be life and health to your husband."

"Yes, I hope so; but one cannot help one's nerves, and I am terribly restless. I mean to go up and see Uncle Jasper to-morrow; and then there is my wedding present to buy for Adelaide—she is to be married in June."

"Why not stay for a couple of nights at Beauchamp Gardens?" suggested Mrs. Disney, with her usual tact. "Mr. Vigne will be so pleased to have you—and you can do your shopping and see your aunt and cousin; it would be a nice attention on your part;" then Christian promised to consider it.

It ended by her taking Charlotte's advice and carrying out this programme. The three days' visit did her a world of good, and she was far less restless when she returned; but a few days at Many Bushes did more than anything else to restore the balance of her mind, and the pleasure was all the greater because it was so unexpected. One afternoon when she returned from an unusually long ride, she heard that Pen had been up to see her and had only just left.

"She was very disappointed at missing you," continued Mrs. Linacre; "but she could not stay longer, as she had promised to fetch Sheila; it is Minna Fergusson's birthday, and the child has been spending the day there."

"Yes, I see; she wanted to save Mrs. Disney a long tramp; but, all the same, I wish I had not missed her. I suppose she had nothing special to tell me?"

" Indeed she had, Christian; she came over to tell you that Mr. Hamill is going to the Vicarage on Wednesday for two or three nights. She thought you would like to know this."

" Wednesday!—the day after to-morrow—I had no idea he was coming so soon. Oh, what a pity! if I had only been at home, we could have asked him to come to dinner."

" I am afraid Penelope is a little disappointed about it, though she did not say so; but why should you not go home for a day or two, Christian; it would make things more comfortable for them?"

" Oh, can you spare me, mater?"

" Yes, of course; Heather and I will get on quite well. If you like to send a line to Penelope to-night, George can easily take it over, and your room can be got ready for you."

" I will write it at once; what a brilliant idea, mater, dear! Pen will be charmed;" and Christian wrote her note, and she and Pen had a few happy days together. As usual, Walter spent most of his time with his sweetheart. Christian did not return to the Stone House until Tuesday morning, and then she brought Pen with her for a couple of days.

And so time wore on, and presently the day came when the *Blair Castle* would be expected in port. Carus had promised to telegraph from Southampton, and one fine May afternoon the message came—a somewhat lengthy one.

Jack wonderfully fit. Sends love. Sleep to-night at Southampton. Arrive Braybrooke to-morrow 4.56.

" Then they will not be here until nearly six," observed Mrs. Linacre; " you may depend upon it, Christian, that they will have luncheon with my brother; Jasper is rather exacting, and Jack will not dare pass through London without seeing his uncle."

" Perhaps Carus thinks it will be better to break the journey," returned Christian; " we must not forget that Jack is still an invalid." Christian folded her work together as she said this and rose from her seat.

" It is not time to dress yet, Christian."

" No, mater, I know," very gently ; " I am only going for a turn in the garden ;" but she carried off the telegram with her. To-morrow she and Jack were to meet after more than a twelvemonth's parting ; she had been his wife for just thirteen months, and since they plighted their solemn troth at the altar they had only been one hour together ; so no wonder that Christian's feelings were a little mixed. Her husband was a stranger to her, and yet she had grown to love him ; but though she longed with all her heart to have him back, and to begin her wifely ministry, she felt a perfect terror at the thought of that meeting. " If I could only be alone with him ; but to be there amongst them all—the idea suffocates me ;" Christian said this to herself as she paced the Bowling Green ; she felt afraid that at the last moment her courage would desert her, and that she would run away and hide herself rather than be present at that public reception. " Jack will hate it too—I know he will ; we think alike on so many things," she went on. " I remember his telling me once how he disliked his mother kissing him when Hitchens was in the room, or any of the servants, and how she always would do it. ' It makes a man look such a fool, Chriss,' were his words ;" for Jack had a holy horror of scenes, domestic or otherwise, being, as Christian well knew, an extremely undemonstrative person.

Christian was late for dinner that evening, but for once there was no word of chiding. " You were too far from the house to hear the dressing-bell," Mrs. Linacre said tranquilly, as Mrs. Jack made her excuses. " Heather was late too ;" and then Heather blushed and looked a little confused. She too had betaken herself to the Bowling Green, but had retired when she caught sight of a gray gown, and had strolled over in the direction of the lake ; Heather too had her fears and tremors ; but she knew that after the first moment things would be well with her.

" Oh, he is so thoughtful, so considerate ; he will make everything easy for me !" she said with a happy sigh. " I will not spoil things by being conscious and nervous ;

and if Aunt Janet notices my ring, I shall tell her that
Carus wished me to wear it."

"Oh, I am so glad it is bedtime!" exclaimed Christian
a few hours later, as she and Heather went upstairs
together; "I really thought the evening would never
end."

"It was rather long, certainly; but Aunt Janet wanted
to learn that new Patience, and then she got so interested over it that she forgot how late it was."

"I was playing Patience too, my dear, and yawning
myself to death over it. Well, good-night; we are
neither of us inclined to talk;" and Christian closed her
door a little abruptly as she heard the soft swish of a
silk dress on the stairs.

After breakfast the next morning, Christian helped
Heather to arrange the flowers in the library and west
wing, then she went off for a long ride, and did not return
until luncheon was nearly over; she found that Mrs.
Linacre and Heather had driven over to Braybrooke to
fetch two or three things that had been forgotten.

"You look flushed and tired, Christian," observed her
mother-in-law kindly; "why did you go far, my dear?
—I am feeling all the better for my little drive—you had
better lie down until tea-time; Heather shall bring you
a cup upstairs if you like;" and Christian accepted this
offer gratefully. The rest she could dispense with, but
the solitude and silence would be soothing; it would be
pleasant to sit by the open window and feel the sweet
May breeze blow in on her.

Heather found her looking refreshed and rested when
she brought up the little tea-tray; as she put it down
a flash caught Christian's eye. "Ah!" with a meaning
glance at the sapphires; then Heather hastily withdrew
her hand.

"It is a quarter-past four, Chriss," she said hurriedly;
"Aunt Janet hopes that you will come down when you
have finished your tea; she thinks they may be here a
little earlier. Shall I help you dress, dear?"

"No, thank you; I shall get on better alone; don't   •
let the mater fuss; they cannot possibly be here for an
hour and a half, and I am never long dressing. Do you

think my white gown will be too smart, Heather—Jack always likes me in white?"

"Then wear it, dear, by all means. I chose this pink delaine because Carus always says it suits me; but it is not very fresh."

"But he is right, and you look like a rosebud in it, and nothing could be nicer; so run away, dear, and let me dress in peace." But for some reason Christian was a very long time over her toilet, and neither did she make her appearance until it was nearly time for the travellers to arrive; and Mrs. Linacre would have sent up more than one message to hurry her, only Heather flatly refused to take them.

"But she will not be ready, and Jack will think it so strange if his wife is not here to receive him," she observed almost piteously. Poor Janet! in her excitement she was more fussy and punctilious than ever, and Heather found it difficult to pacify her; but she grew quiet at once as Christian came down in her white dress.

She found them, as she expected, in Troy, and Hyde and his subordinates already in the porch, while Mrs. Mullins's cap-strings were visible in the corridor; a face or two peeped out of the half-open baize door that shut off the servants' quarters; two or three gardeners were in the drive.

"Come and sit down, Christian," and Mrs. Linacre pointed to a seat beside herself; but Christian shook her head, with a forced smile; she was very pale.

"I would rather be in the drawing-room," she said quietly.

"You must send Jack to her there," whispered Heather hurriedly, for her quick ear had caught the faint sound of wheels; "she would rather meet him alone." Perhaps Janet understood, for she said no more. Christian had heard the carriage wheels too; she had purposely waited until the last minute. The drawing-room was nearly opposite Troy; the door was open, but a *portière* always hung there; Christian stood quite close to it— she could hear everything there.

They were coming up the drive—Locock was whipping up his horses—then the carriage stopped; there was a little hubbub of voices, of exclamations; no doubt Mrs. Linacre and Heather had gone to the porch.

" Where is Chriss?" The deep, well-known tones made Christian's heart beat faster. " Mother, where have you hidden her?"

" Christian is in the drawing-room, Jack; please go to her." It is Heather who speaks; and Christian shrinks back a little among the curtain folds as Jack enters.

To his dazzled eyes, the great, sunny room seemed empty, and he stood for a moment bewildered. Christian gave a little gasp when she saw him; she was trembling from head to foot. Could this poor wreck—this hollow-eyed, emaciated man—be the muscular, well-knit, vigorous, young soldier from whom she had parted on her wedding-day—could this be Jack? Then at that little sighing sound he turned and saw her.

" Why, Chriss!"—but Jack said no more; he only opened his arms, and the next moment Christian was clinging to him.

" Oh, Jack!" she sobbed, " that you should come back to me like this!" And Jack's eyes were a little moist as he kissed her.

" Let me sit down," he said in a shaky voice; " this sort of thing bowls a fellow over;" and Christian, alarmed at the signs of exhaustion on his face, took his arm and led him to a chair.

" Let me go and fetch you some wine, dear; you are faint—the journey has been too much;" but her heart sank as she spoke. She realised now how nearly she had lost him; but, to her surprise, he held her fast.

" No, you must not leave me. It is nothing—a little weakness, that is all—your face is better than any wine. Darling! have you put on that white dress for me?" and then he drew her closer, so that his head rested against her. " Oh, if you knew how I have longed for this—how I have wanted my wife, Chriss!"

XXXVIII

Sweethearts and Wives

Never had man more joyful day than this,
Whom heaven would hepe with bliss.
Make feast therefore now all this livelong day;
This day forever to me holy is.
SPENSER.

The only love, worthy of the name, ever and alway uplifts.—
MacDonald.

THE silence that followed Jack's few pathetic words
seemed too sacred to be broken. Yes—this was the moment for which he had longed as he had lain wounded
in the hospital in Ladysmith, while the shells groaned
and screamed over the town, the one ray of comfort
that came to him, as he tossed on his fever-bed in Durban.

"I don't want to give in if I can help it," he said once
to the chaplain who visited him; "I am going to make a
fight for it;" and then in a choked voice: "I have got a
wife, you see, and that makes all the difference;" and the
chaplain, who was a married man himself, felt quite
touched by these few simple words.

But in the deadly weakness that ensued, poor Jack
would thankfully have turned his face to the wall and
given it all up. When in that collapse of body and mind
kind Sister Death would have been welcome, but the instinct of life was strong within him, and Jack held on;
perhaps the sight of Carus's face was the best restorative,
for he made speedy progress from that time.

"Yes, this is what I wanted," Christian heard him
murmur again. "I have come back to home and rest,
and you, Chriss." Then, as Christian looked down at the
dark, closely-cropped head that rested so heavily against
her, her heart seemed to swell with wifely tenderness and
pity for his weakness.

325

little hubbub of voices, o
Linacre and Heather had

"Where is Chriss?" Th
Christian's heart beat fast
hidden her?"

"Christian is in the dra
her." It is Heather who
back a little among the cu

To his dazzled eyes, th
empty, and he stood for a
gave a little gasp when sh
from head to foot. Could
eyed, emaciated man—be
ous, young soldier from
wedding-day—could this
sighing sound he turned

"Why, Chriss!"—but
opened his arms, and th
clinging to him.

"Oh, Jack!" she sobb
to me like this!" And J
he kissed her.

"Let me sit down," l
sort of thing bowls a fell
at the signs of exhausti
led him to a chair.

"Let me go and fetc'
faint—the journey has
sank as she spoke. Sh
lost him; but, to her su

"No, you must not
weakness, that is all—w
Darling! have you put
then he drew her clos
her. "Oh, if you kn
how I have wanted my

was still holding his
move or speak, but she
e window. " You can
he is yours as well as
n's eyes were saying.
e had been alone with
had been all that she
iet hour of silence had
If Jack had come back
she would have rejoiced
wifely welcome, but he
r as he did now in his
t weeks of nursing and
re her. Jack, broken in
t care; and as Christian
e her heart was register-
ckness and health." Oh,
words! But at least she
o them. " Jack will soon
she was saying to herself
d.

Jack awoke; he smiled as
side him.
?" he asked. " I did not
thought Chriss and I were

or half an hour; you have
d Christian passed her cool
forehead. " Mater, perhaps
ner as well as Jack's; you
you not?"
ief answer.
e went downstairs. After all,
mothers have these moments
ll leave his father and mother
ife," says Holy Writ; and
tiently aside when their son
iger woman.
nts;" there was a brief spasm
t as she said this, but the next
asserted itself. " God forgive

" Jack," she whispered; " don't you know that I wanted it too? The year has been so long without you; I was always longing to have you back."

" Do you really mean it?" There was a flash of joy in the sunken eyes; but Jack had no time to say more, for Carus was beside them.

" You must forgive my interrupting you, Christian," he said gently; " but I dare not let Jack stay here any longer; we must get him up to his room. Winston, his man, is outside, waiting to help him."

" Chriss must come too; you must not separate us, Carus,"—Jack's tone was a little masterful in spite of his weakness—and Carus smiled.

" Christian shall show us the way. I have told my mother that you must be perfectly quiet for an hour or two;" and then the little procession started. Janet watched them from below, her heart aching as she saw how feebly Jack walked, and how, more than once in the ascent, he stood still and panted as though his strength failed him.

Jack uttered a sigh of relief as he sunk on the couch, while Christian placed the pillow under his head; he was too weak and spent to look round at his beautiful room; he took what they gave him and then closed his eyes, but he opened them once to see if Christian was still there.

" Try to sleep, Jack," she whispered as she noticed this. " I am going to sit beside you—indeed, I will not leave you;" and when Carus and Winston had left the room she drew her chair still closer to the couch, so that he could hold her hand. An hour later the *portière* was drawn back and Janet moved noiselessly across the room; she was hungering and thirsting to see her boy again, and the time had seemed endless to her. She stood at the foot of the couch wiping away a few quiet tears as she looked at him; how changed he was! The lean, brown face had grown so thin and wasted that the skin seemed too tightly strained, and the hollowness of the temples and eye-sockets were fearfully apparent; his hands, once so strong and sinewy, were now as white and soft as a woman's. No wonder Janet wept as she stood there, for it seemed to her as he lay there in his sleep that he was only a shadow of himself. Jack was still holding his wife's hand; Christian dared not move or speak, but she motioned to the easy-chair by the window. "You can stay, we can both watch him; he is yours as well as mine,"—that was what Christian's eyes were saying. Christian had had her wish; she had been alone with her husband, and their meeting had been all that she could have desired, and this quiet hour of silence had been full of unspeakable healing. If Jack had come back to her strong and full of life, she would have rejoiced and have been ready with her wifely welcome, but he would not have appealed to her as he did now in his feebleness, when she knew that weeks of nursing and womanly ministrations lay before her. Jack, broken in health, would need her constant care; and as Christian sat there in the evening sunshine her heart was registering its wifely vows: "For sickness and health." Oh, how lightly she had said the words! But at least she would do her best to live up to them. "Jack will soon see how nice I can be to him," she was saying to herself when her mother-in-law entered.

The dinner-bell rang before Jack awoke; he smiled as he saw the two dear faces beside him.

"Have I been long asleep?" he asked. "I did not hear you come in, mother; I thought Chriss and I were alone."

"She has only been here for half an hour; you have had a lovely sleep, Jack;" and Christian passed her cool hand refreshingly over his forehead. "Mater, perhaps you will send me up my dinner as well as Jack's; you would like me to stay would you not?"

"Rather!" was Jack's brief answer.

Janet sighed a little as she went downstairs. After all, she was only human—most mothers have these moments of disillusion. "A man shall leave his father and mother and shall cleave to his wife," says Holy Writ; and mothers have to stand patiently aside when their son turns from them to a younger woman.

"It is only Chriss he wants;" there was a brief spasm of jealousy in Janet's breast as she said this, but the next moment her better nature asserted itself. "God forgive me for my selfishness when my dear boy has been given back to me," she murmured; " shall I grudge those poor children their happiness? Can I not understand their feelings? He has come back to her from the very shadow of the valley of death, and Christian and he know this;" and Janet was so sweet and subdued for the remainder of the evening that no one would have guessed at that brief struggle for herself.

Christian and Jack exchanged very few words together; directly the little meal was over, Carus came up and ordered the invalid to bed.

" You must not let him talk to-night," he said; " he will be better after a good night's rest. You can sit by him until he is asleep if you like, Chriss, and then come down to us; Heather and I want to talk to you."

" Oh, I forgot, Carus! Do wait a moment; I must speak to you?" But Carus shook his head and made her a sign to be silent.

"Come down as soon as you can leave him," was all he said.

" Carus looks ten years younger; I never saw him so fit," murmured Jack dreamily. " What a brick he is, dear old fellow! I wish I could keep awake, Chriss, for I do so want to talk to you!"

" Not to-night, dear Jack; we shall have plenty of time to-morrow—besides, I really must go down now."

" All right; give my love to the mater, and tell her I am asleep—and kiss me again, darling. Good-night, God bless you!" and Jack was asleep almost before Christian closed the door.

All this time she had forgotten Heather. " I have thought of nothing but Jack," she said to herself with sudden compunction; but Christian may be forgiven for her selfishness.

When Janet went into the porch to receive her sons, Heather had followed her and stood a little in the background. Carus was assisting his brother and did not at once perceive her; then she saw him look round as though he were seeking her, and she moved out of her corner; as she did so, a ray of light caught the sapphire and diamond on her hand, and there was a sudden answering flash in

Carus's eyes, but'his greeting was as silent as hers; a mere pressure of the hand that told her that he understood, then he gave his arm again to Jack.

When the invalid had gone up to his room, Heather remained with her adopted mother. After a time Carus joined them; he gave Heather a quick look as he seated himself by his mother, but the girl did not meet his glance; she sat beside them silently, her long lashes fringing her flushed cheeks, looking so indescribably lovely in her sweet, young bloom, that Carus could scarcely refrain from taking her in his arms before his mother's eyes. He heaved a sigh of relief when Mrs. Linacre announced her intention of peeping in on Jack.

"You need not be afraid, Carus; I will not wake him if he is asleep;" and Carus offered no objection. Heather seemed inclined to follow her; she actually rose from her seat, but a detaining hand arrested her.

"My mother does not need you," he said quietly, "and I do. Come with me into the library; no one will follow us there;" and he drew her gently across the hall, and the door closed behind them. "At last I have you to myself!" were Carus's first words. "My darling! my precious child! are you sure you mean it?" and he took the little hand in his, but the shy, upward glance was sufficient answer; the next moment he was holding her to his breast.

Heather nestled against him quite happily; she was like a little bird who found her nest and had ceased to flutter, and who was safe at last. Carus let her stand there silently, his man's nature was too deeply stirred within him for words. "My little blessing," once escaped from his lips, but to himself he was saying that he was not worthy of such happiness. "It is a miracle of goodness, but I have not deserved it; I thank my heavenly Father for this unspeakable consolation."

Presently they were talking together more calmly. Heather was on her old stool; she would have no other place. "Please let me sit here," she pleaded; "I can talk so much better;" but he gave in to her rather reluctantly.

"It is I who ought to be at your feet, sweetheart," he returned; but Heather shook her head.

"I have not ceased to be your child because——" but Heather did not finish her sentence, she only glanced at her ring, but Carus finished it for her.

"Because some day you are going to be my little wife —is that what you would say, Bell-Heather?"

"Yes, I meant that," struggling with her blushes, and looking so sweet in her girlish bashfulness that Carus's self-control was sorely exercised; he could have over-whelmed her with his lover's devotion and worship, but she was so young, and in his tender reverence he feared that she might be less at her ease with him. "Yes, I meant that," she went on; "we must not alter the dear old ways, Carus; you must let me wait on you—it has always made me so happy."

"Yes, darling, I understand; you shall be my little ministering angel, as you always have been; but, Heather, there is something that I want to say before we take other people into our confidence."

"Christian knows all about it," whispered Heather; "she found it out for herself, and is so glad of it."

"Is she, dear? Christian is a sensible young woman, and I have the greatest respect for my sister-in-law; but now listen to me, Bell-Heather: are you quite sure that this is really the right thing for you?"

"How do you mean, Carus?"

"I mean what I said in my letter, when I begged you to think over it all very seriously; that is why I would not let you write to me. Are you quite sure in your own mind, dearest, that you would not like a little longer time? Remember, I am thinking only of you; nothing can be so dear to me as your happiness; and if you wish to be free for a few months longer, you have only to say so, my child."

"But, Carus,"—and there was a distressed look on Heather's face—"I thought we were engaged now?"

"So we are,"—and Carus smiled with tender amuse-ment,—"but all the same, it was my duty to say this. Do you know, when I sent that letter I felt as though I had done a wrong thing—as though I had taken advantage of you; you have seen so few men, Heather, and you are so young, dear; perhaps I ought to have waited another year?"

"It would have made no difference, Carus."

"Would it not, dear? It is sweet of you to say that; but I am so much older—have you noticed my gray hairs, Heather?"

"I like gray hairs," she returned softly; "and I do not care about young men. It is because you are grave and quiet that I like to be with you."

"But my deafness, love——" and Carus's face was a little sad.

"I think that only makes me love you more;" and Heather's cheek rested against his hand. "Carus, I want to say something too. There is no need to wait; you could not set me free if you tried; I think I have always belonged to you. Ever since dear Aunt Janet brought me home, you have been goodness itself to me. I owe all my happiness to you; I never meant to leave you, Carus —nothing could have tempted me; but I never imagined"—her voice faltering—"that you would think of this: that you, who are so much older and wiser, could care for such an ignorant, childish creature; it is this that seems so wonderful to me;" and as Heather said this in her simple, earnest way, all Carus's morbid scruples were set at rest.

"Then I will say no more, darling; shall this be your engagement ring, or would you like another?"

"I shall like none so well as this, Carus; and it has never been worn, you know—at least publicly I mean. I used to wear it in my own room sometimes—I loved it so."

"No one shall interfere with you now," returned Carus fondly. "How I shall love to give you pretty things! Oh, by the bye, Heather, the Vigne necklace!—that ought to have been yours, and now Uncle Jasper has given it to Christian."

"What does that matter?" returned Heather; "I would much rather Christian had it; we are not going to be gay people,—you and I—and I shall not want a lot of jewellery."

" But, all the same, I should like my wife to be well dressed; but, thank Heaven, I can give you all you want! And I also beg to inform you, my dear, that I have not the slightest intention of burying the future Mrs. Carus Linacre. Why are you leaving me in such a hurry?" as Heather started up with an exclamation.

" That is the gong for dinner, and I have not dressed."

" You are dressed to perfection; do you think I would let you change that pink frock, Bell-Heather? Besides, we are none of us in our war-paint to-night. Well, I suppose we must go. Dinners, like time and tide, wait for no man; but what are we to do about my mother?"

" Let us wait and ask Christian" was Heather's response to this; and then Hyde came in search of them, and told them that Mrs. Linacre was already in the dining-room.

XXXIX

"I Have Brought You Your Daughter"

I break a hard thing with patience.—MOTTO.

All one's life is a music if one touches the notes rightly and in time.—RUSKIN.

WHEN Christian at last made her appearance in the drawing-room, she found Carus and Heather alone. Mrs. Linacre had been summoned to the housekeeper's room to interview an old pensioner who had walked over from Braybrooke to see her.

Christian stood before them a moment, gravely scrutinising their faces, then she nodded in a satisfied way.

"So it is all right, you dear people?" she remarked coolly.

"Oh yes, it is all right!" then Heather jumped up from her seat and whispered; "he knows you are glad about it, Chriss; I told him."

"I never was so glad about anything in my life except about Jack's coming home," was her answer. And then a very loving embrace passed between her and Heather. "You will be my little sister in reality, will you not, Heather?" and then Carus claimed his brotherly salute and congratulations. After that they all sat down on the big Chesterfield couch together—Carus like a thorn between two roses, as he said—and talked happily together.

"We want to ask your advice, Christian," he observed presently; "do you think the mother ought to be told to-night?"

"If you ask my opinion, certainly not," returned Christian without a moment's hesitation; "she has had excitement enough for one day—indeed, we all have. You have no idea of the strain it has been these last few days; it would only deprive her of the night's rest that she would otherwise have."

But, all e same.
dressed; bu hank He
And I also ig to info
the slightest intention
Linacre. Wy are you
Heather stand up wit!

"That is is gong fr

"You are refused to
let you chang that pr
we are none of us in
suppose hat
for no man; br

"Let us wit and a
sponse to this and
and told them that Mrs.
room.

ondly. " Well,
a iring day and
upstairs with me,
Carus from under

nr,' he whispered.
comit, Carus drew
w. 'Do not trouble
I sleⴕ sweetly, dar-

as thⴕugh she had a

t, but ⴕould it not be
first— mean without
ⴕifficult ⴕmetimes."
that, Chⴕss? But make
d to spⴕk to my mother

Christiaⴕs surprise she
made a ⴕnfidant of his

us and theⴕhighly amused,
ⴕlings by dⴕling Carus all
a sly dogⴕ knowing old
a cunning, ⴕly old fox, to
—here there ⴕs a weak dig
a prize like ⴕat! Don't tell
ⴕ ot the girl's ⴕoks; you bet,
I always toldⴕhe mater that
r little beautyⴕme day. One
ⴕes and hair anⴕcomplexion."
rotesting that ⴕwas Heather's
ⴕ her lovely face ⴕt had won his
teasing mood. Hⴕtold Christian
never been moreⴕurprised in his
never thought thⴕ Carus would
that they would ⴕok like father
agreed quite meeⴕy. ' Of course
he owned; ' you ⴕed not tell me
of course, I couldⴕot help saying
glad about it. Andⴕ I am. There

" The oracle has spoken, Bell-Heather; I think we had better abide by her advice."

" You would be wise to do so," went on Christian; " you know how excitable the mater is; and she is so utterly unprepared, that the news will be quite a shock to her. A few hours sooner or later will not matter. Why not leave her in peace to-night to think of Jack?"

" I told Heather just now that you were a most sensible young woman, Christian, and I beg to' endorse my words." But Heather sighed; she was evidently afraid of the delay.

" If you are sure Aunt Janet will not be hurt," she returned. " But it does not seem right to hide things from her, even for a few hours; but, of course, if you and Christian think otherwise"—but Heather heaved another gentle sigh, as though even this happy secret oppressed her. For once her loyalty to her adopted mother clashed with Carus's decision.

" We will tell her to-morrow, dearest; there will be little time lost," he said soothingly; but Christian struck in.

" We must use our tact sometimes, Heather. Don't you remember the Vicar's definition of tact—' sanctified common sense'? Well, I consider that this is a case in which you ought to exercise your ' sanctified common sense.' I know exactly how you feel, dear,—you want to get things off your mind; but it would only result in giving the mater one of her neuralgic headaches and a wakeful night."

" Very well, Chriss," returned Heather submissively, and the next moment Mrs. Linacre re-entered the room and asked her to fetch her smelling salts.

" I suppose it is the excitement," she said quietly; " but my head is beginning to ache. You look tired too, Christian. Is Jack asleep, or may I go up and wish him good-night?"

" He was nearly asleep half an hour ago; he sent his love to you, mater. No, you had better not disturb him; Winston is in the dressing-room, keeping guard."

" Then I think the best thing would be for us to go to bed too. Heather, my child, what makes your face so flushed?" and Janet patted the hot cheek fondly. "Well, good-night, my dears; we have had a tiring day and ought to sleep well. Are you coming upstairs with me, Heather?" Then the girl glanced at Carus from under her lashes.

"You had better go with her, dear," he whispered. But as Janet turned her back for a moment, Carus drew her towards him and kissed her brow. "Do not trouble about anything—leave it to me, and sleep sweetly, darling!" and Heather smiled happily.

Christian lingered for a moment as though she had a final word to say.

"Carus, of course you know best, but would it not be well to speak to your mother alone first—I mean without Heather? The mater is rather difficult sometimes."

"Do you think I do not know that, Chriss? But make your mind easy; I always intended to speak to my mother alone."

"May I tell Jack?" But to Christian's surprise she found that Carus had already made a confidant of his brother.

Jack had been first incredulous and then highly amused, and had given vent to his feelings by calling Carus all manner of names: "He was a sly dog, a knowing old beggar, a regular deep one, a cunning, wily old fox, to think of an old bachelor"—here there was a weak dig in the ribs—"snapping up a prize like that! Don't tell me, old fellow, that it is not the girl's looks; you bet, I know a thing or two. I always told the mater that Heather would be a regular little beauty some day. One does not often see such eyes and hair and complexion."

It was no use Carus protesting that it was Heather's sweet nature more than her lovely face that had won his heart. Jack was in a teasing mood. He told Christian afterwards that he had never been more surprised in his life, and that he had never thought that Carus would marry. "I told him that they would look like father and daughter, and he agreed quite meekly. 'Of course I am too old for her,' he owned; 'you need not tell me that, Jack;' and then, of course, I could not help saying that I was awfully glad about it. And so I am. There isn't a better fellow living, Chriss, and Heather is a lucky girl to get him; but he will spoil her to a dead certainty."

"Not more than you will spoil me, Jack," and Christian gave him one of her bright smiles.

"Don't be too sure of that, little woman; I don't hold with spoiling one's wife." But Jack's eyes belied his words, and even as he gave utterance to this marital opinion, he stooped to kiss the hand that rested so lightly on his shoulder. For in those first sweet days of their reunion, Jack found it a delightful and novel occupation to make love to his wife. "I hadn't time to do it before, Chriss," he said once; "but I fancy I do it rather well now." And Christian was forced to acknowledge that Jack's love-making was very much to her taste. Indeed, it would have been hard to say whether the married or the engaged lovers were the happier.

Carus did not hurry matters unduly the next day. He allowed his mother to pay a long visit to Jack, and spent the hour of waiting with Heather in the Bowling Green. But when he heard that she was in her dressing-room, he went to her at once. Mrs. Linacre held out her hand to him with a happy smile.

"Have you come to talk to me, Carus? I have had such a nice time with Jack. He has had a lovely night, Winston says; and really, he looks a shade better. But, as I tell Christian, he is a perfect skeleton."

"We must have Dr. Morton to overhaul him. I have no doubt he will want him to go to some more bracing place when the weather gets warm. It will take time to put him on his legs again. Mother, there is something Heather and I have to tell you, and which we both feel will be a great surprise to you;" and with this grave preface Carus told her in few words of the attachment between himself and Heather.

If Jack had been incredulous when Carus had told him, Janet was even more so. For the first few moments she was literally quite stunned with surprise; such an idea had never entered her head. If it had been Jack— but Carus and that child; somehow her womanly sense of propriety was offended.

"You mean to tell me, Carus, that you have engaged

yourself to that child?" uttering her thought aloud, and the lines of Janet's face grew rigid—astonishment was yielding to displeasure.

"Heather is nearly nineteen, mother."

"And you are forty, and you have done this thing without consulting me, although Heather is like my own daughter. I think that you, and she too, are treating me very badly. What have I done that you should be keeping me in the dark?"

This was a bad beginning, and Carus blessed Christian for her good advice. If he had spoken to his mother the previous night, when she was overstrained from the joyful excitement of Jack's return, her nerves could not have borne it.

"I have cared for nothing but my children's happiness," she went on; "and this is my reward—that my son confides in every one but his mother."

Now it was at this very unpropitious moment that Christian sauntered into the room, not knowing that Carus was there—indeed, she believed him to be with Heather in the Bowling Green. She uttered a slight exclamation of surprise when she saw him and would have withdrawn, but Mrs. Linacre called to her.

"There is no need for you to go, Christian; you are one of ourselves, and I suppose this wonderful piece of news is no longer a secret?"

"Do you mean about Heather?"

Then Janet gave a bitter little laugh. "So you know it already, and I am the last to be enlightened. Well, you are old enough certainly to make your own choice, Carus, and I suppose it is not for me to interfere; but I should have thought that my position with regard to Heather would have entitled me to some courtesy on your part, considering that I am responsible for that child."

"Mother!" stung by this injustice, for Janet never measured words when she was in one of her jealous moods, "will you listen to me a moment before you say scathing things to wound me? Have I ever failed in courtesy to you and yours?" Carus's tone was so hurt, his bearing so proud and indignant, that Janet was brought to her senses sufficiently to say—

" Never before this, Carus."

" Nor have I now. Let me explain things. You know how we persecuted the poor child about Sydney Masters. You got me on your side and made me talk to her, and Sydney, poor chap, was egging me on, and I was so sorry for him, and was convinced that he was the man for her, that I did all in my power to bring them together; you believe this, do you not, mother?"

" Yes," rather hesitatingly; " then you were not in love with her yourself at that time?"

A faint flush came to Carus's face. " If I were I was not conscious of it myself," he returned truthfully; " but I think now that I must always have loved her—but I never grasped that fact until the day before I started for Durban."

Mrs. Linacre looked at him keenly, " Not until then; are you sure of this, Carus?"

" As sure as I am that I went away without a word to tell her of my feelings. But love is not blind, mother, and we could read each other's hearts."

" Heather has certainly not been herself for months," observed Janet musingly; " she never took to any idea quickly. I remember I told Christian that I was sure that after all she cared for Sydney."

" And I told you that you were wrong, mater."

" It seems I am always wrong," she observed pathetically; " I suppose I am growing old and stupid."

" You are growing into a very dear old mother," returned Christian affectionately, as she smoothed the dark hair that was now mixed with gray; " but do let Carus finish what he has to say."

" I have very little more to add," he went on; " I had plenty of time to consider things during the voyage, and when I was relieved about Jack I wrote to Heather."

" Was that wise or right, Carus?"

" I thought so, mother. I had my own reasons for doing so, and I am glad now that I did it. I told Heather to think quietly over things until my return, and begged that she would send me no answer."

" Did you wish her to keep it a secret from me, Carus?"

" I did not say so; but, all the same, I knew Heather never showed my letters to any one, and I was quite sure that she would consult no one. I understand Heather so thoroughly; she is very childish in some things, but I think you have no idea of her strength of character; she would let no one come between us. If Christian had not found it out for herself, she would never have been told."

"Then you did not speak to her until yesterday."

"We were not engaged until then—but there was no need for many words; we understood each other too well. Heather was rather troubled because Christian and I thought it better not to tell you last night; we knew you had had excitement enough, but you will let me fetch her now?"

"Yes, I suppose so," rather dejectedly; "Carus, you must forgive me if I have seemed unsympathetic, but you have taken me too much by surprise; you must give me time;" then Carus smiled at her and went off in search of Heather.

"Mater," observed Christian coaxingly, as she knelt down beside her, "you are going to be good; we shall all be so happy together, and you will have two real daughters of your own;" then Janet began to weep.

"You must all be patient with me; I am getting an old woman now, and I don't see things as quickly as other people. I never thought Carus would want to leave me; I believed that he would never marry, and that I should always have him beside me; my husband brought me here when I was first married, and I hoped to die here, but now I must go away; for how can I remain in this great house without Carus?"

"Mater, how can you talk so! Do you suppose that they will ever consent to leave you? Has Carus ever been wanting in consideration, or Heather either?" Then Janet shook her head, but her tears still flowed.

"If they would only let me stay with them, Christian; I know it is very wicked and cantankerous of me, but somehow I can't bear the idea of Carus marrying."

Then Christian, either in pretence or reality, waxed exceedingly impatient.

"Mater, I do think you ought to be ashamed of yourself; I should have thought that his mother of all people would have rejoiced that Carus—our dear, good, unselfish

Carus—should have the happiness he so well deserves. Think of the dull life he has had, and how his infirmity deprives him of the society he would otherwise enjoy; he has been so patient; and now it seems to me such a beautiful thing, that our little sunbeam is to be his too; I think I love Heather all the better for her devotion to my brother."

"Dear Christian, it is so nice of you to say that, and I know it is all true," but Janet still sighed heavily. Poor woman, her own difficult nature was a sore trial to her; willingly would she have exorcised her familiar demons of jealousy and self-will, but they were too strong for her—her spirits were too depressed to feel the warmth of the sunshine.

"There they come, mater; do please cheer up;" but Janet could do nothing of the kind, and so she lost the sight of Heather's sweet, blushing face as she came in on Carus's arm.

"Mother, I have brought you your daughter;" but Janet's head was bowed. Heather looked at her pitifully for a moment, the next her arms were round her adopted mother's neck.

"Aunt Janet, dear—dear Aunt Janet, say that you forgive me. But how can I help loving him?" Her cheek rested against Janet's, her little hands were almost choking her in her eagerness; "dear—dearest—say something nice to me and him too?"

It was all very simple and childish, but it broke down the hard, prickly barrier in the elder woman's nature. Janet was not proof against Heather's girlish tenderness; she gathered her in her arms, drawing her on to her lap, as she would have done to the child Heather of ten years ago. "Little darling," she murmured; "but how could you have had the heart to keep it from me?" But Heather did not answer this question; she only squeezed Janet's face between her hands.

"Christian calls you mater because Jack does," she whispered; "but I mean to call you mother," and this speech brought the first smile to Janet's face. Their little sunbeam! Christian might well call her so; and Janet would live to bless the day that gave her so sweet a daughter, and Carus a devoted wife.

XL

Jack Has a Brilliant Idea

Love thrives not in the heart that shadows dreadeth.
SHAKESPEARE.

Is it worth while to live?
Be of good cheer,
Love casts out fear,
Rise up and achieve!
CHRISTINA ROSSETTI.

"It was Heather who did the business," Christian observed to Jack afterwards; "the mater had not a word to say after that. It was the prettiest sight in the world to see her, with her artless, coaxing way, dear little soul; she was perfectly irresistible; you should have seen Carus's face."

Carus's first present to his young betrothed was a diamond dove, with an emerald olive-branch in its beak; when Heather showed her treasure to her adopted mother, a faint blush came to Janet's faded cheek.

"You will carry the olive-branch wherever you go, my child," she said gently; "it is very beautiful. Carus must have given a good deal for it."

"It is the loveliest thing I ever saw in my life," returned Heather; "I told Carus that I liked it a hundred times better than the Vigne necklace. Would you believe it, dear, that Chriss actually declared that she intended to give it me as a wedding present, because it had always been worn by the eldest son's wife, and she thought Uncle Jasper would approve?"

"It was really very generous of her, Heather, for I know how proud Christian is of that necklace, and it suits her so well too."

"Yes, she has such a pretty neck; but, of course, I told her that nothing would induce me to wear it; she was very persistent about it until she found that Carus took my side, so now she has promised never to allude to such a thing again."

When Mrs. Linacre got over her first shock of surprise, she soon took very kindly to the idea of her son's engagement; when Mrs. Disney came up the next day to inquire about the invalid, she was soon put in possession of the news, but Janet was rather disappointed that she received it so quietly. " You do not seem surprised, Charlotte; surely no one has hinted at such a thing?"

" Not a creature; but to tell you the truth, dear friend, your news has not taken me a bit by surprise; perhaps I am rather quick to guess at such matters, but the idea came to me a few weeks ago. I think it was something in Heather's manner; she has certainly not seemed happy or like herself, and of course I knew it was not on account of poor Mr. Masters, and then the thought came to me: Can it be Carus? One has heard of more unlikely things, and directly you began to speak, I knew I was right, and that it was Carus."

" And you are not shocked?"

" On the contrary, I think your news charming. Can anything be better arranged for your comfort? You will have your son, and you will not lose your adopted daughter; you will be far happier than if she had gone to Chesterton."

" You are right there; but, Charlotte, would you believe it, when Carus told me yesterday, I made myself quite miserable about it; I thought he had taken advantage of Heather's youth, and that he was far too old for her?"

" Oh, you were not used to the idea, you see, and it seemed rather strange to you at first! But you may be sure of this: that Heather would not have him a year younger."

" She said so herself, but I could not bring myself to believe her; and even now, though I am far more reconciled to the idea, I still find it incomprehensible; I know people say that husbands and wives are often decided contrasts to each other; but for a lively young girl like Heather to refuse that handsome fellow Sydney and choose a grave bookworm like Carus—and with his infirmity too."

" Shall I tell you what I think about it, dear Mrs. Linacre?" returned Charlotte in her earnest way; " I believe that only his wife will ever know what Carus Linacre really is,—not his mother or his closest friend, but only the woman he makes his wife. For years to come Heather will be making fresh discoveries about him; and every day they live together will justify her choice more completely. She knows now that she has made no mistake— a year hence she will be fully assured of it;" and after this magnificent eulogy which Charlotte had uttered out of the depths of her good heart, there was nothing more to be said. When the Vicar came he only endorsed his wife's words; and as for Pen, her delight at the news almost amounted to rapture; no one so dearly loved a love-story.

Jack took it all with easy philosophy, but he was almost too engrossed with his own wife to give much attention to the lovers; and after the first hours of thrilling excitement, Carus and Heather withdrew of their own accord into the background, and were quite content to leave Jack and Christian in possession of the field.

" It is so nice to be quietly together without any fuss," Heather would say, when they took refuge in the library; for her unerring tact guessed how Carus loved these quiet hours.

Christian would have liked to follow their example when visitors invaded the sitting-room. The Vicar and Colonel Bromley often came over for a chat, and many of Jack's friends; but she bore the inflictions good-humouredly, and did the honours of the west wing with much grace.

Jack was always pleased to see his friends; he was sociable by nature, and as he grew stronger, his old cheerfulness returned. He liked to hear all the news, and took an interest in everything, but it was rather difficult to make him relate his experiences. " What is the use of harrowing up people's feelings?" he would say: " it is like a bad dream now—one wonders how one lived through it all," he continued musingly; " scanty rations, enteric, dysentery, and those awful screaming shells, and then Christmas and those poor children, Chriss, and yet we tried to amuse them;" and Jack would look so grave that Christian often changed the conversation. Once when he talked more freely to Colonel Bromley, Christian turned quite sick and looked so pale at the thought of all he had been through, that Jack would say no more until she had left the room.

Jack spent most of his mornings reading the papers, he was a keen soldier, and if his strength had permitted, he would gladly have gone again to the front.

"Lucky fellow," he would say when any one mentioned Sydney Masters; and his sympathy was very great for the officers and men in their dreary prison-ground at Pretoria. "Poor devils!" he would ejaculate; "it is hard lines on them to be out of it all—I think it would have driven me mad, Chriss;" and Jack would grow so restless that Chriss would invite him to pace the corridor with her, or challenge him to a game of bèzique.

In the afternoon they always drove out, and as Jack became stronger, they would often drive over to Braybrooke and have tea with Pen. Christian told him once how she had longed to have him to herself at Many Bushes, and Jack had smoothed his moustache with a gratified smile.

"I shouldn't have minded it myself, Chriss," he owned; "only it would have been rough on the mater. I suppose mothers are all like that; they love to fuss round a fellow, and tuck him up, and do the hush-a-by-baby palaver; but the mater is a good sort after all."

"Indeed she is, Jack."

"You two hit it off splendidly," he went on; "she thinks no end of you, Chriss. Now don't you nod your head in that conceited manner, or it will be my painful duty to take you down a peg; I can't have you getting vain. By Jove! that is a ripping hat of yours, Chriss, and suits you down to the ground;" then Christian executed a sweeping and graceful little curtsey.

"Thank you for the compliment, Jack."

"I think you have grown handsomer," continued Jack complacently,—he had already forgotten his threat,— "anyhow, I like the look of you immensely."

"Even my pince-nez?" in a teasing voice.

"Rather! they make you look *chic,* or what do you call it? Look here, Chriss, if you have got such a fancy for Many Bushes,"—they were sitting on the terrace at that moment as Jack spoke, waiting for Pen to return from the school,—"I expect Carus would let us have it as our headquarters; you know, I can't give up my profession, little woman;" Jack's look was rather wistful as though he were afraid of her answer.

"I never expected you would, Jack; I knew when I married you that you would be no carpet-soldier;" then Jack's eyes brightened—he was evidently relieved.

"What a jolly little brick you are, Chriss! To tell you the truth, I was rather in a funk about it; the mater has been at me once or twice, but I was too cunning to give her a chance. I thought if I could only get you on my side, I could manage her."

"Of course I am on your side," returned Christian decidedly; "do you think that I want you to repent marrying me? I should hate to be a drag on you in any way. You are a free agent, Jack; but you will have to give up thoughts of soldiering for a good many months to come, so I am not going to worry myself about the future."

"You are right, darling; what's the good of crossing the bridge before you come to it. I don't expect they will give me a clean bill of health for ever so long, so we will go to Scotland, as Dr. Morton advises. And, if Carus consents, we will come back straight to Many Bushes. Fancy, setting up housekeeping by our two selves, Chriss!"

"Yes—won't it be just lovely?"

"Ripping! And if they order us to India in the spring, you won't want me to leave you behind—you mean to come with me?"

"Yes, of course, Jack. 'Whither thou goest I will go.' No—don't laugh, but those words seemed to come into my head; but I really mean them. Oh, my dear, do you think I should let you go alone?" and here Christian put down her head on his shoulder and her eyes were full of tears. "That is the worst of a wife—you can never get rid of her;" but Jack's answer to this was so satisfactory that Christian soon dried her eyes.

The next time Jack found himself alone with his brother, he sounded him on the subject of Many Bushes. He soon found it was a foregone conclusion to Carus.

"I always meant you to have it," he returned; "I said as much to Christian. I am not likely to want it again. It is not much of a place, but until you come into your fortune, which I fear will be before long, for Uncle Jasper cannot live more than a year or two, it will just do for you and Chriss. And I will have my belongings removed while you are in Scotland."

"Have you made any plans for yourself, Carus?"

"About our marriage, do you mean? Well, I believe it is settled for October. My mother begged us to wait until the spring; but I soon brought her round to my opinion—that it was better to get it over this year. Have you heard, Jack, that the Stone House as well as the estate is to become mine on my wedding-day? The mother absolutely relinquishes everything to me; she only stipulates that her old age may be spent under my roof."

"How do you suppose that will work?" asked Jack doubtfully. "Heather is a bit young to be mistress; it is a little hard on you, old chap, not to have your wife to yourself."

"Heather and I would not wish it otherwise; you will see that things will work quite smoothly after a time. My mother will keep her old rooms. Do you know, Jack, I have set my heart on turning the end room that we have always kept for visitors into a boudoir for Heather? But she declares that unless she is ill that she will never use it, and that she means to have a corner of her own in the library. I have no doubt that she is right; but, all the same, I shall do it, and the mother quite approves."

"I am sure of one thing: that you two will completely spoil little Heather between you."

"No, she is too good to be spoiled. You will see for yourself, Jack, what a harmonious household we shall be. Oh, by the bye, there is something else I meant to say! Heather has been talking to me about Miss Mervyn and Mr. Hamill; it seems that my mother, and Mrs. Disney, and Chriss are all in a conspiracy to get them married as soon as possible."

Jack nodded his head vigorously.

" The sooner the better, I should say," he returned cheerfully. " I like Miss Mervyn awfully; she is a thoroughly nice girl,—and then Chriss and she are such friends; but we don't want to take her to Scotland; you see, two's company, and three's none, old fellow."

" She can come to us," observed Carus; " my mother would only be too delighted to have her, and Heather would find her extremely useful when she begins to get her things. Miss Mervyn could not very well remain alone at Many Bushes when Mr. Hamill comes to Braybrooke; but we could keep her, and welcome, until the beginning of November; she will be company for my mother until we return."

" And then, I suppose, she must come to us," but Jack did not seem to relish the idea. " You seem amused, Carus," as his brother tried to conceal a smile; " but the fact is, that though Miss Mervyn is a nice little girl, we could both of us dispense with her company—in short, I want Chriss to myself."

" Very proper and laudable in your position, I should say, and nothing could be easier. Why not send her to the Vicarage? Mrs. Disney would only be too glad to have her, and you could easily arrange for her board."

" That's a rattling good idea, Carus. I wonder what put that in your head?"

" Well, you see, we are all very fond of Penelope Mervyn, and none of us want to part with her. As I told you, all the women are putting their heads together to get her married. Hamill has only a hundred and thirty a year, but Christian says that if they could only get some Indian children for Miss Mervyn to mother, that they might venture to be married; and she wants us all to keep our eyes open."

" Well, that is a queer start," returned Jack, twisting his moustache rather excitedly. " You know our major— Major Fothergill—was invalided home with me. His wife is very delicate; and some one told me that she would not be able to live in England; and that they did not know what to do with the children."

" How many children have they, Jack?"

" Four—three little girls, the eldest only nine, and a boy at Wellington. The major has plenty of money, and could afford to pay handsomely, if they could only find the right sort of home they want."

" Could you not write to him and explain things to him?" But Jack demurred to this.

" It would be rather difficult to tell such a long story in a letter; would it not be better for Chriss and me to talk to them?"

" Infinitely better; but I thought you told me the other day that they were at Bournemouth?"

" So they are; they have taken a house there for some months. Let me see how we can manage it. Yes, I have it. You know we are going up to Uncle Jasper's for a few days; why should we not go down for a week-end? Chriss would enjoy it, and I want to see Fothergill; he's quite a crony of mine."

" It would be awfully good of you to take so much trouble, Jack."

" Trouble! pshaw! don't I know how fond Chriss is of the girl? I would do a good deal more to give her pleasure. We will do our best, Carus, to get the children for Miss Mervyn; but I warn you that the Fothergills are rather anxious parents, and the whole thing may fall through."

" Then, in that case, I would not say a word to any one. I believe that Mrs. Disney has already sounded Miss Mervyn on the subject, and found that she and Hamill would be only too thankful to do anything that would bring them together. It would be a pity to raise hopes that may possibly be disappointed."

" All right; I will give Chriss a hint to hold her tongue;" and then Jack went off in high good-humour to find his wife and electrify her with his brilliant proposition.

XLI

A Highland Glen

Oh, the glints an' gleams o' licht
   By the auld burnside!
Oh, the water, amber-bricht,
   By the auld burnside!
Just to see it flashing down
Through the muirland's purple crown,
When the bracken's gow'den brown,
   By the auld burnside!
       HELEN MARION BURNSIDE.

THE secret was well kept; Jack and Christian paid their visit to Bournemouth, and were back at the Stone House before any one suspected that they had left London.

A few days after their return, Christian remarked casually to Pen that a great friend of her husband's—Major Fothergill—was coming down to Braybrooke for a few hours, and would have luncheon at Many Bushes.

Pen seemed a little surprised at this. "I should have thought he would have gone to the Stone House," she said innocently.

"Oh, we would rather have him here!" returned Christian hastily. "I am going to ask Mr. Hamill to join us; and then we shall be a nice, cosy, little party. I shall be over early to help you with the flowers; Jack will go to the station to meet the major."

Walter Hamill had been established for some weeks in his comfortable rooms in the Market Place, and was already reaping golden opinions from his Vicar for his energy and zeal in his work, and he and Pen were as happy as the day was long. As it was impossible for the young curate to go to Many Bushes during Christian's absence, Mrs. Disney arranged that he and Pen should spend two evenings in the week at the Vicarage, and as Mrs. Linacre often invited them to the Stone House, they were a good deal in each other's society.

349

Then there were the frequent services, and the accidental meetings in the town, so a day never passed that Pen did not exchange a few words with Walter. And she thought Christian very kind and considerate to invite him to her luncheon party, little guessing that Major Fothergill's visit was solely paid for the purpose of judging if the young couple were likely to take his wife's fancy. Major Fothergill was a handsome, soldierly-looking man, and he made himself very pleasant to Pen. He talked to her about his little girls, and seemed gratified by her interest, but during luncheon nothing was hinted of the business that had brought him to Braybrooke. The gentlemen were to have their coffee on the terrace, and the ladies were to join them later, but as Christian was about to leave the room, Major Fothergill followed her.

"May I have a word with you, Mrs. Linacre?" Then Christian gave Pen a sign to go into the sitting-room, while they turned into the inner hall.

"Well," rather breathlessly, "what do you think of her?"

"I think Miss Mervyn is charming," he returned smiling. "She is very gentle, and yet she has plenty of character, and I like Hamill exceedingly. I am going to have a talk with him directly, and I shall leave Miss Mervyn to you. But there is one thing I must ask—that they will come down and see my wife and the children. We could give Miss Mervyn a bed for the night, and get one at the hotel for Mr. Hamill; I am going to arrange all this with him." Then Christian nodded as though she quite understood.

Great was Pen's astonishment when Christian unfolded her little plan. At first she was almost too overwhelmed to say much.

"And it is all Jack's idea—you must remember that," went on Christian, feeling that this was *la crème de la crème* of the whole affair. "Carus spoke to him, and he thought at once of the Fothergills."

"But it seems too good to be true, Chriss,"—Pen's face was burning with excitement,—"they must be such nice people, and the children seem such dears; but are you sure that they will think us worthy of such a trust?"

"Well, he is very much charmed with you both, but nothing can be settled until his wife sees you; they both are bent on a personal interview."

"Do you mean that we have to go to Bournemouth?" asked Pen, rather appalled at this idea.

"I do mean it, my dear. Why, what nonsense, Pen, pretending to be shy and frightened! Mrs. Fothergill is such a nice, pretty, little woman—just your sort; and she has such soft, motherly ways. Put yourself in her place, young woman. How would you like to intrust your precious children to a stranger you had never seen?"

And Pen was sufficiently impressed with this argument to raise no further objection, and before Major Fothergill returned to town, the date of the visit was fixed for the following week.

Christian rode over to Braybrooke quite early the morning after Pen's return; she found her just finishing a late breakfast.

"Walter begged me to rest this morning," she said hurriedly. "I daresay it was all the strain and excitement, but I was very tired last night, and we did not reach Braybrooke until nine. It was a long day, but so delightful, and they made us so happy."

"Then it is all satisfactory."

"Oh yes; I think so. Chriss, you were quite right about Mrs. Fothergill; she is such a sweet woman—only so delicate! Do you know, she kissed me when I bade her good-bye, and then she apologised, and said she could not help it? But Walter was so pleased."

"Oh, I knew she would take a fancy to you!"

"And the children are darlings," went on Pen. "The twins—Hilda and Minnie—are such well-behaved, good, little creatures, and I quite lost my heart to that fat, chubby Phyllis; she is only seven, and the twins are nine. I saw a photo of Reggie—such a handsome little fellow; they say he is nearly eleven."

"Yes, I know. But now, what is settled? Are you to have the children?"

"Yes, but not before next April; they are to go with their parents to Mentone. Mrs. Fothergill will not hear of parting with them this winter, but it seems that there is no doubt of their going to India in the spring. Major Fothergill is quite fit for service, and they will be obliged to go."

"Then you will not be married this year, Pen?"

"Not until after Christmas," returned Pen, blushing as she spoke; "but Walter thinks it will probably be early in January. We are to take a house by then, and get it ready, and the children will probably come to us about the end of March. They are going to pay us so handsomely, Chriss, that, with Walter's salary, we shall be able to get on quite nicely. Reggie is to spend all his holidays with us, and there is to be a daily governess for the twins."

"And Sheila could do her lessons with them. You know her governess is going to be married."

"What a splendid idea, Chriss! we must have a regular schoolroom. I am afraid we cannot have a small house, for there is Walter's study; but, of course, we could do without a drawing-room."

"You will do nothing of the kind," returned Christian indignantly. "Don't fidget, Pen; the right-sized house will turn up. The Fothergills are very liberal, but with a good house, and two servants, there will not be much over. Mr. Hamill will have to get a living by and by. What are you going to do about furniture?"

"That is the difficulty," returned Pen. "Walter thinks we shall have to take a furnished house for the first year; he has so little money in hand, and we must just buy things by degrees."

"I am not quite sure that is a good plan, Pen; but anyhow, Jack and I mean to give you the drawing-room furniture, and I daresay some of your other friends will fit up the dining-room. Don't worry; you will find it will all come right," and Christian privately resolved to seek counsel on this point.

After all, it was just as well that Pen's marriage was not to come off this year. She and Jack were to spend August and September in the Highlands, and it would have been impossible to help her; one of Jack's numerous friends had lent him a shooting lodge for two months. They would take Winston with them; he was a handy fellow, and could turn his hand to anything; and the old Scotch body, who was caretaker, could keep the place clean.

"It was quite a homely little shanty," Jack told her, "with one living room and three bedrooms;" "and the kitchen, with a small sleeping apartment leading out of it, had been built on to it. There was a small, square hall, where guns and fishing-tackle could be kept, but it was quite a bachelor establishment. They call it the Log Hut," continued Jack. "Davenant says he can't vouch for your comfort, Chriss; but he declares it a cosy, little hut, and in a nice situation. It is just in a sort of hollow, with a few firs in front, and the moors behind one mass of purple."

"Oh, Jack, it must be too lovely!" whispered Christian. "What does it matter how small and rough it is, when I shall have you to myself for two whole months?"

"We have waited long enough for our honeymoon, have we not, little woman?" and Jack's eyes glowed with strong feeling as they rested on his wife's beaming face. "You just wait till I pull myself together, and we will have a good time yet;" but though Jack's face was still lean and sallow, Christian could note improvement each day.

A few days after Jack and Christian had started, Pen went over to the Stone House and devoted herself to Mrs. Linacre and Heather.

Whenever Walter had a free hour or two, he cycled over to Silverton, and he always spent one evening in the week at the Stone House. Heather was busy getting her trousseau, and there were frequent visits to town; more than once she and Mrs. Linacre spent a night or two at Beauchamp Gardens.

During Christian's absence in Scotland the Cluny Macgregor marriage took place. Christian sent her cousin a handsome present, and expressed her regret that she could not be present at the wedding, as her husband's health was her first consideration, but Adelaide chose to be affronted.

"It is so ridiculous of Christian," she said to her mother. "Captain Linacre has his man with him; he

could easily have been left alone for two or three days.
It is rather hard that one of my few relations should put
such a slight on me on my wedding-day;" but for once
Mrs. Fordham plucked up spirit to contradict her
daughter.

"I am surprised at you, Addie," she said quite
severely; "how can you be so selfish and wanting in
consideration to your cousin? Christian knows her duty
as a wife too well; she is quite right not to leave Jack;
and she has written you a very pretty letter, saying
everything she possibly can."

"Oh, you always take Christian's part, mother!" replied Adelaide crossly, but perhaps her cousin endorsed
her mother's words, for she said no more.

Christian wrote glowing descriptions of the Log Hut
to Pen and Heather. Everything was perfect in her
eyes; the primitive life, the quaint simplicity of the
ménage, delighted them both.

When it is fine (she wrote), we have all our meals out of doors.
Winston puts our table under the firs, and as we eat our smoked
salmon and Highland mutton, or enjoy home-baked scones and
honey, our eyes are feasted by the paradise of purple that seems
to stretch to the horizon. Oh, this delicious moorland air! Jack
is gaining strength every day. He lies out on the hillside for
hours, while I read or talk to him, with the great brown bees
humming all round us.

There was little doubt that Christian was happy, and
for the first month she and Jack were as light-hearted
and free from care as though they were children, but
one morning a letter from Carus to his brother brought a
cloud to Jack's face.

"Is there anything the matter, dear?" asked Christian,
putting down her wild nosegay of heather and rowan-
berries, with which she was wont to adorn their sitting-
room.

Then Jack tugged at his moustache fiercely. "I am
afraid so, Chriss. We did not see yesterday's paper, you
know. Sydney Masters is badly wounded, and is at Deelfontein in the hospital. Carus is afraid it will go badly
with him; he has cabled for news."

" Oh dear !" in a distressed voice; " I do hope nothing will happen to the poor fellow! Heather would grieve so; and it would cast such a cloud over the wedding. Where is he wounded, Jack?"

" Ball in the chest, they say, and they are afraid of the lungs. It looks bad, Chriss,—it does indeed, but Carus has promised to wire."

" I will not write until we hear again, Jack. I want you to come back to the hut now, for I am sure there is going to be a thunderstorm, and it would never do for you to get wet;" but though Jack argued, and dawdled, and declared in a provoking manner that women never did prognosticate rightly of the weather, and that she was thinking more of her clothes than of him, Christian good-humouredly maintained her point.

" Do you think I care about my old serge and Tam-o'-Shanter, you foolish boy? But you walk so slowly, and if you get another touch of fever——" Then Jack rose rather sulkily to his feet, but the ominous bank of clouds behind them certainly verified Christian's fear.

Jack did his best to walk fast, but he soon got breathless; and before they could gain shelter, the storm broke over their heads. Christian flung the plaid she was carrying over his shoulder, and urged him to make haste, and then to her relief she saw Winston with umbrella and macintosh running towards them, and in a few minutes Jack was seated before a wood fire.

Christian assured herself that he was dry before she went upstairs to change her own wet things. A perfect torrent of rain was beating against the hut, and the thunder reverberated like artillery reports amongst the distant hills. " Poor Sydney, perhaps he will die out there all alone !" she thought sorrowfully. " Oh, this dreadful war—when will it be over ?"

Carus's telegram reached them the next morning; there was no better news. A day or two later all was over, and the mortal remains of Sydney Masters were laid to rest in a South African grave.

Christian wrote to Heather at once, and received a very sad, pathetic, little note in return.

Carus is so good to me (she wrote) ; he did not mind at all when I told him that I wished to wear mourning, but I am afraid Aunt Janet thought it rather strange. But, indeed, if Sydney were my own dear brother, I could not grieve more for him; and the idea of his dying in that hospital, all alone, nearly breaks my heart. You see, I cannot forget that it is my fault that he went to that cruel war, for if he had not been so unhappy he would never have gone. But Carus thinks I am probably wrong about this; so many of his friends were volunteers for service, that he says Sydney would have thought it his duty to go too. The chaplain has promised to write, so we shall hear more. Dear Christian, I know how sorry you are for me, for you always understand one's feelings; but as you and Jack will be back so soon, I will not write again.

The two months passed only too quickly, and when the last day of September came, Jack and Christian bade good-bye reluctantly to their Highland glen. But their return was very welcome to the inmates of the Stone House, and Christian was delighted to hear the exclamations at Jack's improved looks.

Heather looked very lovely and pathetic in her black dress. She was rather pale and drooping, as though she had fretted a good deal, but she was evidently making an effort to be cheerful.

Later in the day, when Jack was resting in his dressing-room, with Christian, as usual, beside him, Carus sought admittance; he sat down by Jack's couch.

"There is something Heather wants me to tell you both, if Jack is not too tired to listen," and as his brother eagerly disclaimed this, he went on. "Poor child! she has been very much upset, and no wonder, for such an idea never crossed her mind, though I confess it is no surprise to me. Mr. Horsley, the Masters' family lawyer, has been down here. It seems that Sydney only signed his will the very day he quitted Silverton. He has left Chesterton and all his property to Heather!"

"Great Scot!" exclaimed Jack, but Christian was silent with surprise.

"It seems that I am marrying an heiress!" went on Carus with a queer smile. "Sydney had no near relatives; indeed, as far as we have discovered, he has left no relative at all except a distant cousin—a struggling doctor with a young family in Somersetshire."

" Then there is no reason why poor old Sydney should not have pleased himself," returned Jack. " Heather has every right to enjoy her fortune."

" So we all tell her," replied Carus; " but never was an heiress so ungrateful for the good things that have come to her. If Sydney only guessed the fuss his bequest has caused. At first she refused to touch the money; now she has consented for my sake, if only a third is given to Dr. Masters Williams. Horsley says he is in bad health and needy circumstances, so I think Heather is right."

" And Chesterton?"

" Oh, we can talk of that later on!" returned Carus, and after a little more conversation he left Jack to seek the repose he needed.

XLII

A Port Pleasant

We shall sit at endless feasts,
Enjoying each the other's good;
What vaster dream can hit the mood
Of love on earth.

TENNYSON.

AT first Heather seemed desirous that the wedding should be postponed, but a few quiet words from Carus had their effect.

"Darling," he said gently, "I am sure that our poor Sydney would have grieved if he had known the distress his death would cause you; but, Heather-Bell, you do not need me less because you are unhappy."

"Oh no—no," clinging to him; "I need you more—you are my one comfort."

"Then you will trust me to decide what I think is best for us both?"

"Yes—yes."

"Then, dearest, we will not defer our wedding for a single day. We know it is to be a very quiet affair—we both stipulated for that— and we will go to some tranquil spot—anywhere you wish—and enjoy each other's society."

"It is very soon to put off my mourning," observed Heather doubtfully, but Carus only smiled.

"I shall leave you and Christian to decide that," he said quietly; "my little wife shall come to me in black, white, or gray, or whatever she will." Then his fond tone made Heather blush very sweetly.

Both Mrs. Linacre and Christian were greatly relieved when they heard the wedding was not to be deferred. Heather herself informed them.

"Carus thinks I shall be happier when we are married," she said in her simple way; "and of course I must do as he wishes."

358

" But you will put off your mourning on your wedding-day, Heather?"

" Must I?" in a startled tone. " Do you think it is right after all Sydney has done for me?"

" Quite right, dear; your poor friend who loved you needs nothing from you but tender remembrance, but you owe it to Carus that your new life should be begun as brightly as possible!"

" But he said he did not mind, Chriss."

" Oh, that is Carus's way! Jack is right, and he spoils you dreadfully; but he owned to me once that it made him feel dull to see you in black."

" Oh, Christian, why did you not tell me before? I will take it off at once—I will indeed"—her eyes full of tears. " Oh, how selfish I am!" But Christian detained her.

" No, dear, there is no need to do anything so impulsive; Carus can very well endure the sight of your black frock for another ten days. What do you suppose he will say to your wedding dress, Heather?" for anything more beautiful than Heather in her bridal attire was scarcely to be conceived; and Janet had wept when she saw that innocent young face veiled under soft, cloudy lace.

About a week before the wedding, Carus received the chaplain's letter from Deelfontein; there was an enclosure for Heather. He read his own letter, and then quietly put it with the sealed note into the girl's hand.

" You will like to read this in your own room, dearest," he said gently; " you will see that there are a few lines from Sydney himself." Then, as he saw that she was too agitated to answer him, he pressed her face between his hands with a gesture that was inexpressibly tender. " Do not be too sorrowful, dear child. You ought to be very happy, for you have a lover on earth and another in Paradise." And then he let her go.

The chaplain's letter was a long one:—

The doctors had little hope from the first (he wrote), and I feel sure that Lieutenant Masters quite realised his danger. He suffered much, and it pained him to speak, so a few words from time to time were all he could manage; but he was very patient, and liked me to read and pray beside him. A few hours before his death, I administered to him the Holy Communion. Sister Margaret who nursed him was the greatest comfort to him. Strange to say, all her young days had been spent at Braybrooke; she tells me your mother will know her name—Margaret Ellicott. I think this somehow made Mr. Masters feel as though she were an old friend. He told her that he was very anxious to write a few lines to a dear friend, and though the effort must have been agony to him, he persisted in pencilling the enclosed note. I think he was happier in his mind when he had finished it. A short time before the end he was a little delirious; he seemed to think Sister Margaret was his mother, and once he asked her to kiss him, because he was going away on a long journey. It was a little difficult to understand what he said, his voice was so weak and gasping. There was something about a Bowling Green, and sunset, and lilies, and then more distinctly, "Mother, do you think there will be heather as well as flowers in heaven—I always liked heather best?" Sister Margaret said those were his last words, for after that unconsciousness set in. We were both beside him when he passed away.

And then the good chaplain gave Carus an account of the funeral, and described the quiet corner where they laid him to rest.

Heather's tears almost blinded her before she had finished Carus's letter. Then she opened the sealed note. There was a little sprig of pink bell-heather, with a date affixed, and the words, " Given me on my twenty-first birthday by Heather." It had evidently been treasured. A few pencilled lines had been added :—

DEAREST—I may call you that once more now I am dying—Carus will not mind. I always knew there was some one else, and that was why I had no chance, but I never guessed it was Carus. Dear Heather, you are right to love him; he has the noblest heart, the truest nature. God bless him and you too! You must not be too sorry for me, dear. I am dying for my Queen and country—I would not have it otherwise. I should not care to live without you, Heather; but you must not be unhappy. Take care of my poor Black Prince and the dogs. I love to think everything will be yours; I can write no more. Good-bye; God bless you.—Your devoted friend,

SYDNEY.

Heather was very silent and sorrowful all that day, but Carus was very good to her. He let her sit beside him undisturbed, and only a quiet caress or soothing

word from time to' time told her how well he understood
her depression. Later in the evening they paced the
Bowling Green together, and Heather talked to him in
her innocent, childish way.

"You are sure that Sydney would like me to be happy?"
she asked presently.

"Quite sure, darling. We cannot but believe that he
is happy too; for him the strife is over and the battle of
life bravely fought, and now he is at rest."

"Oh yes; I love to think that," and Heather clasped
her little hands on Carus's arm; "and one day we shall
see him again."

"God grant it, darling," returned Carus reverently.
"Some day when we have finished our pilgrimage, little
one, we may hope to greet those whom we have loved
and lost awhile, and it may be that in some green valley
of that still world we may come upon Sydney, waiting
to welcome his old friends."

"Oh, Carus, you always do say such comforting
things!" returned Heather gratefully. "When I am with
you all the unhappiness seems to roll away, and I feel
quite strong and peaceful;" and then, in the moonlight,
she put her sweet lips to his. "Oh, my darling, my darling, how I love you!" she whispered.

Heather was more like herself the next day, and in the
afternoon she begged Carus to come out with her.

"I want to walk over to Chesterton," she said, "and
see if they are taking proper care of the Black Prince—
and there are the poor dogs—Sydney asked me to look
after them. I should like to bring Rory back with me;
he must be my dog now." Rory was a dachshund belonging to Mrs. Masters, who had attached himself to
Sydney, and as Carus willingly consented to the expedition, they started as soon as possible.

Chesterton was a pleasant, old red brick house about
half a mile from the village of Silverton; it was by no
means grand or imposing, but the rooms were spacious
and comfortable, and furnished with a good deal of taste;
and Heather had a special fancy for the large square hall,
which was fitted up as a living room, and for the quaint,
long drawing-room, with its nooks and corners and cabi-
nets of old china.

The garden was charming, and there was a delightful orchard, where Heather and Sydney had swung as children, between two old mossy, apple trees. A farm, now managed by a bailiff, surrounded Chesterton, and the old-fashioned farmhouse and dairy opened into the orchard. As Heather walked across, with the dogs at her heels, and Rory pattering on his short legs beside her, she pointed out the swing to Carus, and the initials that Sydney had cut in the rough bark of a pear tree. There they were—S. M. and H. B.—notched on a dozen tree trunks. "It was his favourite amusement," whispered Heather, and then she stooped down to caress Rory, who was regarding his new mistress with rapt adoration.

"It is a dear old place, Carus."

"It is indeed; and I think we could be very happy here, little one; but we are bound to live at the Stone House."

"I know that; it is a lovely house,—far better than this—and I would not leave it for worlds; but, Carus, what are we to do with Chesterton?"

"Oh, that is the question?"

"Yes; and I have such a grand idea—it came to me last night when I could not sleep. I just lay in the moonlight and thought and thought until my head ached."

"That is why you had such pale cheeks this morning, sweetheart."

"Oh, but they were such nice thoughts, Carus. You know Chesterton belongs absolutely to me—I can do what I like with it. Mr. Horsley said I could part with it if I chose."

"Sell it, do you mean?. That would hardly be kind, Heather."

"Oh no," in a low, vehement tone; "of course I would never do that—Sydney loved his home so. But, Carus, don't you think it would just do for Christian and Jack? Many Bushes is not nearly good enough; and I want you to give that to Mr. Hamill and Pen."

"Heather, my dear child!"

"Oh, do just listen to me a moment!" returned the girl beseechingly; "I have thought it all out. You know they are not likely to go to India for a year or two,—

Jack will not be strong enough,—so they will want a nice house, and one that they can come back to whenever they like."

"And you mean them to rent it and be your tenants?" Carus's voice was undoubtedly pleased, but Heather meant nothing of the kind.

"I mean them to live here and pay no rent, Carus. I am too rich now—I cannot possibly use any more money—and, you know, you told me yourself that until Mr. Vigne dies, Jack will have only a moderate income."

"Uncle Jasper is not likely to last many months, dear."

"No; poor man! And then they will have all his money; but, indeed, Carus, Chesterton will be quite good enough for them even then, and they could always improve it. Christian does so love the country, and Jack can ride the Black Prince, but he must promise never to take him out of England; he would take care of the dogs too, only I should love to have them myself;" and Heather's voice was very wistful.

"Don't fret, darling; the Black Prince and Gelert and Lassie and Dick shall all find quarters at the Stone House. Jack will have his own horses; and, dear, your goodness to my brother almost overwhelms me."

"You approve then?"

"How can I do otherwise? The place will suit Jack down to the ground; it will give him plenty of scope."

"Oh, I am so glad!" and Bell-Heather looked like her namesake at that moment, with the soft pink flush in her cheeks. "They will just live here and be happy; and by and by, if they still like it, we might give it them altogether—not for two or three years perhaps, but when they come back from India."

"Child—child, what am I to say to you?"

"Only one little yord, 'Yes;' and, Carus, you know you will never need Many Bushes."

"Never! You are right there."

"Well, then, why should you not let poor Mr. Hamill and Pen live in it rent free? You know Christian told us that they were thinking of taking a furnished house, because they had no money to buy furniture; you might give them the furniture as a wedding present, and Chris-

tian and I could do the rest.   Think how convenient for
Mr. Hamill to live next to the church and opposite the
Vicarage, and Sheila coming to her lessons every day
too.   Oh," drawing a long breath, " I know you mean
to do it, for you are just smiling to yourself as though
you loved the idea!"

" I think it is the little idealist I love;" but the rest
of Carus's speech need not be quoted.

The result of the conversation was that Jack and Christian were summoned to the library that evening, and
Heather's generous proposition laid before them.

" Great Scot!" was all Jack could mutter; " do you
really mean this, you two?"

" Of course we mean it, Jack," interposed Heather
softly.   " Do say that you and Christian will take it?   It
will make me so happy; and then Pen and Mr. Hamill
can have Many Bushes."

" Great Scot!" again ejaculated Jack, but Christian
jumped up and looked out of the window; the tears were
running down her face, but Heather, who followed her,
soon kissed them away.

" Dear Chriss—dear sister Chrissy, only tell me that
you like my little plan?"

" Like it!"—Christian nearly choked and then recovered herself bravely—" it is the kindness, the goodness,
the generosity that breaks me down.   Oh, Jack," turning
to her husband, " why don't you say something when you
see a person can't get out a word?"

" Don't worry, Chriss," returned Jack, drawing a long
breath; " just wait a moment until I can pull myself together;" but Jack, when he did speak, managed to express himself with a certain rough eloquence that was very
convincing.

" He and Chriss were awfully obliged, and all that sort
of thing, and they weren't such fools as to refuse a good
offer.   Heather was a little brick; he had always had a
fancy for Chesterton ever since he was a little chap in
Eton jackets, and he preferred it infinitely to the Stone
House."

" You may have the farm too if you like, Jack," interposed Heather; but Jack showed his good sense by refusing this.

" We had better leave it in Stanton's hands," he said; " he is a good fellow, and does his best by the land; and we shall have to go to India, you know."

" I think Jack is right, my Lady Bountiful," observed Carus, with his kind smile; and then some one said that Pen and Mr. Hamill were cycling up the drive.

" Oh, Heather, do tell them about Many Bushes!" exclaimed Chriss excitedly, and Jack was at once sent after them. He found Hyde just throwing open the drawing-room door, and carried them off to the library in triumph.

The feelings of the young couple may be imagined when they learnt Carus's generous intention. Here was an end of all difficulty. The home where Pen had lived so happily for fifteen months was to be hers and Walter's. No wonder that tears of gratitude dimmed her soft blue eyes. Her first coherent speech was thoroughly Pen-like.

" Do you hear that?" Christian was saying to her. " Carus has just told Mr. Hamill that he only means to take his books away, and that he shall leave the study furniture for his use; but surely you will have the largest room for your drawing-room."

" Oh no, Chriss," and Pen dried her eyes; " I always meant Walter to have the best room for his study, and I do so love our little sitting-room;" and this settled the matter.

The afternoon before the wedding, Jack drove Christian over to Chesterton. It had been a busy day, and Carus, who found Heather looking rather pale and tired, had carried her off for a quiet stroll in the Bowling Green.

It was a lovely October afternoon, and in the soft autumnal light the old house looked strangely peaceful. Jack gave his pony to the gardener, and they went into the quaint old hall; as they did so, Christian put out her hand with a quick little gesture to her husband, " Isn't it just lovely, Jack?"

" Ripping," was Jack's answer; and then they sat down together on the old oak settle. No one had heard them, and for the moment they were absolutely alone. A soft sigh rose to Christian's lips as she looked round at the wide staircase and old grandfather's clock and the deers' antlers over the high, carved mantelpiece. What a dear place! How was she ever to tear herself away when their marching orders came?

Then Jack, who could read her face like a book, put his hand on her shoulder. " It is hard lines, isn't it, Chriss? That comes of marrying a soldier; but we shan't have to leave it for a year."

" No, Jack; of course I know that," and Christian coloured as though she were ashamed of her momentary regret. " A year is such a long time; and then we shall always have a dear home ready for us on our return."

" You are sure you don't mind going to India?" and Jack looked at her a little anxiously. Then Christian's beaming smile was a sufficient answer.

" Mind, with you!" she whispered; and then she turned and kissed the hand that still rested on her shoulder. " Oh, Jack, I am so thankful and happy! We have had our Passage Perilous; but I have you safe now—and dear Chesterton shall be our Port Pleasant when our work is finished and we come home to rest."

And Jack's amen echoed his wife's words.

THE END

Popular Copyright Books

AT MODERATE PRICES

Any of the following titles can be bought of your bookseller at the price you paid for this volume

Alternative, The. By George Barr McCutcheon.
Angel of Forgiveness, The. By Rosa N. Carey.
Angel of Pain, The. By E. F. Benson.
Annals of Ann, The. By Kate Trimble Sharber.
Battle Ground, The. By Ellen Glasgow.
Beau Brocade. By Baroness Orczy.
Beechy. By Bettina Von Hutten.
Bella Donna. By Robert Hichens.
Betrayal, The. By E. Phillips Oppenheim.
Bill Toppers, The. By Andre Castaigne.
Butterfly Man, The. By George Barr McCutcheon.
Cab No. 44. By R. F. Foster.
Calling of Dan Matthews, The. By Harold Bell Wright.
Cape Cod Stories. By Joseph C. Lincoln.
Challoners, The By E. F. Benson.
City of Six, The. By C. L. Canfield.
Conspirators, The By Robert W. Chambers.
Dan Merrithew. By Lawrence Perry.
Day of the Dog, The. By George Barr McCutcheon.
Depot Master, The. By Joseph C. Lincoln.
Derelicts. By William J. Locke.
Diamonds Cut Paste. By Agnes & Egerton Castle.
Early Bird, The. By George Randolph Chester.
Eleventh Hour, The. By David Potter.
Elizabeth in Rugen. By the author of Elizabeth and Her
    German Garden.
Flying Mercury, The. By Eleanor M. Ingram.
Gentleman, The. By Alfred Ollivant.
Girl Who Won, The. By Beth Ellis.
Going Some. By Rex Beach.
Hidden Water. By Dane Coolidge.
Honor of the Big Snows, The. By James Oliver Curwood.
Hopalong Cassidy. By Clarence E. Mulford.
House of the Whispering Pines, The. By Anna Katherine
    Green.
Imprudence of Prue, The. By Sophie Fisher.

Popular Copyright Books

AT MODERATE PRICES

Any of the following titles can be bought of your bookseller at the price you paid for this volume

In the Service of the Princess. By Henry C. Rowland.
Island of Regeneration, The. By Cyrus Townsend Brady.
Lady of Big Shanty, The. By Berkeley F. Smith.
Lady Merton, Colonist. By Mrs. Humphrey Ward.
Lord Loveland Discovers America. By C. N. & A. M. Williamson.
Love the Judge. By Wymond Carey.
Man Outside, The. By Wyndham Martyn.
Marriage of Theodora, The. By Molly Elliott Seawell.
My Brother's Keeper. By Charles Tenny Jackson.
My Lady of the South. By Randall Parrish.
Paternoster Ruby, The. By Charles Edmonds Walk.
Politician, The. By Edith Huntington Mason.
Pool of Flame, The. By Louis Joseph Vance.
Poppy. By Cynthia Stockley.
Redemption of Kenneth Galt, The. By Will N. Harben.
Rejuvenation of Aunt Mary, The. By Anna Warner.
Road to Providence, The. By Maria Thompson Davies.
Romance of a Plain Man, The. By Ellen Glasgow.
Running Fight, The By Wm. Hamilton Osborne.
Septimus. By William J. Locke.
Silver Horde, The. By Rex Beach.
Spirit Trail, The. By Kate & Virgil D. Boyles.
Stanton Wins. By Eleanor M. Ingram.
Stolen Singer, The. By Martha Bellinger.
Three Brothers, The. By Eden Phillpotts.
Thurston of Orchard Valley. By Harold Bindloss.
Title Market, The. By Emily Post.
Vigilante Girl, A. By Jerome Hart.
Village of Vagabonds, A. By F. Berkeley Smith.
Wanted—A Chaperon. By Paul Leicester Ford.
Wanted: A Matchmaker. By Paul Leicester Ford.
Watchers of the Plains, The. By Ridgwell Cullum.
White Sister, The. By Marion Crawford.
Window at the White Cat, The. By Mary Roberts Rhinehart.
Woman in Question, The. By John Reed Scott.

Popular Copyright Books

AT MODERATE PRICES

Any of the following titles can be bought of your bookseller at the price you paid for this volume

Anna the Adventuress. By E. Phillips Oppenheim.
Ann Boyd. By Will N. Harben.
At The Moorings. By Rosa N. Carey.
By Right of Purchase. By Harold Bindloss.
Carlton Case, The. By Ellery H. Clark.
Chase of the Golden Plate. By Jacques Futrelle.
Cash Intrigue, The. By George Randolph Chester.
Delafield Affair, The. By Florence Finch Kelly.
Dominant Dollar, The. By Will Lillibridge.
Elusive Pimpernel, The. By Baroness Orczy.
Ganton & Co. By Arthur J. Eddy.
Gilbert Neal. By Will N. Harben.
Girl and the Bill, The. By Bannister Merwin.
Girl from His Town, The. By Marie Van Vorst.
Glass House, The. By Florence Morse Kingsley.
Highway of Fate, The. By Rosa N. Carey.
Homesteaders, The. By Kate and Virgil D. Boyles.
Husbands of Edith, The. George Barr McCutcheon.
Inez. (Illustrated Ed.) By Augusta J. Evans.
Into the Primitive. By Robert Ames Bennet.
Jack Spurlock, Prodigal. By Horace Lorimer.
Jude the Obscure. By Thomas Hardy.
King Spruce. By Holman Day.
Kingsmead. By Bettina Von Hutten.
Ladder of Swords, A. By Gilbert Parker.
Lorimer of the Northwest. By Harold Bindloss.
Lorraine. By Robert W. Chambers.
Loves of Miss Anne, The. By S. R. Crockett.

Popular Copyright Books

AT MODERATE PRICES

Any of the following titles can be bought of your bookseller at the price you paid for this volume

---

Marcaria. By Augusta J. Evans.

Mam' Linda. By Will N. Harben.

Maids of Paradise, The. By Robert W. Chambers.

Man in the Corner, The. By Baroness Orczy.

Marriage A La Mode. By Mrs. Humphry Ward.

Master Mummer, The. By E. Phillips Oppenheim.

Much Ado About Peter. By Jean Webster.

Old, Old Story, The. By Rosa N. Carey.

Pardners. By Rex Beach.

Patience of John Moreland, The. By Mary Dillon.

Paul Anthony, Christian. By Hiram W. Hays.

Prince of Sinners, A. By E. Phillips Oppenheim.

Prodigious Hickey, The. By Owen Johnson.

Red Mouse, The. By William Hamilton Osborne.

Refugees, The. By A. Conan Doyle.

Round the Corner in Gay Street. Grace S. Richmond.

Rue: With a Difference. By Rosa N. Carey.

Set in Silver. By C. N. and A. M. Williamson.

St. Elmo. By Augusta J. Evans.

Silver Blade, The. By Charles E. Walk.

Spirit in Prison, A. By Robert Hichens.

Strawberry Handkerchief, The. By Amelia E. Barr.

Tess of the D'Urbervilles. By Thomas Hardy.

Uncle William. By Jennette Lee.

Way of a Man, The. By Emerson Hough.

Whirl, The. By Foxcroft Davis.

With Juliet in England. By Grace S. Richmond.

Yellow Circle, The. By Charles E. Walk.

Popular Copyright Books

AT MODERATE PRICES

Any of the following titles can be bought of your bookseller at 50 cents per volume.

The Shepherd of the Hills. By Harold Bell Wright.
Jane Cable. By George Barr McCutcheon.
Abner Daniel. By Will N. Harben.
The Far Horizon. By Lucas Malet.
The Halo. By Bettina von Hutten.
Jerry Junior. By Jean Webster.
The Powers and Maxine. By C. N. and A. M. Williamson.
The Balance of Power. By Arthur Goodrich.
Adventures of Captain Kettle. By Cutcliffe Hyne.
Adventures of Gerard. By A. Conan Doyle.
Adventures of Sherlock Holmes. By A. Conan Doyle.
Arms and the Woman. By Harold MacGrath.
Artemus Ward's Works (extra illustrated).
At the Mercy of Tiberius. By Augusta Evans Wilson.
Awakening of Helena Richie. By Margaret Deland.
Battle Ground, The. By Ellen Glasgow.
Belle of Bowling Green, The. By Amelia E. Barr.
Ben Blair. By Will Lillibridge.
Best Man, The. By Harold MacGrath.
Beth Norvell. By Randall Parrish.
Bob Hampton of Placer. By Randall Parrish.
Bob, Son of Battle. By Alfred Ollivant.
Brass Bowl, The. By Louis Joseph Vance.
Brethren, The. By H. Rider Haggard.
Broken Lance, The. By Herbert Quick.
By Wit of Women. By Arthur W. Marchmont.
Call of the Blood, The. By Robert Hitchens.
Cap'n Eri. By Joseph C. Lincoln.
Cardigan. By Robert W. Chambers.
Car of Destiny, The. By C. N. and A. N. Williamson.
Casting Away of Mrs. Lecks and Mrs. Aleshine. By Frank R. Stockton.
Cecilia's Lovers. By Amelia E. Barr.

Popular Copyright Books

AT MODERATE PRICES

Any of the following titles can be bought of your bookseller at 50 cents per volume.

Circle, The. By Katherine Cecil Thurston (author of "The Masquerader," "The Gambler").

Colonial Free Lance, A. By Chauncey C. Hotchkiss.

Conquest of Canaan, The. By Booth Tarkington.

Courier of Fortune, A. By Arthur W. Marchmont.

Darrow Enigma, The. By Melvin Severy.

Deliverance, The. By Ellen Glasgow.

Divine Fire, The. By May Sinclair.

Empire Builders. By Francis Lynde.

Exploits of Brigadier Gerard. By A. Conan Doyle.

Fighting Chance, The. By Robert W. Chambers.

For a Maiden Brave. By Chauncey C. Hotchkiss.

Fugitive Blacksmith, The. By Chas. D. Stewart.

God's Good Man. By Marie Corelli.

Heart's Highway, The. By Mary E. Wilkins.

Holladay Case, The. By Burton Egbert Stevenson.

Hurricane Island. By H. B. Marriott Watson.

In Defiance of the King. By Chauncey C. Hotchkiss.

Indifference of Juliet, The. By Grace S. Richmond.

Infelice. By Augusta Evans Wilson.

Lady Betty Across the Water. By C. N. and A. M. Williamson.

Lady of the Mount, The. By Frederic S. Isham.

Lane That Had No Turning, The. By Gilbert Parker.

Langford of the Three Bars. By Kate and Virgil D. Boyles.

Last Trail, The. By Zane Grey.

Leavenworth Case, The. By Anna Katharine Green.

Lilac Sunbonnet, The. By S. R. Crockett.

Lin McLean. By Owen Wister.

Long Night, The. By Stanley J. Weyman.

Maid at Arms, The. By Robert W. Chambers.

Popular Copyright Books

AT MODERATE PRICES

Any of the following titles can be bought of your bookseller at 50 cents per volume.

Man from Red Keg, The. By Eugene Thwing.
Marthon Mystery, The. By Burton Egbert Stevenson.
Memoirs of Sherlock Holmes. By A. Conan Doyle.
Millionaire Baby, The. By Anna Katharine Green.
Missourian, The. By Eugene P. Lyle, Jr.
Mr. Barnes, American. By A. C. Gunter.
Mr. Pratt. By Joseph C. Lincoln.
My Friend the Chauffeur. By C. N. and A. M. Williamson
My Lady of the North. By Randall Parrish.
Mystery of June 13th. By Melvin L. Severy.
Mystery Tales. By Edgar Allan Poe.
Nancy Stair. By Elinor Macartney Lane.
Order No. 11. By Caroline Abbot Stanley.
Pam. By Bettina von Hutten.
Pam Decides. By Bettina von Hutten.
Partners of the Tide. By Joseph C. Lincoln.
Phra the Phoenician. By Edwin Lester Arnold.
President, The. By Afred Henry Lewis.
Princess Passes, The. By C. N. and A. M. Williamson.
Princess Virginia, The. By C. N. and A. M. Williamson.
Prisoners. By Mary Cholmondeley.
Private War, The. By Louis Joseph Vance.
Prodigal Son, The. By Hall Caine.

Quickening, The. By Francis Lynde.
Richard the Brazen. By Cyrus T. Brady and Edw. Peple
Rose of the World. By Agnes and Egerton Castle
Running Water. By A. E. W. Mason.
Sarita the Carlist. By Arthur W. Marchmont.
Seats of the Mighty, The. By Gilbert Parker.
Sir Nigel. By A. Conan Doyle.
Sir Richard Calmady. By Lucas Malet.
Speckled Bird, A. By Augusta Evans Wilson.

Popular Copyright Books

AT MODERATE PRICES

Any of the following titles can be bought of your bookseller at 50 cents per volume.

Spirit of the **Border, The.** By Zane Grey.
Spoilers, The. By Rex Beach.
Squire Phin. By Holman F. Day.
Stooping Lady, **The.** By Maurice Hewlett.
Subjection of Isabel **Carnaby.** By Ellen Thorneycroft Fowler.
Sunset Trail, The. By Alfred Henry Lewis.
Sword of the Old **Frontier, A.** By Randall Parrish.
Tales of Sherlock Holmes. By A. Conan Doyle.
That Printer of **Udell's.** By Harold Bell Wright.
Throwback, The. By Alfred Henry Lewis.
Trail of the Sword, The. By Gilbert Parker.
Treasure of Heaven, The. By Marie Corelli.
Two Vanrevels, The. By Booth Tarkington.
Up From Slavery. By Booker T. Washington.
Vashti. By Augusta Evans Wilson.
Viper of Milan, The (original edition). By Marjorie Bowen.
Voice of the People, The. By Ellen Glasgow.
Wheel of Life, The. By Ellen Glasgow.

When Wilderness Was King. By Randall Parrish.
Where the Trail Divides. By Will Lillibridge.
Woman in Grey, A. By Mrs. C. N. Williamson.
Woman in the Alcove, The. By Anna Katharine Green.
Younger Set, The. By Robert W. Chambers.
The Weavers. By Gilbert Parker.
The Little Brown Jug at Kildare. By Meredith Nicholson.
The Prisoners of Chance. By Randall Parrish.
My Lady of Cleve. By Percy J. Hartley.
Loaded Dice. By Ellery H. Clark.
Get Rich Quick Wallingford. By George Randolph Chester.
The Orphan. By Clarence Mulford.
A Gentleman of France. By Stanley J. Weyman.

Popular Copyright Books

AT MODERATE PRICES

Any of the following titles can be bought of your bookseller at 50 cents per volume.

Purple Parasol, The. By George Barr McCutcheon.

Princess Dehra, The. By John Reed Scott.

Making of Bobby Burnit, The. By George Randolph Chester.

Last Voyage of the Donna Isabel, The. By Randall Parrish.

Bronze Bell, The. By Louis Joseph Vance.

Pole Baker. By Will N. Harben.

Four Million, The. By O. Henry.

Idols. By William J. Locke.

Wayfarers, The. By Mary Stewart Cutting.

Held for Orders. By Frank H. Spearman.

Story of the Outlaw, The. By Emerson Hough.

Mistress of Brae Farm, The. By Rosa N. Carey.

Explorer, The. By William Somerset Maugham.

Abbess of Vlaye, The. By Stanley Weyman.

Alton of Somasco. By Harold Bindloss.

Ancient Law, The. By Ellen Glasgow.

Barrier, The. By Rex Beach.

Bar 20. By Clarence E. Mulford.

Beloved Vagabond, The. By William J. Locke.

Beulah. (Illustrated Edition.) By Augusta J. Evans.

Chaperon, The. By C. N. and A. M. Williamson.

Colonel Greatheart. By H. C. Bailey.

Dissolving Circle, The. By Will Lillibridge.

Elusive Isabel. By Jacques Futrelle.

Fair Moon of Bath, The. By Elizabeth Ellis.

54-40 or Fight. By Emerson Hough.

Lightning Source UK Ltd.
Milton Keynes UK
UKHW021113220119
335965UK00011B/1087/P